KEE
YOU
SAFE

KEEP YOU SAFE

RONA HALSALL

bookouture

Published by Bookouture in 2018

An imprint of StoryFire Ltd.

Carmelite House
50 Victoria Embankment
London EC4Y 0DZ

www.bookouture.com

ISBN: 978-1-78681-483-8
eBook ISBN: 978-1-78681-482-1

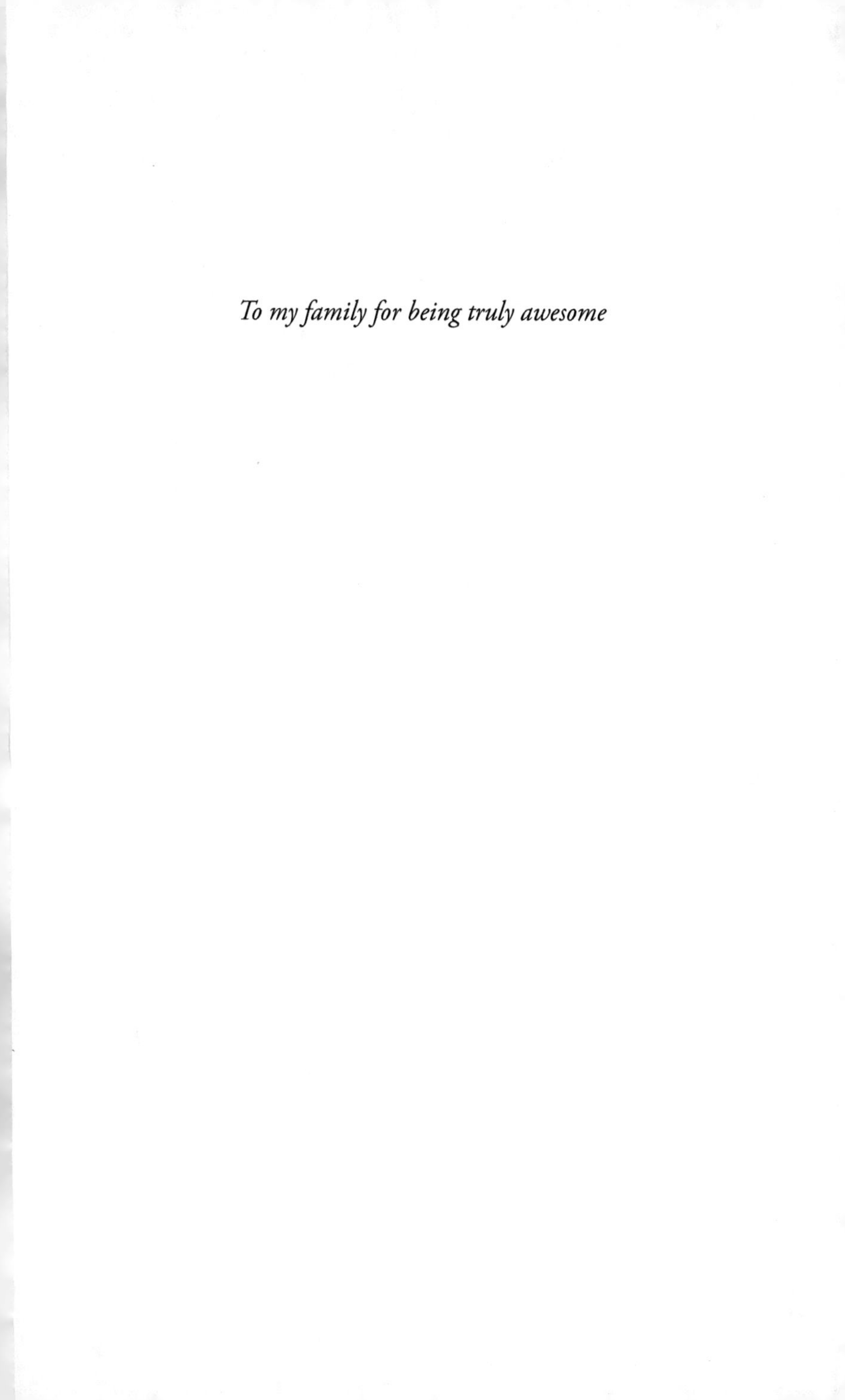

To my family for being truly awesome

CHAPTER ONE

Now

Natalie sits on a metal bench on the top deck of the ferry, watching the mountains of the Lake District glide past. She wonders what her son looks like. Has his hair darkened, his face thinned out? They change so quickly when they're young and she has nothing to go on, not a single picture since he was a baby.

She'll know soon enough, she thinks, with a shiver of nerves, uncertain of what lies ahead but sure that she'll risk everything to have him with her again. She wraps her arms around her chest and imagines that it's her child that she's hugging. She can almost feel his hair against her face, his breath tickling her neck and she hugs tighter, fingers feeling the bones of her ribcage, even through two layers of clothing.

What if things go wrong?

Her jaw tightens, and she knows that she can't let herself dwell on the idea, not for a moment. Confidence is the key to success. She has to believe her plan is possible, has to have faith in herself. After all, she's not the same woman she was three years ago, before she went to prison. Her anger is carved into her heart, is part of who she is now and she's a little scared of what she's capable of when pushed to her limit. If it's happened once, it can happen again, can't it?

She shivers and wraps her fleece a little tighter round her body.

Prison was a place full of raw emotions, a place where it was impossible to relax, where people played mind games, bullied and manipulated to get what they wanted. Or just to pass the time. Fear lurked in every dark corner, every sudden noise, every scream. And fear is an emotion that doesn't disappear overnight. It has to unwind itself, loosen its tendrils until you can ease yourself out of its grasp and finally step away. That's what she hopes will happen, and soon, because living on adrenaline is exhausting, draining the life out of her with the effort of keeping safe.

On the upside, she knows how to fight now, which would be a surprise to everyone who knew her before. She can throw a proper punch, knows which parts of the anatomy require a kick, a stomp or a jab, where the main pressure points lie, and even how to use everyday things as lethal weapons. Spoons to gouge eyes, toothbrushes to jab, pens to stab, shoes to batter and smack. She's seen it all. Even clothing can be dangerous.

It's true to say that she's learned self-defence from some pretty ferocious women, uncompromising in their methods when it comes to protecting themselves and their families. She liked some of them. Admired them for their resilience and sheer determination to survive. And then there was Katya.

Her body gives an involuntary shudder.

She hugs herself harder, shakes the idea of violence from her mind. Anyway, physical skills are not the most important for the task ahead. She needs to meld situations to her advantage, engineer possibilities, mess with people's plans. What's going to be really important is the art of cunning. And the certainty that she will do whatever it takes to be with her son Harry again. No questions, no doubts, no hesitation.

She sits back in her seat, unwraps her arms and stretches out her fingers. *Relax, relax,* she tells herself. *I can do this.* As long as she can stay calm, keep her mind focused and not let anger take control. She imagines Harry as a four-year-old boy instead of the baby she knew. His hair will be brown like hers, she thinks, rather than the dark blond of his father. His eyes, she knows, are wide apart and hazel. And his face? She prefers the idea that it is oval, like hers rather than square like his father's. His nose, of course, will still be a little button of a thing, covered in freckles that spread across his cheeks, just like the pictures of her when she was a child.

Days, weeks, maybe months of her life have gone into building up this mental picture of her child. A child she doesn't know. In the absence of photos, she's used magazines to find pictures of children and build them into a likeness of her little boy. She's invented a voice for him, a laugh, a smile, even his own set of mannerisms. Likes and dislikes. Now the image is so strong, so certain, that she can conjure him at will into her daydreams. And as she closes her eyes, she can feel his little fingers holding her hand, hear his excited voice telling her stories about his day, his life, what he dreams about. And questions! So many questions. She imagines picnics, playing on the swings, the roundabouts, helping him scale the climbing frame. A seed of joy germinates in her heart as she allows herself to create a future that almost seems real.

Soon it will be real. In another place, where her past can't find her and she can start again.

A smile creeps onto her lips and expands into a proper grin, stretching muscles that haven't been used for quite some time. It's a forgotten feeling; this bubbling in her stomach, lightness in her shoulders, laughter in her throat. The movement of the ferry, as it rolls gently from side to side, is a weird but pleasant sensation, reminding her of fairground rides when she was a little kid, when life was simple. She sighs. Is it possible that life can be fun again?

Natalie puts her head back to feel the sun on her face. Goodness knows, she could do with a tan. She's so pale, she looks like a member of the walking dead, veins visible beneath her skin. If she's being really honest, she thinks she looks a bit scary in an unwell sort of a way, with her hollow cheeks and shadows under her eyes.

The wind whips at her hair, flicks it into her eyes and she grabs it, twists it into a knot at the nape of her neck. For some reason, she thought she would feel more light-hearted as a blonde, had decided it would be a good disguise. But she feels like a fraud, a cheap caricature of herself and more obvious than if she'd stayed her natural brunette. That's the first thing that's going to change, she decides as she closes her eyes, trying to visualise a new hairstyle. She needs to look like something else. She needs to look like a mum.

The rocking of the boat lulls her into drowsy daydreams about haircuts, soft beds and the smell of newly washed linen, until a man's voice startles her, his accent northern, but she can't quite place it.

'Do you mind if I sit here?'

Her eyes flick open and her hands grip the edge of the seat, body tensed. Hairs prickle on the back of her neck as she studies the dishevelled-looking bloke who stands in front of her. He is tall and broad-shouldered, dressed in black biker gear, holding a shiny black helmet stencilled with a silver skull and crossbones on the back. Dark hair hangs in lank waves to his shoulders. The start of a beard darkens his face.

It's okay, she decides, heart bumping in her chest. He's not Eastern European, doesn't look or speak like someone related to Katya. *No one knows that I'm out yet,* she reminds herself. But that's not the only reason to be worried. She shouldn't be on this boat, and there's a nagging concern at the back of her mind that a computer system somewhere will have worked out that she's here. Obviously, this is ridiculous, because she didn't book her ticket under her real name, didn't have to show a passport or identification of any sort, but there are CCTV cameras everywhere these days and, well, you never know, do you?

She glances round, sees there is nobody else out on the deck. All the other seats are free. There were lots of people out here when the ferry set sail, but the unseasonably cold wind has driven them back inside. She knows why he wants to share her bench; it's the only place that has any shelter from the wind and she stares at him with her 'I want you to go away' look. He smiles at her, an easy grin. She notices tawny brown eyes, fringed with long dark lashes. Kind eyes. *It's good to share,* she tells herself and shuffles up to the far end of the bench.

'Very wise,' he says as he sits down and puts his helmet and backpack on the bench between them. 'Just been to Glastonbury. Haven't washed in a few days.' He pulls a face, then laughs. 'I'm definitely humming.'

Natalie looks away, clasps her hands in her lap. They sit in silence for a while, watch the sea and the forest of wind turbines, all that's left to see now that the ferry has left the Lake District behind. Out of the corner of her eye, she notices him rummage in his bag, then cringes when he pulls out a harmonica. She hates the harmonica; it reminds her of the endless Bob Dylan tracks her ex-husband used to play. Her teeth grind as Tom's face flashes into her mind and she pushes it away, unwilling to let him sour her day.

'Do you mind if I have a little practice?' the man says. He holds up the harmonica, waggles it in the air. 'I've got a charity gig tonight. Just need to go through a couple of songs.'

She stares at him, blinks. His eyes plead with her.

'I won't take long,' he says. 'Ten minutes, tops.'

'Okay.' Her shoulders scrunch closer to her ears and she decides she'll just have to go and sit somewhere else if she really can't stand it.

He runs up and down the scales a couple of times with obvious expertise, then starts to play. It's a haunting melody, not what she was expecting and against her initial instincts, she's enthralled. It sounds Celtic and reminds her of the Sinead O'Connor's song, 'Nothing Compares 2 U', a song her mother loved. She sighs. The thought of her squeezes Natalie's heart so hard that it hurts and she has to remind herself that it doesn't matter that they're not in touch anymore. Nothing matters except Harry.

The music flows over her, into her, though her, flushing emotions to the surface and by the time he's finished, her eyes are stinging. A tear escapes and runs down her cheek. She turns away from him, wipes at it with the back of her hand.

'That wasn't too bad, was it?'

'Lovely,' she says, with a sniff while she pretends to study a seagull, which glides alongside the boat.

'Mind if I sing something?' He takes a bundle of folded pages from his bag and flicks through them until he finds what he's looking for.

Her whole body goes rigid and she looks around to see if anyone else has appeared on deck, making sure she still has an exit strategy.

'No, no, you go ahead.' She squirms at the thought of this man bursting into song next to her.

She's spotted another bench that might have a bit of shelter and prepares to move, but as he starts to sing, she halts in mid-air and sits back down again. His voice is soulful and sandpaper rough, a perfect match with the song he's singing. 'Sweet Child O' Mine'. All the breath goes out of her and she's aware of nothing but the words hanging in the air. She knows this song, knows every word, every note, because it's the song she used to sing to Harry. She sang it to him while she was pregnant and then to lull him to sleep when he was a baby. Since they've been apart, singing it has kept him close to her. Now she can't stop the tears, so salty they sting her eyes, big sobs catching in her throat, shaking her body.

'Oh my God, I'm so sorry!' he says when he finishes and looks at her. By this time, she's a mess of snot and tears and can feel her cheeks burning. He delves into his bag, holds out a packet of tissues. She takes one and blows her nose, takes another and wipes her face.

'Sorry,' she says to the deck, elbows resting on her knees, hiding her face in her hands as her sobs stutter to a halt.

'No, no. I didn't realise I was that bad.'

She attempts a laugh, which comes out as a snort and takes another tissue to finish the mopping up process.

'Let me get you a cup of coffee or something. Whatever it takes to cheer you up.'

Natalie risks a glance at him, sees the concern in his gaze and has to look away before she starts blubbing again.

'I know!' He slaps his thigh. 'Chocolate always does the trick.'

He lopes off across the deck, leathers creaking, biker boots clanking down the steps as he disappears into the bowels of the boat to find the café. *I should go and hide,* Natalie thinks, but she's welded to the seat by her misery and her legs refuse to move.

The sound of footsteps makes her eyes flick to the stairs, her body tensed, ready to move. But it's just a mother with two children, coming to look at the view. She breathes out and tells herself, once again, that nobody knows she's here.

By the time he comes back, with big cups of coffee and chocolate muffins, she's tidied herself up as best she can, the whole packet of tissues scrunched into a soggy ball in her fist. She squishes it into her pocket as he sits next to her, long legs akimbo, so at ease with himself that she feels a pang of jealousy. She wonders when she'll ever get to feel that relaxed.

'I'm Jack,' he says, with a grin as he bites into his muffin.

'Natalie,' she replies, before it occurs to her she should have made something up.

He's a chatty man, and as they sip their drinks and eat their cakes, Natalie feels the knot of tension in her shoulders start to loosen. He tells her about Glastonbury, the people he met, the bands he saw. It brings back memories, happy memories, of the young woman she used to be. She finds out that Jack was born and bred on the Isle of Man. He's thirty-one, a couple of years older than her, and he fronts a band called Whiplash, who are playing at a charity gig in aid of Youth Arts that evening to help them raise funds to buy musical equipment for local kids.

The coffee is deliciously strong and a forbidden treat because coffee makes her go into verbal overdrive. She savours every sip.

'So, what do you do?' he says.

She drains the last remnants of her drink, taking her time, trying to pick something that sounds cool. It's hard when you have so much choice, and the silence mushrooms between them, her body uncomfortably hot.

'I'm um… I'm a nanny.' Her breath hitches in her throat. *Did I really just say that?* Of all the jobs she could have picked, that was probably the most stupid. She looks like she might eat children, not nurture them.

His eyebrows shoot up. 'Wow, I'd never have guessed.'

'Yes, but I'm er… taking a break.' She shrugs. 'Had a few health issues. So…' She lets the sentence tail off.

'Ah, right.'

It always works, she thinks. *Guaranteed conversation stopper. Because people struggle when they think you're seriously ill.*

He finishes his muffin, licks the crumbs off his fingers and looks out to sea. Her fingers knot themselves together. The idea of spending the rest of the journey in silence seems pretty bleak after the warmth of his conversation.

'But it's a great job,' she says, putting all her energy into sounding upbeat and interesting. 'Been all over the world, looking after rich people's kids.'

He turns and looks at her, curious. 'Have you?'

She nods and before she can stop herself, she's crafted a wonderful web of lies, words flowing like a mountain stream, as she burbles on about the life she might have had if she'd been born to different parents, met different people, and made better choices. *What does the truth matter anyway?* she thinks as she watches him laugh at something she said. *He's just a stranger on a ferry and I'm tired of being me.*

They swap stories until she notices the Isle of Man ahead of them and realises her face is numb from a wind that is ridiculously cold for the end of June. She stands up and stomps around to get some feeling back in her feet, scanning the pretty horseshoe bay lined with its tall, smartly painted Victorian buildings, which run the whole length of the promenade. Rocky headlands rise up on either side of the town, which nestles against the hillside. And there, on that hillside, is the house where her son lives.

She can feel Harry's presence and her heart starts to race. *Not long now. Not long.*

'Here already,' Jack says as he starts to gather his stuff together. 'You didn't tell me… where are you heading?'

'Not sure yet.' She picks up her holdall, watching the harbour get closer, itching to get off the boat now. 'No real plans.'

He unzips a pocket in his backpack and pulls out a pen, rummages around for something to write on.

'Here's my number.' He scrawls figures on the back of a till receipt. 'And this is where we're doing the gig tonight. The Centenary Centre in Peel. Come along, eight o'clock. I'll tell them on the door to look out for you.'

The paper flutters in the wind as he passes it to her and she snatches at it before it's blown away, tucks it in her pocket. *I don't have time for gigs,* she thinks, as the tune of the engines changes and the ferry starts reversing towards the loading bay, but she gives him a quick smile of thanks. Then the call comes for drivers to re-join their vehicles and she waves her goodbye and dashes down the stairs ahead of him.

'Incog-bloody-nito, you useless cow,' she mutters under her breath as she gets into the car she has borrowed, annoyed now that she let her guard slip and at least one person on the boat has had a really good look at her. *He wasn't taking much notice*, she tells herself. *Distracted by the gig. It'll be fine.*

The weight of her mission settles on her shoulders and she jiggles in her seat, fingers drumming on the steering wheel as she waits for her turn to leave the boat. Just the thought of seeing Harry after all this time leaves her breathless and she is drawn to him with a gravitational pull that is as old as time. Nothing is going to stop her. She has to take the threats to Harry's life seriously, doesn't she? Even if nobody else will.

In her imaginings, Elena, the nanny, opens the door, Harry by her side. Elena would still be there, she was sure, because Tom wouldn't cope on his own and he never stopped telling Natalie how brilliant he thought she was. Tom is still at work. His parents are abroad. Harry's eyes widen when he sees her, his face alight with excitement. He knows straight away who Natalie is and runs to her, throws his little arms around her neck and they hold each other tight, neither of them wanting to let go.

He would come with her; just to the playground, she'd tell Elena, no need for her to join them. And they'd make their escape, in a yacht that was ready and waiting in the harbour and they'd sail away, down past France and Spain, through the Mediterranean until they landed in Turkish-run Northern Cyprus, the latest hotspot for fugitives, so she'd heard, to start their new life.

Of course, it won't work out that way. It would be the perfect plan, but it's an obvious fantasy. There is an Irish fishing boat that will take her to Larne, though, and from there she will be picked up by an ex-convict friend and taken to Connemara, where she has the use of a holiday cottage for the rest of the summer, while she sorts out the details of her long-term plan. The fishing boat is her only real hope of escaping undetected, given that the official means of transport off the island, such as planes and ferries, would be policed if a child went missing, and out of the question. She has the contact details of the skipper, who is primed and ready to pick her up and she still has a few thousand left from her divorce settlement. More than enough to pay her way.

The bones of her plan are there, but the timing is critical, the main sticking point being that the fishing boat will arrive in two days' time to land its catch and will be going back to Ireland the following day. After that, her chance to get Harry to safety will have gone.

Natalie's hands tighten round the steering wheel.

Three days. That's all I've got.

CHAPTER TWO

Now

So. It begins.

I know as soon as the phone rings, feel my body tense for some reason. A premonition, if you like.

'Sorry,' I say to the woman on the other end of the line. 'Can you say that again, please. A bit more slowly.' She has an accent and speaks so fast the words blur together into one shrill noise that makes me wince.

I hear her take a breath. 'Natalie Wilson,' she says, enunciating each syllable, 'has been released from prison.'

I knew it, really, because there'd be no other reason for her to ring me. I'm hot, run my finger round my collar to loosen it from my throat. This is too soon. Two months too soon.

'So, where is she?'

'Well, I don't know exactly. I just saw her leave. Yesterday that was. Thought she was going to court or something. Then this morning, I didn't see her, so I checked on the list and found out she'd been released.'

Yesterday? My fist clenches around the phone, my patience a thin veneer. She could be anywhere by now. What is the point of knowing that she's been released if I don't know where she is?

'Can you find out?' I try not to sound sarcastic.

The woman breathes out, a big huff that crackles in my ear.

'I don't know.'

If she was in the room with me I'd slap her. I thought she had more to her than this. Did I choose the wrong prison officer? I loosen my jaw as my brain clicks into gear.

'I would be very grateful,' I say. 'Five hundred pounds more grateful than I am already, if you could give me her exact location. Quickly. Like today.'

'I'll see what I can do,' she says. Then whispers, 'I've got to go.'

She hangs up.

I stare at the phone, my heart racing as though I'm running, thumping so hard I can feel my body vibrating.

The hunt is on.

CHAPTER THREE

Then

The last time Natalie saw her son was three years, four months and five days ago, when he had just turned eight months old.

They were in their home on the Wirral, located in an area favoured by Merseyside footballers, financiers and assorted celebrities. It was just after seven o'clock on a Tuesday evening when she heard the knock at the door, firm and insistent, making her jump. She made a mental note to ask Tom once again if they could replace the knocker with a doorbell, something that made a softer sound, a tune maybe, that wouldn't startle her quite so much.

'Tom, can you get that?' she called from the family bathroom, a room that was the same size as the lounge had been in her childhood home. In her opinion, it was the best room in their newly built house, one that she'd helped to design, insisting that it should be child-friendly. A tiled mural of sea creatures ran along one wall above a double-ended bath, rounded fittings everywhere, no sharp corners to bang little heads, cushioned flooring underfoot. It was a cheerful room, playful in its decoration and fixtures, quite different from the rest of the house, which, in all honesty, was more to Tom's taste than hers.

She wrapped Harry in a towel, rubbed his downy hair and blew raspberries on his chubby tummy, making him squirm and giggle. It was her favourite time of day, the one time when she could properly relax, made all the more precious now that she was back at work.

She loved the warmth of his little body next to hers, his delicious sweet aroma, the feel of his peachy skin, soft against her face.

The door knocker thumped again, this time harder, louder, impatient. Who on earth could it be? They rarely had visitors and those that did come were always expected, her husband being a man who didn't like surprises.

'Tom!' she shouted, louder this time. 'Can you get the door, please?'

Maybe it was the lack of a 'please' that had prevented him from responding the first time round. He was a stickler for proper manners, drilled into him at boarding school, he said, whereas her upbringing had been more slapdash in that department.

She heard footsteps, the click of the front door opening, the murmur of voices. A little while later there was a thump, thump, thump on the stairs, and Tom appeared at the bathroom door. He came inside, closed the door behind him, a frown on his face. Handsome, she'd always thought, in a neat and tidy way. His jaw worked from side to side, as he chewed on his words, getting ready to spit them at her. She tensed, fingers fumbling with the poppers on Harry's baby suit, struggling to finish the job as she wondered what she'd done wrong this time.

Natalie knew that she hadn't been easy to live with in recent months, but surely she was allowed a little leeway, after the trauma of Harry's birth and then his illness, which had dragged on for months. She was allowed to be tired, wasn't she? A little tetchy at times. Forgetful. Struggling to settle in back at work when her mind was at home with her son. Wasn't that all part and parcel of having a new baby?

She flashed Tom her best smile and wondered if they could ever get back to the way they used to be, when she was the centre of his world. He used to buy her presents, bring flowers, take her out for lavish dinners. Tell her she was beautiful, perfect, that he loved her. But that was years ago now, and such a faint memory that she wondered if she'd imagined it all.

'Nearly finished.' She forced a lightness into her voice and gathered Harry into her arms, kissing his cheek and giving him Mr Bunny, a toy that he never allowed far from his grasp.

'Natalie,' Tom hissed, blond eyebrows joined as his frown deepened. 'What have you done now?'

She stopped and stared at him. A chill tip-toed down her spine. *What had she done?* She searched her memory, but nothing came to mind, nothing that would get him this cross anyway.

'What do you mean?' she said, voice quivering, as she got to her feet, Harry clasped to her chest like a shield.

'The police are downstairs.' She could see now that it wasn't just anger in his eyes; there was a glint of something else. Beads of sweat were visible on his brow. Natalie swallowed, her heart beating faster as his stare bored into her, drilling for the truth. 'They want to talk to you.' He folded his arms across his chest, leant against the door. 'You need to tell me. Why are they here?'

'What?' She clasped Harry tighter, defiance in her voice. 'How would I know?'

'What weird stuff have you been up to now?'

She stepped back, his words striking her with the force of a slap. Her mind frantically sifted through her actions over the last few days, but her memories were so blurry, it was hard to know what was real and what was daydreaming.

'What do you mean, weird stuff?'

'I mean, like ordering that bloody great BMW, which you say you can't remember buying. Or sending five thousand pounds, which we can't afford, to Syrian refugees. You say you can't remember doing that either. So, what the hell else have you done that you "can't remember"?'

His voice was scathing, his fingers putting inverted commas round the end of the sentence, making it clear he thought she was lying. But it was true. She had no recollection of doing those things, although she must have done, because they had really happened. The donation had been paid for with her card, the car signed for with her signature.

She'd been living in a strange world since Harry had been born, doing things she couldn't remember, for reasons she couldn't fathom. Was she going mad? This was not a concern she could possibly admit to a health visitor or doctor, and definitely not to her husband, her hope being that these blanks in her memory were merely a combination of tiredness and hormones, that everything would settle down. In the meantime, she was very careful about every pound she spent, compulsively viewing her bank transactions to reassure herself that she hadn't done anything stupid. And recently, she was sure that she hadn't.

'Have you walked out of a shop without paying? Stolen something? Is this why the police are standing in my hallway?'

She buried her face in Harry's neck, not able to look at Tom's accusing stare.

'You didn't hit someone with the car and not stop, did you?'

Her head snapped up. How dare he suggest such a thing?

'No! No! I haven't done anything.' She glared at him, a man she no longer seemed to know, more distant from her by the day.

His face was going red and she could sense his anger building, noticed his hands clenched into fists by his sides. He wouldn't hit her, she reassured herself as she backed away, but knew that he wanted to, could see it in his eyes. Harry started to cry and she realised she was crushing him. Tears pricked at her eyes, as she cooed to her son, who sobbed and snuffled while she rubbed his back.

Maybe I haven't done anything. Maybe there's been an accident.

The thought made her freeze.

Her heart skipped a beat as the faces of her family flickered through her mind; mother, stepfather, absent father, brother. She clutched the towel rail to hold her world steady.

'Mr Wilson?' A voice floated up the stairs. 'Mr Wilson?'

Tom opened the door, strode towards her and took Harry from her arms.

'I just hope for your sake this is not another of your little attention-seeking stunts.'

His words pierced through her, shards of venom, delivered in his clipped public-school tones, making him sound like he was in the right. He nodded towards the door as Harry looked at her, clearly confused and on the verge of a protest. 'They're waiting. You better go and see what they want.' He cuddled the child to him, swaying from side to side to try and stop the imminent wail. 'I can put Harry to bed.'

Her mind worked through the possibilities as she hurried down the landing, sure that it had been years since she'd done anything illegal. Not since she'd met Tom, in fact. That meant it had to be an accident, didn't it? She stopped for a moment, trying to calm herself, before she made her way down the long, curving sweep of the stairs.

A squat policeman, rugby player type, all shoulder muscles and no neck, looked up as she headed towards him, pale-grey eyes following her until she got to the bottom step. She licked her lips, swallowed. His face was blank, no sympathetic looks and she dared to hope. His partner was a severe-looking woman in her forties, grey hair scraped back from an angular face. She had a misshapen nose, which had obviously been broken at some point and a forehead covered in squiggly lines, like a reporter's notepad.

'Mrs Natalie Wilson?' she asked in a nasal Liverpudlian twang.

Natalie nodded and teetered on the last step, dreading what she might hear if she went any further.

'We would like you to accompany us to the station,' the policewoman said. 'Our colleagues would like to ask you some questions.'

'Questions?' Natalie let out a long breath. *Thank God. Nobody's dead.*

'We can explain everything at the station,' the policewoman said.

'Explain what?' Natalie frowned.

'There are some queries about a client you have been dealing with. At Wilson Wealth Management,' the young policeman said. 'That's where you work, isn't it?' His partner frowned and flashed him a look that told him to shut up.

'What sort of queries?' Natalie's hand tangled in her hair, pulling hard. 'I've only been back from maternity leave for a couple of months. I'm just getting back into the swing of things.' She looked up the stairs. 'It's my husband's business. Perhaps you need to speak to him if there's a problem at work.'

'Save all that for when we get to the station,' the policewoman said, moving towards her, as the policeman opened the front door.

'But… my husband… He can sort this out, no need for me to go anywhere.' She glanced up the stairs again, willing Tom to appear, heart galloping so fast that she started to feel dizzy. She grabbed hold of the banister to steady herself, root herself to her home.

'It may just be a mix-up, a misunderstanding,' the policewoman said, in a gentler tone. 'But you need to come to the station so we can sort it out.'

'Tom!' Natalie shouted as the policewoman got hold of her elbow, fingers digging into Natalie's arm. 'Tom!' she shrieked, so loud it hurt the back of her throat. Surely, he could hear?

However benign the policewoman tried to make it sound, Natalie knew something was very wrong. She didn't want to go, couldn't bear to leave Harry. Tom hadn't much of a clue about his routine. He'd cry. The nanny, Elena, was out for the evening. Tom wouldn't cope. Natalie clung to the banister, tried to resist, but she had a police officer at each elbow now. They prised her fingers from the wooden rail and as much as she writhed, Natalie had no chance of escape.

She was bundled into the back of a police car and turned to see Tom standing at the window of Harry's bedroom. In her mind, she could hear Harry's cries, his bedtime routine being a thing of precision and she knew he wouldn't settle without her there to sing him to sleep. Her hands tugged at a door handle that refused to work.

'My son, he needs me!' she shouted at the police officers sitting in front of her, but they didn't turn their heads.

'Calm down, madam, or we'll have to cuff you,' the squat policeman said, as he started the car.

She banged on the window, shouted Tom's name, but he obviously couldn't hear her. A sob caught in her throat as she watched her house recede into the distance.

CHAPTER FOUR

Now

It is fortunate that Natalie has a good memory for the geography of places and it doesn't take her long to navigate through the town centre towards the house that is owned by Tom's parents. She remembers each turn with a satisfied 'aha'. *Nearly there, nearly there.*

Tonight, her plan is to do a bit of reconnaissance. A bit of snooping round the house, remind herself of entrances, exits and the lie of the land. Hopefully, she'll get a glimpse of Harry. The thought of seeing him is growing inside her, filling her up, making her heart thump so hard her body shakes with each beat. She would like to drive faster, but is careful to stick to the speed limit, constantly checking her rear-view mirror, just to be sure that she's not being followed.

Ten minutes after leaving the ferry, she drives past the large cream house, a modern mansion, which sits on a hillside at the edge of Douglas. This is where the rich people live. People like Tom's parents, who run a shipping business and are wealthy beyond belief, having moved here for tax reasons before Tom was born. They travel all over the world on a regular basis, with other properties in tax-havens like Kuwait and the Cayman Islands, leaving this house empty for long periods of time. Plenty of space for Tom, Harry and the nanny.

This is where Natalie thought her son would be, where her solicitor had said they were living, but the house appears to be empty. No curtains or blinds at the windows, no lights on, no cars in the drive. It has that forlorn air, which settles over properties when they are bereft of humanity; slightly tatty round the edges, the lawns uncut, flower borders tangled with weeds, a flyer poking out of the letterbox. Then she notices an estate agent's board by the gate, sees the red letters stating that the property has been sold and her chest tightens.

'No! No! No!' She smacks her hands against the steering wheel in a furious drumbeat until her palms are burning and stares at the empty house, willing it to burst into life. *Have I got the wrong address?* She looks around, but knows that she's in the right place, having been here several times with Tom.

A few deep breaths help to steady her. *They're on the island.* She knows this for sure, because her ex-husband registered as a director of a business here three years ago, and the business is still operating. She rang to make sure just yesterday and spoke to his secretary.

'Mr Wilson's in a meeting, I'm afraid,' his secretary had said, her voice a pleasant sing-song, with the hint of a foreign accent. She'd sounded apologetic, sincere. 'I'm not sure when he'll be available. Would you like to leave a message?'

Natalie had chewed on her lip. *As if he'd respond to a message.* For the last few months she'd been bombarding him with messages, warnings that their son was in danger. Tom hadn't believed her. He was sure it was all a ruse to get access and said he wasn't going to fall for her melodramatic games.

'Um… no, it's okay,' she'd said. 'I'll try again later.'

'Are you sure? Can I take your name, let him know you called? It's no trouble.'

'No, no, it's fine.'

A car horn jolts her back to the present and she realises that she's blocking the road. She holds up a hand in apology and pulls over to the pavement. *What to do now?* For a moment her mind is blank, but then she suddenly remembers something that the musician on the ferry had said, something that hadn't registered as important at the time, but now it shines like a beacon of hope and she starts the engine and heads towards Peel, glad of the scrap of paper tucked in her pocket.

The conversation runs through her mind.

'It's nothing fancy,' Jack had said. 'Just a charity do. A friend of our drummer works in wealth management and he's managed to persuade a bunch of firms to put their hands in their pockets and sponsor the thing. Should be a fun night though.'

Tom works in wealth management, she thinks, *and he was always a sucker for a charity do. Thought it was good publicity. Maybe this friend knows where Tom lives. Maybe Jack does.* The Isle of Man is only a small place, after all, no more than thirty miles long and ten wide. There are a lot of interconnections when you live in a place that size.

The more she considers it, the more her spirits lift, certain that Jack will be able to help. She drives across the island, down lush, tree-lined roads, between the rolling hills, the tug of her connection to Harry feeling stronger than ever, pulling her, she's sure, in the right direction.

Twenty minutes later, she arrives at Peel marina, a pretty place, full of all manner of boats, bobbing on the tide, masts swaying, lines clanking in the breeze. Behind them, Peel Hill rises in a long, low ridge, protecting the town from north-westerly winds. To the north, on a rocky island, attached to the mainland by a short causeway, stand the ruins of a red sandstone castle, jagged against the skyline. A long, high breakwater reaches out from its walls into the Irish sea, forming a harbour and providing a protective arm to keep the worst of the weather from the mouth of the marina.

Officially Peel is a city because it has a cathedral, but she decides that's a ridiculous concept when she sees the size of the place. Even the label of town is pushing it, given that it takes her five minutes to do a circuit, ending back where she started, by the marina, outside a tiny chippy. Her window is open and the enticing smell drifts into the car, reminding her that she's only had a chocolate muffin to eat since breakfast. She checks her watch, sees that she still has an hour to kill, and decides she might as well be eating. *Refuel while I can.* Who knows how the evening will pan out? There might not be another chance. She parks up, and gets herself some fish and chips, then walks round to the promenade to find somewhere to sit and eat.

She passes a rowdy group of teenagers playing volleyball on the crescent-shaped beach. There are dog walkers, couples walking hand in hand and, out in the bay, a small fleet of kayaks, like a line of ducks. On the horizon, fishing boats are coming home. There's something very innocent about the place. Time wound back by thirty years.

Although it's evening, a handful of children still play on the beach and she watches a toddler as he tries to shovel sand into a bucket, fascinated by the concentration on his face, his determination to accomplish his task. She imagines what it might be like to be one of the mothers, holding her child's hand as they stand in the sea, screaming at the chill of the waves as they break over their legs. Laughing and playing together.

It's a bitter reminder of all the time that she's missed, the stages of development that Harry has been through without her, the things she'll never remember because she wasn't there, the days like this one when they should have been together. She shifts her gaze, aware of the hollowness inside her; the empty space where shared experiences should be, filled with a seething mess of anger.

Halfway down the promenade, she finds a shelter, with a bench seat and view out to sea. But as soon as she starts to eat, she feels imaginary eyes burning into the back of her neck, making her gulp down her food. Distracted by the children on the beach, and the thought of finding Harry, she hasn't been as vigilant as she should have been and she glances round, looking for faces that don't fit. She swallows big chunks of fish, moist and slippery, no need to chew.

A seagull perches on the sea wall in front of her. Quiet at first, just watching, then, as she eats, it starts to shriek, strutting to and fro. Several other birds fly down and now she has an audience. She eats faster and they hop closer, surrounding her in a noisy rabble of hooligan birds. They are quite big, close up, scary with their sharp orange beaks. One flaps up onto the bench next to her, beady eyes focused on her fish and she rears back, a protective hand over her food as she moves away. It follows and she snatches up her meal, jumps to her feet, setting off a cacophony of screeches as the birds watch their dinner disappear.

They follow her down the promenade, an embarrassment of flapping wings and noisy, gaping beaks, until she escapes across the road, which appears to be some sort of magical barrier because they don't follow. She breathes a sigh of relief as she hurries towards her car, keeping her head turned away from the curious people on the promenade, annoyed to have drawn so much attention to herself.

That's when she spots the notice, stuck with sticky tape to the front window of a whitewashed cottage. Bed and breakfast, fifty pounds a night, it says. She hasn't booked anywhere to stay; her intention was to find a hotel in Douglas, but now that her search has led her here, she feels that she should stay. For tonight, at least. She could sleep in her car, but it's very small and has a strange, musty smell about it. A bedroom has much more appeal, and would feel safer.

Will this do for the night?

She steps back and looks at the house, one of a row that lines this side of the road. It looks small, narrow, hardly big enough to have more than one bedroom, but she knocks on the door anyway. No harm in asking. Nice and cheap, and after prison she reckons she can sleep anywhere.

An elderly lady opens the door, a glass of something in her hand. She is small and dumpy, her round face framed by short, straight hair, her cheeks flushed. The hand holding her glass is crinkled like crêpe paper, dotted with liver spots.

'Hello,' the lady says, friendly. She gives Natalie a glassy-eyed smile.

'I was just wondering if you have any vacancies,' Natalie says, no pleasantries to warm up the conversation, having already convinced herself she's wasting her time. The lady looks her up and down, takes a sip from her glass, then opens the door wide.

'Come and have a look, lovey. It's just a small room, but it might suit you.' Natalie hesitates, then follows her inside. *Why not?* She can always say no.

The cottage is Tardis-like in its dimensions, the hallway stretching back into what must be an extension. Natalie follows the lady up steep, creaking stairs, lit by shell-shaped wall lights, along a landing with cream woodchip paper on the walls and a purple swirly carpet on the floor, into a cosy little room at the front of the house.

There's a small double bed, draped with a patchwork quilt, in shades of heather, cream and blue, a pine wardrobe and a chest of drawers with a mirror on the wall above. A sheepskin rug lies on varnished floorboards by the side of the bed and pretty floral curtains hang at the windows. She can hear the sound of the waves, rhythmic and soothing as they break on the beach.

'It's perfect,' she says. *Much better than a hotel. Who would think to look for me here?* 'I'll take it. A couple of nights, would that be okay?'

'That's fine, lovey.' The lady gives her a wan smile and walks over to the window. 'It's going to be a beautiful sunset.' She turns to Natalie and her eyes glisten. 'My husband loved the sunsets.' She sniffs and takes a hanky out of her sleeve, blows her nose with a loud trumpet.

'Mmm,' Natalie says, unsure where the conversation is heading.

'Four years today since he died.' The lady's chin wobbles. 'He was a lovely man. Lovely.' She puts her glass down on the windowsill and takes a picture out of her cardigan pocket, holds it out for Natalie to take a look.

It's a wedding photo of a middle-aged couple laughing as they cut into a single-tiered wedding cake. He's a large man by all definitions, with several chins and a bald head, and their happiness shines out of the picture.

'I'm so sorry for your loss,' Natalie says, handing back the photo.

'He was my second.' The lady sighs. 'Heart attack. My first husband had a stroke. Absolute sweethearts, both of them. Really good to me. I've been very lucky.' She looks at Natalie's hands, which clasp the remains of her chip supper to her chest. 'You married, lovey?'

'Not anymore.' The bitterness is clear in Natalie's voice.

'You'll find someone else.' The lady picks up her drink and finishes it off in one big gulp. She holds up her empty glass and gives it a wiggle. 'Fancy some wine?'

Natalie looks at her watch and gives an apologetic smile. 'That's so kind of you. I'd love to, really, but I'm meeting a friend. Maybe another time?'

The lady sighs and walks towards the door.

'Just have to drink it myself, then' she says, sounding disappointed. 'Before you rush off, though, I'd better give you a key. I keep the front door locked, you see. With it being on the prom. Get pranksters sometimes.'

'Okay.' Natalie nods and smiles, following the lady as she sways down the hallway. She watches as she takes the stairs sideways, one careful step at a time.

'I'm Mary, by the way.' She looks up, stopping for a breather after a few steps. 'And you are…?'

'Natalie.'

'That's a pretty name.' She winces, clearly in pain. 'It's my knees, lovey. I'm fine going up, it's the coming down that's the problem. But, you know, I'm seventy-four this year so I suppose you've got to expect a bit of wear and tear.' She eases herself down a few more steps, grunting with each movement. 'Nearly there.'

Natalie checks her watch. Twenty past seven. She passed the Centenary Centre on her lap round Peel so she knows it's only a five-minute walk. Plenty of time to get into the venue, find Jack, see what he knows and get out of there before the gig starts.

Finally, Mary reaches the bottom and Natalie hurries down. She sees the rack of keys hanging by the door but Mary walks past and through a doorway into the front room. Natalie follows into a pleasant, square-shaped room with pastel-pink walls and roses on the curtains. A rectangular table and chairs are set up by the window and a couple of leather armchairs sit in front of a fireplace. A large dresser fills the back wall and Mary puts her empty glass on it.

'So, this is the dining room. You'll have your breakfast in here and you can use it as a sitting room if you like.' She points. 'TV in the corner, over there.'

'Right, yes, that's lovely.' Natalie hopes she doesn't sound impatient, but this is all happening at a snail's pace.

Mary turns to her.

'That your supper?' She nods at the parcel of food, which is leaking the unmistakable aroma of fish and chips. 'Feel free to tuck in. I can get you some cutlery, if you like.' She gives an encouraging smile but the thought of soggy chips makes Natalie feel queasy.

'Oh, thanks, but I've finished,' she says, and Mary holds out a hand out to take it off her.

'Right you are, then. I'll just show you the kitchen where you can make a cuppa whenever you like, then I'll let you get off.' Natalie hides a sigh of relief and follows her down the hallway.

If the rest of the house is dated, the kitchen looks like it hasn't been altered since the nineteen fifties. Open shelves, stacked with tins and jars, line the painted yellow walls. Wooden worktops are fitted around two sides of the room, and cream floral curtains, hanging on strips of coated wire, hide more shelves underneath. Terracotta lino covers the floor, pretending to be quarry tiles. A fridge-freezer hums in the corner, next to a washing machine. But although the room is basic and a bit tatty round the edges, every surface is spotlessly clean and the smell of citrus hangs in the air.

A clock chimes in the hallway. Natalie checks her watch. Half-past seven.

'I'm so sorry, Mary, I don't want to hurry you, but I've really got to go.'

Mary purses her lips a couple of times, like she's sucking a sweet. 'Oh, okay,' she says, holding up a finger. 'I better give you that key.' She ambles to the row of hooks by the door, takes a key and presses it into Natalie's hand.

'Have a nice time, lovey,' she says, opening the door for her.

Natalie smiles her thanks and heads outside, speed-walking up the hill towards the Centenary Centre.

CHAPTER FIVE

Now

My phone rings. I snatch it up and look at the screen.

'Hello,' I say, not even trying to hide my impatience. 'So, where is she?'

I know where she's heading. It doesn't take a genius to work that out, but I need to know how close she is. How much time I have.

'Right. So, she went to a bail hostel in Bangor.'

'Bangor? In Wales?'

'North Wales. Yep.'

'Why would she go to North Wales?'

'Well, I dunno, do I? That's where there was a space, I suppose. Or maybe she's got family there.'

'Right.'

Silence. I sense there's a but coming.

My shoulder muscles tighten.

'But I rang the hostel where she's staying and she did arrive, the manager confirmed that. But when he went to check for me, 'cos I wanted to make sure I was giving you proper information… well, she wasn't there. No bag in her room, nothing.'

Listening to this woman is making my jaw ache and I massage the muscles before I speak again.

'So, she's done a runner?'

'Well, it looks like that might be a possibility. But then again, she might come back. Maybe just didn't want to leave her stuff there while she went out to get a few bits and pieces.'

'So,' I say, carefully, 'you don't really know where she is?'

'I've informed the authorities here, and they're waiting for the manager to call back when she turns up.'

'If she turns up.'

'Well, if she doesn't come back, I suppose they'll go looking for her.'

'But it could be days before anyone bothers to do that?'

She sighs. 'Yes, you're probably right. It's not like she's a dangerous criminal or anything, so I don't suppose she's a priority. But if it gets to Friday and she misses her appointment with her Probation Officer, then I suppose someone might do something.'

'So,' I say, realising that an opportunity has arisen, 'nobody knows where she is and until she misses an appointment in three days' time, then nobody is going to bother looking for her? And even then, it might take a while for something to happen?'

'Exactly.'

I disconnect. And smile. That's actually very good news.

CHAPTER SIX

Then

After Natalie was delivered to the police station, she was led to a small, airless room furnished with a metal table and four metal chairs, all bolted to the floor. The room was painted a pale green, no windows, only a rectangle with what she supposed was a two-way mirror on one of the walls. The grey vinyl floor was worn and damp in places, the smell of bleach floating in the air, stinging her eyes.

She sat down, the door banged shut, and she was alone.

The silence pressed down on her, the rhythm of her heart shaking her body against the hard edges of the chair. She shifted in her seat, trying to find a comfortable position, but realised it wasn't possible, the furniture design having nothing to do with comfort.

It was too hot, heaters pumping blasts of warm air through vents at floor level. She could feel it on her ankles and she plucked at her joggers, peeling them away from sweaty skin. She wished she'd been able to change into something more presentable, something that didn't smell of body odour and wasn't dotted with stains. The fluorescent lights hummed and flickered, giving off a glare that made her head ache.

After a while, the door opened. Someone brought her a cup of coffee, and then, without saying a word, they left. She was numb, her thoughts floating up in a bubble of disbelief. But as she drank her coffee, the questions started to form, crowding into her mind and demanding answers. What was going on? How had she ended up alone, in this room, in a godforsaken frigging police station? And where the hell was her husband? If this was about work, they should be talking to him, not her. It was his sodding business, wasn't it? She fidgeted in her chair, sat up straighter, less sure now that she was here because of something she'd done. Surely it was all a bloody great mess, a mistake.

She clung on to that thought. A mistake. Or… another possibility emerged from the maelstrom of her thoughts; perhaps one of her clients had attracted police attention. Perhaps she was here as a witness, not a suspect. She stopped breathing for a moment as the implications registered. Yes! The idea had merit, because everyone knew that a proportion of people with money were less than honest. In her mind, she scrolled through a list of her clients, trying to identify the most likely culprits, a welcome distraction from the doubts that still lingered.

An hour later, she swirled cold coffee around in her polystyrene cup, an attempt to convince anyone who might be watching that she was bored, unconcerned and obviously not guilty of anything. She looked at her watch again. What were they doing for all this time?

Finally, the door to the interview room clicked open and two men walked in. They could almost be clones, with the same shaven heads, matching black suits, white shirts and plain dark ties, like in *Men in Black*. She put them somewhere in their late thirties, early forties.

Here we go, she thought, her hands suddenly slick with sweat, making her lose her grip on the cup, spilling the remnants of her coffee all over the table. She watched as the pool of dark liquid spread, like a bloodstain, horrified by her clumsiness and the impression she was making.

'Sorry,' she said, jumping to her feet as the coffee started to drip off the table and onto her legs. 'You startled me.'

'Geoff, get something to wipe this up,' said the first man who'd come in, his thin lips hardly moving when he spoke. Geoff sighed and went back out of the room.

The man looked at her, a cold stare, and her heart started to beat a little faster. Geoff came back in, cleared up the mess, and eventually they were ready to start. She wiped her hands on her joggers and took heart from the fact that they didn't seem to be in a hurry. That meant it wasn't too important, didn't it?

'I'm Detective Inspector Alan Morgan,' the man said, giving her a ghost of a smile, gone before it properly arrived. 'And this is my colleague, Detective Sergeant Geoff Adams.' Geoff nodded a greeting, staring at her with icy blue eyes.

Her hands locked themselves together in her lap. She sat up straight, forced her shoulders back and tried to look confident.

'These are preliminary questions,' DI Morgan said. 'You're not under caution.'

She breathed. That was good, wasn't it? She dared to imagine that she'd got it right, that this was about one of her clients, but her heart still raced.

DI Morgan opened a file and spent a moment flicking through the papers until he found what he was looking for. He pulled out a single sheet, looked at her and ran his tongue round his lips. 'Okay. Let's just clear up the basics, shall we?'

She nodded, wanting to appear helpful so they could get this sorted out and she could go home.

'Do you work at your husband's firm, Wilson Wealth Management?'

She nodded. 'Yes, I do. I manage investment portfolios for a number of clients.'

'And were you at work on Monday twentieth of February?'

She had to think about that, days and dates all merging together into an impenetrable mass of forgotten events. What date was it today? She looked at her watch. February twenty-seventh. A week ago.

She nodded. 'Yes, yes I was.'

'And what are your working hours?'

'Nine to five generally.'

He raised an eyebrow. 'So, you never go in earlier?'

She shrugged. 'Occasionally.'

'What about on that day?'

She thought about it, shook her head. 'I honestly can't remember.'

He stared at her for a long moment. She swallowed, gripped her hands together a little tighter.

'Okay, let's move on.' DI Morgan's eyes locked with hers. 'Do you have a client called Ballios Christopoulos?'

She raised her eyebrows, breathed a quiet sigh of relief, surprised that he was the subject of investigation. Because that must be what this was about. She'd never considered his finances suspect, but there was obviously no way of telling just by looking at somebody. The nicest people could still be criminals, couldn't they?

'Yes, I do,' she said, her body aching with the effort of sitting up straight, determined that her posture should present a professional persona even if her clothes were letting her down. 'Is he in trouble?'

DI Morgan's lips tightened. 'We ask the questions, if you don't mind just answering.'

'Yes, yes of course.' Her cheeks flushed.

'And you look after his investment account with your firm?'

'Yes, that's right.'

He handed her a sheet of paper. 'Would you mind having a look at this, please. Tell us what you think it means?'

She looked at the columns of figures and was about to hand it back when she realised that something wasn't right. She frowned, put it on the table in front of her, looked at it again and suddenly knew what this whole thing was about.

A bead of sweat worked its way down her spine. She swallowed, and met DI Morgan's gaze, giving him what she hoped was the look of an innocent woman.

'It's my husband's business. Maybe you should be asking him about this?

DI Morgan smiled, but there was a challenge in his eyes. 'We believe it's your client and you're the only person he deals with, so we're asking you.'

'Well, I'd like to speak to my husband, please.'

He stared back at her, and the seconds ticked by, but she wasn't going to break eye contact first, knew it was important to appear strong, however weak she felt inside.

'I'm afraid that's not possible,' he said. 'But now you know what this is about, I'll leave you to have a think about things, shall I?'

He stood and left the room, Geoff not far behind him.

The door clicked shut and she was alone again, shaking and clammy. How the hell was she going to explain her way out of this one?

CHAPTER SEVEN

Now

The Centenary Centre, where the gig is being held, is a squat but tidy building, with an Art Deco feel about it. People are waiting to get in and Natalie attaches herself to the end of the queue, careful not to catch anyone's eye.

She tells herself there's safety in numbers, the best place to hide is in a crowd, but these platitudes are a nonsense because she senses people sneaking glances at her. She wishes she'd taken a bit more trouble getting ready, at least put on some make-up, or changed her clothes but it's so long since she's been to a social gathering, it hadn't even crossed her mind. Now her lack of effort makes her stand out. She shakes out her hair, combs it with her fingers to tidy it up, hoping it will shade her face a little, make her less obvious. She stares at the pavement while the queue shuffles forwards, hands tucked in her pockets, trying to look relaxed.

A few minutes later, she's at the front of the queue, looking at the middle-aged woman who is manning the door. She has a severe haircut, short and angular, that does nothing to flatter her prominent nose and she reminds Natalie of a Russian assassin in one of the old James Bond films.

'I'm Natalie.' She lowers her voice, aware that several people are listening. 'Jack invited me. From the band. He said he'd mention it to you.'

'Have you got a ticket?' The woman's face is a picture of disapproval. 'It's a sell-out tonight and you won't be able to come in if you haven't got a ticket.'

Natalie stares at the woman, who stares back, then lifts her eyes to the next person in the queue and beckons to him. Natalie's been dismissed, the woman's demeanour making it clear that there's no potential for negotiation. She clamps her jaw tight, and turns to go, eyes on the ground as she wonders what to do next. *I can ring him later*, she thinks. *But then I'll have to wait until the gig's over.* A couple of hours at least. *Too much wasted time.*

'Excuse me!' A strident voice calls out, making Natalie stop. 'Excuse me.' She turns to see the assassin woman waving at her, Jack standing at her shoulder, a grin on his face. Everyone in the queue looks at Natalie as she scurries back to the entrance door, relief flipping in her stomach.

'Hey! You made it,' Jack says.

She smiles and decides he's scrubbed up pretty well. His hair is a lighter brown now that it's clean and falls in shiny waves to his shoulders. His face is freshly shaven, only a faint hint of stubble remaining, allowing his dimples to show when he smiles. He smells of something spicy and fresh, looks bigger out of his biker gear, a plain white T-shirt showing off a toned torso and muscular arms.

'Auntie Beth, this is Natalie,' he says, turning to the woman manning the door.

'I know,' she snaps and turns to deal with the next person in the queue.

Jack shrugs.

'Daft old bat,' he murmurs in Natalie's ear as he leads her away from the door.

Natalie gives him a tentative smile and opens her mouth to speak, to tell him that she's not staying, but Jack speaks first.

'We might be running a bit late,' he says, as she follows him into a small bar area that is jam-packed with people, the hum of conversation a few decibels louder than comfortable. 'Just waiting for the drummer to turn up. Want something to drink?'

She shakes her head. 'I can't stay.'

He leans towards her, hand cupping his ear. 'Sorry, you can't what?'

'I can't stay,' she says, louder. 'I just wanted to ask about Tom Wilson. From Excalibur Wealth. I think they might be one of your sponsors.' But he's not listening, his head turned, distracted by the shout of his name.

'Jack! Jack!' A bearded young man with big holes in his ears, like an African tribesman, is at the door, waving tattooed arms above his head. 'Craig's here!'

'Right, gotta go,' Jack says, eyes alight, looking nervous and excited at the same time. 'I'll see you at the interval. Okay?'

Natalie watches, helpless as he pushes his way out of the room, the chance of finding Harry going with him. The noise of excited chatter hammers inside her skull, making her wince while her mind spins through her options. *Stay or go?*

Her eyes to do a sweep of the crowd and she glimpses a familiar face, a woman standing at the other end of the room, on the edge of a noisy group. She does a double-take, thinking she must be mistaken. But she'd recognise Sasha anywhere; her profile, that mane of strawberry-blonde hair. She used to be her best friend.

She remembers the postcard she received in prison a few weeks ago, a picture of a woman in Elizabethan dress on the front, posted from Liverpool:

Cool part in a period drama, posh frocks and everything. Should be back before you come out. Confirm date and time and I'll try to be there to pick you up. Not long now. Can't wait to see you.

Love Lady Catherine (Okay, Sasha to you) xxx

In all honesty, she hadn't believed that Sasha would come and pick her up, because filming schedules were variable, and she'd been disappointed so often in the past when arrangements had fallen through, so she'd put it out of her mind.

In any case, Natalie's release had been sudden, a bit cloak and dagger, due to the death threats and even Natalie hadn't known what was happening until the morning she'd been freed. Then they'd taken her to a halfway house in Wales, which had been a surprise and had prompted her to make a flurry of phone calls to get everything organised. She hadn't thought about Sasha, and where in the world she might be filming.

This is a sign, she tells herself. *Forgive and forget.*

Sasha will help her find Tom and Harry, she's sure of it, because Sasha has promised that she'll support Natalie in any way that she can. She pulls herself towards her like a drowning woman pulling on a lifeline, twisting and turning as she tries to find a way through the mass of people crammed between them.

She's about to call out to Sasha when she stops, sandwiched between two overweight men, and the cacophony of conversation fades away, to be replaced by the thudding of her pulse in her ears: a drumbeat that signals caution.

Is Sasha still a friend?

It's something Natalie has asked herself more than once over the years.

Theirs was not a natural friendship, more an attraction of opposites, but somehow it had worked, having bonded at secondary school when they'd had to sit next to each other as new girls. Sasha had always wanted to be an actress, while Natalie had wanted to be a journalist and they'd shared dreams of successful careers, celebrity boyfriends and beautiful houses in London. After school, when Sasha had gone off to the Liverpool Institute for Performing Arts, still chasing her dreams, and Natalie had abandoned hers and went to work in a casino, they'd kept in touch. Even when

Sasha's work had taken her backwards and forward to America, their friendship had remained strong.

Until Natalie had been sent to prison.

'I'm so scared,' Natalie had said when she'd rung Sasha, voice wavering. 'Please come and see me. You will, won't you?'

'What?' Silence for a long moment. 'Oh, Nats.'

Silence.

'Sash, you still there?'

'Look… I'm so sorry, but… I can't.' Natalie had heard a shuddering sigh. 'I can't come to a prison. You know what it was like when… when Dad was inside. Panic attacks like you wouldn't believe when I tried to go and see him. Couldn't breathe, blacked out and ended up in hospital. You remember, don't you? I can't do it. Honestly, you know I want to, but I just… I just… physically I can't.' Sasha's voice had been thick with emotion. 'I'm letting you down, I know I am, but…'

Another silence had filled Natalie's ears. She'd swallowed back the words she'd wanted to say. 'It's okay,' she'd said instead and leant against the wall, her legs weak. Sasha's father had been in prison when Natalie had met her and it was something she'd rarely spoken about. But it had happened when Sasha was a child. Surely, Natalie had reasoned, things were different now she was an adult?

'It's going to be fine.' Sasha had sniffed, tears in her voice. 'I'm here for you. You know that, don't you? Ring whenever you want.'

Natalie had huffed, her fist thumping the wall behind her. 'Yeah,' she'd said.

Sasha had cried then. 'Hang on in there,' she'd sobbed. 'I'm thinking about you. I want you to know that. Always. Sending positive vibes. Don't you worry. It'll all work out.' Natalie had heard Sasha blowing her nose.

'Yeah,' Natalie had replied, then slammed down the phone. She hadn't tried to call her again; the idea of everything unsaid, all the emotion was too much to contemplate and she'd found it was easier to write.

Over the years, Natalie reminded herself that it wasn't Sasha's fault. Reality wasn't her strong point. As an actress, she lived in a pretend world and the practicalities of ordinary people's lives were often beyond her. Natalie had always been the sensible one, the comfort that Sasha gravitated towards when her own world was shaky. The idea that Sasha was still her friend was the important thing, the life jacket that stopped Natalie from drowning in a sea of loneliness and resentment.

Natalie thinks about this now, and wonders what constitutes friendship when one of you is locked away. *Is the idea of it enough?* Or would a friend have made more of an effort to come and see her? They would at least have tried, wouldn't they? She would have done it for Sasha. No question.

There's still a nugget of hurt, tucked away in her heart, that makes her want to keep Sasha at a distance, but if she's going to find Harry, she needs Sasha's lateral thinking, and another person would make the task so much easier. It's an opportunity that she can't throw away, for Harry's sake.

The movement of people brushing past Natalie shakes her out of her thoughts and she realises that the bar is emptying as people make their way to the hall. She's swimming against the tide and decides it'll be easier to go with them as far as the door, where she can stand to one side and wait for Sasha to come through. She glances over to where Sasha had been standing, and her eyes widen when she realises she's not there anymore. Her pulse quickens. She glances around the room but can't see her anywhere.

Oh no! What if she's left? Gone back to wherever she's staying?

Natalie detaches herself from the tail end of the crowd, hurries towards the exit, and bumps into Sasha coming the other way. Literally walks into her. Flesh bumping flesh. She gasps. Sasha frowns, looks annoyed and steps round her before Natalie can say anything, leaving a waft of perfume in her wake as she hurries into the hall, where loud cheers signal that the band has come on stage.

Natalie lets out a long breath, her hand on her chest. She frowns. *Doesn't that tell me everything I need to know? She didn't even recognise me.*

Annoyed with herself for wasting time, she decides to go back to Mary's and start on some Internet research. Then she'll ring Jack later. She's almost at the exit when she hears footsteps behind her and before she can turn, a hand grasps her by the shoulder. Her heart leaps and she reacts without thinking, survival instincts kicking in. She swings round, body hunched low and punches whoever it is in the stomach with as much force as she can muster, ready to run as soon as they hit the floor.

CHAPTER EIGHT

Then

Natalie stood in the police station, fidgeting with her hair, her chaperone standing a few yards away, as she waited for John Bergman to come to the phone. Technically he was Tom's solicitor, they were buddies from school, but she'd met him at several social events. She'd had to ring his home number, given the late hour, and his wife answered, not too pleased about the interruption to their evening. She'd tried to fob Natalie off and it took a few minutes of pleading to persuade her that it was important enough to disturb her husband.

'Natalie?' His booming voice filled her ear. She registered a note of caution and cringed. She didn't really know him well enough to be asking for a favour, but he was the only legal person she knew.

'Look, John, I'm so sorry to ring you at home…'

'We're having a dinner party.'

'Yes… yes, your wife said.' Natalie's hand tightened round the receiver, almost ready to put it down. 'I'm so sorry to disturb you, but I have a problem. I need your help.'

'Oh?' He sighed.

'I think… I think I've been arrested.' Her cheeks were burning.

'Ah.'

There was a silence. She waited for him to ask her why, but he didn't, so she stumbled on.

'Something to do with the business.'

'Look, Natalie, I have to stop you there. It would be a conflict of interests for me to speak to you.'

'What?'

'Anything to do with the business, I'm afraid I act for Tom.'

Was this man being deliberately obtuse? 'Okay, but we're married, so don't you act for me as well?'

'I'm sorry, Natalie. I can't discuss my client's business or personal interests with you.'

His words were harsh and unexpected, taking her breath away.

'Okay, I understand that,' she said, carefully changing tack, keeping her voice as calm as she could. 'But is there someone in your firm who could act for me?'

The phone buzzed. She'd lost the connection and she cursed the battered handset she was using. She dialled again. The number was engaged. She tried again and again and it wasn't until her fifth attempt that it dawned on her that he'd taken the phone off the hook. She stared at the handset like it had just bitten her, a sense of foreboding draping itself around her like Dracula's cloak.

'No luck?' asked her chaperone.

She shook her head and chewed at her lip. *What now?*

'Would you like the duty solicitor?'

He lifted the receiver, fingers ready to dial. She nodded. What else could she do?

Shortly after midnight, a young woman in a black suit and white shirt turned up, looking hot and flustered, eyes bleary and red. Natalie thought she must have got dressed in the dark because her shirt was buttoned up wrong and her dark hair was clipped in a comb thing, with a clump falling out at the back. She looked cross. Natalie was furious, like an animal backed into a corner.

'Steph Bradley,' the solicitor said, holding out a hand, no smile, a hostile look in her eyes, like Natalie had wronged her in some way. 'Right.' She looked at her watch. 'We've got half an hour to go through everything, then you're in for an interview under caution.'

Natalie swallowed. 'Can I speak to my husband?'

'No,' the solicitor said, frowning at Natalie as if she was stupid. 'And you won't be able to speak to him while this case is ongoing, given that he's your employer and is a potential witness for the prosecution.'

Natalie gripped the edge of her seat. She really hadn't considered that aspect to their relationship. But that couldn't be right. *He wouldn't give evidence against me, would he?* Her mind stuttered as it tried to process the idea that her husband would do such a thing. *No. He just wouldn't.* However strained their marriage, he'd been brought up in an old-fashioned way and considered himself to be the protector of his family. His loyalty to her was an undeniable fact. Her thoughts paused for a second. *Unless they make him.*

Her solicitor sat down and dropped a large shoulder bag to the floor with a thump, then slapped a folder onto the table before taking a notepad and pen from her bag. She opened the folder, read a sheet of paper and frowned before looking at Natalie.

'Okay, so you're accused of taking one point two million from one of your clients' investment accounts.'

Christ! That sounded so bad when it was said out loud. The tension in Natalie's shoulders notched a bit tighter, her heart thudding in her chest. In the hours that Natalie had been waiting for her solicitor to turn up, she had come to the realisation that there was no way for the money to have disappeared that didn't involve her. It must have been a mistake, a transposition of numbers. So easy to do when you were tired and had your mind at home with your baby, rather than at work with your clients' fortunes. But she hadn't stolen the money. No way. It was an honest mistake. That was all. A mistake.

'I didn't do it,' she said. It sounded feeble, even to her ears. She tasted blood as her teeth nipped at her lip, her heart rate picking up. *What happens if nobody believes me?*

Her solicitor gave a humph and put down her pen. She crossed her arms, a weary look in her eyes. 'You're going to have to do better than that.'

Natalie stared at her and wondered why she was a defence solicitor. *Isn't she supposed to be on my side?*

'This is a mistake,' Natalie said, tapping the table with a finger. 'A clerical error of some sort. I don't know what's happened, but if I could go to the office and look at my client's records, then I'm sure I could sort it out.'

The solicitor stared at her, silent for a long moment. Natalie could feel her nostrils flaring, breath puffing out of her as her frustration mounted. *Why isn't this woman listening?*

'Well, you're going to have to give me something. Tell me how you're going to prove that you didn't steal the money because the trail leads back to you. The police have evidence, which they want to discuss with you in—' she looked at her watch '—fifteen minutes.'

Natalie stared at her, lightheaded.

'I… um…' *Christ, I need to say something, anything to try and get this woman to work with me rather than against me.* 'Okay, so I've just come back from maternity leave and have started to pick up my clients again. Mr Christopoulos—' she nodded to the piece of paper in her solicitor's hand, which was a summary of Mr Christopoulos's investment account with the business '—he was one of the first clients I ever dealt with, and he insisted I should carry on looking after his portfolio. Wouldn't let anyone else near it, even while I was off on maternity leave.'

Natalie thought about the small, slender man with a shiny head and bulbous nose, who'd made his money in shipping. A friend of Tom's father. He had money stashed all over the world, and the few million pounds he invested with Tom's company was just play money. He liked to take risks and she'd enjoyed doing the research, finding the right companies and funds for him to invest in, advising him when to buy and sell.

The solicitor nodded, made a winding motion with her hand.

Natalie sat up straight, more comfortable now that she had a clear picture of her client in her mind. She could visualise their meeting, hear the conversation in her head. She nodded, her confidence rising. Somebody had made a mistake somewhere, but that somebody wasn't her. It could be the banking system. Unusual, but it wasn't unknown for there to be occasional problems.

She looked at her solicitor. 'We had a meeting a couple of weeks ago. Decided things were going well and we wouldn't make any changes for the time being.' She frowned as she replayed the meeting in her mind.

'So, you are the only person in the business who has dealings with this client?'

'Yes. I'm the only person with the passwords to his accounts.' *That doesn't sound good, does it?* 'We have a strict procedure, for client security. That's why this has got to be a mistake. I haven't done any work on his account for over six months. I know I haven't.'

'So, who transferred a lump sum of money into an account in the Cayman Islands if it wasn't you?'

Natalie started to feel unbearably hot. Beads of sweat blossomed on her brow.

'The Cayman Islands? Are you sure about that?'

'Why? Does that mean anything to you?'

Little black dots invaded her vision. She took a sip of water, tried to calm her breathing. Did she remember signing forms to open an account there?

Her fingers rubbed at her temples as she tried to get things clear in her mind. 'Maybe. I don't know.'

The solicitor gave her a searing look.

Then the door opened and Geoff poked his head round.

'We'd like to interview your client now,' he said, as if Natalie wasn't there.

The interview under caution was very short. A slam dunk for the police because they'd done their homework and had more than enough evidence. Very neat and tidy.

She stared at the police officers as they read out the charges, their voices sounding far away as she shrank inside her body, like a snail retreating into its shell. It had all happened so fast. *This can't be real, can it?* Maybe she'd misunderstood the proceedings in some way? She turned to her solicitor, expecting her to say something to stop the process, but she didn't. She just nodded and left the room along with the police officers.

Left alone once more, Natalie slumped forwards, her elbows on the table, hands cradling her head. She pulled at her hair, using the pain to blot out the thoughts of what might happen next.

She'd been charged with theft.

What was Tom going to say when he came to take her home? And her mother? She shuddered at the thought, unable to work out how it could have happened, no recollection of making the transfer. *But I must have done, mustn't I?* She was going to have to go and see the doctor about these blanks in her life, no doubt about it. This was getting scary now. Worse than scary. She'd just ruined her career, possibly her marriage and goodness knows what effect it would have on her family, the business and their reputation. Had she ruined her son's future? She lay her head on the table, welcoming the cool metal against her forehead, tears trickling off her nose.

Eventually, her solicitor came back in, grim-faced, looking as weary as Natalie felt.

'I'm sorry, but you've been denied bail. They're going to be taking you to Stanbridge Prison.'

Prison? Natalie looked at her like a startled rabbit. *Was that what she just said?*

Natalie shook her head, her heart forgetting its rhythm. 'No way am I going to prison! No way! I can't. I've got a baby.' Her chest was tight and she was panting like she was about to give birth. It hadn't entered her mind that she wouldn't be going home, not for a minute.

'I'm sorry, but that's what's happening. Apparently, some airline tickets were found in your desk at the office. One-way tickets for you and your son to Brazil.' Natalie stared at her solicitor, unable to speak. 'As you may know, the UK has no extradition treaty with Brazil. They think you might take your son and do a runner, so they won't risk letting you out on bail. You'll be held at Stanbridge on remand.'

'But... but...' The words stuck in her mouth as her world dissolved. 'I didn't book any tickets.' She shook her head. 'I didn't.' The solicitor was packing up her stuff and Natalie grabbed her hand to make her listen, sobs catching in her throat. 'Please, you've got to believe me.' The solicitor shook Natalie's hand off hers and slung her bag over her shoulder, giving her a hard stare.

'Look, Natalie, I'm afraid begging is not going to work with me. The tickets were booked with the Co-operative travel agents in town. The police have been to see them, and they picked out a picture of you as the person they had sold the tickets to. Really, there's no point lying to me because the only way I can do my best for you is if you tell me the truth.'

'But I am,' Natalie sobbed. 'I am telling the truth.'

The solicitor pressed her lips into a thin line, then turned and walked away, while a police officer escorted Natalie to a cell to await transportation. Alone in an alien world, she huddled in a corner, aching for her son, her husband, her home while fear and misery held on to her like clammy hands.

CHAPTER NINE

Now

Natalie's hands fly to her mouth as Sasha hits the ground with a thump, arms hugging her stomach.

'Sasha! Christ, I'm so sorry,' she says as she crouches beside her, hands flexing, unsure whether to touch her or not. 'You startled me.'

'Fucking hell, Nat!' Sasha forces the words through clenched teeth. She turns onto her side and gets onto her knees. Natalie stands, biting her lip as she watches Sasha struggle to her feet and lean against the wall, still hugging her stomach. 'Christ!'

'I'm sorry, Sash, honestly... it's just that...' Heat flushes round Natalie's body as she hunts for the right thing to say.

'Just what?'

'Where I've been, if somebody comes at you from behind, you know they're up to no good. Pointy object in the kidneys, or neck or something.' She shuffles from foot to foot, appalled by what she's done, not sure how this is going to work out.

They stand and look at each other for a moment.

'Oh, Sash, it's so good to see you.'

The years of being apart fall away and she wraps Sasha in a hug, drawn to the memory of their friendship like iron filings to a magnet. They're about the same size, which makes hugging that much easier and Natalie clutches Sasha to her, breathing in her perfume, relishing the feel of Sasha's cheek against her own.

Tension flows out of her in a sigh that goes on and on until her lungs are empty, the warmth of a familiar body making her feel giddy as she embraces the idea that she's back in the real world. A world where she has a proper friend.

'I'm so, so sorry,' she says and hugs Sasha harder. 'Please forgive me.'

After a moment, Sasha hugs her back and Natalie's muscles start to relax. Eventually, it's Sasha who pushes away. She shakes her head.

'Fuck, Nat! I can't believe it's you.' Her eyes travel up and down Natalie's body. 'You've… er… Wow, I honestly didn't recognise you.'

'I know.' Natalie flaps at her clothes. 'Lost a bit of weight. Thought I'd have a go at being blonde.' She shrugs, her throat too thick with emotion to speak.

Sasha narrows her eyes, puts a hand on Natalie's shoulder and gives it a gentle rub. 'Are you okay?'

Natalie laughs instead of answering because that's a really stupid question. *Of course I'm not okay.*

'Wow,' Sasha says again, eyes searching Natalie's face, a smile playing on her lips. 'You're out already. I thought it was going to be… well, I didn't know when they were going to let you out. Why didn't you tell me?'

'It was a surprise for me as well,' Natalie says. 'Ran out of space to lock up dangerous women, I think.' She laughs. Sasha frowns. Natalie runs a hand through her hair. 'I would have told you, but I don't have your number anymore. Would you believe they lost my phone? All my contacts gone, so I couldn't have told you.' It's a poor excuse, she knows, because it would have been easy enough to track down Sasha's mum who could have given her the number. She stumbles on. 'And you said you were away filming for a few months, so I… um…' She smiles at Sasha. 'Thought I'd surprise you when you got back.'

Sasha raises her eyebrows and rubs her stomach. 'Yeah, it's a surprise all right.'

The band hits a crescendo of screaming guitars and crashing drums, making Sasha wince. She takes hold of Natalie's arm, wheels her round and starts walking her towards the exit. 'Come on, you mad cow, we can't talk with this racket going on, let's go and get a drink.'

She steers Natalie out of the building, fingers clasping Natalie's elbow like a claw. Natalie's mother used to drag her along the road like this when she was cross with her and Natalie understands Sasha's reaction, accepts that she deserves it after that punch.

'I can't believe you were at that gig,' Natalie says. 'Not your sort of thing, is it?'

Sasha laughs. 'No, you're right about that. I was dragged along, didn't have much choice, to be honest. The producer of this film I'm in is a director of the charity that organised the event, so he forced us all to buy a ticket.' She lets go of Natalie's elbow and links arms with her instead, pulling her close. 'Glad to have an excuse to get out of there, to be honest. As you know, I'm a Lady Gaga kinda girl.' She flicks a puzzled glance at Natalie. 'Come to think of it, rock music's not really your thing either, is it?'

Natalie stops and pulls away from Sasha, stuffs her hands in her pockets. She doesn't want to go to the pub, hasn't got time for a cosy chat. Enough time has been wasted already. She needs to know, right now, if Sasha's going to help her or not.

'I'm in a bit of a rush, Sash. I'm sorry but I can't go for a drink.'

'You are joking, aren't you?' A flicker of hurt crosses Sasha's face. 'After all this time…'

'Look, I've got to find Harry.'

Sasha looks puzzled for a moment. 'Harry? Oh God. Of course. They moved here, didn't they? I had totally forgotten. But that makes sense now, why you're here of all places. Is that where you're off to in such a rush?' She sighs, clearly disappointed. 'It's okay, I suppose we can have a drink another time.' She puts out a hand and rubs Natalie's shoulder. 'Don't worry about it. I understand.'

Natalie takes a deep breath. 'No. I'm sorry but you don't understand. I um… I haven't spoken to Tom yet.' She pulls a face. 'You know how things are between us. The problem is…' Natalie hesitates, then her words come out in a rush. 'I don't know where Harry is. I thought he'd be at Tom's parents' house, that's the last I heard, but the house is empty. It's been sold. Can you believe it? So, once I found that out, well… I didn't know where to go. Ended up here because I met some bloke on the ferry, who's in the band. I thought he might know something, because I figured Tom's company might be one of tonight's sponsors. I couldn't think of anything else to do and, well…' She throws her hands up.

Sasha frowns. 'Oh no! So, you've no idea where they are?'

'Not yet, no.' A knot is forming in Natalie's stomach, clenching tighter as the difficulty of her mission becomes clear.

'Oh dear.' Silence for a moment. 'So, what are you going to do?'

Their eyes meet and Sasha's steady gaze makes Natalie's heart lurch. 'Sasha, would you help me?'

She looks puzzled. 'Help you with what?'

'Getting Harry back.' Natalie's chest tightens as she watches Sasha's blue eyes widen. 'I need to get him safe.'

'Safe? What do you mean?' She frowns. 'Why wouldn't he be safe?'

'He's in…' Natalie stops herself. Remembers that Sasha doesn't know about Katya. Or Katya's brother, Lech, and the death threats. *How could she understand?* Natalie takes a deep breath. 'He needs to be with me, Sash. Tom can't look after him properly. He's not fit to be a parent, you know that.'

'Oh Nat.' Sasha's eyes are full of concern. 'Don't you think… Look, don't take this the wrong way but, after all this time, don't you think Harry might be settled in his own little world? I mean, he won't know you, will he?'

Her words rip at Natalie's heart and she stares at her. 'Of course he'll know me.' She taps her chest. 'I'm his mother. What are you saying?'

Sasha grasps Natalie's hands, her face soft with sympathy. 'I just… Oh, I know how hard this has been for you. I do. All your letters… I feel for you, honestly, I do. But sometimes it's better to leave well alone, you know. Hard as it is, sometimes you just have to let go and move on.'

Natalie snatches her hands away.

'Being without him for over three years has been hard enough.' Disbelief sharpens Natalie's voice. 'You think I can just walk away and forget him? You think that's even possible? I can't live another day without him, let alone a lifetime. Honestly, you've no idea. Not even a… a bloody clue.' She folds her arms across her chest. 'Anyway, forget it. I can manage by myself. Can't be that hard to find them on a little island like this, can it?'

Natalie glares at Sasha, reminds herself that she still has Jack to ask for help. And there's plenty of information on the Internet. She hasn't really started with that yet. Sasha's an optional extra, a non-essential part of her plans.

Sasha sighs. 'Look, I'm sorry, I didn't mean to upset you. I just… I'm thinking about what's best for you. Maybe better to get yourself back on your feet before you do anything rash. You know, adjust to being out. Take it slow.'

'I said, forget it.'

Sasha holds up her hands in a gesture of surrender. 'Okay, okay. I don't want to fight. Look… it's your life. If you need me to help, then—' she gives Natalie a warm smile and nods '—of course I'll help you. You know I will. Whatever you need.'

They stare at each other for a moment and Natalie looks away. A worm of doubt wriggles in her mind because you don't want someone on your side who's not fully committed to the cause and she's not convinced that Sasha really is, not yet anyway.

Harry won't know you. How could she even think that? Of course, he'll know me. He's part of me, isn't he? Made from my own flesh and blood. Her hands clasp her arms tighter to her chest. *Of course, he'll know me.*

She looks up, catches Sasha watching her, eyes narrowed, like she's trying to work something out.

'I wondered, just so I know what we're doing here… are you allowed?'

Natalie frowns. 'Allowed what?'

'To be here. Are you supposed to be here? On the Isle of Man. I thought you'd be…'

'Be what?' *Here we go*, Natalie thinks, *undermining me before we've even started.*

'Sorry, Nat,' Sasha puts a hand on her shoulder, 'I just thought they'd want to… you know… supervise you in some way. Give you work to do, community stuff.' She shrugs. 'Tag you with one of those electronic thingies, so they know where you are.'

Natalie looks away, kicks at the pavement.

'Okay, so technically I'm not supposed to be here, but it's only for a few days and nobody's going to know and…'

'You're not going to get me in trouble with the police, or anything, are you?'

Natalie opens her mouth to speak and closes it again. *Am I? Asking her to get information, act as a decoy, a distraction. No, I'm pretty sure she'll be able to talk her way out of trouble.* Natalie returns her gaze. 'I'm not asking you to do anything illegal,' she says. 'Not really.'

Sasha nods. 'Okay, so what's your plan, then? What do you need me to do?'

Natalie's heart is racing now and she wonders where to start. But before she can speak, Sasha's phone rings. She takes it out of her pocket, looks at the screen and tuts.

'Sorry, got to take this,' she says and walks away a few steps. Natalie clamps her mouth shut and strains to hear, catches snippets.

'Mel… what, no better? Okay, don't panic… Try that… What?' She sighs. 'Okay. Okay. Yes. I'm on my way.'

Sasha walks back to Natalie, looking annoyed, her mouth pinched at the edges. 'Look Nat, I'm really sorry but I've got to go. One of the actors – my leading man, would you believe – has taken something he shouldn't and he's completely out of it. I left someone babysitting him, but she's panicking and—' she throws her hands up, clearly upset '—he'll get thrown off the production if we can't sort him out. Ruin it for all of us.'

Natalie sighs. *Typical, just when I was getting somewhere.*

'Oh. You're still filming, then?'

Sasha taps and swipes at her phone, frowning. 'What?' She looks up, mouth a thin line. Then her eyes soften a little. 'Yes, yes, still filming. But look, I've got to go. Give me your number and I'll call you. Find a time tomorrow when we can meet, get a plan together.' Sasha hands Natalie her phone and waits while Natalie finds a card with her new phone number on it and types it in. Then she wraps Natalie in a sudden hug and when she pushes away, her face is serious. 'Don't you worry. We'll find Harry. You and me.' She gives Natalie a quick smile, then she's off, trotting down the road. 'See you tomorrow,' she calls over her shoulder.

Natalie watches her disappear, up towards the cathedral and realises that she can't just let her go, relying on her to call. *What if she doesn't?* Tomorrow can mean many things with Sasha. On rare occasions, it can actually turn out to mean tomorrow, but usually it can mean in a day or two, next week, in a few months. Perhaps never. She dashes after her, wanting to make a definite arrangement to meet, but when she gets into the cathedral grounds, Sasha's nowhere to be seen.

CHAPTER TEN

Then

The morning after her arrest, having spent all night at the police station, Natalie was shown into a small, rectangular waiting area with black metal benches fixed against pale-green walls. The van would be here soon, she'd been told, once it had finished its pick-ups from a couple of other police stations.

Goosebumps prickled her arms as she felt the presence of all those who had been there before her. She could see it in the grubby line that ran around the room, where people had leant greasy scalps against the walls, and on the grey-painted floors, scuffed with the passage of hundreds of feet. Her thoughts went to Harry. Was Tom managing to get him dressed and give him breakfast? She reminded herself that Elena, Harry's nanny, would be back home by now, told herself that she would look after him. *But he'll be missing me.* Her chest tightened. She could see his crumpled face, crying, the image locked in her mind, taunting her until she was close to tears herself.

A young woman, early twenties at the most, was brought in, mascara smudged around her eyes, long black hair tied in a high ponytail. She looked oriental, exotic, wearing a sparkly silver dress that rode up her thighs as she sat down, showing a tattoo of a dragon. No shoes on her feet. She was tiny, making Natalie feel bloated in comparison. They sat in silence for a while, the space between them filled with the acrid smell of sweat.

'You been before?' the girl asked in a Liverpudlian accent, her voice as light as her frame.

Natalie shook her head, hands gripped together in her lap, her head held in the vice of a throbbing headache.

'I have.' The girl sighed. 'This is the third time for me.'

'What?' Natalie's eyes opened wide. She looked away, focused on the girl's bare feet, small as a child's, her nails painted ruby red. *Where are her shoes?*

The girl nodded. 'First time was possession. Not my stuff, I was just doing some dude a favour but, well, who's going to listen? Then it was shoplifting. I put my hands up to that one. But, you know, when you're desperate for something to eat…' She looked at her feet, wiggled her toes, then her eyes met Natalie's. 'And now… GBH. I think that's what they said. Or was it ABH? I can't remember. But I don't see how you can class a stiletto as a weapon, do you? Not like a knife, is it?'

Natalie looked away, aware that her mouth was open and hoped her expression had been noncommittal. Like it wasn't a big deal, heard it all before. Who was she to judge, anyway? *But Christ, grievous bodily harm? With a stiletto?*

'I'm Mali, by the way.' The girl folded her arms across her chest, eyes defiant. 'And in case you're wondering, it was self-defence.'

'Oh, yes, right.' Natalie swallowed, looked at the girl, so as not to appear rude, but couldn't quite manage a smile. 'Right… I'm Natalie.'

They lapsed into silence again, Mali fiddling with her nails, while Natalie tried not to look at her; difficult when you're sitting opposite each other. She wondered how an attractive young girl came to be in and out of prison. What sort of life had she led? What sort of people would Natalie be locked up with? She wiped clammy hands on her joggers. The girl was staring at her.

'Don't look so scared,' she said. 'It's not so bad. You'll be fine.'

'I didn't do anything.' Natalie's voice was plaintive, like a lost child. 'I shouldn't be here.'

The girl laughed, a high tinkle of a sound. 'None of us should fucking be here. Crap sort of a system if you ask me. We're the victims, aren't we? But—' she held up her hands, raised her eyebrows '—what can you do? It's a man's world, isn't it?' She lowered her eyes, started picking at her fingernails again. 'Just got to get on with it.'

When the van finally arrived, Natalie was surprised to find that the inside was divided into small compartments, each with a reinforced window, too high to see through, and a grey plastic bench seat. The smell of disinfectant, vomit and body odour made for a heady mix, the stuffy compartment almost devoid of breathable air. She slid up and down the slippery seat as the vehicle was thrown round corners and roundabouts by a driver in a hurry, her body hurled against the sides of her compartment, banging elbows and knees, shoulders and hands.

At their final destination, she emerged from her box shaken and pale, gulping a lungful of fresh air. She felt like she'd been on a fairground ride for the last forty-five minutes and thought she might be sick. She frowned as she took in her surroundings, a hand over her mouth as her stomach heaved. *Have they brought me to the right place?* It didn't look like a prison at all.

Behind the high gates and the tall metal fence stood a red-brick Victorian building, large and imposing, but so much better than she'd been expecting. She could see other similar buildings in the grounds, double-fronted houses, surrounded by trees and lawns. Flowerbeds sang with colour. It looked like a private school. Or a small village. She let out a breath. *Maybe Mali was right. Maybe it won't be so bad after all.*

Mali put on a cocky act and started a bit of banter with the guards, but Natalie could hear the quiver in her voice, a hint of fear that made Natalie's heart beat faster. She followed Mali into the reception area, which opened out into a large waiting room. Lounge seats with padded cushions were arranged around coffee tables, magazines strewn across their surfaces. A large TV hung on the wall. Next to that, a water cooler. It was bright and airy with a big bay window looking out over the well-tended gardens. It felt benign. Like a community centre.

Natalie sipped a cup of water while Mali was led into another room. She locked her eyes on the TV, losing herself in some show about buying houses from the auctions. Her heart bumped to an erratic beat and her legs wrapped themselves around each other, as her body shook with intermittent spasms.

Stop it! she told herself. *Get a grip. There's nothing scary about this place. At all.* She tended to her fear, poking and prodding it until she was able to pull it up by the roots, like a weed. She straightened her shoulders, told herself she was going to get through this.

Tom would have been interviewed by now, she expected. Her cheeks flushed at the thought of him telling the officers how much she'd been struggling at work, telling them his theory that she had mental health problems, probably postnatal depression. That's what he kept telling her, anyway, trying to get her to take something for it, so there was no reason to believe he wouldn't tell the police. Then they'd have to accept it was all a mistake.

People were allowed to make mistakes, weren't they? Must happen all the time. She'd be out of there in a matter of hours. A day at the most.

'Alright?' A skinny woman with short, bleached-blonde hair, dressed in an oversized pink T-shirt, black leggings and sneakers plonked herself in the chair next to Natalie. She smiled. 'I'm Lisa,' she said. 'I'm the peer mentor on meet-and-greet duty this morning.' Natalie could see scars spotting Lisa's arms, like white measles. *Are those needle marks? Is she a druggie?* She couldn't stop herself from staring. *And the white slashes on her wrists. Has she tried to…?*

'Sorry,' Natalie said, lifting her eyes to the woman's face. 'You're a what?'

'Peer mentors, we're called. Here to help you get settled in.' The woman's voice was rough round the edges, like a torn cloth, but her smile was friendly and now that Natalie looked at her properly, she could see that she was middle-aged, her face covered with a web of fine wrinkles.

The woman held out a carrier bag. 'This here,' she said, 'is what they call a reception pack.' Natalie took it and peered inside. 'It's got a few toiletries to get you started. Shampoo and soap and stuff.' Lisa leant over. 'Toothpaste's a bit strong. Better than nothing though. I hate it when me teeth need cleaning.' She pulled a face.

Natalie managed a flicker of a smile and pulled a booklet out of the bag.

'That tells you all about the place, what the rules are and everything.'

Natalie nodded.

'So, I'll give you the spiel, then you can ask me whatever you want. And then I'll see you again when you've had your assessment and seen the doc.' Lisa tucked her legs up under her, took the booklet from Natalie, turned to the page she was looking for and started talking, pointing to pictures as she went along, as if she was reading to a child.

HMP Stanbridge had an operational capacity of four hundred and eighty women, accommodated in twenty large houses set in the countryside, just south of Liverpool. As well as the houses, there was a modern block called the Therapy Wing and various other facilities. For much of the day they would be able to roam about the grounds as they wanted, go to educational classes, the library, the gym, join various groups and access whatever healthcare they needed, including various therapy groups.

After her assessment, Natalie would go to the First Night Centre, where new inmates were taken through an induction process and monitored for the first day or two. Then she would be assigned to a house.

'So, I can go outside?' Natalie couldn't keep the surprise from her voice.

Lisa smiled. 'Yep.'

'I won't be locked up all day?'

'Oh no, not all day. They've just had to change the rules, mind. Staff shortages. So, we're locked up over lunch and then after evening meal. About five thirty, it is.'

'And will I be sharing a room?' The pictures of the bedrooms in the booklet all showed bunk beds. *Bunk beds? For grown women. Really?*

'Oh yeah. That's the worst part. Three or four to a room is a bit of a tight squeeze. Just got to hope you don't get a farter. Or a snorer.' Lisa laughed, covered her mouth. 'Or a sleepwalker. They're the worst.'

Sharing with three other people? *What if I don't like them? If they don't like me?* Natalie's stomach griped, her insides clenched together as tight as her fists. She doubled up, the pain catching her by surprise and when she sat up again, there was a sheen of sweat on her upper lip. Nausea unleashed itself, throwing bile up her throat.

'You okay?' Lisa studied her, frowning. 'You look a bit peaky. Do you need anything?'

Natalie's stomach lurched. She put a hand over her mouth but it was too late and a stream of vomit spewed over the floor in a foul-smelling mess. Natalie gasped as another spasm tore through her.

Lisa jumped to her feet and ran off across the room, reappearing a few minutes later carrying a mop and bucket, followed by a prison officer.

'Right, love,' the prison officer said, a plump young woman, of a similar age to Natalie, with a short brown bob and a sympathetic smile. 'Not feeling so good?'

Natalie shook her head, cheeks burning, her throat so tight she was unable to speak.

'First time here?'

Natalie's stomach lurched and she swallowed the bile back down, nodded again.

'Okay, well let's get you sorted out then, quick as we can. Then you can have a shower, get yourself cleaned up. I think we'll get you checked out by the doctor first. Okay?'

Natalie held her head in her hands for a moment before hauling herself to her feet. *What is wrong with me?* She was too hot, but shivered, her back damp with sweat, her body so heavy she struggled to keep herself upright. She followed the prison officer to the medical room, where a nurse took control and Natalie slumped in a chair, hardly feeling the needle as blood samples were taken.

Eventually, she found herself being led into a small, cluttered room where the doctor sat behind a desk. Her black shoulder-length hair was streaked with grey. Lively eyes looked at Natalie over the top of lime-green bifocals, which matched the colour of her tunic and complemented her olive skin.

Natalie squinted, the light too bright, a headache pulsing behind her eyes.

'Okay, Natalie. From the samples, we can see that you have been taking opiates,' the doctor said, no preamble, as if this news was to be expected. She looked at Natalie with a raised eyebrow, waiting for her to say something. Natalie looked back, clutching her stomach, the doctor's voice a bouncing echo.

Opiates? Is that what she just said?

The doctor leant forward, her hands flat on the desk and raised her voice a little. 'I need to know exactly what drugs you've been taking, in what doses, so we can wean you off them safely.'

'Sorry? I've... I've what?' *How could this woman think such a thing?* She shook her head, immediately regretting it as the room spun in front of her eyes.

The doctor peered over her glasses and sighed. 'This isn't going to get you in any more trouble. Look, there's no point denying it; your blood and urine samples tell their own story.'

The clock ticked. Something electrical hummed. There was nothing Natalie could say. She'd never taken any tablets. Never injected anything. Why would she?

'I'm trying to help you,' the doctor said.

Natalie stared at her.

'Okay,' she continued, 'have you been prescribed anything? '

'No! No, you've made a mistake.' The volume of her own voice made Natalie wince.

The doctor pursed her lips and carried on. 'Anything for depression? Insomnia? Anxiety?'

A memory flashed into Natalie's mind. When Harry was poorly. She frowned as she tried to remember. 'My doctor gave me something a few months back, but… I decided not to take them.' Her voice was a whisper, but even that jarred.

'Can you remember what they were?'

She forced herself to think, scrunching her eyes against the pain. 'The names of all these medicines… It's hard to remember.'

'What were they for?'

'Um… well, my husband said…' She sighed at the memory of his words, embarrassed to admit it. 'I wasn't coping… after the birth of our son and he, well, he said I should go and get something to help me sleep. Calm me down. I don't know…'

The doctor gave her a small smile of encouragement.

'Well, we can contact your GP, ask for a copy of your notes, see exactly what was prescribed. Then we can work out how to help you cope without them.'

'But I didn't take any of them.' She absolutely knew this to be true, didn't she?

'Natalie.' The doctor's voice was a firm, cut-out-the-crap tone. 'You've definitely been taking something. And from the looks of things, from your withdrawal symptoms, you've built up a bit of a dependency and we need to wean you off gradually. Make it easier for you. Believe me, you don't want to go down the cold turkey route.'

Natalie slumped back in her chair, head in her hands, unsure of herself now.

Have I been taking the tablets?

She could visualise the bottle, sitting in the bathroom cabinet and she remembered looking at it a few times, wondering if one would do any harm, but then her mother's experience with sleeping tablets and antidepressants would tap on her conscience, tell her it wasn't worth it. Maybe she did succumb to the lure of a calmer reality.

Did I?

She shook her head. 'I just… don't remember. Why can't I remember anything?'

'A lot of these drugs can affect your memory; it's one of the side effects. As well as making you nauseous, moody, depressed, erratic. All sorts of things. They affect everyone differently depending on the specific drug, the dosage, your metabolism.' The doctor wrote something, looked up at Natalie. 'We'll start you on opiate substitute treatment today and when we have information back from your GP we can reassess if needs be.'

The doctor looked at the guard before flicking her eyes back to Natalie. 'And I think we'll put you on the Therapy Wing, so we can keep an eye on you. It's a separate unit where we look after people with drug dependencies and… other problems.' Natalie's heart skipped a beat. Lisa had mentioned the Wing. *Isn't that where all the nutters are held? Self-harmers, people with mental health issues.*

'It'll be easier for us to assess your medication levels. And you can have your own room. Which we don't have available in the First Night Centre at the moment. Bit of a glut in admissions these last couple of days.'

The prison officer led her back into the waiting room.

'I'm fine,' Natalie said, eyes pleading. 'Honestly, I'll be fine in the First Night Centre. It's just the shock of being here.' She tried a smile, but it wobbled from her lips. 'I don't think I need to go on the Wing.'

The prison officer sat her down. 'If you just wait here, I'll be back when I've sorted out a room for you. It's for the best, you know.'

Natalie tugged at her hair, hyperventilating.

How the hell did I become a drug addict?

CHAPTER ELEVEN

Now

It's late when she calls again and I let the phone ring a few times before I answer.

'Yes.' Do I sound bored enough?

'I have more information.'

'Go on.' I close my eyes. Please, God, just make her give me something that I don't already know.

'Okay, so I rang the hostel in Bangor again. She didn't go back but the CCTV picked her up getting into a car. I've got a number plate as well.'

'Right,' I say, casual as you like, wondering how that information is going to be any use to me at all.

A heavy breath echoes over the line. 'You still there?'

I smile to myself. All information is useful. 'Okay, give me everything you know about the car she's driving. Make, model, colour and number. You give me that, and you'll get your money. Tonight.'

When I hang up, I have a little debate with myself, but after a moment's hesitation, I transfer the money. A deal's a deal, at the end of the day. Then I delete her contact details and call history.

That's one bitch out of my life.

Now it's time to work on the next.

CHAPTER TWELVE

Now

Natalie is woken by the sound of drawers opening and closing, a door banging, the chatter of a breakfast show.

She's lying on the bed fully clothed, her phone still clutched in her hand, showing that it's six fifty-two. It's the first time she's slept right through the night since she was sent to prison and she tries to blink her eyes awake. But sleep drags at her, not quite ready to let go. It was a nice dream she was having, playing on the beach with Harry, like the mothers she'd seen the evening before. They were making a sandcastle together and she wants to go back and finish it, hear Harry talk to her as he carefully shovels sand into a bucket and pats it down hard.

After a moment, she jerks awake again, and sits up, heart pounding with the idea that she should be doing something, should be somewhere and is late in some way. She swings her legs over the side of the bed, bereft now that Harry's presence has faded away, and leans forward, elbows resting on her knees, while she waits for her heartbeat to steady.

Today I'm going to find him, she tells herself. *So, where am I up to?*

She'd tried ringing Jack last night, but a woman had answered his phone, telling her that he was out at a gig and had forgotten to take his phone with him. Natalie didn't leave a message. Then she'd searched the Internet for several hours to try and find information on Tom's whereabouts and had come up with a big fat nothing; she'd obviously fallen asleep still looking.

Her brain feels numb, paralysed by too much sleep. There is nothing but fog where her thoughts should be, a feeling of hopelessness making her body lethargic and heavy.

She checks the time again and puffs out a few breaths to wake herself up a bit. It's too soon for people to be in offices, for her to ring anyone. She rummages in her bag and finds her running gear, knows from experience that exercise is the best way to get her thoughts moving, and a shot of endorphins will give herself the lift she needs. *Just a short run. Twenty minutes max.* Then she can come back, get an action plan together, and go and get her son.

She trots downstairs, feeling more positive.

'Sleep well, lovey?'

Mary pops out of the kitchen doorway as Natalie reaches the bottom step. She's wrapped in a fluffy blue dressing gown, wearing slippers shaped like monster feet, hair already done, nice and tidy, make-up on.

'Ready for some breakfast? I'm making coffee if you want some. Or tea.'

Natalie tries to smile but her face hasn't woken up yet. 'I'm just off for a run.'

Mary raises her eyebrows. 'Oh, okay. Well, you have a nice time. I'll do breakfast whenever you're ready.' She gives a little wave, fingers wiggling as Natalie lets herself out of the front door.

The view out to sea, the hugeness of the world, swells in Natalie's chest. She breathes it in, a deep lungful of salty air, before starting a series of warm-up exercises. Then she looks at her watch and sets off at a brisk jog, pushing down through her legs, making her muscles work. *I can find him, I can find him, I can find him,* she says in time with her strides, a mantra to focus her thoughts. Her stomach lurches and growls, making her wince, but she pushes on.

The day is calm, the sun already smiling in a sky the colour of duck eggs, the air warm against her skin. The long, low ridge of Peel Hill looms in front of her, the marina to the left of it, the castle and the sea to the right. It seems the obvious route. *Not all the way up to the top,* she tells herself, *just ten minutes' worth*, then she'll come back down. She starts up the steep path.

She imagines herself walking up here with Harry, her little person trotting along beside her, holding her hand and chattering away like children do. *Where might he be?* Still in Douglas somewhere, close to Tom's work? Or have they moved out to a place in the countryside… one of the villages? Realistically, she has to assume he could be anywhere in the two hundred and twenty square miles that make up the island. She grits her teeth, calf muscles on fire as she pushes her legs harder, until she finds herself on top of the ridge. She stops to catch her breath, then checks her watch. Ten minutes left. *A quick breather,* she thinks, *then I'll run back down.*

She sits on the grass, chest heaving after the exertion of the climb, and looks down the coast towards the south of the island, taking in the rounded hills, edged by soaring cliffs that drop into a restless sea. Gulls wheel and cry below her, the rocky shelves and crevices busy with fluttering, noisy life. She lets her mind drift on the waves, soar with the gulls, linger in the fluffy clouds that are forming above her. She can see mountains in the distance, across the sea. Ireland, possibly? More to her right, which must be the edge of Scotland.

Exercise has weaved its magic on her mind and a stream of ideas starts to flow. The estate agents might have a forwarding address. And she can try the Post Office. Manx Telecom? Schools? Harry should be registered for the reception class now, if they have such a thing over here. She needs to find that out as well. What about nurseries? Then there's Jack. She can try him again, see if he can help.

Oh yes, lots of positive things to do.

Perhaps Sasha might be easier to track down than Tom, she thinks, given that she must be staying in a hotel. And there aren't that many hotels in Douglas. Or she could call Sasha's mum and get her number that way. She picks at the grass, letting the stalks float on the breeze. They were a good team, her and Sasha, back in the day, before adulthood chopped their lives into pieces. *How good would it be to feel that closeness again?* The thought squeezes her heart and she sighs.

Funny what we dream about when we are young and don't have a clue. At least Sasha's dream had come true, a successful actress, and she'd recently found true love at last, in Marco, whose name had filled her recent letters. But, Natalie thinks, what happened to her own fantasies? In all honesty she'd realised that they weren't what she really wanted and had been more a function of hanging out with Sasha, trying to fit in. She'd discovered that what she really wanted was to be a wife and mother. Not a popular view amongst her circle of friends, but that was the truth of it. A husband to love her, children to nurture, and a house to make into a home. For a little while, she'd been living her dream. Until…

He won't know you.

Sasha's words bounce into Natalie's head, knocking her thoughts off track. Tension creeps into her shoulders. *How could she even suggest I should forget about Harry?* Her fingers dig into the soil. *How could she? But then, what would she know? She can't possibly understand what it's like when a piece of you is missing. Stolen.*

She stands, brushing grass off her legs, ready to go back down.

A wave of dizziness catches her by surprise and she leans forward, hands grasping her knees, her heart suddenly racing. She knows these sensations; the dull thudding across her forehead, the spots in front of her eyes. The earth moves under her feet, making her lose her balance. It's happened before and the only way to stop it from developing into a full-blown migraine is to eat something. She looks at the route she came up and gulps. *So steep.* Sweat beads on her forehead as she starts inching her way down, stumbling and swaying like a drunkard, a show of flashing lights exploding in front of her eyes.

'Hey! Hey!'

A man's voice, the rustle of clothing.

She turns to see a figure walking behind her. Tall and dark-haired. *Where did he come from? Has he been watching me? Following me?* Her heart quickens.

It's not Lech. He can't know that I'm here, she tells herself. But she doesn't believe it. Not in her heart.

Her pulse pounds in her ears as she stumbles on, trying to go faster, but when she looks behind, she sees that he's getting closer. Turning too quickly, she loses her balance, trips over a rock and crashes to the ground. Gorse and heather scratch at her face, her arms, prickling through her clothes. She hears his footsteps. Closes her eyes.

It's done. Over. Will he be merciful?

Why would he be? His culture is Old Testament, an eye for an eye, a tooth for a tooth and the words from his letter appear in her mind.

> *'I will make you suffer what I have suffered. You will watch me do to your child what you did to my sister, my Katya. And then you are dead.'*

Her body tenses, hands shielding her head.

Shuffled footsteps.

A child's laughter, an excited squeal, a man's voice murmuring something. She turns her head to see a little boy crouched on his haunches, looking at her with big hazel eyes, curly blond hair, cheeks pink from exercise. Natalie's breath rushes out of her. She squints to get the child's face into focus, sees a smile full of tiny teeth.

'Harry,' she whispers, wondering if she's hallucinating. If she's already dead. She squeezes her eyes shut, opens them again and the child is still there. *He's real.* And all thoughts of being attacked are forgotten, dismissed from her mind by the appearance of this child. Her child. *Could it be?* She squints, conjures up her mental image of Harry and compares it to the child in front of her. The only feature she is certain of is the hazel eyes. It's possible that he has his dad's blond hair, instead of her brunette. She could have imagined him all wrong, couldn't she? After all, who knows what a baby will look like nearly three and a half years on?

'Harry!' she sobs, emotion clogging in her throat, blurring her speech.

The boy gazes at her and she stretches out a hand to touch him, but he's too far away. She rolls onto her side and tries to get onto her knees, but her vision fizzes with unidentified objects.

'Connor, come here,' the man says and the child runs off.

It's not him.

Disappointment weighs heavy in her chest and she slumps back down, pain thudding in her forehead in time with her pulse.

'Steady,' the man says, kneeling beside her. 'Are you okay? Can I do anything to help?'

'Blood sugar,' she says to the ground, fighting back a wave of nausea.

'Ah, right.' He sounds relieved and unzips the top pocket of his rucksack. A piece of white stuff is thrust into her hand. She tries to focus on it… decide what she's supposed to do with it.

'Kendal mint cake,' he says. 'Pure sugar. Have you on your feet in no time.'

She shoves it into her mouth, feels the minty sugar melt into a pulp and ooze its way down her throat. He passes her another piece, then another and a few minutes later she feels her energy start to return, the dizziness and nausea fading. She turns onto her knees, sits back on her heels and squints in the brightness of the morning light. They are both staring at her, the man and the child. She squirms under their scrutiny, cheeks burning and struggles to her feet.

'Hey, wait a minute,' the man says, his hand on her shoulder. 'I'll walk down with you, make sure you're okay.'

'I'm fine, honestly,' she says, then stumbles as her legs buckle. The man catches her before she falls.

He tuts and shakes his head. 'What's up with you women? Just accept a little help, will you?'

Natalie gives him a tight smile, hangs on to his arm and they start to walk down the path at a geriatric's pace, the little boy running around in front of them like an excitable dog. Thankfully, few words are spoken and no questions are asked, because Natalie would have felt terrible having to lie to this man after he's been so kind.

Near the bottom of the hill, she sees a number of benches dotted around; she lets go of the man and points to the nearest one. 'Um, you know what? I think I'll just sit here for a bit, enjoy the view.'

'Are you sure? I don't mind seeing you back to your house. Honestly, it's no trouble.'

She plonks herself on the bench, flaps a hand. 'I'll be fine here. Absolutely fine.' She smiles at him. 'Thank you so much for your help.' She folds her arms, leans back on the seat and looks out at the view of the castle in front of her, hoping he will get the message and leave her alone. Which he does.

Her thoughts whisper on the breeze. *That was stupid. Stupid.* She has to look after herself better, keep herself strong and vigilant, because if it had been Katya's brother following her, then who knows what might have happened. *Over the edge of the cliff and who would be any the wiser?* That's how easy it would have been.

Still. The worst didn't happen. No point dwelling on could haves. *And anyway, it's Harry he wants. He can't torment me if I'm dead, can he?* Just thinking about it, putting the words into her head, makes her shiver.

Focus on finding Harry and getting him to safety. No distractions, no diversions. Two and a bit days to go.

Her plan is suddenly clear and she wonders how last night's panic managed to addle her thoughts so thoroughly. It's obvious. Find Tom and follow him home. He's the key to everything, and where he lives, Harry lives. She can bin the rest of her ideas, because this is the only one that has real merit. And she knows exactly where he works.

CHAPTER THIRTEEN

Then

The Therapy Wing was exactly how Natalie had thought a prison block would look and was a complete contrast to the house where she'd initially been taken. The architecture pressed down on her the minute she walked through the door, making her feel small and fearful.

Unlike the Victorian houses, the Wing was a modern, two-storey building, with cells arranged down both sides of a double-height corridor, maybe fifteen feet wide, a set of metal stairs at one end. On the ground floor, the corridor was used as a communal area, set out with leather sofas and big round tables with blue seats attached; adult versions of the sort of thing you might find in a primary school. The ceiling was a metal grid, allowing light to filter through from the glass roof above while stopping prisoners from throwing things, or themselves, from the first floor. They'd tried to brighten the place up by painting the cell doors dusky pink and lavender, the walls magnolia. The floor was concrete, painted red and covered with a wide strip of blue carpet. It was undeniably a prison, and however much they'd tried to jolly it up, it still looked dismal, the air filled with the acrid scent of cleaning fluid.

The communal area was empty when Natalie was escorted to her cell on the ground floor but the place echoed with screams and shouts. She shivered and folded her arms across her chest, hugging herself tight.

Her cell was a magnolia box, no bigger than her utility room back home. It was furnished with a metal bed, the thin mattress covered with pale-green sheets, a blanket and a peach bedspread. There was a cupboard above to store her belongings, with a shelf underneath. The toilet and washbasin were stuck in the corner at the end of the bed, behind a half screen. Against a side wall, there was a small table and a chair. And opposite the door, at the other end of the room, was a mullioned window with five narrow slits of glass that you couldn't really see out of, but which let in a bit of light.

She stared around her, stomach clenched as tight as a fist. *Is this it? This tiny little room?* The smell of disinfectant was so strong she could taste it. Her stomach lurched, bile stinging her throat.

'Here we are, Natalie,' the prison officer said, with a tired smile. 'Now let's just have a little chat, then you can get yourself settled in and get a bit of rest.'

Natalie shook her head, eyes wide. 'I don't need to be here, honestly, I'm feeling much better now, thanks. Bit of nerves, I think. That's all.'

'Well, the doc thinks you need to be here, so here you will stay until we're told otherwise. Not my decision, pet.' She gestured for Natalie to sit on the bed, while she sat on the chair.

The springs creaked as Natalie lowered herself, slowly, as if the bed was going to bite her. There was no duvet, no bounciness and the meagre covers felt devoid of any capacity to create warmth. *I can't sleep here,* Natalie thought, feeling crushed by the closeness of the walls.

Her eyes stung and she tucked her hands between her thighs. There was a buzzing in her head, like a bee trapped against a window and she was finding it hard to concentrate. *It's not for long,* she told herself. *They'll work out they've made a mistake. Tom will make sure of that. He'll want this sorted as quickly as possible so it doesn't affect the business. I've got to be brave, get through this. For Harry's sake.*

'So, I just need to tell you about the regime on the Wing.' The prison officer smiled at her and took a breath. 'We get you up at seven forty-five in the morning. Then you have breakfast and a half hour exercise in the yard. Now I think you'll be kept in your cell while we see how the meds are working, but once you start feeling better, there are work groups you can join to keep you busy. Cleaning and cooking and gardening. Painting and decorating. All sorts of things.' It was clearly a well-practised briefing, the woman trying her best to make it sound interesting. 'And you can go to the CALM Centre where you can get your hair and nails done, join a therapy group. They even do acupuncture if you fancy it. And then there's the gym. Whatever activities you think you might like to do, lots of choice. You've got to do at least an hour of physical exercise a week. But you can do more if you like. And then, in the evenings, there's what we call association for an hour and a half, when the cells are open and you can chat to the other girls for a bit. If you want.'

Natalie nodded, watching the officer's lips move, the words flowing over her but not sinking in. The fact that she was in prison had suddenly become real to her. All she could think of was Harry and the gap that was opening up between them. She felt like she was floating, on a boat that had been cut from its mooring and was drifting out to sea, leaving her son on the shore, helpless to do anything as she watched him fade to a dot in the distance. She squeezed her eyes shut. *Just a few days at the most,* she reassured herself. *No more than that.* Her hands clasped together in her lap, as if in prayer.

'Now for the rest of the day, we're going to keep you locked up, as I said, but we'll be checking in regularly to make sure you're okay. Lunch has just finished, evening meal will be at five, but I don't think you're really up for food right now, are you, pet?'

Natalie didn't answer, her eyes still closed, blotting out the harsh reality of her cell.

The prison officer leant forwards and shook Natalie's knee. 'Earth to Natalie, are you receiving me?' Natalie dragged her eyelids open, a violent shiver shaking through her body, making her teeth rattle. 'Aw, not feeling so good, are we?' The prison officer's face softened. 'Let's get you tucked up in bed, eh?'

She helped Natalie take off her trainers, then flicked back the covers so she could lie down, and gave her a quick smile. 'I'll be back in a bit.'

Then she was gone, with a clang of the door and a clunk of the lock.

Although Natalie felt weary to the core, there was no chance of sleep. The unfamiliar sounds of prison life made her eyes dart round the cell as she tried to decipher what was going on. Somebody was shouting, close by. Maybe the next cell. A stream of obscenities that made Natalie flinch. Then a loud banging. Rhythmic and insistent, from the first floor, she thought. Someone else, further down, screaming and screaming. More shouting, urgent this time. Then the sound of running feet, up the stairs, along the metal corridor above her, the rattle of keys, a door slamming open. More shouting and screaming and banging.

Throughout the afternoon, the noise went on, a wave of sound that ebbed and flowed, punctuated by rushing feet and crackling radios as prison officers darted about, sorting out emergencies and bad behaviour.

Finally, Natalie drifted off to sleep only to be startled awake some time later by a commotion in the next cell. The woman who'd been shouting earlier. 'Ligature,' a voice said, outside Natalie's door. 'I'll start CPR. Get an ambulance. Quick.'

Natalie's eyes widened. *The woman had tried to kill herself?*

She cowered in her bed, covers over her head as if this might block out the reality of what was going on her around her, not daring to move even though she was desperate for a pee.

Who knew that minutes could stretch out like days, each one longer than the last?

She used thoughts of Harry to block out the bedlam, hugged his imaginary body to her chest. He'd be missing her; she was sure of it. Thank goodness Elena would be there by now; at least she knew he was being looked after properly. She thought back to when she'd last seen him, imagined his laugh when she blew raspberries on his belly, his pudgy little arms waving around, grabbing her hair. *Be strong for him*, she told herself, gritting her teeth as tears trickled down her face. *Be strong.*

The following morning, after a sleepless night, Natalie was called in to see the doctor again.

'Sit down, Natalie,' the doctor said, nodding to the chair in front of her desk. She looked at her for a long moment. Natalie clasped her hands in her lap and tried to relax her face into a neutral expression. A tic flickered by her left eye. 'How are you feeling?'

'Fine,' she said, forcing her lips into a bright smile. 'Absolutely fine. I don't think I need to be on the Wing anymore, taking up space.'

The doctor gazed at her, eyes scrutinizing every inch of Natalie's face. Natalie forced herself to be still, while her stomach churned and griped.

'Hmm,' the doctor said. She looked at an open folder on her desk. 'I've got the results of your tests here and I'm a bit puzzled. It looks like you've been taking Oxycodone.'

'Oxywhat?' Natalie frowned.

'It's a highly addictive opioid-based painkiller.'

Painkiller? Why would I have been taking a painkiller?

Natalie stared at the doctor, the tic twitching faster. She rubbed her face. 'Sorry, I don't think I understand.'

'Okay.' The doctor sat back in her chair. 'So, the tablets you've been taking are a synthetic form of morphine. But twice as strong.'

Natalie put a hand to her mouth, eyes wide. 'Morphine? As in… like heroin?'

The doctor nodded. 'That's right. Hillbilly heroin, it's called in the US because of the abuse problems they have over there.

It's usually prescribed for people in late stages of cancer. Or after surgery. And for chronic pain.'

Natalie's frown deepened and she shook her head. *A heroin substitute?* 'I don't understand. Why would I be prescribed something like that?'

The doctor didn't answer immediately, her eyes boring into Natalie's. She clasped her hands together, tried to hold the doctor's gaze.

'That's the puzzle, Natalie. It's definitely not what your doctor prescribed for you. He gave you Valium.'

Natalie blinked. 'But I didn't…' Her chest tightened, the idea so shocking she started to shake. 'I don't remember taking anything.' Natalie studied the expression on the doctor's face, and ran her tongue round dry lips.

The doctor sighed, her voice softer. 'Natalie, the evidence is here. You can tell yourself whatever you want, but that doesn't change the facts. There's no getting away from the results of your blood tests. You have definitely been taking Oxycodone.'

She stared at Natalie, who looked down at her hands, her mind struggling with this new information. Was this yet another thing she couldn't remember? Had she been taking something, and blocked it out? Because that would make her weak, wouldn't it, and that was something she tried so hard not to be. Tom despised weakness, had struggled to know what to do with her when it was obvious she wasn't coping. Her teeth clamped together. Another thing she'd done wrong. What a mess she'd made of everything. What a Godawful mess.

'Okay, well, we'll carry on with the withdrawal treatment,' the doctor said, writing something in her notes. 'At least we know what we're dealing with now.' She looked up and nodded to the prison officer, who'd been standing by the door, ready to escort Natalie back to her room. 'I'm afraid you'll be on the Wing for a couple of weeks, until we get you stabilised, then you'll be transferred to one of the houses. I'll see you again in a week or so, see how things are progressing.'

Back in her cell, Natalie sat on her bed, and let her mind wander through the alleyways of her memory, trying to identify how things had gone so wrong. For two years she'd been living the dream, before her relationship with Tom had slowly started to crumble. She'd tired of the endless weekends entertaining clients, the awkwardness she'd felt with Tom's upper-class friends; and when he was stressed, Tom could be so pernickety it had made her feel claustrophobic. She'd been so sure that a baby would repair the cracks, would refocus their lives. But it hadn't been the answer.

Motherhood had changed her, there was no doubt about that. It had also changed everything else about her life. After Harry was born, Natalie had hardly seen Tom. He'd worked longer hours to cover for her absence from the business and when he was home she'd either been busy with the baby or taken the opportunity to sleep. She'd thought the distance between them was a phase, a few short months, then things would change.

And she'd been right – they did, but not for the better.

Harry had fallen ill, a bad cough that hadn't responded to any of the medication he'd been given. The coughing had gone on for weeks, and she'd become exhausted; a tearful, angry mess, unable to make the simplest of decisions. Then, as soon as Harry had started to get better, Natalie had become ill with flu, which had taken weeks to disappear. It had left her feeling weak and anxious, never quite in control of her emotions.

Before she was ready, Harry was six months old and it had been time for her to go back to work.

'Maybe it's too soon,' Natalie had said to Tom as they'd discussed her hours over breakfast. He'd wanted her to start work on Monday, less than a week away. Full-time. He'd lowered the *Financial Times* so he could see her, his mouth twisting from side to side as he'd pondered his response.

'I'm short-staffed,' he'd snapped. 'I don't have the manpower to look after all our clients properly and I need you back in the office.' He'd sighed and flicked his paper, ready to continue reading. Then he'd lowered it again, folded it carefully and laid it on the table next to his plate. He'd fixed her with a hard stare. 'I thought we were a team.'

'We are, Tom, but I've got Harry to think about now. He's not been well, and—'

'He's better now, though, isn't he? You said so yourself. As did the doctor when he went for his check-up. He'll never be independent if you don't let go a little.'

'Yes, but—'

'We've got the nanny lined up. We both agree she's perfect, with excellent references, and Harry took to her straight away.'

'I know, Elena is lovely but—'

Tom had slapped his hands on the table, making her jump. 'I just don't know what the problem is!'

'Nothing… nothing, there's no problem.' Natalie's mouth had suddenly gone dry. She'd shrunk back in her chair. 'Just… probably just a bit nervous, that's all.' She'd wiped her hands on her joggers, up and down her thighs. Then she'd realised what she was doing and clasped them together instead.

He'd stared at her, lips a thin line, a frown emphasising the groove in the middle of his forehead.

'What's to be nervous about? You know everyone at the office, all your clients.' He'd folded his arms across his chest. 'I just don't understand.'

She'd flashed him a smile, eager for the conversation to end, feeling like she'd done ten rounds with Mike Tyson.

'It's fine, just me being silly.' She'd started clearing away the plates. 'You're right. I'm ready for work now. Next Monday will be fine.'

His gaze had softened as he watched her.

'I'll take you shopping, if that'll make you feel better. We can go this morning, get you some new clothes for work. I can go into the office a bit later and stay a couple of extra hours tonight.'

She'd looked down at herself and pulled a face. She used to be slim and beautifully turned out, confident that she looked the part. Now she was a shapeless blob, dressed in joggers and maternity T-shirts. She still looked pregnant and hadn't need reminding that none of her work clothes would fit. She'd told herself he was trying to be kind and forced another smile.

'That would be great. Thank you.'

He'd gone back to reading his paper and she'd gone to weep in the shower.

There had been times when she'd felt their relationship was like a war casualty, disabled by resentment as they'd each battled to get their own way. Both of them struggling to be themselves in a relationship that didn't fit. It was the birth of their son that struck the fatal blow. Not that Tom didn't want children; it was more that the timing was wrong. He'd wanted to wait until their business was more established, when their finances would be stronger, but she'd ignored him, causing many an argument as their life together had changed shape in ways they could never have imagined.

He would surprise her, though, with moments of tenderness, a reminder of the charming, chivalrous man she'd married. And at these times, she'd felt like they were different people, living in a parallel universe.

Twice a day, she'd seen him at his best. First thing in the morning they would sit together over a coffee and share their plans for the day ahead, then last thing at night they would have a drink and go through everything that had happened.

Now, in her prison cell, walls scratched with graffiti, the sound of wailing, shouting women filling her ears, she remembered how she lived for those moments, for the glow that she'd felt as she basked in his love. Remembered how the hours between seemed to stretch out longer and longer, as though she was addicted to him, to his attention.

She sat up straight, a hand to her forehead, trying to catch hold of a thought that had raced through her mind.

Night and morning, she took a tonic, something that a friend of Tom's had suggested, to give her a lift after she'd had the flu. Apparently, it was all the rage in London, a favourite of Gwyneth Paltrow's, full of valerian and chamomile, ginger and ginseng, amongst other things. It tasted disgusting, so Tom would put it in her drink and it did seem to make her feel calmer, more able to cope and it definitely helped her to sleep.

But was that the only thing he put in my drink?

The idea developed like a photograph until it was clear in her mind. *Tom's been drugging me.* No wonder she'd felt so good and then so wretched, as if she was waiting for her next fix. She fought to catch her breath, like the air had been punched out of her.

But why? Why would he do that to me?

She clenched her jaw. This was just the sort of thing he would do, a panicked effort to take control of a situation that was beyond his comprehension, trying to improve her moods, help her sleep, make her someone he could live with. Perhaps he'd tried putting Valium in her drink and decided it wasn't working, and had got the medication from a friend but hadn't realised how strong it was.

She covered her face with her hands. If only she'd done as she was told for once and followed doctors' orders, none of this would have happened.

It's my fault. All of it.

CHAPTER FOURTEEN

Now

Natalie waits on the bench for a few minutes, time enough for the man to disappear down the path, before she heads back to Mary's. The jangling of her phone makes her jump. She'd change the ringtone if she knew how, but it's a new phone and she hasn't quite got the hang of it yet. The number on her screen has no name attached. Not surprising when the only numbers currently in there are the skipper of the fishing boat and her friend in Ireland.

Perhaps a wrong number. *Should I even answer?* It carries on ringing and she can't help herself.

'Hello?' she says, her voice tentative.

'Nat? That you?' A woman's voice buzzes through Natalie, like an electric shock, making her jump to her feet and start walking.

'Sasha?'

She rang! The tension seeps out of Natalie's shoulders. *Maybe I'm not alone in this after all.*

Her gaze flickers across the marina as she descends from Peel Hill, and catches on a handsome yacht moored directly below her, about sixty feet away. It bobs up and down with the swell of the tide, light sparkling off its white paintwork. As she gets closer, she notices the name, *Smooth Talker*, written on the bow. And then she notices something else. On the deck. Something that makes her stop.

The woman is facing the other way, but her hair is unmistakable, tumbling down her back in reddish-blonde waves. Natalie takes a few steps forward, has another look and her breath catches in her throat. *It's Sasha!* Natalie frowns, puzzled. *What's she doing on a yacht?* It looks expensive, bigger than any of the other yachts in the marina, with a mast than must be thirty feet high. *Maybe they're using it for filming?*

'Sorry I had to dash off last night,' Sasha says, all breathy in Natalie's ear. 'Bit of an emergency, but it's all sorted now.'

Natalie watches her fiddle with her hair as she talks, a familiar habit that pulls Natalie closer with each twirl of her finger, tugging at her like a fish on a line.

'No worries,' Natalie says as she starts walking again, excitement bubbling in her stomach, because it's all feeling more possible now. *A problem shared is a problem halved. Isn't that what Dad used to say?*

An idea blooms in her mind. An idea that makes Natalie speed up, berating herself for not having thought of it before. *If the producer of the film that Sasha is working on is a director of the charity that organised last night's gig, and Tom sponsored the thing, surely the producer might know where Tom lives?* And if they're filming on the yacht, then the producer may be around somewhere and her search for Harry could be sorted in a matter of minutes. Her pulse quickens, along with her feet, and she hurries down the path.

'So, Nats, where are you?' Sasha says.

Natalie reaches the bottom of the hill, Sasha out of sight for a moment as Natalie negotiates the steps that will take her down onto the road.

'Oh, I'm ah… just out for a run.' She doesn't want to be too specific about where she is just yet. Not until she's sure about the situation with the yacht.

Sasha laughs. 'You're joking, right? You? Running?'

'Strange but true.' Natalie reaches the road and turns the corner, but then she stops, because Sasha's not alone anymore. A man has joined her on the deck, his arm around her shoulders. Natalie ducks behind a stack of lobster pots, her excitement transformed into a different emotion altogether.

'Yeah, right. So… you didn't say last night, but I'm assuming you're staying in Douglas?'

It's not a bad assumption because that's where most of the hotels are. Natalie ignores the question. 'So, are you filming today?'

'Oh, um… not until later,' Sasha says. 'I'm out and about in Douglas this morning.' She flicks her hair over her shoulder. 'Doing a few errands.' The man nuzzles her exposed neck, but Sasha squirms away from him, shaking her head, pointing to the phone. 'I thought we could meet up for lunch. I'll come and pick you up from your hotel if you like.'

Marco. This man must be Sasha's boyfriend, the man she says she's going to marry.

Natalie's jaw clenches and she can't speak, needs a moment to decide how to respond. *Lunch? Where's the urgency in that?* But Sasha won't realise, she reminds herself, has no idea that Harry's life is in danger. *I'll have to tell her everything,* she decides, if she wants her to be fully on board. But she doesn't want to tell Sasha anything with Marco there. Another person in the mix isn't what she needs right now. And Sasha's just told her a blatant lie about where she is. *Dammit!* The moment she's written Sasha into her plans, she's gone and prioritised herself once again, even though she knows there's an urgency to Natalie's mission. *Unreliable as ever.*

'Okay,' Natalie says. *No point arguing.* That would be wasting time. She'll just pretend to go along with it. 'No need to pick me up though, just choose a place and I'll meet you there.'

'Oh, fantastic! I really, really want to see you!' Sasha's jumping up and down in a circle and as she turns towards her, Natalie can see a broad smile on her face. Then Sasha stops, her face suddenly serious. 'And we need to have a proper talk, don't we? Plans to make and all that. You know, I've been thinking about what you said last night and you're right. Tom's not fit to be a father. He never was any good at it, was he? Impatient, grumpy bastard. And after what he did to you, well… there's no question in my mind, Nat. I'm with you all the way.'

Natalie's unsure what to do now, mixed messages pulling her mind in circles. *Should I ask her?* In the end, she can't help herself. 'Look, Sash, I just had a thought. Do you think you could ask your producer if he knows where Tom lives? He's a director of the charity that last night's gig was all about, isn't he? And I think Tom was a sponsor. So I thought perhaps he might know him. Could you do that?'

Sasha stands still. 'Wow, you're right! I hadn't thought of that.' She's silent for a moment and Natalie holds her breath, waiting. 'Sorry, I'm just thinking… thing is, I'm not sure when I'll get the chance to talk to him today.' Sasha sighs and starts fiddling with her hair again. 'He hates being interrupted when we're filming and he's such a scary man when he's cross. But… look, don't you worry, Nat, I'll do my best. Catch him after this morning's session.'

A maybe rather than a no, Natalie thinks. At least it's another lead being followed up, something Natalie can't do herself.

'Let's meet at the café in the sea terminal, shall we?' Sasha says, pacing around the deck now. 'If we make it one o'clock, then I should have spoken to Nige by then, have some info for you. That's not too late, is it?'

Natalie chews her lip, still frustrated by how long she's going to have to wait, but decides that it's better than nothing. *A contingency.* 'Yeah, one's fine.'

'Brilliant! I'll see you then, sweetie.'

Natalie watches Sasha being led down the steps into the cabin and can guess what sort of errands she's going to be doing for the rest of the morning.

Sweetie.

Their term of endearment, pinched from *Absolutely Fabulous,* a favourite TV programme when they'd been teenagers.

Sweetie.

The word connects with something in Natalie's brain, triggers forgotten moments, exploding images into her mind, so clear she can see every detail. Getting glammed up to go out, helping each other with hair and make-up, swapping clothes, walking to the bus stop arm in arm. Dancing. Laughing. Singing all the way home. Sleepovers, illicit hangovers.

Sweetie. How powerful a word can be.

Is Sasha trying to tell her that she's still that friend and she wants things to get back to how they were?

More images flicker to life. Images of a time when their lives had been stretched apart, not seeing each other for a few years while Sasha was working in America. Then Sasha had turned up unannounced, just when Natalie had needed her most, showing a side to her personality that Natalie had never known was there.

'Natalie. Natalie.' Tom's voice had been urgent, his hands shaking her shoulders to wake her from a fitful sleep. Her eyelashes had fluttered, stuck to each other and it took a moment for her eyes to focus, her mind still woolly, body slick with sweat as it tried to fight off the flu.

'What?' she mumbled and studied his face, realising straight away that something was wrong.

'There's a woman at the door. Says she's your friend.' His stare was accusing.

'What woman?' Natalie's mind ran through a short list of friends, but she knew that none of them would turn up without ringing first, given the remote location of their house, right on the edge of the Wirral.

'Said her name was Sasha.'

'Sasha?' Natalie sat up, her head spinning, body weak from lack of food.

'Hey,' Tom said, sitting next to her on the bed, putting an arm around her shoulders. 'No need for you to get up. I just wanted to know if you knew her. I wasn't sure…'

Natalie looked at him and wondered if he ever listened to a word she said. She was too uncomfortable to be patient, a nagging headache squeezing her brain so hard there was little room for thought.

'Oh, Tom, you must remember me talking about her? I've shown you pictures, for Christ's sake.'

Tom frowned.

Natalie bunched the duvet in her hands.

'My childhood best friend? Supposed to be Maid of Honour at our wedding? Surely you remember? She had food poisoning and couldn't make it.' Natalie rubbed her temples, already tired of the conversation, and fumbled on the top of her bedside table for the painkillers. Tom took the packet from her, pressed two capsules into her hand and passed her the glass of water. She swallowed them down and looked at him, eyebrows raised.

'So? Where is she?'

Tom stared at her. Natalie's hands went to her face, eyes wide.

'No. You haven't left her outside, have you? Tell me you haven't.'

Tom's face reddened but his voice was firm. Defensive. 'I didn't know who she was. Could be a con woman for all I know. Neighbourhood Watch have been on the phone about burglaries all around the area in the last few weeks.'

Natalie sighed, then swung her legs over the side of the bed, a small part of her finding the energy to wonder why Sasha had turned up. But it didn't really matter. Any distraction was welcome… anything that could lift the despondency that crushed her a little more every day.

A loud wail burst from the next room, followed by another and another, the fractious screams magnified and distorted, hammering inside Natalie's head until she felt her skull would burst. Tom sat on the bed, looking at her, and she knew that expression, knew what he was thinking. She glared at him. *Why couldn't he do it? Would it kill him to change a nappy or sort out a feed?*

Suddenly, the crying abated, reduced to stuttering hiccups, accompanied by a woman's voice cooing and shushing. Tom and Natalie stared at each other, frozen. A moment later Sasha appeared in the doorway, cradling Harry in her arms, a bright smile on her face, looking every inch the movie star she had always yearned to be.

'Hope you don't mind me letting myself in.' Sasha looked at Tom, a challenge in her eyes. She swayed from one foot to the other, rubbing Harry's back as he sucked on his dummy, snuggling his head into her shoulder. She beamed at Tom and Natalie. 'Just look at this gorgeous little man. So cute!' She bent her head and leant her cheek against his hair. 'And this house! Wow! I mean, wow! It's fantastic.'

Tom stalked out of the room, Natalie burst into tears and Sasha rubbed Natalie's shoulder, looking thoroughly confused about the swirl of emotions she had unleashed.

After that, Sasha had realised Natalie needed support and had stayed close; she'd got a job in a theatre group in nearby Liverpool and was always ready to look after Harry if Natalie had needed a bit of time out or had appointments to keep, ready to listen and sympathise with her rants about Tom. Their friendship had become stronger than ever.

Natalie walks back towards Mary's house, remembering that feeling of closeness and how good it had felt.

Was it such a bad lie? Sasha was probably just covering her tracks, trying to hide the fact she was somewhere she wasn't supposed to be, sneaking a bit of time out with her lover. *Does it really mean I can't trust her?* Natalie's glad now that she's left her options open. A new surge of hope flushes through her and she opens the door, runs upstairs, keen to get on with her plans for the day.

CHAPTER FIFTEEN

Then

On her third day in prison, Natalie had an unexpected visitor.

'Hi there.'

The voice startled Natalie out of her stupor and she turned to see a young woman leaning against the door frame of her prison cell. She was wearing black jeans and a funky patterned shirt. Her long, wavy hair was dark, almost black, her brown eyes set close together in a pale face with high cheekbones and a thin, straight nose.

Natalie turned her head back to where it had been, eyes staring at the wall, no energy to move from her prone position on the bed and in no mood for a conversation. It was the first day her cell door had been left open for association and several of the other inmates had looked in on her, but nobody had spoken and she'd ignored them all, making sure her back was always turned towards the door. A clear signal, she'd thought, that she wanted to be alone. What the hell could she talk to them about anyway? Theirs was a world she knew nothing about, no common experiences to spin into the threads of a conversation.

'Not talking?' Natalie heard the woman's clothes rustle as she moved and willed her to go away. She closed her eyes tight, her body tense with the effort of mentally removing the stranger from the doorway. It had always worked before, but she could sense that the woman was still there.

'I'm Katya, by the way,' the woman said as she walked into the room and sat on the bed.

Natalie wriggled her arms up across her chest, rounding her back against the intruder like a protective shell. *Can't the woman take a hint?*

'Aw, feeling rough?' Her voice was soft with sympathy. 'What are you on?'

'Nothing,' Natalie muttered.

Katya laughed, a staccato burst of sound, devoid of any joy, that ended as fast as it had begun. 'Sure, you're on something. You wouldn't be here otherwise. We're all on something, aren't we?' Her English was fluent, but there was an accent in the background; clipped words, guttural pronunciation.

'Go away,' Natalie said, teeth clenched.

'It's good to talk.' She patted Natalie's leg. 'Didn't they tell you that?'

'I don't need to talk.'

'Sure you do. We all need to talk.'

Natalie felt the bed move as Katya hitched herself across the mattress until her back was against the wall, legs stretched out in front of her, thighs touching Natalie's feet. Natalie opened her eyes, startled when she saw Katya staring at her. She was different from the others. Wore nice clothes for a start, rather than faded hand-me-downs. Her hair was shiny and well cut, her complexion flawless, eyes bright and curious. She was beautiful, and acted with a poise and confidence that was out of place. They looked at each other for a while, both of them silent.

Maybe she's a member of staff. A psychologist? She was certainly acting as if she had a right to be there, in Natalie's cell.

Natalie sat up and shuffled to the opposite end of the bed. She sat on her pillow, knees hugged to her chest as she frowned at Katya, head throbbing with the beat of her pulse. She didn't need some sort of psychologist trying to twist her words, telling her that she was in denial, making her doubt herself any more than she already did.

'What are you doing in here? What do you want?'

Katya smiled at her, picked at the bedspread, removing invisible specks of fluff. 'Just wanted to say hello. See how you're getting on.'

'I'm fine.' Natalie closed her eyes, leant her forehead on her knees. 'I don't need a therapist. Go away.'

Katya laughed again, the sound jarring through Natalie's body like a jackhammer. 'I'm not a fucking *therapist*. My God! Is that what you think? That's quite an insult, right there.' Despite the forcefulness of her words, there was amusement in her voice.

Natalie bristled, the pounding in her head increasing. 'So, who are you then?'

'It's a hell of a thing, isn't it?'

Natalie lifted her head, noticed Katya's sympathetic gaze. 'What is?'

'Coming out of an addiction.'

'What would you know about it?'

Katya stared at her, mouth pressed into a thin line. 'Oxy,' she said, holding Natalie's gaze. 'You too?'

Natalie nodded.

Katya sighed, flapped her hand. 'I know, I know. A silly mistake, I bet, just like me. I had an accident and paracetamol just didn't do it. I needed something stronger. A friend gave me some Oxy and then, wham! Before I know it, I'm hooked.' She gave a rueful smile. 'So, what's your story?'

Natalie was intrigued, felt a connection with the woman. *Can I tell her? Should I?* And before she knew what she was doing, the whole sorry tale came bursting out, like steam from a pressure cooker, until there was nothing left to say and silence filled the space between them.

'So, your husband has been drugging you and you didn't even know?' Katya's voice rises with every word.

Natalie nodded, her cheeks burning. 'I honestly thought it was a health tonic.'

Katya frowned. 'But you must have noticed that feeling, you know, that lovely warm feeling. All your troubles gone. Whoosh!' She flung her arms wide.

Natalie thought about it. 'Well, yes, I did. But I just thought it was the tonic.'

'Fucking good tonic, eh?' Katya laughed.

Natalie looked away, tugged her socks up her ankles, suddenly aware of her unkempt appearance; the hairs on her legs, the shapeless tracksuit, the smell of sweat. 'Anyway, why are you in here? You're not like the others, are you, so what's your story?'

Katya waved her hand in a dismissive gesture, looked around the bare cell. 'Oh, you know. The usual.'

Natalie frowned. *What the hell did that mean?* Something in Katya's eyes made her decide not to ask. Another time, maybe, when she'd got to know her better. But really, what did it matter?

She winced as her stomach started its usual griping. She could time her day by it, knew when the medication was wearing off and braced herself for the chills and tremors that would surely follow. She was feeling sick now, the pains in her head reaching a crescendo. She lay her forehead on her knees again, closed her eyes, ready to sit it out for the next few hours until she got her evening pills.

'Aw,' Katya said as she wriggled closer. She put out a hand, stroked Natalie's hair. 'It's tough, isn't it?' Natalie flinched, then relaxed into the rhythmic caress, found she liked it, this show of comfort, distracting her from the pains. 'Don't worry, it'll get better. Another week or so and you'll be coming out of it. All the physical shit'll wear off. Just the mindfuck left.' Katya sighed. 'That takes a bit longer.'

Just the mindfuck.

But that was the worst of it, constantly agitated and anxious, tears springing from nowhere, making her body shake with the force of her sobs. Dozens of unanswerable questions queueing up to ambush her mind, making her head ache with the effort of trying to work out answers that disappeared into a fog of confusion.

She felt so weak and ill she just wanted to evaporate, become nothing.

'Hey,' Katya said, her voice silky and soothing. 'Don't worry. You'll get through this. I'll look after you. Stick with me and you'll be fine.'

Her arms snaked round Natalie's shoulders and Natalie clung to her, all her worries coming to life in her head, worries about losing Harry, her home, her life; teasing and taunting her, until it was all she could hear.

CHAPTER SIXTEEN

Now

I'll admit I didn't sleep well last night, my head so full of plans. But I feel like I could crush the world in my hands today. That's how pumped up I am. Amazing stuff, adrenaline. And caffeine. Not to mention that little snort of coke, just to top it up. I'm buzzing around at ninety miles an hour, getting everything sorted.

My bag is packed with everything I might need, including a new tracking device, a little magnetic thing that I can stick under her car.

I don't think I've felt this good in ages. I feel almost invincible.

There's no escaping me now.

CHAPTER SEVENTEEN

Now

Mary puts a huge plate of food in front of Natalie. 'There you are. Set you up for the day, that will.'

Natalie's eyes widen. Bacon and eggs, beans, sausage and toast. It smells delicious and saliva is already filling her mouth, but the thought of wading through such a massive amount of food horrifies her. Even though it's early and nobody will be answering phones yet, she's on edge, anxious to get out and about, trying to find Harry.

Her stomach grumbles.

How long since I had a proper meal? she wonders as she looks at her plate. It's been snacks on the go ever since she left prison, and after the incident this morning, she knows she needs to organise her eating better. If she fills up now, then she won't have to worry about food for the rest of the day. She looks at the clock on the mantelpiece. *Ten minutes. Whatever I can eat in ten minutes, then that's it. I'm out of here.*

Mary bustles out of the dining room and comes back a minute later with a large pot of tea and a jug of milk.

'This should keep us going for a while,' she says as she settles herself in the chair opposite, pouring two mugs of tea. Natalie checks the clock again. Seven forty. Twenty minutes until there's any chance of people being in offices. People who might lead her to her son. She eats faster.

'Well, this is nice,' Mary says, wiggling in her seat, hands wrapped round her mug. 'A bit of time to get to know each other. So, where are you from, lovey? I don't think you said.'

'London.' Natalie squirms, wonders if she should have made something up.

'You don't have a London accent.'

'Well, I was born in London, but I've lived all over the place.' She talks between mouthfuls of food, hardly chewing before she swallows, desperate to get breakfast done with. 'My dad gave up teaching, then had loads of different jobs, kept getting made redundant. We couldn't afford to live in London, so we had to move to Manchester, then Sheffield, then Leeds.'

Mary tuts. 'That's not easy when you're a child, is it? Always moving schools. Leaving your friends and having to make new ones.'

The sympathy in her eyes brings a lump to Natalie's throat. She remembers the horror she'd felt each time she was taken to a new classroom by a different head teacher and introduced to the rest of her class. The way they'd looked at her, curious and assessing, as if she was a newly discovered species of sea creature. She'd learnt that children are mean and horrible to each other, and especially horrible to new kids who have a different accent and don't talk proper. She takes a sip of tea, shudders.

Thank goodness she'd sat next to Sasha on her first day of term and was able to stay at the same school all through her teenage years. *Some things are meant to be*, she thinks. *Me and Sasha.* Tied together by shared experiences, by defining moments, even though there have been times when their lives have gone in different directions. *But isn't that the test of a true friendship?* That it can survive the times when you don't see each other; is there to be picked up, like a dropped stitch in a piece of knitting. Part of the fabric of your life, whatever the pattern turns out to be.

'Where's your family live now then?' Mary's voice breaks into her thoughts and Natalie looks up to see curious eyes watching her.

She takes a last bite of toast and pushes her plate away, wondering how to explain that she's lost her family along the path of life, when she veered off in an unforeseen direction, and none of them came with her.

'Oh, all over the place,' she says, as if it doesn't matter that she's got no idea where her father or brother live. 'Mum lives in Lytham St Annes.' *At least I think she does.*

'Oh, nice.' Mary nods. 'Posh there, isn't it?'

'Oh yes. Definitely posh.' She takes a gulp of tea, no desire to continue with Mary's gentle interrogation. But her nosiness has given Natalie an idea. An idea that might help her find Harry. Her pulse quickens with new hope and she gives Mary a smile, puts her mug down.

'I wonder if you could help me, Mary?' She leans forwards, elbows on the table.

Mary's eyes twinkle. 'Of course, lovey. If I can.'

'Well, the thing is, I wanted to visit an old friend of mine.' Natalie laughs. 'Actually, he was my employer. But he's moved and I don't know his new address.' Mary tuts. 'You might know his family? The Wilsons? Gordon Wilson owns a shipping company. His wife Marian does lots of charity work, always used to be in the news. Their son is called Tom.'

Mary looks at the ceiling, then at Natalie. 'Ooh now, I can't say they sound familiar. In shipping, you say?' She frowns, lips pursed together as she thinks.

'That's right. Tom runs a company called Excalibur Wealth Management. They used to live in Douglas but when I got there I found out the house has been sold. Empty.'

Mary's eyebrows shoot up towards her hairline. 'And they didn't tell you?'

Natalie sits back in her chair. 'Oh, I've um… been working away. We lost touch for a while, but I thought it would be nice to pop in and see them while I'm on the island.' She looks away, finishes the rest of her tea and thinks, *I'm wasting my time here.*

She glances at the clock. Almost eight. 'Gosh, Mary, I'm really sorry but I've got to go.' She gives her an apologetic smile. 'I'm meeting up with a friend. I'll have to dash or I'll be late and she hates being kept waiting.' She stands and pushes her chair back in against the table. 'Thanks for a lovely breakfast.'

'I can do dinner, if you like.' Mary looks hopeful, eyes big and round, like a lost kitten. 'And... and by then I will have had a chance to talk to my friend Margaret. Her daughter does a chat show in the afternoons. On the radio. Talks to anyone and everyone. I'm sure she'll know who you're talking about. Might be able to point me in the right direction.'

Natalie stops, hands on the back of the chair. *Do I risk it? Or is it time to move on, find somewhere else to stay. Make it harder to be traced?* But she feels safe tucked away with this old lady. Nobody will think of looking for her here. And who knows, Mary might just come up trumps. *Another line of attack can't hurt, can it?*

She smiles at Mary. 'Okay, that'll be great.'

Mary beams at her. 'I'll make it for six, shall I?'

'Six will be fine, but give me your number just in case there's a problem.'

Mary recites her number and Natalie taps it into her phone, thinking that Mary reminds her of a great aunt that she was fond of as a child. A weight settles in Natalie's stomach and she holds back a sigh. There's no chance she will ever be part of a family now. All that has gone. *It will always be just me and Harry.* Because who would want to have anything to do with her once they found out what she'd done?

CHAPTER EIGHTEEN

Then

In prison, Natalie woke from a dream, anxious and alert. She could hear Harry crying and swung her legs out of bed, stopping for a moment as the world whirled around her. She closed her eyes to steady the dizziness and when she opened them again, she remembered where she was. With a groan, she slumped back on the mattress.

It wasn't Harry crying, it was some crazed woman. Maybe a self-harmer who'd slit the flesh of her arms with broken plastic. Another one of the determined few, who attempted to kill themselves every single day and wept because they were not dead. Because they had to carry on living their hopeless lives.

Natalie's cell was near the control room and she listened to prison officers come and go outside her door, on a constant mission of damage limitation. She heard what these women did to themselves. It wasn't just ligatures. It was knives and razors and plastic bags over their heads. Anything could be a weapon of self-destruction, it seemed, and these people were inventive. Last night, a woman had stuffed a pair of knickers down her own throat, hoping they'd choke her to death.

Their misery hung in the air, seeped through the walls, the floor and into Natalie's heart. *What's the point in keeping quiet?* Her pain found its voice, a wail, loud and visceral, full of the desperation to be with Harry again. A sound that welled up from the depths of her soul and flowed out of her until she was spent, drained of all feelings, an empty vessel with nothing left inside, except the ache of separation.

It took her a long time to go back to sleep, and then she was disturbed several times by the soundtrack of anguish that played on a constant loop around her.

The next morning, a prison officer opened her cell and popped her head around the door. It was the same woman who'd brought her to the Therapy Wing, her face jolly and round, blonde hair tied back with a scrunchy at the base of her neck.

'Morning, Natalie. Just thought you might like to come out for breakfast today. Start getting to know the girls.'

Natalie didn't move. Withdrawal from the drugs made paranoia a constant companion and Katya's words of warning made her scared to venture out of her cell.

'Don't be fooled,' Katya had said, the night before, when she was giving Natalie the low-down on how to survive on the Wing. 'They're not nice people. It's an act. Just remember that. You can't trust them. Not any of them.' Katya's eyes were fierce, teeth clamped together as she hissed her warning. 'Everyone wants something from you. Do you understand? Everyone. And if you don't give it, then, believe me, they will take it.' She smashed a fist into the palm of her hand. Natalie winced.

'Let me tell you what has happened.' Katya wagged a finger, nodded. 'Then you will know for sure.' And she proceeded to reinforce her message with example after example of the nastiness Natalie might expect to encounter. Until she started to cry and Katya stopped.

There was no reason not to believe her.

Now, Natalie looked at the prison officer and shook her head. 'I think I'll just stay in here.'

'Oh, come on, they won't bite, you know.'

That's not what Katya said. Natalie looked away, stared at the window. 'No thanks.'

'Look, you need to get up and get moving. It's not good to stay in bed all day.' The prison officer took a couple of steps into the cell. 'I'll sit with you at breakfast for a bit if you like, just for today. Introduce you to some people. You'll soon get chatting.'

The prison officer came closer, and Natalie wondered if she would be manhandled out of her cell if she didn't go voluntarily. She let herself be led to where breakfast was being served, then to a table with a few other women.

The woman sitting opposite her was scrawny as a plucked chicken, with bad skin, rotten teeth and wild eyes. The girl next to her had scars all the way up her arms where she'd cut herself. On the next table sat a woman covered in piercings and tattoos, who looked hard and mean on a level Natalie had never come across before. She realised she was shaking, her spoon clinking against her dish.

She pushed her food away. 'I'm sorry, I'm... I feel a bit sick. I think... I just... need to lie down.' Heart racing, she hurried back to her cell, closing the door behind her.

How can I survive in here with these people? They spoke languages Natalie didn't understand, used slang she'd never heard of, making her feel like she'd landed in an alien world.

Her door opened and the prison officer came in.

'You okay?'

Natalie nodded, eyes stinging. She sniffed, wiped her nose with the back of her hand.

'Ah, you're not okay, are you?'

Natalie shook her head and fiddled with her hands in her lap.

'Look, I know it can be a bit scary, but these women are not a bad bunch when you get to know them. Most of them anyway. A lot of them have never had a decent chance at life, you know. Not really their fault they've ended up in here when you get to know their situations.'

'I'd rather...' Natalie clasped her hands together, as if in prayer. 'Can I... just stay in here?'

''Course you can, pet. Till lunch, then we'll have another go. Get you acclimatised slowly. How about that?'

Natalie nodded, her body sagging with relief. 'Thank you.'

'I'll get your meds for you, shall I? Then you won't have to queue. Be about twenty minutes, okay?'

Natalie lay on her bed, exhausted and drained, feeling as though she'd run a marathon. She closed her eyes and waited for the day to end. Tomorrow she was seeing her solicitor. *Maybe she'll be able to tell me when I can see Harry.* She clung on to the thought of being with her little boy again, and he came to life in her mind, took over her daydreams, taking her away from the nightmare of reality as she drifted into sleep.

CHAPTER NINETEEN

Now

It's been a promising start to the day, and Natalie runs up the stairs, fortified by a hearty breakfast and the knowledge that she now has four potential leads. She knows where Tom works, so she can wait until he leaves, and follow him home. That must be her surest route to success. Sasha has signed up as her accomplice, which will make everything so much easier, and the fact that the producer might know Tom makes for a good plan B. If both those leads draw a blank, Mary might have some information for her this evening and, as a last resort, she still has Jack's number. Surely, at least one of these possibilities is going to come up trumps?

But what if Tom's not in the office today? The idea that the mainstay of her plans might be a non-starter brings her to a halt in her bedroom doorway. She chews at her lip. *Only one way to find out,* she decides as she slips inside, closes the door and pulls out her phone. It's just after eight, but she gets an answer straight away.

'Good morning, Excalibur Wealth Management,' Tom's secretary says.

'Oh, hello.' Natalie sounds all cheery, as if she hasn't a care in the world. 'I just wondered if Mr Wilson's in the office today?'

'Oh, I'm afraid he's out at a meeting, won't be back until later this morning. Can I take a message?'

'Oh, no. No.' She's too quick off the mark and slows herself down. 'No, thank you. It's a... personal matter.' She cringes. She shouldn't have said that; the secretary will be curious, but it's too late now. 'I'll er... call back later. Is he in for the rest of the day?'

'Just let me have a look for you...' She hears keys tapping, then the secretary comes back on the line. 'Right, so he'll be in from ten forty-five until twelve, just popping back for a quick meeting, really, and then he'll be working at home this afternoon.'

Her stomach jangles with nervous energy, the need to be doing something making her pace the floor. She checks her watch. A couple of hours until Tom comes back to the office. *Dammit.* She pulls at her hair, trying to think of something she can do to speed up the process of finding Harry and getting him to safety, but draws a blank.

She decides to get herself into Douglas and stake out Tom's office, ready for his arrival. *Just got to be patient,* she tells herself. *One step at a time.* And the first step is to make herself look more ordinary. Invisible.

She sits in front of the mirror, backcombs her hair on the top to give it more volume, braids it over one shoulder and pulls out wisps on either side of her face to soften the angles of her jaw. Then she opens her new make-up bag and gets to work. It's been so long since she's worn make-up she'd forgotten what a hassle it is to get all the layers in place. Concealer, foundation, blusher, powder, mascara, eyeliner, eyeshadow, lipstick. But her hands remember the drill, quick and precise, and ten minutes later a glamorous face peers back at her. She allows herself a satisfied smile. *Much better.*

The new outfit she bought in Bangor, a flowery calf-length dress she found in a charity shop, matched with an olive tailored jacket, makes her look presentable enough. In a yummy mummy sort of a way. Comfy leather sandals finish the outfit in case she has to do a bit of standing around. She even has a sunhat and shades, should she need to hide her face.

She's sure that nobody who saw her yesterday will recognise her today. Tom presumably thinks she's still in prison and Katya's brother, Lech, met her when her hair was brunette, her face chubby. Neither of them will be looking for an elegant, skinny blonde.

But that niggly feeling in the pit of her stomach refuses to go away and she knows she has to trust her instincts. *Got to stay alert,* she tells herself. After all, Lech runs an international operation, has contacts all over the place and although her release was supposed to be kept a secret, she knows that prisons are leaky places when it comes to information, because prison officers are only human and they have families to protect.

The threat rears up in her mind, an ugly truth that needs to be addressed. Up to now, she's been running towards Harry, rather than running away from Lech, because she'd thought that her early release would mean he wasn't ready, wasn't looking. *But I need to keep both things in mind,* she tells herself. *Plan for all eventualities.*

Her eyes fall on the composite picture that's propped in front of her, the best she can do without any photos to go on. *Harry.* She strokes his face with a finger, trying to imagine what his skin feels like. *Is it as soft as when he was a baby?* Soon, she'll know and her heart swells with love for her child, filling her chest so she can hardly breathe.

'Not long now, Harry,' she whispers, kissing his picture before putting it back on the dressing table. Then she picks up her handbag and hurries downstairs.

So much of life is about luck, she thinks as she drives towards Douglas. The friends you make, where you live, job opportunities, the people you meet. Chance events that shape moments in time and change the direction of your life forever. It's all about luck. And something tells her that her luck is changing.

Being released two months early was lucky, the result of a Home Office initiative to reduce overcrowding. And the fact that she was getting death threats made them push her to the front of the queue. Having the use of this car was lucky. Borrowed off a friend, an ex-convict who had been willing to let her have the use of it in return for a hefty chunk of money. Meeting Jack, a chance encounter, led her to Sasha and to Mary's house. *Yes, lots of lucky things have been happening recently,* she thinks, with a flicker of a smile. *Maybe I'll be lucky today.* Her hands tighten round the steering wheel. She's got to be. Harry's in danger, time is flitting away and she's not even at square one yet.

Once in Douglas, Tom's office proves easy to find, but locating somewhere to park is a different matter. Eventually, she ends up in a multi-storey car park at the back of Marks & Spencer, which is not ideal because it's a bit of a walk to where Tom works. She takes a deep breath, steadying herself for the task ahead, puts her hat and sunglasses on and walks with a confidence that belies the churning in her stomach.

She takes the stairs out of the car park, a couple of flights down to street level. When she's almost at the bottom, she hears the tap of feet coming down behind her. Purposeful and quick. *Is somebody following me?* The thought takes hold and grips like a vice, leaving no room for doubt. Her heart leaps, as though it's been jump-started and she gallops down the rest of the steps, bursting out of the door at the bottom.

She finds herself in a pedestrianised square, a place she doesn't immediately recognise. But she can't stop, not for a moment, and hurries on. She enters the narrow street that houses the main shopping area and is relieved to see that it's busy today, crowded with shoppers. She starts to sweat as she weaves in and out between people, can almost feel breath on the back of her neck. She imagines a hand reaching out to grasp her shoulder. Her heart skips, her stride lengthens, she speeds up.

You're overreacting, she tells herself. *You're in a crowd of people, for Christ's sake.* But her body takes no notice. She starts to run.

There's a small shopping centre up ahead on her left. A good place to hide. But as she gets to the doors, a scream and then a shout makes her glance back the way she has come. She stops for a second. People are looking round, murmuring to each other, craning their necks to see what's going on.

A child's buggy has been knocked over and a woman in a baseball hat crouches on the floor next to a child. For a few seconds, there is no movement, no sound. A young man in skinny jeans and a grey hoodie stands with a hand over his mouth, his other hand pulling at his long hair. 'My baby! Oh, God!' he starts shouting, over and over, panic in his voice. An older man stands next to him in a blue patterned shirt, his eyes raking through the crowd that is gathering around the scene.

A frown darkens his face, his lips drawn back from his teeth in an angry snarl. His eyes meet hers. For a moment, she is paralysed. *Is that him? The man following me?* He doesn't look like Lech, but then, she realises, he might have sent one of his men to do his dirty work. It hadn't occurred to her before, but now it seems a likely scenario.

She dashes into the shopping centre. Her eyes flick around as she gets the measure of her surroundings; a circular courtyard that houses a handful of shops, an atrium letting in natural light. An escalator in the middle leads up to another floor with the same layout. Adrenaline courses round her body, her mind alert to every movement, every sound. Nowhere to hide, she's going to be cornered if she stays here. Then she sees another set of doors, leading outside at the back of the building. It's her only escape route and she runs through them, emerging in a back street. She glances around. *Is he behind me?* Her pulse rate spikes. Her dress sticks to her back. She daren't look, can't waste a second. Nothing to do but push on and hope she loses him.

In front of her, a steep set of steps runs up the hillside next to another multi-storey car park. *Places to hide up there*, she decides, and dashes across the road, taking the steps two at a time, leg muscles burning. She grits her teeth, pushes through the pain, but when she reaches the top, she has to stop, hands on her knees, pulling air into her lungs as if she's drowning.

A waist-height wall provides a hiding place in front of a single-storey building, once a shop but now closed. The left side of the street is lined with Victorian houses converted into office buildings, and the steps have brought her out at the start of the terrace. Across the road is a covered parking area, lined with cars, dark at the back, providing a perfect hiding place. She can dash over there and be out of sight in a matter of seconds. Feeling more secure now, she questions her reactions.

Is it paranoia or is it real?

Her heart says real, her head says not.

Gut instinct. She tells herself. *Believe it.*

Hidden from view, still huffing and puffing, she makes herself peek over the top of the wall, looking back the way she's come. She can see the tops of people's heads, but not their faces. Nobody is on the steps. Then a man exits the shopping centre. Tall, dark-haired. His shirt looks familiar. A brightly patterned blue Hawaiian print. *Is that the man from the street?* He looks up the steps. Her breath hitches. *It is! It's him.* She ducks down, pops her head back up and sees him head off in a different direction.

Then a woman comes out, a mother with a double buggy. An elderly couple. A gaggle of teenagers. A few women with children of assorted ages. Older women on their own. A young man. Gradually, her breathing slows. *See? Nobody there to worry about. Christ, you need to get a grip.*

Still, a doubt wriggles in her mind.

Sirens blare, filling the air. She stiffens. *Ambulance or police?* A woman dashes out of the shopping centre and runs down the road. Natalie watches her duck into a shop further down. Then two policemen appear. They stop and look around, then split up, one heading towards the steps. Natalie's eyes widen.

Dammit! Time to go. She wheels round and bumps into a dumpy middle-aged woman in gym gear, almost knocking her over.

'Sorry,' Natalie says. 'You alright?' But she doesn't wait for an answer, and sets off across the road, cursing under her breath. She wipes sweat from her forehead. *Is the woman still watching me?* It feels like it. *Has the policeman caught up? Or is it somebody else?* She glances over her shoulder, but the woman's gone. *Nobody is looking.* She ducks into the covered car park, crouches behind a chunky four by four, hidden in the shadows. She kneels on the floor and waits. It smells of piss and engine oil and she tries not to breathe through her nose, her ragged breath rasping in her ears.

CHAPTER TWENTY

Then

On her fourth day in prison, Natalie had a meeting with her solicitor, and her first question, as soon as the woman walked through the door, was when could she see Harry.

'I'm sorry, Natalie, but your request has been refused,' her solicitor said, not even looking at her while she got a bundle of paperwork out of her bag and started sorting through it on the desk.

Refused? Not for one minute had Natalie imagined that she wouldn't be able to see her son and it took her breath away like a blow to the chest. *I'll go mad if I can't see him.* She could hear herself hyperventilating. *Oh God, I'll end up like the rest of them.*

The woman settled in her seat and started flicking through papers. When she glanced up and caught Natalie's eye, her expression was calm and business-like. 'I'm afraid there's nothing more I can do. Let's move on, shall we?'

'Can't I appeal? What do I have to do?'

Surely, I've got rights? And Harry, he has the right to be with his mum, hasn't he?

'Unfortunately, I can't be much help, I'm afraid. Family law isn't my field, you see.'

'But I'm his mother.' Natalie stood up, started pacing up and down the windowless box of a room where their meeting was being held. 'Don't you see that he needs me?'

Her solicitor sighed. 'Well, as far as I'm aware, you still have a live-in nanny, so I'm sure your baby is being well looked after.' She gave Natalie a conciliatory smile. 'I'm sure he's fine. I know this is difficult for you, but there's absolutely nothing I can do.'

Natalie was in no mood to be placated and glared at the woman who was supposed to be helping her. 'He's not fine! How can he be? He needs to be with me.' She tapped her chest for emphasis. 'Me! Not some… nanny!'

'Well, he can't be with you in here.'

'Why not? Other mothers have their babies here.'

'Yes, but there are special circumstances which mean that's the best option for the child.' She was talking to Natalie with a forced patience, as if Natalie was a belligerent two year old.

Natalie opened her mouth to say something, but her solicitor held up a hand to stop her, a frown sharpening her face.

'No, I'm sorry, there's nothing more I can do for you with regards to seeing your son. You'll have to believe me on this one. Your husband is in control in that department and if he doesn't want to bring your baby to visit, well, that's his call.'

Natalie stopped pacing as it suddenly dawned on her that Tom couldn't come to visit, even if he wanted to. He was a potential witness, her solicitor had said. Maybe that's what this was about. Not that he didn't want to bring Harry, but he wasn't allowed. That made sense. But the nanny, Elena, she could bring him, couldn't she?

'But…'

'There are no buts!' Her solicitor pointed to the chair, a hand clasped to her forehead. 'Please sit down. You're making me nauseous. I cannot cope with you pacing about like some… some caged animal.' There was a weariness in her eyes, an edge to her voice. 'Sit down, please, or this meeting is over.'

Natalie's hands clenched by her sides.

'I mean it.' Her solicitor started shuffling papers together, getting ready to leave.

Natalie sighed. However much she disliked the woman, she needed her and she walked back to her chair, sat down with a thump, her hands knotted together in her lap.

The solicitor's jaw was working as if she was chewing a toffee that had stuck to her teeth.

'Okay, Natalie. I don't think you understand your situation here. So, let me make it clear for you.' Her eyes narrowed as she spoke. 'You are a prisoner.' Her finger jabbed the air. 'You have no say. Your crimes have denied you that right, as well as the right to have contact with your son if your husband doesn't think it's a good idea. And, given that you're a drug addict, not many people would disagree with his decision.'

Words of protest stuck in Natalie's throat as the truth of her situation was laid out before her. She was helpless, at this woman's mercy, and it seemed that she'd already decided that having contact with Harry wasn't important. The solicitor fiddled with a pen, clicking the point in and out, in and out. She leant forward.

'Just be glad that your child has a good home with his father and is being well looked after. Most women in here don't have that luxury. Their children are in care, or left with relatives and goodness knows who else.' She put the pen on the desk. 'Your child is the lucky one. You need to remember that.'

Natalie opened her mouth, too astounded to speak. Her mind wrestled with the idea of more time without Harry, the pain of separation aching through her as though he was a missing limb.

Her solicitor kept staring at her. Natalie closed her mouth and stared back.

'I can refer your case to a colleague who deals with family law. That's the best I can do, okay?'

Natalie nodded. 'Thank you,' she murmured, happy that she'd forced some progress; the most she was likely to achieve today.

'Right,' her solicitor said. 'Let's move on to the case against you, shall we?'

Natalie brought her mind back from its fluttering panic and forced herself to concentrate. She had to do everything in her power to make these people listen to reason and make sure she was released as soon as possible. It was the only way she was going to be with Harry again. She sat up straight. Perhaps there'd been progress in the police investigation. Perhaps somebody had taken notice of her comments after all. Perhaps Tom had…

'Okay, so this is the situation.' Her solicitor paused to make sure Natalie was taking notice. 'If you plead guilty, act remorseful, send an apology to your client and tell them where the money is, then we have a better chance of getting a more lenient sentence. We could probably do some work around the effects of pregnancy, something hormonal, maybe see if we can get a diagnosis of postnatal depression.'

Plead guilty? Natalie put her hands to her temples, pressure building into a headache. *What is the woman talking about?*

'But I haven't done anything wrong.' Natalie's voice was a whimper. 'I don't know where the money is. Honestly, I don't. I'm not guilty. I might have made a mistake, but I haven't stolen any money.'

She wondered, as she said it, whether this was actually true. Or had she actually done it and blanked it out, acted out a recurring fantasy to get away? She shuddered at the thought. No. She'd know, wouldn't she? She'd remember. A chill ran through her as she thought about the new car and the payment to the refugee charity and the airline tickets. She had absolutely no memory of any of that. But those things had happened. She tried to swallow her unease away, unable to look her solicitor in the eye now.

'I'm afraid the evidence says otherwise, Natalie. Look, you have to be realistic here. There's a convincing trail of evidence that leads, very clearly, to you.' Natalie looked up to see a sly smile on her solicitor's face. 'The money went into an account in the Cayman Islands with your name on it. Then it was moved on again and the police are still trying to track where it went. It's a lot of money to give up, I understand that, but they'll find it eventually, you know. However clever you think you've been.'

Natalie's hands gripped each other as she stared at the table. Her fingernails dug into her palms, the pain enough to tell her that this was real.

'Natalie!' The solicitor smacked the table. 'Natalie, are you listening?'

She raised her head, blinking.

Her solicitor's face softened. 'Okay, I know this is a shock. Tell you what, let's get a cup of coffee, have a bit of a breather. I'll give you a few minutes, shall I? Then we'll carry on.' She walked over to the door, had a word with the guard and slipped out into the corridor. The door clanked shut behind her.

Natalie gazed around the stuffy little room, with its horrible green walls, scuffed floor and stark fluorescent light. She was going to be convicted of a crime she couldn't remember committing and there was nothing she could do about it. *Harry.* Her heart lurched. Poor little Harry, how confused and upset he must be without her. How long before she would get to see him again? An image of his crumpled, tear-stained face filled her mind, the sound of his cries rang in her ears and she lay her head on the table, unable to hold back the tide of her misery, letting it flow over her, engulf her and drown out the pain of her thoughts.

Ten minutes later, her solicitor came back holding two polystyrene cups of coffee, the smell of cigarettes floating in with her, polluting the air.

Natalie pulled her leaden body upright and wiped her face on her sleeve. She accepted the tissue that her solicitor passed over the table and blew her nose, then took a sip of coffee.

'Right. Feeling better?' Her solicitor gave a thin smile. 'Okay. So, we're on a damage limitation exercise here. Let me tell you how it works. As it is, you're looking at a maximum, and I do stress this is a maximum, of six and a half years.'

Natalie gasped, rocked back in her chair. *Six and a half years? No, no, no!*

'If you plead guilty to a crime straight away, your possible sentence is reduced by a third. If you wait until the trial date is set, that goes down to a quarter and if it's on the day of the trial then you only get a reduction of a tenth.' Her solicitor straightened up the pages in her file, tapped them together and put them back on the table, giving Natalie a moment to absorb what she'd just said. 'So, you can see that it's much better to plead guilty at the earliest opportunity.'

They stared at each other. All Natalie could hear was the scream in her head.

'The other consideration, of course, is overwhelming evidence. Which there is in your case. And that makes the reduction only one fifth instead of a third. But that's open to interpretation.' The solicitor picked up a newspaper clipping, waved it at Natalie. 'Here's some guidance. A recent case. The sum stolen was two point three million. The woman was given just over three years. But—' she held up a finger '—the money was recovered and she pleaded guilty as soon as she was arrested. Saves police time and resources, you see. So… in your case, unless the money is recovered, I would anticipate a sentence in the region of… well, let's say five years max? Maybe less.'

Natalie's eyes widened. *She's telling me to plead guilty?*

'Of course, you will be eligible for parole, which means you'll only serve half of that time. So… probably two and half years? Less if we can work on mitigating factors, which I think we probably can. I've got a brilliant psychologist we can use for an assessment. So, let's say two years. Doesn't sound so bad, does it?' She smiled at Natalie.

Two years? Not so bad?

Natalie's hands gripped her chair, as if this would stop her from falling into the black hole that had appeared where her life used to be. Her body started to tremble. She was staying here, locked up in this prison. Separated from Harry. For years.

Natalie stared at the wall in front of her, unable to focus on anything but her hopeless situation.

'You're in court tomorrow to enter your plea.' Her solicitor started to tidy her papers away. 'I suggest you think about our chat overnight and I'll see you in the morning.' She gave Natalie a curt nod before she got up and left the room. Natalie stared after her, mouth gaping.

Tomorrow? No, it can't be that quick.

She had to work out a defence. But she could only do that if she had someone on the outside to help her, to agitate and make a nuisance of themselves. Get the people who mattered to listen. Fast.

Knowing she wasn't allowed to talk to Tom, and Sasha was abroad, the only other person she could ring was her mother. She'd been putting it off until she felt mentally robust enough, hoping things would be resolved, but she couldn't delay it any longer. Desperate times called for desperate measures. Even if her solicitor wouldn't listen, then her mother surely would. And her mother was an expert at getting her own way.

'Mum, I'm in trouble,' she said at lunchtime, when she finally got to the front of the queue for the phone, and the story flowed out in one long, breathless sentence.

When Natalie finished speaking, the silence was thick and ominous. She swallowed, hugged her arms to her chest.

'Oh, Natalie. I've had Tom on the phone. He's already told me.' Her mother let out a long sigh. 'There's no excuse for it, though. You can't go blaming other people for everything all the time. You never were good at taking responsibility, were you?' Natalie tensed. 'And the story you've just told me is so far-fetched, honestly, no wonder nobody believes you.' Her mother tutted.

Natalie couldn't speak, could feel the blood draining from her face. This was her last hope. Her last chance of getting someone to help her.

'Tom has been wonderful to you, Natalie. Treated you like a princess. I mean, that house you live in is gorgeous. All those lovely clothes. That new BMW. And the job he gave you… It's more than I ever hoped you might achieve. Honestly… what more did the man have to do?'

A list of things flashed into Natalie's mind, but it was not the point of the conversation. What she needed was for her mother to talk to people; the police, solicitors, human rights campaigners. Make them understand, get them to do something that would question the validity of the evidence and get her out of prison.

'I haven't done anything wrong.' Natalie's jaw ached from being clamped shut. 'I've just told you.'

'There's no smoke without fire.' Her mother snapped. 'Tom tells me there's piles of evidence and frankly it sounds like your behaviour has been more than a bit suspect.' Her voice took on a weary tone. 'I'd trust that man with my life, Natalie, but you… well, you've always been difficult.'

'What?' Natalie's heart skipped a beat. *Did she just say that?*

'Oh, you know what I'm talking about. It's not the first time you've been in trouble with the police.'

'I was fourteen,' Natalie said, astounded that the incident had been dredged up again.

'A leopard doesn't change its spots.'

'It was a couple of lipsticks from Boots.'

'It. Was. Still. Stealing.' Her mother's voice was laced with distaste.

Natalie bristled. 'Oh, come on. I wasn't even charged with anything, just cautioned.'

Silence.

'It was just a dare.' Natalie had never told her that before, hadn't wanted to get Sasha into trouble as well.

'I didn't bring you up to be a thief. Honestly, when this gets out… I think we might have to move. I couldn't face them up at the golf club. Not now.' She could hear a strangled sob. 'You've ruined everything, Natalie. Again.'

Natalie leant her forehead against the wall. Why had she imagined her mother's reaction would be any different? She slammed the phone down, letting out a scream that a werewolf would have been proud of.

'Gets you like that sometimes,' the prison officer said, giving her a comforting pat on the shoulder. 'Don't worry, you'll soon settle in.'

Natalie gazed at her. She didn't want to settle in. She wanted to go home to Harry.

CHAPTER TWENTY-ONE

Now

Those bloody parents! What a fuss they made. It was an accident, for God's sake! I couldn't have avoided that buggy even if I'd wanted to. They just pushed the thing straight out of the shop, right in front of me.

They made such a fuss, even insisting on taking the child to hospital.

Christ, she'd better be okay. Can you imagine the fuss if she isn't?

And who decided to call the police? Fucking do-gooders. In the space of five minutes, the street was packed, everyone gawking, muttering as if I was to blame. I pointed them towards the real culprit, though. Let them chase after her for now, I thought.

I get back in my car, fiddle around in the glove compartment and pull out the little flask I keep for emergencies. Take a nip.

Time to get that magnetic tracking device on the car. Then she can't slip away again.

Right. I take another gulp. Things to do. Better get going.

CHAPTER TWENTY-TWO

Now

Legs and feet move up and down the pavement, all Natalie can see as she peers out from underneath the car. Nobody is running and gradually, her pulse steadies. The rough concrete digs into her knees. Her feet start to cramp and after ten minutes she creeps out of her hiding place, glances up and down the road. The back of the policeman gets smaller as he walks away from her, down the hill. There's nobody else in sight. She lets out a long breath.

See? Everything's fine. She watches for a moment longer. *Everything's fine.*

She heads off up the road, still unsure whether she was actually being followed or not. It felt like it, but she may have been imagining things, scaring herself into thinking what was in her mind was actually real. She realises that she has no idea where she is now and stops to try and get her bearings. For a moment, she feels a flush of panic. *Your phone, you idiot. There's a map on your phone.*

In the three years that she's been in prison, technology has come on a long way and she's not used to all the apps at her disposal. It takes her a moment to get the thing working, then, with a sigh of relief, she realises Tom's office is only a couple of streets away. She checks the time. Twelve minutes until he arrives, and he will arrive on the dot. She knows this, knows all his little obsessions, and she walks a bit faster.

Oh, God! I'm going to see him.

She's tried not to think about it, because her memories of him have been scarred by resentment and she has no idea how she will react. She forces herself to take deep breaths. It's not like she has to speak to him, or even get close. All she has to do is observe and find out what car he's driving. The hairs prickle the back of her neck and she looks over her shoulder, stomach feeling decidedly queasy.

A few minutes later, she's standing outside the building where Tom works. This is the road where lots of solicitors have their offices, along with some banks, finance companies and other business service providers. The architecture is a mixture of sombre stone terraces and modern buildings with fancy glass entrances. Upmarket. Smart. Tom's office building is on a corner, a shared space with a number of other businesses by the looks of the sign on the door, where there's a buzzer for each one.

Natalie sees her reflection in the glass doors and does a double take, her breath catching in her throat. She stands out like a sunflower on a gloomy day in this street full of dark suits and she fastens her jacket. But it's still far from ideal, he'll spot her a mile off. She turns and strides down the road, trying to behave like she belongs there while she looks for somewhere suitable to wait. She spots a seat tucked around a corner on the opposite side of the street, a smokers' area by the looks of it and she hurries across the road. The entrance to Tom's building is still visible but she's partially hidden from view. Perfect.

She perches on the seat. Tension grabs at her shoulders while she pretends to look for something in her bag, keeping one eye on Tom's office. A woman clicks past on impossibly high heels. A man on the other side of the road, with his head down, looking at his phone. A couple, holding hands, chattering, excited. They don't seem to notice her, but she is aware of all the windows. Of people in offices, eyes watching. A bead of sweat inches down her spine. How long can she stay here, exposed like this? She checks her watch again, glances around.

Tom should be here by now, shouldn't he?

A man walking towards Tom's office building catches her attention. Initially, she discounts him because, although he's the right height, his shape's all wrong; a paunch hangs over the belt of his trousers, his body is hunched, shoulders sloping forwards, like he's carrying a heavy load. But as she watches him walk, notices the slight limp on his left leg, the way he twists his hip, she realises, that it's him. *It's Tom.*

Her body reacts as if she's been slammed against the wall, the breath forced out of her. A maelstrom of emotions swirls inside her, and a silent howl fills her head. Oh, how she's longed for the day when she could make him feel even a fraction of the pain he's put her through. *But today is not that day.* Her hands grip the bench to tether herself to the spot, body shaking with the effort of keeping still.

She pretends to look the other way, but keeps him in her peripheral vision. *Being strong is not about giving in to impulse,* she tells herself. *It's about weighing up risks and being brave. Doing things you don't want to do with conviction. Total commitment to achieving the goal.* And getting Harry back is what she lives for. Keeping him from harm is something she'd die for. Her chest tightens, her breathing quick and shallow.

Natalie squashes her fury at what life should have been back into the bunker in her mind. She has to think about the now, this minute, what she's just seen, and use it to her advantage. Tom looks so low and downtrodden that she hardly recognised him. He's not the demon she's seen in her nightmares. Not even close. In the real world, he looks like a broken man and that changes everything. *One-to-one I could take him out,* she thinks, with a satisfied smile, knowing that her task might be a little easier than she'd thought.

She watches as he presses the entry buzzer, notices a glint of gold on his left hand. *His wedding ring?* She can't believe he still wears it, having dropped hers down a drain as soon as it was possible to dispose of it. But then a question blossoms in her mind.

Has he remarried? It's not an idea she's ever considered, because, in her eyes, he's so obviously flawed. The thought of another woman bringing up her son scratches through her, ripping at her heart. *Does he call her Mummy?* Her throat tightens, a surge of emotions threatening to undo her illusion of calm.

How can she possibly love my son like I do?

Natalie's breath quickens.

Maybe she doesn't. Perhaps she's mean to him.

She sees images of her little boy, frightened and confused, cowering away from a ranting banshee of a woman who has no patience with a child who isn't hers. Prison gossip was full of such horror stories, where complicated families were the norm. The images darken and her imagination escalates the abuse until she has to shake herself back to reality. She reminds herself that it's just a theory. *A distraction.* Her eyes widen as a new thought burrows into her head. *Elena.* The nanny. She remembers how his eyes had followed Elena, his appreciation of her youthful good looks and curvaceous figure clear in his expression. And he was always remarking on how wonderful she was with Harry. *Maybe he married her?*

She gives herself a mental shake.

Get a grip. Focus. There are things to do.

She breathes herself into a state of calm while she watches Tom disappear into the building, then she crosses the road and retraces his footsteps.

There's a private car park behind his building, the obvious place for him to be parked and she walks round all three floors, trying to work out which car is his. He always drove a Jaguar and she finds two. Black or maroon? She can't decide which colour he'd prefer and peers through the windows but both are spotless inside and there are no clues as to ownership. She feels the bonnets, but neither is warm. A weight settles in her stomach. *They can't be his.* She taps her forehead with the heel of her hand while she thinks, willing some ingenious idea to spring out of nowhere.

The only way is to go round the whole car park, feeling the bonnets for the warm ones, then try and narrow it down. It sounds like an impossible task. She hears the slap of footsteps and hides behind a pillar. A car door slams. *Somebody leaving? Or…* The roar of an engine coming up the ramp drowns out her thoughts. She glances towards the ceiling. CCTV cameras. The idea that someone, somewhere is watching her, wondering what she's up to, brings her skin out in goosebumps. They might think she's about to steal a car and decide to take action. She has to go. Right now, she has to go.

She darts down the stairs, out of the car park, and round a few corners until she feels far enough away to be safe from curious eyes. She leans against a wall, panting, feet throbbing in sandals that were not designed for running. Her head is pounding, her plan in tatters, because how can she follow Tom home when she doesn't know what car he drives?

CHAPTER TWENTY-THREE

Then

The evening after her meeting with the solicitor, Natalie was sitting on her bed, staring at the wall, when Katya put her head round the door.

'So how did it go with the solicitor?' She walked into the room and sat down next to Natalie.

'I'm in court tomorrow.' Natalie's voice sounded far away. She stared at Katya, not really seeing her. After the revelations of the morning and the conversation with her mother, she had to accept the inevitable; prison was going to be her home for a couple of years. She imagined endless days in this scary, soulless place, while Harry grew from a baby into a walking, talking little person. Without her. All those development milestones that she would never witness, never be able to delight in or remember. And his memories of her would fade to nothing. She felt hollow, a shell, so fragile that the merest knock would shatter her into tiny pieces.

Katya frowned. 'Well, you can't wear those.'

Natalie looked down at her baggy T-shirt and grimy joggers, caught a whiff of body odour. She realised how sticky and grubby she felt, her scalp itching to be washed. She sighed. *What does it matter?* There was nothing she could do to change her fate; she just had to turn up, a mere witness to the proceedings.

'Well, they'll have to do. I haven't got anything else.' She pulled her knees up to her chest, wrapped her arms around her legs.

Katya wrinkled her nose. 'You need a shower.'

Natalie nodded, chewed on her bottom lip. She'd made do with the wash basin up to now, but there were limits as to what you could do with a flannel. And washing her hair was impossible because bending over the sink made her feel dizzy. It all seemed like too much effort. Natalie dropped her head onto her knees. It was hard to function at this time of day. Hard to have the energy to breathe. Another hour or so until it was time for her meds. The longest hour.

'It's important to look smart. Look like you care. It'll change how the judge thinks of you. Maybe get you a shorter sentence.'

Natalie looked up and frowned. 'You think so?'

'Judges are only people, you know.' Katya wagged a finger at her. 'We all make up our minds about people on appearance.'

Natalie thought about it for a moment, a spark of hope igniting in her heart. There were lots of things she could nothing about, but this... this was something she did have control over. And what if Katya was right? *I've got to try, haven't I?* For Harry's sake. She swung her legs over the side of the bed, swayed as dizziness flashed over her.

'Tell you what—' Katya put a hand on Natalie's arm '—I know you're still a bit wobbly. I'll go and ask for some clothes for you, shall I?'

'Would you?'

'Now, let's see... size sixteen?' Katya's eyes narrowed. 'Eighteen, maybe?'

Natalie sighed. 'Probably.' It wasn't something she liked to think about.

'Okay, I'll see what I can get. There's not always much choice. Black, I think, for court. White shirt, maybe? Something light anyway. And shoes? Shall I see if I can get something that isn't trainers?'

Natalie nodded. A headache thumped at the base of her skull. 'Yeah, that would be great, thanks.'

Katya smiled at her. 'Right, then. Won't be long. Then I'll come with you down to the showers, if you like. Stand guard. Make sure you're safe. Okay?'

'Thanks, Katya.' Natalie winced as her stomach griped. 'You're a star.'

Katya smiled. 'It's what buddies are for, isn't it?' Then she was gone, leaving Natalie alone with her thoughts.

Natalie realised that Katya was the only real buddy she had. Her life, as she knew it, was over. Just like that. And there was nothing she could do about it. She closed her eyes while pain crept out, like a rodent, to chew on her joints.

An hour or so later, when she'd cleaned herself up, she felt a little better.

'My solicitor wants me to plead guilty.'

Katya stopped teasing the knots out of Natalie's wet hair. Apparently, she knew a lot of people who had been convicted of crimes that they didn't do. It had been the subject of a long conversation just yesterday. And it had happened to Katya's brother, Lech, although Natalie hadn't liked to ask for details because there'd been tears in Katya's eyes.

Now, Katya gave Natalie a fierce hug. Then she pushed away, held her at arm's length, hands grasping her shoulders. She looked like a wildcat, eyes burning.

'What you have to remember is that the justice system is not about justice. It's about the police finding someone to blame for the crime so their clear-up rates look good. It doesn't have to be the right person. And pleading guilty doesn't mean that you are guilty, does it?'

Natalie was hypnotised by Katya's passion and she clung on to every word.

'Sometimes you just have to know when you're beat. Lose the battle to win the war, you know? Make the sentence as small as you can.' Katya nodded. 'And then… then you plan your revenge.'

Revenge? It wasn't something that Natalie had thought about. When all was said and done, it was becoming increasingly apparent that this was her fault. Some little fantasy that she'd acted out under the influence of the drugs that Tom had been giving her. Everyone she cared about seemed convinced. The police were convinced. There was evidence, her solicitor had said, and even if she didn't remember transferring the money out of her client's account, she must have done. Another thing to add to the long list of things she didn't remember doing.

Later, when Katya had gone and the meds started to work their magic, a plan began to take shape. One that planted a seed of hope in her heart. It was time for her to fight her corner instead of rolling over in defeat. Harry was more important than that. She had to try, or she'd never forgive herself for what might have been. If she pleaded not guilty, then her case would go to trial and she'd have time to get someone to gather evidence of her own. Prove that this was a mistake, a simple clerical error that had collided with a little holiday she'd planned with Harry, to a place she'd always wanted to visit. Nothing more sinister than that. It was hard not being able to speak to Tom, but loyalty was one of his strengths and she knew that whatever mess she might have got them into, he would be working his hardest to sort it out.

She stopped herself, and turned that idea over in her mind so that she could study it a bit more closely, scowling when the realisation hit home. Tom couldn't help her even if he wanted to. He'd been giving her prescription medicine that he must have bought from an illegal source somewhere, because her doctor sure as hell hadn't given it to her. If she took this to trial, then all that would have to come out. Instead of her being a criminal, he would be. She screamed her anger at the ceiling. He'd done this, not her. If he hadn't given her those drugs then she wouldn't have been so out of it, wouldn't have made the mistake in the first place. She covered her face with her hands. It was all such a mess, filling her head until it felt like it would explode.

Eventually, her thoughts began to settle. Once she'd been to court, she'd talk to the advisors in the prison, she decided, see what they could do for her. Maybe they could help to untangle this in a way that would allow her to go back to her life. She needed a new solicitor, that was for sure. One that would do a proper job. Get the police wondering about the evidence and whether it could be interpreted in another way. And when they realised their mistake, they'd have to release her. Hopefully, it would be sorted in a matter of weeks. Definitely not two years.

That night, she actually slept and woke feeling more positive than she had since her ordeal began.

Natalie walked into the court building with her head held high, more presentable in her white T-shirt and black pin-striped suit, even if it was a bit eighties with the big lapels and padded shoulders. The trainers let her down a bit, but at least they weren't white and there was only a flash of luminous pink on the navy background.

'Ah, Natalie,' her solicitor said, spotting her in the huddle of people waiting to be processed. 'Good news, you're on second, so there'll only be a quarter of an hour or so to wait once we get started.'

Natalie's heart started racing. *Quarter of an hour? Fifteen minutes.* She wiped clammy hands on her trousers.

Her solicitor led her to a quiet spot. 'Let's just run over the order of events,' she said. 'Very simple today. They'll want to verify your identity, then the charges will be read out and you'll be asked for your plea.'

'I can't...' Natalie started to say, but she was silenced by her solicitor's raised hand.

'Just let me stop you there,' she said, eyes narrowed. 'I've got something to tell you. And you really need to listen.'

Natalie swallowed, nodded.

'Some CCTV footage has come to light.'

'What CCTV?'

'Outside your office.'

Natalie was puzzled. 'We don't have any cameras.'

'No, but the office next door does. And your door is right next to theirs, so it shows up clearly on their footage.'

Natalie frowned. 'So?'

'So, it shows that on the day that the money was transferred from your client's account, at seven twenty in the morning, you unlocked the office door and entered. The money was transferred thirteen minutes later. And nine minutes after that, you were seen leaving again, locking the door behind you.'

'But...' Natalie shook her head, eyes wide. 'No! I didn't do that. I didn't. And anyway, it can't be right. I never go to work that early.'

Her solicitor frowned at her. 'Sorry, Natalie, but I've seen the footage and there's really no mistaking it. The person is you. Your hair, tracksuit, trainers, everything. Then you were seen arriving again, an hour and a half later, different outfit, after everyone else had come in to work.'

'That's not right! Ask my husband. We have breakfast together every—'

'He says you went jogging, trying to get rid of some weight.' Her solicitor stared at her, waiting.

Natalie's legs struggled to keep her upright. Was this another of the things that had happened that she didn't remember? *Why would I be in the office that early?* She rubbed her temples with the heels of her hands. *Going to the office in a tracksuit? Never. Jogging? No, that hadn't happened either.*

She stared at the floor. It didn't really matter now. The evidence was there and it sounded like the police believed it. Her solicitor believed it. A jury would believe it.

Her solicitor was watching her, arms folded across her chest, eyes narrowed, as if she knew what Natalie had been thinking.

'Let me remind you—' her voice was snippy and sharp '—that judges don't take kindly to people wasting police time, or taxpayers' money, going to trial when there's overwhelming evidence.'

Their eyes locked and Natalie withered inside as her words hit home.

'Natalie Rose Wilson!' The shout of her name made them both turn. Her solicitor placed a guiding hand on Natalie's back and steered her towards the courtroom, while Natalie's heart thrashed in her chest, pressure building in her head.

The judge went through the formalities, then the charges were read out to her.

'What do you plead?'

The room was silent. Someone coughed, feet shuffled, clothes rustled. She looked at her solicitor and remembered what she'd said about deductions from her sentence. How the evidence against her was overwhelming. It all ticked through her mind, a convincing checklist. Natalie felt unbearably hot. *Who's going to believe a drug addict?*

Katya's words threaded their way into her thoughts. *Know when you're beat. The justice system isn't about justice.* She swallowed and looked at the judge.

'Guilty,' she said, almost choking on the word as she forced it out of her mouth, hands clutching the edge of the dock. It was the sensible thing to do, wasn't it? *Or have I just made the worst mistake of my life?*

It was all over so quickly, and she felt lightheaded, disorientated, as a man led her out of the court, leaving her in the corridor with her solicitor.

'Sentencing will be in four weeks.' Her solicitor slung her bag over her shoulder. 'Just a formality, but we'll see what we can put together in terms of mitigating circumstances before then. Make sure we get the shortest sentence we can.' She gave Natalie an empty smile. 'I'll see you next week. Okay?'

Natalie hoped the woman might have died a horrible death before then, but she nodded, and watched her walk down the hallway, the fury of injustice pumping through her veins.

That evening, Katya came to see her, suggesting a game of cards to take her mind off things.

'I've been thinking,' Katya said, as she dealt their hands. Natalie looked up. 'You know how you laid it all out for me, what's happened to you. I've been thinking that your husband set you up.'

Natalie stared at her. Now that it had been said, she couldn't ignore the possibility anymore. It had occurred to her when she was first arrested, but she'd talked the idea out of her mind as being fanciful, because if it was true she wouldn't be going home. And that was a truth she couldn't bear. But now? Now she had to face the facts, however much they may hurt.

'It's gotta be about money.'

'But he's got loads of money. His family is literally dripping with the stuff. Houses all over the world. A shipping empire. To be honest, I don't even know what half his dad's businesses are. We're talking multi-millions, here.'

Katya looked up, a curious gleam in her eyes. 'Whoa. That rich?'

'Oh yes.' There was bitterness in Natalie's voice. 'But money's a curse sometimes, isn't it? Tom was sent to boarding school when he was seven, while his parents travelled around the world running their businesses. Don't get me wrong, nice enough people. Perfect manners. But they're not close. Tom was always trying to prove himself.' She sighed. 'He would never ask for help. Always trying to show his dad that he was just as good as him. Better, even.'

Natalie put her cards down, unable to concentrate on the game. Her eyes met Katya's intense gaze.

'But you have money? You and Tom?'

'Well…' Natalie stopped to think about it. She remembered Tom being snippy about her spending in recent months. Did Harry really need all those clothes? Why did she need to change the car? Couldn't she do the cleaning herself instead of employing someone? 'You know,' she said, slowly, 'I thought we did, but I don't suppose I ever knew the full picture. Perhaps we didn't have as much as I thought.'

'What? You don't know?' Katya's voice had risen an octave, her brow crumpled into a frown. 'How does that work when you're married?'

Natalie sighed, her hands picking at the bedspread. 'I didn't like to ask. My mum drilled it into me that you don't ask people about money.'

Katya laughed. 'Yeah, but it's different when you're married, isn't it? Everything gets shared then. Fuck, I wouldn't marry anyone until I'd seen all their bank statements. Made sure they could look after me properly.'

Natalie's cheeks burned. It all sounded so stupid now. Naive. 'My salary went into a joint account that we used for household bills. I dealt with all that. And Tom looked after the business finances. Paid for holidays and treats out of his own bank account. Put money into investments for us. That's how we shared things out.' She shrugged. 'It worked. I always had more money than I needed and Tom was… well, he was generous. Always buying me things.'

'So, you didn't know how the business was doing?'

'Well, I saw the annual accounts. So, I know that six months ago we had the best part of a million in reserves.'

Katya's eyes widened. She tossed her cards down, looked around, put a finger to her lips. 'Sshh,' she said, her voice a harsh whisper. 'For fuck's sake! Keep your voice down. You don't know who might be listening. Christ! You can't go shouting about stuff like that in here. Haven't you understood anything I've said to you about these people?'

Natalie bit her lip. Katya shuffled across the bed so she was next to Natalie, her face just inches away.

'So, I'm not understanding this,' she whispered. 'The business has a mill in the bank. You pay all the bills. Maybe it isn't about money.'

'No, no, I think it is.' Natalie squeezed her eyes shut, picturing the scenario that had painted itself in her mind. 'You see, when I was on maternity leave, I had to keep asking for money to cover the housekeeping because there wasn't enough in the account. When I checked, Tom had been putting business lunches and a whole load of other expenses through there, which was a bit odd. Then, when I spoke to him about it, he made me feel awful for asking. So… that makes me think he was short of money himself and…' Natalie stopped, working through her train of thought again, making sure it rang true.

'Go on.'

'And the only reason for that would be…'

Why didn't I see it? All those late nights. The tension that had crept onto his forehead. That hunted look in his eyes. She'd thought it was pressure of work, with her being out of the office and Tom having to take the strain. The struggle to accommodate the needs of a new baby in their lives. *But what if it wasn't?*

'Would be what?' Katya said, her hand rubbing Natalie's shoulder.

'If he'd started gambling again.' There, she'd said it and the moment she did, she knew she was right.

Katya gave Natalie's shoulder a squeeze. 'Ah. He had a problem?'

She sighed. 'I thought we'd sorted it out. When we met, he said I was an antidote to the casino.' She gave a hollow laugh. It sounded ridiculous now, but it had charmed her at the time. 'He said, because he had me in his life, he didn't need to go there anymore. He could flash me around instead. He loved me getting all dolled up, taking me to fancy restaurants, down to London for shows.' Natalie closed her eyes and could see Tom's face, alight with pride as he introduced her to friends and contacts.

When she spoke again, her voice sounded far away, as distant as the memories.

'When we set up the business, he started getting his buzz from making money rather than winning it. It was still gambling in a way, but with clients' money instead of his own. And I made sure I did thorough research, lowered the odds of us making a mistake.'

Katya was quiet for a moment. 'Makes sense, doesn't it?'

Natalie nodded. 'Like you said. Feels neglected when Harry comes along. Hooks up with his high roller mates again. Gets sucked back into the whole casino thing.' She let out a long breath, leant her head against the wall.

'So,' Katya said, working through the logic, 'he runs out of his own money and starts gambling with his clients' money. Makes losses, takes more money.'

Their eyes met, the convincing narrative opening Natalie's mind to the truth. 'Then he needs to pay it back, but he can't. And he can't face up to the truth. So, he pins it on me.'

'The lying bastard,' Katya said, kicking the cards all over the floor.

'And he's stitched me up so well, hasn't he? Making it look like I'm a drug addict. Nobody believes a word I say. Then he's so charming, so well connected, that everything he says is taken as the truth. And I'm the liar.' Natalie thumped the wall in frustration.

They sat in silence for a moment as Natalie thought it all through. She'd trusted Tom so completely, had even made herself believe that he'd drugged her to help her cope. But what if she trusted herself for a change? What if all those holes in her memory weren't holes at all? She could hear her teeth grinding.

It was all Tom. I didn't do any of it.

Anger surged through her like water from a burst dam. How could she have been so blind, so stupid? None of this was her fault.

Katya tucked an arm round Natalie's shoulders and pulled her close. 'We'll get your money back, hun. Don't you worry. We'll get it all back.'

But it wasn't the money that Natalie wanted. It was her son. And now she understood the game that Tom was playing, he felt further away than ever.

In the following weeks, she struggled through several frustrating and difficult conversations with the detectives, who were determined that she knew where the money was, until they'd given up, with threats that her sentence would be increased to the maximum possible for her crimes.

Four weeks later, it was all over.

Natalie walked out of court towards the prison van telling herself that she'd got off lightly. She'd been given a three-year sentence. In eighteen months, she'd be eligible for parole. Seventeen months, if you took off the time that she'd already served. Harry would still be a toddler when she got out. *He'll soon remember I'm his mum.* Forget that she'd ever been away. She leant her head back in her seat as the door closed, fingers twisted together in her lap. *It could have been worse.*

CHAPTER TWENTY-FOUR

Now

Natalie ends up in a short pedestrianised street that links the main road and the back of Marks & Spencer, puffing and panting after her latest exertions. There's an odd selection of little shops down either side and she gazes at the costumes in the window of a fancy-dress shop, not really seeing them, as her breathing starts to calm and her mind begins to function once more. There's another puzzle to solve now; how to follow Tom if she doesn't know which car he's driving.

The only solution is to park somewhere near his office, wait for him to come out and follow him on foot back to his car. Then she'll have to hope she can dash back to her own car in time to tuck in behind him when he leaves the car park. And that will only be possible if she gets a parking spot in the right place.

Possible? She chews her lip. *Unlikely. But you never know until you try, do you?* Worst-case scenario, she'll at least know which car is his and can try again tomorrow. She leans her head against the window, weary with all these false starts. She's like a greyhound running around a track after a hare, never quite able to reach it.

Another day before I find Harry? It's too long. Puts him at too much risk from Lech. She refuses to ignore the death threats, even if Tom has dismissed them.

She stands up straight, pushing herself to keep going even though her body is exhausted with all the adrenaline that's been flushing round her system since she got out of prison. Her jaw clenches. *I've got to make this work.*

She's distracted by her phone, making one of its beeping noises, a language of its own that she hasn't yet learned. It's a reminder of an event: a meeting with Sasha at one o'clock.

She frowns. If she's following Tom at twelve, she can't be meeting Sasha at one. Anyway, there's no guarantee that Sasha will even turn up. Not if she's been shagging Marco all morning. It would be easy to lose track of time, and – knowing what Sasha is like – Natalie calculates that the odds on her being there are fifty-fifty at best. Given that Tom is the more reliable of the two, she decides that following him will have to take priority. She sends Sasha a text. Tells her that she's not feeling well, is going back to bed and will ring her later to rearrange.

A few seconds after she's pressed send, her phone rings. She looks at the screen and groans. Sasha. *Can I ignore her?* No, not really, she reasons, not if she wants her help. And she can't tell her the truth either, not now that she's lied. Sasha would throw a fit.

Talk about weaving tangled webs. Too many lies, constantly putting her on edge as she tries to keep one step ahead of whoever it is she's talking to. All this running around isn't helping either. Her mind feels like a jungle, thoughts tangled around each other like the undergrowth, obscuring the best way forward.

She takes a deep breath. *Harry.* Her priority is to get to him before Lech does and not worry about who she upsets in the process.

'Hi,' she says, drawing out the word to give herself time to work out her story. 'Glad you rang. I wasn't sure if you'd be free to take my call and I didn't want to interrupt filming or anything, so I—'

'Oh, Nat, I'm so sorry that you're not feeling well. You poor thing. You haven't eaten something dodgy, have you?' Sasha's voice is full of concern and Natalie feels even worse for lying.

'Well… maybe that's it.' Natalie grasps her phone tighter, one arm folded across her chest, hand pinned under her armpit, holding the lie together. 'I've been throwing up all morning. It's been horrible. I can't go near food. Just the smell… and I'm so dizzy, I don't feel safe driving.'

'What a bummer. I can't believe it.' Sasha's sigh rattles down the phone. 'It's been a hell of a thing getting time off at all today. Had to make all sorts of promises. And I really wanted you to meet Marco. Just to say hello before he goes back to London.'

A rush of guilt travels up Natalie's neck and burns her cheeks. 'I'm really sorry to stand you up like this, but I'm afraid I'm stuck here. Near the toilet.'

'Okay.' Sasha sighs again. 'I do understand. Honestly, I do. It's just I've got such a heavy schedule I'm not sure how much time I'm going to have or when I'm going to be free. They keep changing the order of everything. And this lunchtime is the only bit of freedom I've been able to wangle for definite.' Sasha huffs, clearly frustrated. 'God knows how the rest of the week's going to pan out. Never worked with such a bunch of cowboys, you wouldn't believe… We're way behind schedule, got night-time shoots and everything. And on top of all that, Marco's going, and I'm so pissed off, because I'm really going to miss him.'

The silence is punctuated by the sound of Natalie's breathing. She holds the phone to her chest while her thoughts flutter around like butterflies, unable to settle in one spot long enough for her to make a decision.

Sasha or Tom? Sasha or Tom? Sasha or Tom?

'You still there?' Sasha says, her voice muffled against Natalie's clothing. 'Nat? Nat?'

'Yes, yes,' Natalie's says. 'Still here. Just thought I might have to dash off for a moment.'

'Oh, Nat. What a pain. I was dying to meet up again. Could hardly sleep thinking about it. You know, seeing you yesterday, it made me realise how much… well, how much I've missed you, sweetie.'

There's that magic word again and Natalie is swayed by the emotion in Sasha's voice. It's a rare thing and tears prick at Natalie's eyes. She shuffles from foot to foot. *Should I go?*

'Look, I've been wanting to…' Sasha starts, then stops. Natalie thinks she hears a sniff. 'Wanting to say I'm sorry for not visiting.' Sasha's voice cracks. 'I should have made myself do it. I should have. Christ! Honestly, I hate myself sometimes. I should have come. I know I should. Faced up to my stupid phobia.' Sasha blows her nose. Natalie blinks and swallows, her throat tight as her own emotions threaten to overflow. 'I want to make it up to you. Help you get your life back on track after your… your time out. Anything I can do to help, then I'm up for it, but it's not going to happen unless we can get together and talk it through, is it?'

'I know, I know.' Natalie's legs feel weak at the thought of a friend to rely on and the memories of their closeness are tugging at her, making her waver. 'Couldn't have happened at a worse time, could it? And I…' A sudden thought makes her stop. 'Look, I don't suppose you've been able to speak to the producer, have you, Sash? About Tom's address?'

'What? Oh, no. Not yet. But I've spoken to his PA and she promised to get back to me before one. I told her there was a deadline.'

Natalie's mind ticks through her options. There's no doubt that Sasha means well, but hasn't she just been going on about how badly organised the film company are? And that means the PA might be fobbing her off.

Tom's going home and that's where Harry will be. If I follow him, I'll see my son. Today.

The pull of that thought is too strong and she knows there's no choice to be made. *And if I fail at following Tom, I'll still have time to meet up with Sasha.*

'Tell you what, Sash, I'm going to have a lie down for half an hour. I'll ring you back in a bit. Maybe I'll be feeling better by then. And if I am, I'll get a cab.'

Natalie's pretty sure Sasha can't argue with that and she doesn't. They say their goodbyes and there's a lightness in Natalie's heart that wasn't there before. For a moment, she felt that connection with Sasha again, the rekindling of their old friendship.

She's fastening her bag when a hand grabs her neck and pulls her backwards. A muscular arm wraps around her body, pinning her arms to her sides.

'Gotcha,' a gravelly voice whispers in her ear.

CHAPTER TWENTY-FIVE

Then

Five weeks after Natalie was arrested, she had a meeting with Mr Higgins, her new solicitor. Tom had filed for divorce. No surprise there, given everything that had gone before, and Mr Higgins was dealing with that aspect of her legal affairs. He was a funny little man, Scottish-Asian, all dapper and tight-lipped. Old-fashioned in his immaculate grey suit and shiny shoes. His accent was gentle; Edinburgh, she guessed.

She knew there was something wrong the minute he walked into the room and his eyes slid away from hers. His mouth puckered a couple of times before he spoke and Natalie tucked her hands between her thighs, suddenly nervous.

'Well, Natalie, I've some… um… unexpected developments to discuss with you.'

'Okay.' She dragged out the word, because his tone was ominous.

He opened the file and found a page of notes, then looked up at her. 'So, it appears that Mr Wilson, your husband, has wound up his business.'

'Oh. Right.' She studied the table as she processed the information. Was it that much of a surprise? Having stolen the money, he'd want to distance himself from the scene of the crime, wouldn't he?

'He's also put the family home up for sale.'

She sucked in a breath, puzzled. *How can he possibly have done that so quickly?* 'Well, at least all our assets will be liquid then,' she said, all snippy. 'Should make it easier to share them out properly.'

Mr Higgins grimaced. 'Ah, well, that's where we have a problem. It appears he has moved to the Isle of Man.'

Natalie frowned. *Okay, so things are happening at twice the speed of light, but as problems go, it's not that bad, is it?* 'His parents live there. It's not like it's a million miles away. He'll still be able to see his son.'

Mr Higgins sighed. 'I'm afraid that, legally, it creates a big problem for us, Natalie.' Mr Higgins caught her eye and looked down at his notes. Her stomach clenched as she waited for the inevitable punchline. 'It's a different jurisdiction, you see. They have their own legal system, and we have no rights to access finances… or children, for that matter.

Her eyes flicked around the room as her mind repeated what Mr Higgins had just said.

No right of access to Harry? Oh no! No, no, no. Her eyes widened, hands covering her mouth.

Mr Higgins looked sympathetic. 'I'm afraid there's more.' He sighed. 'Apparently, the house was in his name.' Natalie nodded, dreading what was coming next. 'And the business was in his name.' She closed her eyes as she realised what he was going to tell her.

It's all gone. Everything.

'As soon as the house sale completes, your husband will have no assets in this country. So I'm afraid we're limited as to what we can achieve in terms of a financial settlement. And he's arguing that the majority of the assets were already his before he even met you.' Mr Higgins took a neatly folded handkerchief out of his pocket and mopped his brow. 'He's also saying that your criminal activities forced him to close his business and relocate. At great expense, apparently. According to him, he will need all the residual funds from the house sale to set up a new business venture so he can earn a living. He claims he won't even be able to afford to buy a property and he's had to move back in with his parents.'

Natalie spluttered and jumped up, fingernails digging into her palms as her hands balled into fists. She paced up and down, felt the urge to hit something.

'So, the last bit of news is—' Mr Higgins winced '—he's refusing to pay our requested financial settlement. I think we'll be able to get a few thousand out of him, but realistically, I don't think we can expect more than that.'

Natalie put her head back and howled. A noise that came up from the tips of her toes, pulling all the threads of her misery together and bundling them into a great ball of sound. *How could he be so heartless? How could he?*

Mr Higgins leant back in his chair, perspiration on his brow. 'Why don't you sit down while we discuss everything.' His eyes slid towards the door.

'Discuss?' Natalie walked back to the table and leant towards Mr Higgins. 'Discuss what? Sounds like a done deal to me.'

She didn't believe a word about Tom's situation, suspected that he had money squirrelled away all over the place in offshore accounts. But that was the problem, wasn't it? Offshore accounts were secret and nobody but him knew where the money was hidden.

Her fists slammed onto the table, again and again, battering out a thunderous rhythm, imagining it was her husband's face she was hitting. Eventually, a prison officer came. Mr Higgins moved out of the corner he'd retreated to and walked away, while Natalie was led back to her cell. She burrowed under her covers, blotting out the light, desperate to be anywhere but here, for reality to be different.

Tom had taken Harry away from her, to another country, with no intention of letting her see him ever again. And the law was on his side. She howled until her throat was raw and when the sound of her heartache finally faded, she sobbed herself to sleep.

That evening, at association time, Katya was sitting on Natalie's bed, animated, talking about what she was going to do when she was released. But Natalie wasn't listening. Her solicitor's words were wrapped around her thoughts, like a clenched fist, refusing to let go. Her head ached, her throat was sore and her body felt leaden, exhausted with the hopelessness of her situation. Even her chest ached, as if her heart had been ripped out. A tear trickled down her face, no energy to wipe it away. She looked at Katya, who stopped mid-sentence and frowned.

'What is it?' Katya put a hand on Natalie's shoulder, concern in her eyes. 'What's happened?'

'He's taken Harry.' Natalie's voice was a hoarse whisper. 'Made it impossible for me to be with him when I get out.' A sob caught in her throat. 'And he won't give me any money. I won't be able to afford to rent anywhere to live. I won't be able to get a job. I don't know what I'm going to do. How I'm ever going to get him back.'

There was nobody she could turn to. Definitely not her family. And her close friendships had withered over the years, like neglected houseplants. She only had Sasha. A supposed best friend who wouldn't even visit her.

Katya put an arm round Natalie's shoulders and pulled her close. 'Hey, hey. You let it all out, hun.' She rubbed Natalie's back as she cried onto Katya's shoulder. 'Tell me all about it. Let's see what I can do to help.'

Once the story of that morning's meeting was out and Natalie's sobs had subsided to sniffles, Katya sat back against the wall, her eyes staring into the distance as she thought, fingers tapping on her bent knees. She stopped, held up a finger. 'First thing you have to do is find somewhere to live. Somewhere nice, so there's no argument about Harry coming to live with you. That's step one. Then you can try to get him back. You can't get him back if you have nowhere to live, can you?'

Natalie thought about it and nodded.

'So. You can come and stay with me.' Katya beamed at her. 'I'll be out in a few months. I have a big house. Honestly, loads of room.'

'Oh no,' Natalie said, eyes wide. 'No, I couldn't do that.'

'Sure, you can. I want you to come.' There was something in her tone, a firmness that made Natalie pause and consider the offer properly.

Would it be such a bad idea? A few weeks, just until she got herself on her feet again. Better than the alternative, which was what? Some scabby apartment or halfway house. She cringed at her mental image of desperate people, all crammed together, like unwanted animals, hoping that someone might come and rescue them one day.

'It's a really big house. Let me find you pictures.' Katya pulled an envelope out of her bra, tipped out the photos and sifted through. She waved one in front of Natalie until she took it. 'See, it's massive.'

Natalie studied the sprawling white villa, designed in a U shape. The middle section, which she presumed housed the living room, was glass-fronted, opening out on to a huge limestone patio, set with palm trees in enormous planters. Beech trees shaded each wing of the house and mature gardens tumbled in colourful terraces into the distance. Genteel and serene, it oozed class and Natalie wondered again what Katya's story was. It was a subject she couldn't broach, a mystery that couldn't be solved by questions, because questions made Katya get up and leave.

'That's very kind of you, Kat, but I need somewhere my son can live too.' Whatever her solicitor said about jurisdictions, she was going to find a way to get him back.

'No problem. No problem at all. We love children.'

We? Now that was curious. Katya had never mentioned a partner. 'Who's we?'

'My family, of course. I live with my brother, Lech.' She smiled at Natalie, eyes shining. 'You'll like him. Tall and handsome. And he works out.' She held up her arms, flexed her biceps like a body builder and started doing a routine to show off different muscle groups. Natalie felt a smile twitch the corner of her mouth, a bead of hope swelling inside her. *Is Katya giving me a solution, a new start?*

Katya sifted through her photos and handed one to Natalie. It was a picture of a huge man, standing next to a younger Katya, with his arm round her shoulders. There was something about the look in his eyes, the set of his face, that made the hairs on Natalie's neck stand up. *What if I don't like him? Or he doesn't like me?* She looked at the picture again, and knew that she didn't want to live with them, however beautiful their house.

It's time to make my own way. Just me and Harry. That's how it was going to be. Nobody else. She'd had enough of depending on other people. It was time to do things her way. Nobody else to shape her life and try and make her into something she wasn't.

'Oh, I couldn't…' she said, handing back the photo.

'He'll look after us.'

'I don't need looking after.' It came out fast, sounded ungrateful and Natalie shrivelled inside as soon as the words had been spoken.

'Sure, you do.' Katya's face was serious, a hard glint in her eyes. 'We all need looking after. No arguments. You come and live with me. I promise, you'll like it.'

Natalie squirmed. An unfamiliar tension hung in the air, awkwardness pushing them apart. Katya leant over and picked up the pack of cards from Natalie's bedside cabinet. Natalie moved her legs and changed her position on the bed while Katya dealt the cards ready for a game that Natalie didn't want to play.

'Rummy?'

Natalie shook her head, her mind full of Harry. Whatever course of action she took, she was going to need money and that was something she didn't have. Mr Higgins had said it might take years to get a settlement out of Tom. She sighed, dragged down by the weight of her worries. *I'll always be Harry's mum,* she reassured herself. *Nobody's ever going to take that away from me.* But how could she be his mum if he wasn't with her?

'Oh, come on,' Katya said. 'Moping won't do any good. What about blackjack, then?' She gathered up the cards, pressed them into Natalie's hand. 'You shuffle. Do that fancy croupier stuff.' Natalie looked at the cards as if she didn't know what to do with them, her mind taken back to her past, when life was everything she'd hoped for and more.

Blackjack.

Tom's favourite game at the casino. That's where they'd first met. She'd been the dealer when he sauntered into the room, looking handsome and confident in an old money sort of way. You could spot them a mile off, she'd realised, after a year of working the tables. The way they dressed. Hairstyles. And especially in the way they talked. Old money people had such lovely manners, always articulate and polite. Completely charming.

'Good evening, sir,' she'd said with her brightest smile, because he was the most attractive man she'd seen in a long while, and part of her job was to flirt a little, get the punters coming to her table.

'Good evening,' he'd replied, his eyes finding hers and holding them for a delicious moment, sending an unexpected glow round her body. He'd looked like James Bond in *Casino Royale*, his voice smooth and sexy and she'd felt her heart beat a little faster when he'd taken a seat. The table had been empty, so it'd just been the two of them. He'd held her gaze while she'd shuffled the cards, putting on a show for him.

An hour or so later, Tom had left the table with a broad grin on his face and thirteen hundred pounds in his pocket. He'd come back the next day and the next, making her laugh with his dry wit and she'd found herself looking out for him. On the fourth night, he'd asked her out to dinner.

It had taken her two weeks to fall in love and after they'd been together for five months, Tom had proposed. 'I want to look after you, my love. Always.'

And look how that had turned out.

Natalie's jaw worked from side to side. The last thing she needed was a man to look after her. And Katya's brother looked as easy to get along with as a scorpion. No, living with Katya was never going to work; she'd just have to think of something else.

Natalie stared at the cards as she shuffled. There had been such a seismic shift in her life, she was finding it hard to think without gusts of panic scattering her thoughts like tumbleweed, blowing them this way and that so she couldn't catch hold. How was she ever going to cope without being able to even see Harry? What if Tom wouldn't co-operate with access? The walls started closing in on her. She couldn't breathe. The room started to spin. She dropped the cards and clambered to her feet, gasping. 'I've got to get out of here.'

Katya frowned, picked up the cards and started dealing their hands. 'Sure you do. We all do.'

Natalie lurched towards the door, and grabbed the doorframe for support, hand on her chest as her heart hammered at an alarming rate. 'No, I mean now. I need to go outside. Get some fresh air.'

Katya was up in a flash, blocking the doorway. 'Oh no, you don't want to do that. Not on your own.' She sounded cross, her voice sharp. 'Haven't you been listening?'

'I just want to go outside.' Natalie ducked under her arm. In all the time she'd been on the Wing, she'd only been outside once on her own. Since then, she'd waited for Katya to go with her. But now she was desperate, she didn't even think about it and started to walk down the corridor.

Katya caught her by the elbow. 'Hold on,' she hissed. 'You need protection. You know what I've told you about the people in here? You're not safe on your own.' Natalie glanced around the corridor at the groups of women standing chatting. They turned and stared at her, suddenly silent. A chill settled between her shoulder blades as she took in the faces ravaged by drugs, alcohol and abuse. Skin defaced by crude tattoos and self-harm. She huddled closer to Katya and made sure that her eyes stayed on the floor.

'You don't want to mix with them,' Katya said when they emerged into the crisp air of the exercise yard, which reminded Natalie of the old tennis court at her school, with its tarmac surface and high wire fencing. A breeze lifted Natalie's hair, stroked her face and her chest expanded, allowing her to breathe properly again. She leant against the fence, gulping in air and it was only when her panic attack had passed that she noticed curious eyes staring at her, and was glad that she wasn't alone.

Maybe Katya was right.

'You know, Katya, I think that was a good idea. Me coming to stay with you for a few weeks when I get out. If it's still okay.'

Katya beamed at her and linked her arm through Natalie's. ''Course it is! And Lech's coming to visit in a couple of days. I'll get him to book to see you as well, then you'll get to meet him.'

Natalie nodded. *Yes, a meeting in the flesh might put my mind at rest.*

The visiting room was loud with chatter when they entered, Friday being a popular day for visits. The visiting suite had been recently refurbished and was an open, airy space filled with rows of Formica-topped tables, each with two chairs on either side. At one end of the room was a play area for children and another area set out with leather sofas. To one side there was a serving hatch for drinks, next to a vending machine full of snacks.

All the prisoners had to be settled at tables, in their seats, before visitors were shepherded in by the Visits Officer and led to the correct table. Natalie and Katya sat side by side, studying the door as each person was brought in. Katya's hand found Natalie's and she held it tight.

'Don't worry. He'll be here,' she said, a hint of nerves in her voice, something Natalie had never heard before. Then the door opened and in strode Lech, a big lump of a man, just like the picture Natalie had seen, but visibly older. His short, dark hair was greying round the temples, his beard grey flecked with black. It softened his face, Natalie thought. But his eyes were still like a hawk, deep-set and piercing as they raked the room, flicking over Natalie, before settling on Katya. That's when his face changed, transformed by a huge smile full of perfect white teeth.

'*Kiciu*,' he said as he was shown to their table. 'I thought I was never going to get through the door. So many people today.'

Katya had jumped up as soon as she saw him and was waiting with open arms. He wrapped her in a hug, kissed her cheek and let her go.

'*Zabko*,' she said, as they sat looking at each other, obviously delighted to see each other again. 'What's that on your face?'

He stroked his beard, eyes wide in mock offence. 'You don't like it?' He shrugged. 'Is fashion.'

Katya giggled. 'What do you think, Nat? Does it make him look old?'

Natalie blushed as Lech turned his attention to her, not wanting to say anything in case she got it wrong.

'You must be Natalie.' He held out his hand and gave her a firm handshake, amusement flickering in his eyes. His hand was hot and sweaty, and she had to wait for him to let go, which took several seconds longer than she would have liked. 'I have heard so much about you. And any friend of Katya's is a friend of mine.' He gave a little bow. She was stuck for something to say, hadn't expected him to be charming. She smiled and looked down at her hands.

His accent was there, stronger than Katya's, but his English was very good. He talked to Katya about their childhood, bringing up funny stories about mishaps and misunderstandings that made them all laugh. Sometimes the two of them would slip into Polish and Natalie would have to wait for them to realise and switch back to English. He was the opposite of what Natalie had expected, and was quite the clown, entertaining them both for the best part of two hours.

When he was gone, Katya turned to Natalie. 'There, I knew you'd like him.'

Natalie smiled. 'Yes,' she said, to keep Katya happy. But it wasn't true.

At the time, she couldn't put it into words, but later, when she was alone in her cell, able to replay the meeting in her head, she came to understand what it was about Lech that bothered her. He didn't seem real. *Had it all been an act?* And there were the intense bursts of Polish conversation that pushed her out on a limb and left her wondering what they were talking about. He had that air of a powerful man in more than the physical sense. She'd met many of them in her job at the casino and then in finance, but she'd never felt comfortable with them. Had never liked them. And now she was going to go and live with one.

Beggars can't be choosers, she told herself as she lay in the dark, listening to the noise. *It'll only be for a few weeks.* She'd be gone as soon as she could make other arrangements, of that she was sure.

CHAPTER TWENTY-SIX

Now

'I knew I'd catch up with you eventually,' the man says. 'Led me a right merry dance, you have.'

Natalie screams as his hand tightens around her. But the man is quick and his hand slaps over her nose and mouth. Her eyes widen, lungs bellowing in and out, unable to think beyond the need to breathe. She sucks in the skin of his hand instead of air. Sweaty and rough, it tastes of salt and tobacco, making her stomach lurch. Instinctively, her teeth clamp round his flesh, tearing at it like a zombie, but his skin is tough as leather, a working man's hand and her teeth make little impression. She nips instead, as hard as she can, her canines finding a softer patch at the base of his thumb, breaking the skin.

'Aargh!' he snarls. 'You vicious little…!'

He pulls his hand away and wipes it on his trousers. She draws in air, eyes searching for someone to help as she gets ready to try another scream. But his arm tightens around her body, strong as a boa constrictor, squeezing her chest so hard there is no room for her ribs to move or her lungs to expand. She hears crunching, as bones compress, the force of his grasp shooting the remaining air out of her mouth. She breathes in little gasps and starts to feel lightheaded, the buildings swaying and swirling in front of her eyes, her legs weakening.

Dammit! Relax, she tells herself, as panic flutters against her ribs. *Remember what you were taught: by fighting him, you're fighting yourself.* She has to bide her time, wait until his concentration lapses. *Which it will*, she reassures herself. *It will.*

Against all her natural instincts, she forces herself to stop struggling and after a moment he loosens his hold a fraction, enough to allow her to take deeper breaths and the world starts to settle into its normal order.

'Look, none of that funny business,' he says. 'Or you'll be off to hospital in an ambulance.'

His voice is a gruff smoker's rasp and his accent is not what she was expecting. Katya and Lech both spoke with a slight American twang, a product of learning English from the television and Internet. But this man's accent is northern. Flat vowels. Yorkshire maybe?

It's not Lech, is it? It's hard to be sure, given that it's three years since she met him and at the time she'd felt he was putting on an act. Which may have included an accent. He's older than Katya, so maybe he's been in England longer, learned his English while working in the north somewhere? *Doesn't matter who it is*, she tells herself. *The important thing is to escape.*

Screaming is probably not a good idea, she decides. The last thing she wants is for the police to turn up and complicate things. She swallows and closes her eyes, thoughts flipping through her mind as if they're on fast forward.

So, what's his plan?

If he's even got a plan. Because there's not much he can do to her in the middle of town, is there? Her pulse begins to steady. Even on this back street, somebody will come. It's a cut-through. Office workers are bound to use it, to and fro, getting their lunch. And it's almost lunchtime.

Her eyes flick open and she catches the man's reflection in the shop window. With a jolt, she recognises the shirt. A blue Hawaiian thing. *It's the man I saw earlier! The one in the street by the baby who was knocked out of its buggy.* He turns away and she doesn't have time to study his face, compare it with the mental image she has of Lech. *Would I even remember his features after all this time?* She's not good at recognising faces at the best of times, but his eyes, she thinks, she'd definitely remember those eyes. The look of a predator.

His grip relaxes, just a smidge, but she's alert to every tiny movement, every indication that his concentration is not what it should be. She stomps on his instep, hard as she can, but sandals are not the right tool for the job and a stabbing pain shoots up her leg. He doesn't flinch. She scowls and tries to kick his shins, his knees, but he's wise to her moves and keeps turning her round so she can't make contact.

'Right little firecracker, aren't we?' he says from between clenched teeth. He squeezes her harder. Lack of oxygen makes her head spin. A sob of frustration catches in her throat. Then a movement catches her eye. Someone walking. *Oh, thank goodness!* She thrashes her legs and tries to scream, but his reactions are quick and he clamps his hand over her mouth again. He moves his body round, so his back is towards the pedestrian and she can't be seen.

'Citizen's arrest,' he shouts to the person, over his shoulder. 'This one's wanted by the police for reckless endangerment. Just waiting for them to get here.' He sounds authentic, very believable. Like he's in the right.

'Oh, okay, mate. Nice one.' A man's voice says. 'Need any help?'

'Nah, mate. Got it covered.' He sounds calm, as if this is an everyday event.

'You sure?'

'Yeah, mate. Cops should be here any minute.'

Cops? She frowns. He hasn't had time to ring them, has he? And anyway, why would he want the cops involved? *It's got to be a bluff.* But whatever his plans might be, she's got to make her move quickly. *Quickly.* Because Tom will be leaving his office soon and if she doesn't get away from this man, her chance to follow him and get to Harry will be gone.

The thought fires up her resolve like putting a match to a bonfire.

The bystander walks on and she listens to the sound of his footsteps as they fade away, clear in her mind what she has to do.

'Right, then. So, we're going to take a little walk,' he says.

He has to change his grip, and she suddenly lets her body go limp, so he's holding all her weight. It takes his balance, because he's not expecting it and he lurches forwards, his shoulder and head smacking into the wall. He grunts and stops, clearly dazed. She grits her teeth and throws her head back with all the force she can muster. *Crunch!* She cries out when her skull hits bone, a sharp pain slicing through the back of her head.

He snuffles and groans. *Did I get his nose?* His hold on her loosens. She wriggles her arm free and gives him a punch to the face with the back of her knuckles, bone connecting with bone. He shouts out and she gasps at the burning pain that engulfs her hand. *Ignore, it, ignore it,* she chants to take her mind off the throbbing. This might be the only chance she's going to get.

She slithers out of his grasp and runs.

CHAPTER TWENTY-SEVEN

Then

Stuck in prison, with nowhere to go, no place to be and hours on her own, Natalie became a writer of letters. It was a distraction, a focus and something she became obsessive about, writing slowly and neatly, no crossings out, thinking it through before she allowed herself to put pen to paper. Her main correspondent was Sasha, the only person she considered a friend anymore, but it also became a way to create precious moments with her son. By writing to him, telling him about what she saw in her daydreams, her imaginary version of him became three dimensional and for a time, almost real. It was the only way she could make life bearable, the only way to stop herself from becoming one of the self-harmers, the screamers.

Of course, she didn't send Harry the letters. She wouldn't want Tom or the nanny reading them; they were much too personal for that. No, they were just for her and Harry. She kept them all, neatly stacked in her locker and one day, when he was older, she might show them to him. But for now, they allowed her to live in a dream world for hours at a time, a world where he was with her and she could play with him, feed him, bathe him, cuddle him. She could enjoy him, all to herself.

Today, he'd be nine months old. She drew him a picture, spending an age designing it and colouring it in. In her mind, she baked a cake – banana, of course, his favourite. She could see him, sitting in a living room that didn't exist, in a house that she'd bought and furnished in her imagination. There was a long Persian rug, patterned with hues of red and blue, Harry sitting at one end, her at the other, holding Mr Bunny. He'd do anything to get that toy and today was the day he worked out how to crawl.

She could see the look of determination on his face, could hear her cries of encouragement as he pushed himself up on hands and knees and started moving towards her, swaying and unsteady, but getting closer. He flopped onto his belly for a rest, but after a few moments, he was up and trying again, tongue poking out, like it did when he was working something out. Once he'd set his mind on something there was no stopping Harry, and when he finally reached her and grabbed his prize, she was rewarded with a beaming smile and his laughter as he waved Mr Bunny in the air, watching his long ears flapping about.

She finished her drawing of rabbits, a whole family of them and wrote him a message at the bottom of the page.

Lovely Munchkin,

I think about you every minute of the day, hoping you are being looked after. Know that I love you as much as any mother can love their child, even though we are miles apart. I hope you feel my love warming you when you're cold, holding you when you're upset, laughing with you when you're having fun. I am a part of you and you are a part of me, little one and nobody can take that away from us. Nobody.

A tapping sound distracted her and she looked down to see tears dripping from her chin onto the card, smudging the ink, her chest aching as though she'd been squeezed too hard. She wiped her face with her sleeve and went to lie down on the bed, conjuring Harry up again to lie with her, in the crook of her arm, his head snuggled in to her neck, baby-soft hair tickling her face.

'*You are my sunshine...*' she sang, softly, the lyrics flowing until she got to the line about taking her sunshine away, when her voice cracked and it was a struggle to finish.

In her mind, she stroked his hair as she sang, felt him settle, his breaths deep and even. She sighed, hollowed out by a desolation that was impossible to fight. So many milestones she was going to miss. His first steps, a mouth full of teeth, his first words, learning how to run and jump and climb up and down steps. All without her.

How could Tom even think about doing this to me? How could he? But she knew the answer. He'd done it to preserve himself with no thought about her. No thought at all. Her body shuddered as she cried herself to sleep.

Five and a half weeks into her prison sentence, Natalie actually received a letter. It had taken thirty-eight days for someone to write to her, if you discounted Sasha's scribbled postcard, and it felt more like a year. Her heart swelled with hope when it was handed to her because it meant that someone out there was thinking about her. Maybe a response to one of her letters. Then she studied the writing and sighed. *Not Mum, then.* Well, what did she expect?

The sound of her mother's disapproving voice was never far from Natalie's mind. Maybe because she knew that it was a voice she was unlikely to hear again.

Natalie was never her mother's favourite; that would be Martin, her younger brother, who was so clever he'd been put up a year into Natalie's class, an embarrassment she'd never come to terms with during her time at school. They had never got on, were the opposite of close and he delighted in showing her up at every opportunity. In her mind, he was the wedge that drove her family apart.

The pivotal moment had happened after a memorable parents' evening. They'd all been to school to discuss performance and the subjects Natalie and Martin were going to choose for GCSEs. The more teachers they spoke to, the more the tension built and their parents had started arguing as soon as they got in the car to drive home.

'She's not stupid,' her father had said.

'I didn't say she was,' her mother snapped. 'She just needs to apply herself. Like Martin. Put some effort in.' She looked round to where Natalie sat, open-mouthed, on the back seat and caught her eye. Her mother's face hardened. 'It's the truth.'

Martin sniggered.

Natalie swore under her breath.

Her father thumped the steering wheel and the car swerved dangerously close to a hedge.

'Natalie is just as clever as Martin. The problem is…'

'Eyes on the road, Roger, please.' Her mother hung on to the door with one hand, her seat belt with the other.

'I know how to drive,' her father said through gritted teeth, knuckles white as he tried to strangle the steering wheel rather than her mother. 'The problem is teaching methods. Natalie's a bright girl, but she needs to be engaged in the subjects. All this national curriculum, it's like a straitjacket. Makes lessons boring.' It was her father's hobby horse. An ex-teacher himself, he felt he had the high ground on the matter and he glared at her mother.

'It's about application. And drive. And determination.' Her mother folded her arms across her chest. 'Things you could show a bit more of. Perhaps if you'd set a better example…'

The car screeched to the kerb before she could finish her sentence. Natalie's father got out, slammed the door with a force that made the car shake and headed into the Golden Lion. None of them spoke. Her mother sighed, shuffled across to the driver's seat and drove them home in a silence that demanded not to be broken.

It was a couple of days before her father came home and then it was to announce that he was leaving. As far as Natalie knew he was living in France somewhere, teaching English. But that information was thirteen years old. Maybe he was still there. Maybe he wasn't.

Natalie never blamed him for wanting to get away from her mother. What made her angry was that he didn't take her with him. Her mother refused to have anything to do with him once he'd gone, and had moved the family without telling him their new address. They'd lost touch and she didn't even know where he lived anymore. It was a sadness that she found hard to bear because he'd always stood up for her. And she could really do with him now.

She could do with somebody.

Anybody.

Which brought her full circle back to the letter in her hand, written in Sasha's big curly script. *Perhaps she hasn't deserted me after all. Perhaps I can still count on her as a friend, whatever Katya might think.*

She tore open the envelope, delighted to find several pages of stories about Sasha's life, the tour she was on with the theatre group, places they'd been and people she'd met. It made Natalie smile and she read it several times, warming herself in its gentle embrace, hearing Sasha speak the words, seeing her face, hearing her laugh. She savoured each word, each sentence, especially the last one:

'*Love you always, better than a sister, Sweetie x.*'

It was only later, when the day had been and gone, that she realised that today was the first day since she'd been on the Therapy Wing that she hadn't seen Katya. And that troubled her. That was really odd.

CHAPTER TWENTY-EIGHT

Now

Natalie doesn't look to see if her attacker is following, but dashes through the back door of Marks & Spencer, her heart racing. She slows to a speed-walk and weaves her way through several departments until she finds herself by the front exit. Then she's back on the main shopping street. She glances over her shoulder, can't see him and hurries on.

What to do? What to do?

She needs to get to Tom's office, but equally, she needs to make sure she's not being followed. As she passes a charity shop, she has an idea and slips inside, glad now for her flowery dress because it shouldn't be too hard to make herself look different. *He can't follow me if he doesn't recognise me, can he?* It's her only option. She glances at her watch. Twenty minutes until Tom leaves. It's doable but she's got to be quick.

The shop is long and narrow, widening out at the back where the clothes section is located, so she's hidden from people passing on the street. Her legs are shaking with all the effort of the morning and as she flicks through the clothes rack, she realises how close she came to being caught. Her heart skips at the thought. *I can't let that happen again, got to stay sharp.* She picks out a few items, darts into the changing room and whips the curtain closed as if it has the power to make her invisible.

She struggles to get changed, fingers fumbling with buttons and zippers, the hand that punched her attacker already bruised and starting to swell. A white blouse and black trousers fit well enough and there's a pair of navy shoes in her size, a bit clumpy in an old lady way, but they'll do. Then there's a black handbag, old-fashioned, but it hangs over her shoulder and tucks under her arm, so it's not too visible.

She shakes her hair out of the braid into a wavy mane and fluffs it around her face, then scrubs off her make-up with a couple of tissues and a good dollop of spit. Finally, she finds the dorky glasses with thick black rims that she already had in her bag. They cover half of her face and when she looks in the mirror, she sees a different person. One that looks hot and stressed. Like she works in an office.

She checks her watch. Twelve minutes. *Quick, quick.* She transfers the contents of her handbag, leaves her old clothes in the cubicle and heads towards the exit. Fortunately, the volunteers who are manning the shop are more interested in a bag of books they are sorting through than what she's doing and there are a couple of customers milling around the till, hiding her from view as she strolls out of the shop.

A glance up and down the street reassures her that her attacker's not there and she sighs with relief, checks her watch. *Dammit!* Ten minutes and Tom will have left his office. She sets off at a run, back to her car.

The car park is quiet, only a couple of women draped with loaded shopping bags heading towards their vehicles. She does a quick scan. *Is that him? In the far corner?* A man standing beside a big, black four by four, talking on his phone, his back towards her, foot scuffing something on the ground as he talks. He's wearing the same coloured shirt as her attacker and her senses fizz. *It's got to be him!*

Hardly daring to breathe, she slips into the driver's seat of her car while the man is still focused on his conversation. She's parked right by the exit and pulls away before he notices. *Or did he?*

She looks in her mirror. A silver estate car is at the top of the exit ramp, nothing behind it. Acrylic clothes stick to her sweaty skin.

It only takes a couple of minutes to get to Tom's office, but she constantly checks her mirror, muscles pulling at her neck and shoulders. So many black four-by-fours around, it's hard to tell if he's following her or not. She didn't see what make it was and has no interest in cars, so even the shape didn't register as anything particularly memorable. Big and black, that's all she has to go on. Not even a number plate.

The only available parking space is at the end of the road, too far away from Tom's office for her to see him leave. She'll have to get out and loiter somewhere until she sees him come out.

She checks her watch. A couple of minutes to go. Can she stay and wait?

But what if… Her eyes widen as an unwelcome thought crawls into her mind. Whoever attacked her is also looking for Harry and if she follows Tom now, she could end up leading him right to his prize. She'll be putting Harry in more danger.

Gripped by fear, she drives away, glancing behind her. *Something black. Two vehicles back.* She urges the people in front to go faster. The black car is still behind her as she gets to the edge of town and she takes a sudden left at a mini roundabout, no idea where she's going. She checks her mirror, hands so slick with sweat she can hardly steer. Just a silver estate car, nothing black, and she weaves her way through a residential estate thinking that she must have lost him. Then a black car turns into the bottom of the road behind her. Her throat tightens. She turns right and nips in front of a lorry, camouflaged for now.

A retail park looms on the right and she whips her car off the main road, pulling in behind a burger van, at the far end of B&Q's car park. Satisfied that she's hidden from view, she slumps forwards and rests her forehead on the steering wheel, her body shaking as if she's drunk a six pack of Red Bull.

Her throat feels raw with the force of her breath. Her head throbs where she head-butted the man, and her hand is so swollen now that her fingers will hardly bend. She rummages in her bag, and finds a packet of painkillers, swallowing a couple down in the hope that it'll take the edge off the pain, enough to stop it from distracting her at any rate. Her eyes flick between her mirrors, but nobody comes and gradually, her pulse starts to slow.

Dammit! What went wrong?

It occurs to her then that her car is the problem. It has UK number plates and stands out as a stranger amongst the local vehicles. And it was borrowed from an ex-convict friend. Could Lech have found that out, through his network of contacts? *Maybe that's how he found me?* Because the man in the car park can't have been there by accident. He must surely have known the car was hers. *Has my timescale shrunk?* Is today the only chance she has to get to Harry and sneak him off the island?

She works through her options. *Dump the car?* No, she needs transport and won't be able to get Harry without it. *Maybe hire something?* But then she'd need to give identification. *Change the number plates? That's it! Disguise the car.* She sits up and a sense of calm drapes itself over her, like a magic cloak, returning life to her limbs and purpose to her thoughts.

She hops out of the car and peers round the edge of the burger van, eyes sweeping the car park. There are a few black cars, but nothing as chunky as the one her attacker was driving. She double-checks, just to make sure. *No, not here.* Inside the shop, she finds an assistant who's stacking shelves with paint.

'Number plates? No, we don't do them here, but if you go out of the car park, turn right and right again, you'll find a motor supplies place up the road on your left. They'll do them for you. Fit them as well if you pay a bit extra.'

Natalie runs back to her car and within half an hour, she's on her way, her car now camouflaged, not only with Isle of Man number plates but with a white stripe on the bonnet and boot, some fancy hub caps and fluffy tiger print seat covers for good measure. It was the best she could do, and overall, she's happy with the effect. It's surprising what a difference little details can make to a car's appearance, she decides. Surely, he won't recognise her now?

Cat and mouse. I can do this, she thinks as she navigates her way back to the main road. As long as she doesn't panic, and keeps sharp, he won't find her again.

So, what now? She can't go back into Douglas, so that rules out meeting Sasha. Her best option, she decides, is to go back to Peel, get changed into a new disguise and see if Mary has come up with anything useful. And she can ring Sasha, see if the producer's PA has come up with Tom's address. If she hasn't, then she'll ring Jack.

She takes a deep breath. *It's all okay,* she reassures herself. *Only lunchtime. Still plenty of hours left in the day.*

She chews at her bottom lip as she drives, her mind stuck in the car park, with the man in the Hawaiian shirt. *Was it Lech?* She doesn't think so, but maybe that's who he was speaking to on the phone. She nods. *Makes sense.* Icy fingers walk down her spine. *But that means... Crap! There's two people to look out for.*

Her eyes flick to her rear-view mirror, but there are no black cars in sight. Just a silver estate. A sleek thing with tinted windows. *Silver estate?* She looks again and her heart skitters. *Isn't that the car that followed me down the ramp at Marks & Spencer?*

CHAPTER TWENTY-NINE

Now

Well, that didn't go as well as I'd hoped. Best laid plans and all that. All gone to shit. That bitch is a slippery fish. I really thought I had her.

I mean, I know she's in Peel somewhere, but she parked in the central car park then scarpered before I could see which direction she went. Those bloody mobility scooters, getting in the way. Two abreast at two miles an hour, for fuck's sake!

Anyway. Stiff gin and then I'll have to work out what to do next.

Can't get downhearted, though.

If nothing else, she'll be spooked as hell after today. And frightened people make mistakes, don't they?

CHAPTER THIRTY

Then

On the third day, when Katya didn't come to visit, Natalie knew she had to do something. *Maybe she's ill?* It was an appealing idea, better than worrying that she might have offended her, and the thought that she might be able to repay Katya's kindness became motivation enough to track her down.

At association time, she crept out of her door and flattened herself against the wall.

Women were gathered in twos and threes, leaning against the walls, or sitting together, chatting. Natalie looked up and down the corridor, but couldn't see a guard anywhere. She swallowed and told herself there was nothing to worry about. *I've managed to get food and meds the last couple of days, haven't I?* But she'd had a prison officer with her then, so everyone was on their best behaviour. Now, on her own, she felt like a tourist who'd strayed into a foreign ghetto.

She slinked her way along the wall and hadn't gone ten yards before a woman caught sight of her, walked over and blocked her way. Red-rimmed eyes challenged her from no more than a couple of feet away. The woman was tall and gangly, all bones and joints with no fat to soften her skeletal shape. Her thin brown hair was scraped back, emphasising the length of her face. Tattooed tears dripped down her right cheek, ending at a gash of a scar next to her mouth. A spider's web decorated her neck.

'Natalie, isn't it?' She spoke with a lisp, her front teeth missing.

Natalie nodded and resisted the temptation to wipe the spray of spittle off her face. The stories Katya had told her about bullying, rape and torture flashed through her mind and she held on to the wall with sweaty palms. She glanced behind her, but the path back to her cell was blocked now by a huddle of curious women. They inched closer, crowding round her until she was at the centre of a semi-circle. Natalie's heart clenched.

'You're Katya's new girl, aren't you?' the woman said.

It sounded like an accusation. Natalie pressed against the wall, the cold seeping through her clothes as she tried to create some distance between herself and the crowd of women.

'Cat got your tongue?' The woman grabbed Natalie's chin with a bony hand, lowering her face so she could peer into Natalie's eyes. A bead of sweat worked down Natalie's back. More faces crowded round, bodies pressing closer. Rancid breath and the smell of body odour filled her nostrils. The woman's nails dug into Natalie's skin, but she couldn't react, was frozen in time, staring into the woman's steel-grey eyes, like a mouse hypnotised by a snake.

Hands clawed at Natalie's clothing, grasped her shoulders, her arms. No sound would come out of her throat and her eyes darted back and forth, searching for the prison officer but all she could see was a row of menacing faces.

'It's so rude not to answer when you're spoken to, isn't it, girls?' The woman's eyes narrowed, jaw set.

'Slap her!' another woman shouted. 'That'll loosen her tongue.'

The force of the first blow whipped Natalie's head to the side, banging it against the wall. She cried out, unable to think or even move, her breath pumping in and out. Hands started slapping at her from all directions, stinging her skin like a swarm of wasps. The first punch caught her unawares, as a fist drove into her stomach and her breath whooshed out of her. She doubled over, a second punch glancing off her cheek.

In slow motion, she felt herself fall to the floor, was aware that she banged her shoulder, smacked her hip onto the concrete. But the pain didn't register, like she'd been reduced to a bubble of thoughts, floating above her body. Sounds muffled, blending together into a background murmur. She felt tears trickle down her face, into her mouth. Her body curled into a ball.

Is this how it's going to end?

She could hear herself whimpering.

'I love you, Harry,' she whispered. *'Love you, love you, love you.'* If these were to be her last words, then she hoped they would reach him somehow, work their way through the ether and root themselves in his baby mind, to grow with him, so that he would always feel his mother's love, could draw on it whenever he needed her.

'Oi, Mags! Leave her alone!'

The shout broke through the melee. Between the women's legs, Natalie could see the booted feet of a prison officer getting closer, could hear her smacking a baton against her palm. The women started to inch away.

'I'll see you lot later,' the prison officer said, pointing the baton at them, one by one, sounding like a teacher telling off naughty schoolgirls. 'Go on, clear off.'

Natalie blinked, watched feet shuffle away, heard excited voices fade into the distance. She felt the cold of the concrete floor against her cheek.

'It's okay, they've gone now.' The prison officer held out a hand to her. 'Come on, up you get. Doc wants to see you.'

Natalie winced as her bruised body was heaved off the floor. Her skin burned where she'd been struck, her shoulder and hip ached from the fall. Blood pulsed in her ears. She straightened her clothing and wiped her face on her sleeve, but her legs struggled to move and she hung on to the arm of the officer as she was escorted away, aware of eyes watching her every step.

The doctor flicked her eyes up from the desk as Natalie entered the room. Behind the doctor, shelves bowed with the weight of files and books. Piles of papers sat in a tray on the desk, next to a computer screen. Filing cabinets scrunched together in a grey metal row down one wall. The doctor gave Natalie a quick smile and pointed to a chair. Natalie sat and the prison officer stood next to her, leaning against a filing cabinet.

'Let's have a chat, shall we? See where we're up to.'

Natalie stared at her. She wasn't in the mood for a chat. What she needed was answers.

'What have you done with Katya? Where's she gone?' Natalie's voice was shaking as much as her body. There was no way she could survive prison without Katya. And the thought of being sent back into that place, that corridor, on her own with those feral women, made her shake even more.

'Let's talk about you first, shall we?' The doctor's voice was all sing-song with the hint of a Welsh accent. She caught Natalie's eye and peered at her, assessing, scrutinising, like a judge at a dog show.

Natalie looked away and wrapped her arms around her chest, hugging tight. She was cold now and the shaking in her stomach was making her feel sick.

'Where is she?' she said, eyes frantically searching the room as if she'd find Katya tidied away in a corner somewhere.

The doctor looked at the prison officer, eyebrows arched. 'What on earth's gone on in there, Jan? The girl's terrified.'

'Oh, just Mags and her cronies.' The officer was chewing gum, hands in her pockets, clearly unconcerned. 'A little "getting to know you" session.'

Natalie turned to stare at her, mouth open. *She thought that was okay?*

The doctor frowned.

'They were going to kill me.' Natalie's chin wobbled with the effort of holding her emotions in check.

The prison officer shook her head. 'Bit of a scuffle, that's all.'

'What makes you think they were going to kill you?' the doctor asked, frowning.

Natalie's head was aching, all of her was aching and she pressed her fingers to her temples, head bowed, as she tried to put a coherent account together.

'They surrounded me. Kicking, punching, stomping. If this officer hadn't come, then… I don't think they would have stopped.' She looked up at the doctor. 'Katya said that would happen. She told me what they'd do to me. That's why she had to protect me.' She looked at the officer. 'What have you done with her?'

'Oh, come on, it wasn't that bad.' The prison officer stood up straight now, looking at the doctor. 'Just a bit of roughing up. You know, the usual stuff. Establishing the order of things.'

The doctor nodded, slowly, mouth a thin line. 'Ah, right. I see what's going on here.' She laid her pen on the desk and leant forwards, hands clasped together in front of her. 'Okay, so paranoia is part of the withdrawal from Oxycodone. Seeing events through a suspicious frame of mind, if you like. Interpreting normal events as threatening.'

Natalie glared at her. *Paranoia?* She didn't think so. That woman had looked mean. Had acted mean. They'd all ganged up against her. There'd been nothing normal about it.

'They were beating me up.' Natalie spoke slowly, letting each word find its place.

The doctor looked at her for a moment. 'Well, you don't look beaten up. No blood. No broken bones.'

Natalie stared at the doctor.

'I know you're feeling better in yourself,' the doctor said, 'but mentally, it takes a bit more time for the effects of these drugs to wear off. So… I think we'll start sessions with Dr Patel. She'll help you talk it through.'

The words skimmed over Natalie, making no impression. There was only one thing on her mind now, only one thing that could help her get through this ordeal.

'Where's Katya?' Natalie's jaw clenched. 'I'm not going anywhere until you tell me where she is.'

The doctor shrugged. 'Okay. It's not a secret. Katya's in the Unit.'

Natalie frowned. 'What's that? I don't know what you mean.'

'It's the secure unit we have here for people who are severely disturbed. She had a… there was another… let's call it a psychotic incident.' The doctor flicked a look at the prison officer. 'So, we're keeping her in solitary for now, until we sort out her medication. Get her stabilised again.'

Natalie's eyes widened. *Psychotic incident?* No. Not the Katya she knew. Natalie's eyes travelled between the prison officer and the doctor as they sent each other glances that surely held a message.

What's really going on?

The doctor checked her watch, stood up and walked round the desk, perching on the edge. 'But the good news, Natalie, is that we're moving you into a house.' She smiled at her, like she'd just given a child a sweet. 'We need your cell for a new admission, and you've been making good progress, so…' She gave Natalie's arm a pat. 'Happy?'

Happy? Natalie glared at her. *What on earth is the woman thinking?* After everything else had been taken from her, now Katya was gone too. Katya, her protector, who was going to give her a home and help her get Harry back. She couldn't imagine ever being happy again.

CHAPTER THIRTY-ONE

Now

Natalie hurries away from the car park in the centre of Peel and down the narrow streets towards the promenade, her clothes damp with sweat. She glances over her shoulder but the street behind her is empty and she's pretty sure she's lost whoever was in the silver estate. *If it was even following me*. It could have been a coincidence, couldn't it? She shakes her head at the naivety of the thought. *It was following me, alright.*

If she can get herself to Mary's, then she'll be safe while she works out her next move. And who knows what information Mary might have for her. *It could all get sorted out today.* It's got to. After the events of the morning she is shaken to the point of exhaustion, her nerves rubbed raw with the effort of escaping whoever is following her.

At the end of the street, she peeks around the corner, relieved to find she's just fifty yards from Mary's house. The promenade is quiet; only a few dog walkers, a couple of old dears pottering along on mobility scooters and a handful of families on the beach. Cars are parked along the road and she takes a minute to check. *No. No silver estates.* She stops holding her breath and turns towards Mary's.

A man crosses the road in front of her, a white poodle trotting at his heels and she squints at him. *It can't be, can it?*

'Jack!' she shouts, before she can stop herself, clutching at the chance meeting before it slips from her grasp. *Thank God!* It would have been awkward to have to ring him, but now she has a chance to tick another lead off her list.

Jack frowns and Natalie wonders for a moment if he's forgotten her, then she remembers her disguise and takes off her glasses, smiles at him.

He laughs. 'Oh no! Natalie! I don't believe it.' Jack picks up the dog and tucks it under his arm. 'Not mine,' he says, arching his head back as it tries to lick his face. 'Meet Butch. He's my mum's, but she fell off her bike at the weekend. Bashed herself up, so I said I'd walk him for her.'

Natalie steps back a pace, into the shadows of the narrow lane, and leans against the sandstone wall of a fisherman's cottage, hiding her injured hand behind her back. The presence of Jack makes her feel safer; nobody's going to attack her while she's with him, are they? And all the emotions that have been parcelled up inside suddenly burst out, wrapped in a coating of laughter. Jack cocks his head and her cheeks burn. She points at the dog.

'Sorry,' she says, her laughter subsiding as quickly as it came. 'It's just… well…' She wrinkles her nose, shrugs.

He gives a wry smile. 'Yeah, I know. Not cool. He's a rescue dog, but God knows why she chose a poodle.' He puts the dog down and stuffs his hands in the pockets of his jeans while it sniffs around her feet. 'I nearly didn't recognise you.'

Her blush deepens and she plucks at her clothes. 'Disgusting, aren't they?' Her mind scrambles for a plausible explanation and she takes a breath while the tale lays itself out in front of her. 'I was meeting a friend this morning and I wasn't looking where I was going, bumped into this guy and spilt two skinny lattes all over myself. Honestly, I was dripping. So… I decided to see what I could find in the charity shops. Just to get me back here, so I could change. But there wasn't much that fitted me and…' She looks down at herself and does a ta-dah movement with her hands. 'This is the best I could do for a fiver.' She gives a little laugh. 'So here I am dressed in acrylic, on a boiling hot day, sweating like a pig.' She flaps a hand in front of her face, hoping he believes that her burning cheeks have something to do with her clothes.

She feels exposed, jittery, sure that the person in the silver estate must be trawling the streets of Peel for her. She changes her position, so Jack is hiding her from the view of anyone driving along the promenade. It'll do for now, but she needs to hurry things along. She opens her mouth to speak, but he beats her to it.

'So…' he says, his eyes dropping to look at the dog, 'I hoped I'd see you after the gig last night.' He looks up and squints at her. 'Not your thing?'

The gig. She'd almost forgotten she was there. 'Oh, no, it was… I loved the music, that was great, but…' She winces. 'Sorry, I'd had a long day and I just—'

'Hey, no worries,' he says, chopping off the end of her excuse.

He turns away and looks at the sea for a few moments.

She fidgets. *Come on, get on with it. Ask him.*

'Jack, I don't suppose you know someone called Tom Wilson, do you?' He turns to look at her. 'I think he might have been one of the sponsors at your gig last night. Runs Excalibur Wealth Management in Douglas.'

Jack's eyes narrow, and she realises that her question is pretty random, given everything he thinks he knows about her.

'I used to work for Tom, a few years ago. I was…' Thankfully she stops herself at that point, remembering that she told Jack she was a nanny, a job that had allowed her to travel the world with her families. 'He has a son. Harry. I looked after him when he was a baby. Such a lovely child…' She looks down, unable to speak for a moment and when she tries again, her voice is thick with emotion. 'I wanted… I wanted to see him. But they seem to have moved and I don't know where they are now.' She blinks and chews her lip, watches the dog while she gathers herself. 'I don't suppose you know his address, do you?'

Jack frowns. 'Hmm. I wasn't involved with the sponsors, Craig sorted all that out, but I know who you mean. Know him by sight, that is, but not to talk to.'

Natalie's eyes widen. She puts a hand on his arm. 'So, I don't suppose your friend Craig knows where Tom and Harry might be living then? Could you ask him?'

He rubs his chin and she hears the rasp of stubble. 'Well… as far as I remember, it was all done by email. We had a whole list of people we sent begging emails to. And I'm pretty sure Craig doesn't know him, either. Not well enough to have his home address, anyway.'

She sighs, euphoria waning as she realises this could be another dead end.

'Wait a minute, though.' He holds up a finger. 'I'm sure there was an article about a local businessman's wife in one of the papers recently, you know, a profile sort of thing. Tom Wilson, did you say?'

His wife. Natalie's skin prickles. Could it really be their nanny, Elena?

'Oh?' she says.

'Yeah, I'm just trying to think…' She waits, holding her breath. 'To be honest, I don't take much notice of those things. It's my mum and sister who rabbit on about them. Gossip central, their house is.' He scrunches up his face. 'Sorry, I'm not being very helpful, am I?'

''Course you are.' She's sure he knows more than he thinks he does, because people absorb information by osmosis, without even noticing, then it pops out and surprises them. She just needs to coax it out of him. 'What's her name, can you remember?'

'Um…' He rubs his chin. 'I know she hasn't taken his surname, but…' He squeezes his eyes shut as he dredges his mind, but when he opens them again he looks a bit crestfallen. 'Nah, I'm really sorry, but I honestly can't remember.'

She tries another tack. 'Do you know what she does?'

He shakes his head. 'Umm… sorry, that's another no. I only took notice because she was wearing… well, not a lot, to be honest and my mum showed it to me, thought she looked like a slapper.'

She pictures the nanny in her mind, tall and brunette, with a full figure. Definitely all the physical assets you'd need to draw a man's attention.

He laughs. 'One thing I do know, though… if it is the same guy, my mum and sister said they reckoned they wouldn't be married for too much longer.'

She frowns. 'Why's that then?'

'I think there was a rumour they might have separated. Or were about to. I don't know.' He shakes his head. 'Marriage on the rocks, anyway.'

'Oh, right.' It would explain why Tom looked so rough, but if they are separated, who is Harry living with? Tom or Elena? Her jaw clenches. *Christ, is nothing ever simple?*

'I don't suppose that's too helpful either, is it?'

Elena what? Her surname was something foreign, more or less unpronounceable and she'd never managed to store it in her mind. She reminds herself that she's making assumptions. She doesn't know for certain that Tom did marry Elena. The wife could be someone completely different. Anyone.

She shakes her head and studies the pavement as she thinks it through. If Harry is living with the wife, how will she ever find him, especially if she doesn't even know her name? The thought of losing him forever swells in her mind, growing bigger and bigger until there's no room for anything else. Her body wilts against the wall and she's oblivious to her surroundings for a moment, deaf to Jack's voice.

'Natalie?' He touches her arm, and she jolts back to the present. 'Look, I've got to go now, get this dog back to Mum's, then I'm off to work. Can I walk you back to where you're staying?' She thinks for a moment, and decides it's not a bad idea, his presence providing her with a camouflage of sorts.

'Thanks,' she says as they start walking. 'I'm only down the road a bit. Just there, that cottage with the blue door.'

'Oh, you're at Mary's.'

'You know her?' She doesn't know why she sounds so surprised, given the close-knit nature of small communities.

'Yeah, yeah. She's my mate's nan. Daft as a box of frogs.'

'Is she?'

'Well, renting rooms out to strangers. At her age. That's not something a sane person would do, is it? Could have all sorts of nutters staying.'

'Hmm,' she says, thankful they have arrived outside the front door.

'Present company excepted, of course.'

'Thanks.' She glances up at him, catches his eye. He looks like he's going to speak, then stops himself.

'Bye then,' she says, after an awkward moment.

'Um…' He hesitates. 'I was going to suggest… I don't suppose you fancy having a drink tomorrow night, do you?

Yes, she wants to say, a sadness aching inside her. It would be lovely to meet up with him again, but she can't drag him into her mess.

She shakes her head, knows she can't be here tomorrow night, not with Lech and his henchman breathing down her neck. 'I'm sorry, Jack. It's not that I don't want to, but I don't think I can. I'm hooking up with a friend; it's the only time she could manage.'

He looks disappointed and she knows in another life her answer would have been different.

'I was going to see if I can find that address for you. See what Mum and Fliss know. And there's people at work who are into all the gossip.'

There's hope in his eyes and she makes herself reconsider. *Surely somebody in his network will know where they live?* It's such a small place, everyone knows everybody else's business. And her story may touch someone's heart; a nanny who wants to meet the child she cared for. She gives him a smile. 'Maybe I could rearrange. Tell you what, can I call you later? Let you know?'

He smiles. 'Yeah, okay. I'm on lates tonight, though.' He purses his lips while he thinks. 'Be better if I ring you. Probably after seven, but who knows what might kick off at work?'

'Oh, okay.' She finds the card with her number on and he taps it into his phone. Sooner would have been better, but if he's at work, she hasn't much choice. His words suddenly register in her brain. *Work?* She frowns, puzzled. 'But I thought you were… isn't being in a band your job?'

'God, no. Be lovely if it was, but, no…' He looks at the ground for a moment. *Is he embarrassed?* Then he looks her straight in the eye. 'Okay, no easy way to say this, so I'm just going to put it out there.' He swallows, looks worried. 'I'm a prison officer.'

Christ alive! She leans against the wall, wishing she was sitting down.

'Oh,' she says, her pulse steadily rising. *Can he see the imprint of prison on me, or is that just an internal injury?* Then she thinks about all the lies she's told him and feels a little weak. *They're trained how to spot lies.* She's sure they are.

'Yeah, I know.' He sighs. 'Bit of a conversation stopper, but it's not a bad job. Pays well.'

He doesn't know. Hasn't guessed. She starts to breathe again.

'Wow.' She nods enthusiastically. 'Must be rewarding.'

He looks relieved. 'Oh yeah, it really is. I work with the juvenile offenders and, you know, they're not bad kids. Most of them. There's the odd little sod, obviously, but most of them are just a bit… you know, lost.'

Suddenly, she understands where his interest in her may lie. She must remind him of his clientele. Another lost soul for him to nurture.

'Anyway, I better be off.' He pulls on the lead. 'I'll ask around, see what I can find out and I'll ring you later.'

She manages a feeble smile, watches him walk down the road and out of her life because a prison officer is not the type of person she can be interacting with in any shape or form. And now he knows where she's staying, she's got to move on.

CHAPTER THIRTY-TWO

Then

The day after her conversation with the prison doctor, Natalie was taken to one of the houses by a prison officer called Beryl, a long streak of a woman, like an upside-down exclamation mark, with a tidy black bob and a face punctuated by a hook nose that drew your eye. Natalie clutched her bag of belongings to her chest, eyes flickering over the unfamiliar landscape. It was weeks since she'd been out in the open like this and she felt like a tortoise without its shell.

I should be happy to get out of that place, she told herself, but still her body tensed, apprehensive about what was round the next corner.

'Now let me tell you a bit about the house,' Beryl said. 'A lot of the women are recovering from drug addictions, so it's very supportive, everyone helping each other. And there are therapy groups you can go to, just so you can, you know, sort out why you found your way to addiction in the first place.'

'I'm not an addict.' Natalie came to a halt as anger flared up inside. 'My husband drugged me. Didn't they tell you?'

'Right.' Beryl nudged Natalie onwards. 'Well, like I said, the support's there when you're ready.'

Natalie sighed. *She doesn't believe me either.*

They stopped in front of a two-storey red-brick Victorian building with two pointed gables at the front, like an M.

'Here we are, then.' Beryl led her inside and up a broad flight of stairs. 'We'll get you settled in first, then I'll give you a tour of the facilities. Okay?'

Natalie's eyes widened when she entered her room and saw the two sets of bunk beds. She looked round the cramped space. *Four of us, in here?*

'Now then, Natalie, I think this is yours.' Beryl bent over a small cabinet and opened the door. 'Yes, this one's empty. You can put all your stuff in here.'

'So…' Natalie turned in a circle, taking in the rectangular room, with a toilet and washing facilities at one end, a large window at the other. 'There's four of us in here?'

'No, love, not at the moment. You'll be sharing with two other girls, so you're lucky, you get to pick which top bunk you want.' She made it sound like a treat.

Natalie swallowed. *Sharing a room with strangers? No privacy.* That thought alone gave her goosebumps. And where was she going to write her letters? There was no table. No space to think. Her heart clenched. *How am I going to spend time with Harry?*

'Don't look so worried, love. Linda and Mel are alright. Nice women when you get to know them.' She gave Natalie's shoulder a squeeze. 'You'll be fine. Better than on the Wing, anyway.'

Natalie realised then that everything was quiet. Calm. No screaming or shouting, no running feet and she had to admit that the absence of drama would be a relief. She could actually see out of the window and if there hadn't been a metal grille over it, she'd think she was in a park or on a private estate. She pressed her face to the glass and watched a group of women outside doing an exercise class. Others were sitting on the grass, chatting. Women walking to places and from places. Another group weeding a flower bed. She ached for fresh air and thought she could join them. One day. Maybe. *Or is that asking for trouble?*

'So, the routine's a bit different in here.' Beryl leant against the door frame while Natalie unpacked her meagre belongings. 'I think you'll find it's more relaxed. Same breakfast time. Then we don't have lock up again until after lunch. Just for an hour. Then you've got all afternoon until teatime and association before evening lock-up.' Like the doctor, her voice had a Welsh lilt to it, sentences flowing up and down in a hypnotic rhythm. 'And in your free time you can do courses and join work groups. If you use your time wisely you can go out of here with all sorts of qualifications.' She tucked her hair behind her ears and smiled at Natalie. 'Or you can train as a peer mentor. I'll give you a list of everything when we go downstairs. And there's the library and the gym.'

Beryl's words jumbled together, too much information for Natalie to absorb, but one word caught her attention. *Library? That's where I can write.* And outside, she could surely find a quiet space to be with Harry when the weather was good. Natalie's hands unclenched and she smoothed them on her joggers, wriggling her shoulders to ease out the tension. This wasn't sounding too bad now.

Beryl came to stand next to her. 'Did I mention the other support groups? There's legal advice, and one for mothers to maintain access with their children and then—'

'What did you say?' Natalie was definitely taking notice now. 'I can get help with access arrangements?'

'Oh yes. Most of the women in here have kids. They're a very active group. Lots of experience and they get very good results. They do special recordings for mothers to send to their kids on their birthdays as well. You know, reading favourite stories. Singing songs. All sorts. Put it on a CD, then they design a proper cover for it. Lovely, they are.'

Natalie's heart lifted and she smiled for the first time in days. This was getting better all the time.

At lunchtime, after a tour round the site, she was shown to the dining room, a large room, half the width of the house, with a high ceiling and a bay window at the front. It was set out with five tables, four chairs at each and she was placed on a table with three other women. Beryl pointed out Mel and Linda, her roommates, but was called away before she could introduce them.

Natalie's good mood disappeared in an instant, to be replaced by a familiar unease. She crept to the table and slid into her seat, looked at her plate of food, determined not to catch anyone's eye. She was the new kid at school again, new to the routines, the cliques, the order of things. Her stomach clenched, in no mood for eating. Her head filled with the clatter of knives and forks, the clack of plates being stacked, every sound amplified until it was almost too loud to bear. She wondered when she could leave. *Do I have to ask, or can I just get up and go?* Her eyes flicked around the other tables and came back to rest on the congealed mess of shepherd's pie on her plate.

'Natalie, isn't it?'

She glanced towards the voice and there was the girl she'd arrived with all those weeks ago. Natalie's lips cracked into a smile.

'Mali, wow! I didn't know you were still here.'

Mali rolled her eyes. 'Oh yeah, like, for the duration.'

'Right.' Natalie nodded, as if she knew what that meant.

'Do you want to sit on our table?' Mali pointed to the window, where a couple of young women sat, looking at her. One of them wiggled her fingers in a wave and smiled. 'Come on over. Get to know them.'

Natalie rubbed the back of her neck aware that the women on her table were staring at her, their conversation hanging in mid-air as they waited to see what she would do.

She ran her tongue round dry lips and looked at her plate. 'Another time, maybe,' she said, and put a forkful of lukewarm slop into her mouth. Her stomach growled and she silently thanked it for its collusion.

Mali laughed. 'I'll let you get on. Sounds like you're ready for that. Not a bad meal for a change.'

Natalie watched Mali weave her way across the dining room and as she glanced back towards her plate, she caught the eye of the woman sitting opposite her. Mel. She was probably Natalie's age, skinny to the point of being malnourished with a pointy face and big brown eyes. Thin, sandy hair hung to her shoulders. *Don't trust anyone.* That's what Katya had told her. Natalie glanced away, took another forkful of food.

'Natalie?' Mel rolled the name around her tongue like she was tasting wine. Natalie nodded, suddenly hot. 'You're Katya's new girl?'

Natalie frowned, flustered, a blush reddening her cheeks. *Does she mean girl as in girlfriend?* 'Friends. We're just friends.' She put her knife and fork down, pushed her plate away. Her right leg bounced under the table.

The women glanced at each other and laughed.

'What?' Natalie looked at Mel, surprised to see that her expression was one of concern.

'Katya doesn't have friends,' said Linda, who was sitting next to Mel. She was at least sixty, her face wrinkled and worn, white hair cut short and teeth so even they had to be dentures.

'Well, she does now,' Natalie said. 'She's been brilliant to me.'

The women gave each other knowing looks.

'So, where is she? This friend of yours,' Mel said.

'She's... she's not well.'

'You're right about that. Fucking psycho, that one.' The women erupted into cackles, like a burst of static.

Natalie pressed her lips together and looked for the exit but all she could see were dozens of pairs of eyes watching her. Her leg bounced faster.

'You know what she did, don't you?' Linda said, leaning towards her. 'She stabbed a girl in the eye with a fork.'

Natalie gasped. 'No, she didn't!' She leant back in her chair, away from the woman and her spiteful words. 'You're making that up.'

Linda shook her head. 'Eighteen, the girl was. First time in prison. Now she's blind in one eye.'

'No! She wouldn't do a thing like that. Not Katya.'

'Listen, love. You need to keep away from that bitch. She's the fucking devil.' Heads nodded around the room, a low murmuring of voices, everyone having something to say on the subject.

Don't believe a word they say. They all want something from you. Katya had warned her, hadn't she? And she'd been proved right so many times.

Natalie's eyes found the door and she dashed round the tables, feet pounding up the stairs and into her room. She climbed onto a top bunk, turning her back to the door, pulse racing. What a terrible thing to make up about someone. *Horrible, horrible women.* And she had to share a room with two of them.

'Natalie? Is everything okay?'

Natalie turned her head and saw Beryl standing in the doorway.

'I heard there was a bit of a commotion in the dining room. Someone been bothering you, love?'

Natalie wiped her eyes and swallowed. 'They were slagging off my friend.'

Beryl walked towards her and rested her arms on the edge of the bunk, her face level with Natalie's. 'Right, so which friend would that be?'

'Katya.'

Beryl's mouth hung open. 'You're friends with Katya?'

Natalie nodded. 'They said she stabbed a girl in the eye.' Natalie wiped her nose on her sleeve. 'Why make up stuff like that?'

Beryl sighed. 'Well, love, it's not made up, I'm afraid. That's exactly what happened. They haven't got to the bottom of why she did it yet. But the truth will come out eventually.'

Natalie's body curled in on itself, the news like a dose of poison. *Katya had really done it? But why?* She must have been in danger, been threatened. It happened all the time. Katya had said so herself.

'I've heard there's going to be an inquiry,' Beryl said. 'Somebody's going to get into trouble. Probably the doc, because it's not the first time that Katya's hurt someone. That's why she was on the Wing, you see. Where we've got a better staffing ratio.' Beryl tutted. 'Too kind by half, the doc is, if you ask me. Always giving people the benefit of the doubt, then one of us has to pick up the pieces. And now that poor girl has been maimed for life.' She patted Natalie's arm. 'You've had a lucky escape, love. Katya turns, you see. In an instant. Jekyll and Hyde, that one.' She tapped the side of her head. 'Unstable.'

'But… but I can't believe it. She said she was on the Wing because she was coming off Oxycodone, like me.'

Beryl shook her head. 'She's a convincing liar, isn't she? You know what she's in for, right?'

Natalie swallowed. 'No, she… she didn't say.'

'She runs a brothel. Her and her brother. Several brothels, if you listen to what the girls have to say. She's got charges pending for kidnap, extortion and money laundering. As well as dealing Class As. And a couple of years ago she got away with murder, literally, on the basis of diminished responsibility.' Beryl pursed her lips, her eyes clouded with anger. 'But then she can afford the fancy barristers. And that means you can get away with just about anything. Can convince the jury black is white, those fellas.'

Natalie frowned. 'Are we talking about the same Katya?'

Beryl snorted. 'Only one Katya ever been in here.'

'But she has a beautiful house. She showed me. It wasn't a brothel. No way was it a brothel. I was going to go and stay with her when I got out.'

Beryl's eyebrows lifted. 'Honestly, I don't know what they're thinking over there. Letting her groom you like that.'

'What do you mean? She wasn't grooming me.'

Beryl huffed. 'So, what do you think would have happened when you got to her house? And her big brother stuffed you full of heroin. Brought in a party of businessmen?'

Natalie's chest tightened, Beryl's words wrapped around her like barbed wire.

'It's what happens.' Beryl leant forwards, eyes narrowed. 'Believe me. I've seen Katya's girls. And you definitely don't want to be one of them. Whatever her plans are for you, they're not going to be good.'

Natalie shrivelled against the wall.

'But don't worry, the girls you're sharing with are fine. Nothing nasty about them. And I'll look out for you now that I know what Katya's been up to, put the word round the other officers.'

Beryl pushed herself away from the bed, smoothed her uniform and gave Natalie a tight smile.

'Just watch your back, love. Katya doesn't work alone. She's going to be in the Unit for a while now, I would imagine, but… strange things happen in here. Things that make no sense at all.'

CHAPTER THIRTY-THREE

Now

Natalie lets herself into Mary's house, relieved to be inside and out of sight. She runs upstairs to her bedroom, closes the door and dashes to the window, checking up and down the prom for the car that was following her. *It's not there.* She gives a sigh of relief, sweaty hands leaving their imprints on the glass.

She flops on to the bed, running the events of the morning through her mind. If Lech was in the black car, who was in the silver estate? Or was that Lech, and his henchman was in the black car? That theory makes more sense, and would explain why Mr Hawaiian Shirt had a northern accent.

Wait a minute.

Her body stills.

Maybe it was Tom. Could he have seen her when he'd arrived at his office? It's possible, isn't it? And then he could have followed her to the car park. The thought circles in her mind. He hadn't been subtle, the person who'd been following her. The car had been with her all the way from Douglas to Peel. Nothing covert about it. More of a message than a threat. 'I know you're here' sort of thing. Lech wouldn't do that, would he? She shakes her head, confused.

Time to ring Sasha, she decides, *see what she makes of it all.* She gets her phone out of her bag, but after pressing all the buttons, it's unresponsive and she throws it onto the bed, frowning. *Useless thing!* What has happened to phone batteries while she's been in prison? Her old phone would go for a couple of days without being charged, but this one only seems to last a few hours.

She's plugging her phone into the charger next to the bed when she hears the creak of footsteps on the landing, followed by a sharp knock on the door.

'Natalie? Can I come in?'

Before Natalie has time to reply, the door opens and Mary pokes her head round. Her smile sags into a frown as she looks Natalie up and down.

'There you are.' She sounds a bit edgy. 'I must have heard you wrong this morning. I thought you weren't coming back until teatime.'

Natalie manages a quick smile. 'Oh, well… yes. My friend wasn't feeling so good, so we cut it short.' She checks her phone, shoulders sagging with relief when she hears it buzz back to life.

'Oh, that's a shame.'

'Yes, well, we'll see if she's better tomorrow and do it all then.' She really needs Mary to leave now, so she can get on with her phone call but Mary edges into the room and shuts the door behind her.

Dammit! Natalie taps at her phone, finding Sasha's number in the call log, hoping that Mary will realise that she's busy.

'I'm just having a bit of soup for lunch if you'd like to join me?'

Natalie freezes. *Lunch?* She hasn't got time for that and is just about to say so when Mary speaks again.

'I also found that address for you.' Mary's benign smile is back on her face. 'It's downstairs. If you come and have a bite to eat, then I can explain how to get there.'

The address! Oh, thank God, thank God, thank God.

Natalie's heart jumps around like a child at Christmas and she beams at Mary, while she wonders how fast she can eat a bowl of soup. *Ten minutes?* Then she can be gone. Gone to find Harry and get him to safety.

'That sounds great, Mary.' Her smile widens. 'Thank you. I've just got to make a call, then I'll be right there.'

'Okay, lovey.' Mary turns and disappears down the landing.

Natalie pulls the door closed, sits on the bed and calls Sasha, but after a few rings it goes straight to voicemail. She stares at the phone and tries again. And again. After the third attempt, she realises she has no choice but to leave a message.

'Sash, it's me,' she says, after the beep. 'Look, I've got Harry's address.' Her breath hitches in her throat, because saying it makes her realise how close she is now. 'And… well, there's a couple of other things I need to talk to you about. Anyway, call me as soon as you can. Please. Thanks… bye, sweetie.'

Sweetie. It feels strange, saying that word after all this time and it leaves a peculiar taste in her mouth. The taste of something dead. She sighs. Tells herself that she needs to give Sasha a chance. She did say she was going to be busy with filming or whatever else she's doing and Natalie knows that she can't rely on her too much. But, there's bound to be a quiet moment when she'll be able to return Natalie's call. *And maybe she'll be free later?* Be able to help with their getaway. Her hands clasp together, as though she's praying.

It's all okay, she tells herself. She hadn't planned on Sasha's help, and is more than capable of sorting everything out for herself should Sasha be busy. Especially now she knows that Tom is a shadow of the man he used to be. But it would be so much easier with two of them.

Harry's address!

Her heart celebrates with a couple more skips.

I'm going to see him today. This afternoon.

She springs off the bed with renewed vigour and catches her reflection in the mirror. It holds her attention like a magnet and her jaw drops. No wonder Mary was staring. She looks ragged without the camouflage of make-up, and her hair is a horrible, tangled mess. *I'd scare the life out of Harry if I turned up looking like this*. He's got to recognise her as his mum. That's the important thing, or he'll never go with her.

Okay, new plan, she decides, tearing herself away from her reflection. *Get the address from Mary, even it means having to guzzle a bowl of soup, then dye my hair afterwards. While the phone charges.* She'll need her phone to contact the man with the boat, tell him they're on their way. She works through the timings. *An hour if I really pull my finger out. One chance, that's all I'll get. Better to prepare properly.*

'Soup's going cold, lovey,' Mary shouts up the stairs.

'Yeah. On my way,' she calls and heads down the landing, her jaw set. First things first. Without Harry's address, she's not going anywhere.

Natalie finds Mary in the kitchen, where she's set the table for the two of them. She's filling the sink for the washing up and she looks round as Natalie enters, wiping her hands on a tea towel that's slung over her shoulder.

'Ah, there you are.' She smiles. 'I thought we could eat in here. Bit cooler with the back door open.'

She points Natalie to a seat and brings over two bowls of soup, which have been sitting ready on the worktop. There's a basket of crusty bread in the middle of the table, glasses of iced water with lemon and red serviettes folded like fans.

'This looks lovely and the soup smells fantastic.' Tomato and basil, Natalie guesses by the rich aroma.

'Tuck in,' Mary says, sitting opposite and they eat in silence for a while, spoons clinking against their bowls as Natalie shovels the hot liquid into her mouth as fast as she can.

'That's a nasty bang you've had there,' Mary says, staring at the bruise that covers Natalie's knuckles.

The statement holds a question and Natalie slips her hand under the table, shakes her head. 'Oh, it's nothing. Just trapped it in the car door.'

Mary's stare makes her wriggle in her seat and she pushes her bowl away, eager to change the subject. 'That was lovely, thanks. Fresh basil, makes such a difference, doesn't it?'

But Mary doesn't respond and seems distracted. She stands and takes a Tupperware container off a shelf, brings it over to the table. 'I've got some arnica if you want. It'll take out the bruising.' Bandages, plasters, safety pins, boxes of tablets line up on the table. Natalie watches, aware that precious minutes are ticking away, but unable to work out how to demand the address, when it's the result of a favour.

'Aha! Here we are.' Mary holds up a mangled tube of ointment. 'Still a bit left. Marvellous stuff. Just dab a bit on and rub it in.'

Natalie takes the tube and does as she's told, wincing as she strokes the cream onto her swollen flesh. Mary watches every move. 'Should start to feel better in a few minutes.' Natalie looks up and finds herself locked in a gaze that makes her scalp prickle.

'Look, I know this might sound like a strange question,' Mary says, 'but those aren't the clothes you were wearing this morning, are they?'

Natalie licks her lips, feels a blush creep up her neck.

'Oh no… I er… just spilt coffee on myself in town and couldn't walk round dripping wet, so I—'

'It's just that…' Mary leans forward. 'Look, I don't want you to think I'm judging but…'

Natalie's stomach quivers. 'But what?'

'You're not in any trouble, are you?'

Natalie lifts her chin, eyes wide. 'What? No. Why would you think that?'

Mary fiddles with her napkin before answering. 'That dress you were wearing this morning. So pretty. But unusual. And I heard on the radio…'

'Heard what?' Natalie holds her breath.

'Well, there was an incident in town. And—' Mary frowns and starts to break a piece of bread into pieces '—a baby ended up in hospital.' She looks up, straight into Natalie's eyes. Natalie looks straight back, not even daring to swallow. 'It was a shoplifter. They were chasing after her and a baby's buggy got knocked over.'

Natalie can see the scene in her mind. Like one of those mannequin posts on social media, everyone suspended in time. And in the centre of the picture, the man staring at her, accusation in his eyes.

'They gave a description. And the person they're looking for… well, she was wearing a dress like your one this morning. Blonde, like you. Thin.'

Natalie's feet gather under her. She looks at the back door, wide open. Blinks. *Crap, crap, crap!* She can't go anywhere without Harry's address. She feels like she's on a high wire, fighting to keep her balance after a sudden gust of wind.

'Oh, that's terrible,' she says, keeping her eyes on Mary. 'But it wasn't me.'

Blood pulses in her ears. *Shoplifter? Where's that come from?*

'Apparently, the child's uncle was a volunteer officer and nearly managed to do a citizen's arrest on the woman when he spotted her a bit later, but she escaped before the police could get there to help him.'

Natalie manages to keep her face still, masking the commotion in her mind. *The child's uncle? It was the uncle who'd grabbed me, not Lech, or his henchman!* Her mind recalibrates, trying to undo all her false assumptions. *Forget black cars, all I have to worry about is the silver estate.* And that could still have been a coincidence, not following her at all.

'Police are all over the place trying to find her.' Natalie's mouth twitches. Mary nods, her gaze steady as her words paint Natalie into a corner. 'And they've put out a public appeal for information.' She taps a piece of paper tucked under her placemat. 'Got the number right here.'

Natalie rubs at her injured hand, letting the pain spike through her and sharpen her mind. A thick silence settles between them.

'The front door's locked. And the back gate.' Mary folds her arms across her chest. 'I've hidden the keys. So, you're staying here until we get to the bottom of this.'

'Okay,' Natalie says, taking a sip of water. She puts her glass down carefully and sits back in her chair. 'I haven't been completely honest with you.'

'No,' Mary says, popping a morsel of bread into her mouth. 'I don't suppose you have.'

'But I'm not a shoplifter.'

Mary chews and swallows, her stare unwavering.

'So, what are you then?'

CHAPTER THIRTY-FOUR

Then

Life went on in prison and Natalie went with it, floating along like a log in a river, aware that at some point she would come to the end of this part of her life and arrive at something different. Something better, she told herself, because it would have Harry in it. She treated prison as a dream. Not real. Not something she wanted to get involved with. Instead, she practically lived in the library with her memories of Harry, wrapped in a dream world, a place where she was still there as his mother and she could keep him close. It seemed the only way to cope.

It was surprising how quickly being in the house became the norm, the limits of Natalie's life accepted and ignored. Conversations revolved around the before and the after, the now being something that everyone struggled through, day by lengthy day. Unless there was an incident. Then it was pounced on and picked to pieces, chewed over until there was nothing left to say, the subject abandoned like the bones of a dead animal when all the edible bits were gone.

'So, Natalie, what are you going to do when you get out?' Linda asked one night, when it was too early for sleep. She was a fussy woman and clucked over Natalie like a surrogate mother, always making suggestions. Every other sentence seemed to start with 'Why don't you…?' and it was becoming a bit wearing, but Natalie kept telling herself it could have been worse. She could have ended up with someone like Mags. So, she usually smiled and nodded and went along with whatever the suggestion might be. 'Mel's doing her hairdressing and I'm learning to do accounts. Why don't you come with me? The teacher's ever so good.' She laughed. 'I mean, if me, at my age, with only half me brain cells working can understand it, then anyone can. Get you a good job after, as well.'

Natalie choked on a laugh. Clearly, her career in wealth management and financial services was over, a criminal record making her unemployable. But she had avoided talking about her past, so the women weren't to know.

'Thanks, Linda, but I've tried it.' She pulled a face. 'Didn't work too well.'

The question awakened something in her though, reminded her that she needed to be prepared for life after prison. *A year and a quarter isn't that long, is it?* Once she got out she was going to need a job, something that earned decent money, and that would require qualifications of some sort.

'There's loads of stuff going on,' Linda said. 'Why don't you give hairdressing a go? You can always earn money if you can cut hair.'

Mel nodded. 'Thing is, time goes much faster if you're doing something. Worth it just for that, isn't it, Lin?'

'It's the truth,' Linda said. 'And the parole board likes to see you trying to move on, you know. Why don't you have a look at the list, see what takes your fancy?'

'Okay,' Natalie said, staring at the ceiling, her mind already working on what she might like to do. 'I'll do that tomorrow. Have a think.'

And think, she did. Now that the drugs were out of her system, her mind was less prone to wander and she wanted something to aim for, instead of sitting around counting the minutes and hours, adding them up into days and weeks and months. She had to believe that she could support herself and Harry. That she could make a good life for them.

It's time to do something different, she decided. Something that was true to who she really was, not be the person who put on an act every day. Dressed in a costume, saying the right things, mixing with a load of people she didn't even like. What she needed was something she could do as a business, on her own. Something she could train for while she was in prison.

The next day, she found the list of courses on offer, something she'd been given and ignored weeks ago. And Linda was right, there really was loads of stuff going on. She found herself smiling while she worked down the list, an unfamiliar buzz tickling the back of her neck at the thought of learning something new. Preparing for her new life. *Just me and Harry.* And for the first time since she'd been in prison, it felt like something positive was happening. She grabbed the opportunity with both hands and flung herself into learning.

She tried hairdressing with mixed results and she certainly wasn't good enough to take it any further than the two-week taster course. Then she tried massage, and although she liked the idea of soothing other people's pain, she found the experience of kneading the flesh of strangers distinctly unappealing. Beauty therapy was fun, like an art class really, but it seemed so irrelevant, it was hard to summon the motivation to take it seriously.

Downhearted, she went back to the library and her daydreams, feeling a little empty inside. What if she couldn't get a job when she got out? What would happen to her then? And how could she look after Harry?

At the end of Natalie's second month in the house, she spent her time trying to get away from Mel and Linda, who were constantly on at her about doing some course or another and it had got to the point where she was in danger of losing her temper. She'd tried, hadn't she? There just didn't seem to be anything she could do.

She gravitated towards Mali and her crew, as Mali liked to call them. And in the end, it was Mali who changed her life.

It happened on Harry's first birthday. She woke up feeling hollow and dejected, a soggy mess of sadness, overwhelmed by the fact that she was missing this major milestone in her son's life. Lethargic and cold, she stayed huddled in bed while Linda and Mel went down for breakfast. As soon as she was alone, she got out her writing pad and pen, sure that talking to Harry through a letter was the only thing that would make her feel better.

Happy birthday, Munchkin!

One year old today and you have to celebrate without Mummy, but I'm sure you'll have a wonderful time. I bet you have a big cake, with a number one candle on it. Can you blow it out? I think you can. And I think you can clap your hands as well now, can't you? It will be so much fun, opening your presents. All that paper to tear and scrunch and boxes to explore and Granny and Grandad will have bought you lots of wonderful things.

I hope you like the CD I sent you. The Very Hungry Caterpillar *is such a lovely story and I know you have the book at home, so I hope someone will look at that with you.*

I'm sorry that I can't be with you, but it's not because I don't love you. In fact, my present to you is eternal love. How about that? A love that will never end, one that grows stronger every day and keeps you safe and well because love is a magical thing. Did you know that? My love for you can't be kept in prison, it can't be locked up. What a silly idea! My love can flow through walls, across the sky and zoom straight into your heart, little munchkin. But the best bit is, because you are the only person on this earth that I love, you get to have it all. Imagine that? All that magical power, just for you.

Even though I can't be there I want you to remember me, Harry. Don't ever forget that you have a mummy.

The pen dropped from Natalie's hand when she saw her worst fear written down on paper and she stumbled out of bed, throwing the writing pad into her locker. *Of course he'll remember,* she told herself, Dr Patel said so, didn't she?

'You mustn't worry about that, Natalie,' Dr Patel had said during one of their counselling sessions. She'd rubbed Natalie's arm. 'It only takes a few months for a toddler to accept a mother back into his life and in a short time, he'll forget there was a period when you weren't there.' She'd smiled at her and Natalie had wiped the tears from her face. 'Children are very adaptable. You'll see. Ask the other mothers here. They'll tell you.'

So, she had, and it seemed that Dr Patel was right. She reminded herself of this now, made herself get dressed and get on with her day. She couldn't give up, couldn't wallow in self-pity. *That won't make me a good mother, will it?*

'Come on, Nat,' Mali said after breakfast. 'Why don't you come to the gym with us? It's fun, isn't it, girls? You'll enjoy it.'

The other girls sharing the table looked at each other, then burst out laughing.

'Yeah, right,' Chelsea said, a chubby young woman, with long red hair and terrible skin. 'But it beats doing nothing.'

'That's the point,' Mali said, dragging at Natalie's arm. 'Stops you moping. And it makes you feel better.' She checked the clock on the wall and stood up. 'Time to go, girls.' She pulled at Natalie's arm again. 'At least give it a try. Come on,' she wheedled, 'just the once.'

Natalie pulled a face. She'd had a peep in the gym a few weeks ago, had seen a room full of sweaty, red-faced women doing things she knew her body couldn't do and had gone straight back out again, afraid to make a fool of herself. But she was slimmer now, had lost a stone or so while she was coming off the drugs. Maybe it was time to tone herself up.

'Oh, alright. If it stops you going on at me, I'll come with you.'

And that was the start of something quite unexpected.

She found out that she actually enjoyed exercise. The fact that it was a surprise had a lot to do with her PE teacher, who she'd hated with a passion and had managed to avoid for much of her time in school, persuading Sasha to skip her lessons and accompany her instead on illicit trips into town to try on make-up and perfume.

Once Natalie had done aerobics and Zumba, yoga and spin classes, she knew that her life had changed forever. She had something to look forward to, something that occupied her mind and distracted her from her worries. In the gym, she could imagine that she was anywhere in the world. It didn't feel like she was in prison. In her daydreams, Harry was in a crèche, in a nearby room while she worked out. She could imagine that she was a normal mother, having a little time out for herself. Her body shape started to change and with some element of self-respect restored, a virtuous circle had begun.

A few months after her exercise regime started, Mali stopped in the entrance to the gym and pointed at the wall. 'Hey, have you seen this? We could get a qualification.' She looked at Natalie, eyes gleaming. 'What do you think? Personal trainers!'

Natalie studied the notice and grinned at Mali. *Personal trainer.* It had a nice ring to it, it really did. And wouldn't it be the perfect job for her? She bumped Mali's outstretched fist and a plan was born. A future in the making and a chance that she could come out of this experience, not just in one piece, but with something exciting ahead of her. A new career that would make a life with Harry possible.

She wasn't to know that it would lead her to the worst day of her life, a day that would scar her forever and put her son's life in danger.

CHAPTER THIRTY-FIVE

Now

So now I need to see if I can work out exactly where she's hiding. Mind you, it might be better to wait in the car park, then when she takes off I'll be right behind her.

Hmm.

The problem is, she knows my car now. That was stupid to tail her so close. But I couldn't resist. I could see the panic in her eyes when she looked in her rear-view mirror and realised she was being followed. It was worth it just for that.

What to do? I don't know. It's hard to be here doing nothing.

The thing is, I need to get her somewhere quiet. Which won't be a problem. So many secluded spots to choose from. And then… and then.

I haven't quite decided.

It would be so easy to make her disappear. Then all my worries would be gone with her. It's tempting. I mean, who would even know? Who would miss her? Nobody. That's who. Fucking nobody.

CHAPTER THIRTY-SIX

Now

When Natalie finishes speaking, her life story laid out on the table between them, Mary tuts and shakes her head. 'That's a sorry tale you've got there.' She fixes Natalie with a beady-eyed frown and leans forwards a little, hands on the table. 'But I know you're not telling me everything.'

'But I have, Mary. I have told you everything.' Natalie feels like she's back in school, in the headmistress's office, and looks down at her hands, clasped in her lap.

'No,' Mary says, firmly. 'No, you haven't. I brought up five girls, lovey. I know all about half-truths and things not said.'

Natalie bites her lip to stop the missing bits from coming out. It would be so easy, a relief even, to tell her. The words push their way up her throat, but there's no doubt that telling the truth would destroy this slim chance she has of persuading Mary to let her go without a fuss. There is no way she's going to hurt this woman, but if it's a choice between her and Harry... She swallows what she wants to say and tries something else.

'What I didn't tell you is... I jumped parole.'

Mary gives a derisive snort and shakes her head. 'I'm sorry but that's not it, is it? You jumping parole is flippin' obvious. There's something else.' She wags a finger at Natalie. 'Look, I might be old, but I'm not daft. I've read detective stories. Loads of them. I know the signs to look out for when someone's lying. The body language, the direction of the eyes.' She flaps a hand. 'All that stuff and...' She gives a sigh. 'Look, it's not that I don't believe your story, because I do. So far. But I'm wondering if the bit you haven't told me is the bit I really need to know.'

Natalie keeps her eyes on Mary while her mind starts inventing. 'Okay. Okay, you're right.' Her hands twist under the table. 'There is more. My ex-husband knows I'm here. I think he's been following me. I was running away from him in Douglas. That's what I was doing. But I didn't knock over the buggy. He must have made up a story about me being a shoplifter, so that guy would chase after me and the police would be looking for me.' She leans forwards and grasps Mary's hand. 'I'm... I'm frightened of him. What he might do.'

In her mind, she substitutes Lech's name for 'my husband' in the hope that she'll foil the lie test. *And anyway, it's not that far off the truth, is it?* It might have been Tom in the silver estate, following her. It's a theory that can't be discounted.

Mary's gaze softens. 'See, that wasn't so bad, was it?'

'I just want to see my son, Mary.' Natalie's voice wobbles, then her bottom lip joins in. 'Surely there's nothing wrong with that?'

Mary sighs. 'No, lovey. I don't suppose there is.' She tuts. 'What a mess. What a terrible mess.'

'I know. I know.' Natalie leans back in her chair and drops her eyes, which are aching with the effort of staying still. She picks at her fingernails, listening to the silence. Waiting for Mary's verdict.

'Do you think you could keep this quiet, Mary?' Natalie's voice is hardly audible, as though the whispers in her head have sneaked out on their own. 'Let me have Harry's address and I promise you... I honestly promise that once I've seen him, I will contact the police, hand myself in and take whatever consequences there might be.'

Her body feels limp. *Have I done enough?* She risks a glance at Mary and catches her wiping a tear from her eye. Her hopes lift themselves off the floor and her hands wrap themselves tighter. She waits. Mary fidgets with her napkin, then puts it on the table and looks at Natalie.

'Okay. This is what we'll do.' Mary takes a folded piece of paper out of her apron pocket, opens it out and pushes it across the table. 'We're going to have to compromise. I've got my conscience to live with, you see, not to mention my neighbours.' Natalie holds her breath and stares at the paper, her heart jiving with joy. She can't quite believe it. *Harry's address! Nearly there, nearly there.* 'I'm going to let you have until… let's say eight o'clock this evening. Then, if you haven't rung to tell me you've done what you said… then I'm going to have to tell the police what I know.'

Natalie pulls the piece of paper towards her, lightheaded with excitement. She glances at the address and her eyes widen. Peel. Not far then. Her heart pumps faster. Eight o'clock. Just over six hours. Not very long. But… the sooner the better, given that Lech is out there somewhere, hunting her down and Tom may already know that she's close.

'Thank you, Mary,' she says as she folds the piece of paper, clutching it in her fist. 'Thank you so much.'

'That's alright. You deserve a break after what you've been through. But I'm going to have to ask you to leave my house.' Mary reaches across the table and puts her hand on Natalie's arm. 'Not that I want to, you understand. But it wouldn't look right if I let you stay tonight. There'd be talk. I could be an accessory to… something.'

Natalie nods and runs her tongue round dry lips. 'Okay, okay, no problem. I just need to tidy myself up, then I'll be off.'

'Well, I'm going out in a bit. And will be out until later this evening, after eight sometime, I expect.' Mary winks. 'I've remembered that I was going to visit my daughter up in Ramsey, you see.'

Natalie gives her a slow smile. 'I can't thank you enough, Mary.'

'You're welcome. Just make the most of the time you have and don't... well, you just take care.'

Natalie pushes her chair back and gives Mary a sudden, fierce hug before running up the stairs.

Six hours.

Not long at all. Then it dawns on her. A new problem. The boat won't be here until tomorrow and now she can't stay with Mary, where's she going to go with Harry until she can escape off the island? *Sasha.* Now she really needs her help.

In her room, she grabs her phone and calls Sasha again, pacing the floor as it rings, then goes to voicemail. *Dammit!* Her fists clench as she waits for the beep and leaves another message.

'Sash, it's me again.' Her voice rushes on, like a river in flood. 'Ring me, please. Look, there's been a new development. I've only got six hours to get to Harry. I'll explain later. But just... Please. Ring. Me.'

Okay.

She starts to change her clothes, deciding that she'll just go. Now. No point waiting for Sasha, or the palaver of a new disguise. *In a few minutes, I could see Harry. Just a few minutes.*

Mary's words scuttle into her mind, and make her freeze for a moment. *The police are looking for a long-haired blonde woman. An alert has been put out.* She turns and looks in the mirror, shocked again by her reflection. If she's going to have any chance of foiling Lech or Tom or the police, or the public for that matter, a new disguise is essential. Her jaw tightens and she chews on her frustration, swallows it down and knows that she has no alternative. *Short and brunette it is then. Quick.*

She sits in front of the mirror, digs in her make-up bag for her nail scissors, then grabs a clump of hair and cuts it off. Then another. And another until she's engrossed in a frenzy of snipping, hair falling around her feet like autumn leaves. In films, people on the run cut their own hair and it looks just fine, but when you're doing it yourself, everything's back to front in the mirror, the angles all wrong. Heat percolates through her body, rising up her neck as she struggles to make good her mistakes, trying to remember what she learned on her course. Seconds turn into frantic minutes and half an hour later, her hair is much shorter than she was aiming for. A variation on an elfin crop is the only option and actually, once she's finished, it doesn't look too bad. Except for the tacky blonde colouring.

It'll look better when it's washed she tells herself, turning her head this way and that to inspect the damage. *And anyway, now it's short, it won't take long to colour.* She pulls the box of dye out of her bag and rushes to the bathroom.

By the time the dye is ready to wash out, she's left Sasha three more messages and Googled Harry's address so she knows how to get there. It's a mile or so out of Peel, on a little lane, a property set on its own a few hundred yards beyond a cluster of houses. Which is perfect. *Nice and secluded.* Nobody to see what she's doing.

She thinks it through while she has a quick shower to wash the dye out. Harry could be playing in the garden. On his own. And if Tom was going to be working from home, that suggests his wife is out. *So, just Tom to deal with.* And given the shape he's in… A determined smile creeps onto her lips. *I can take him out, no problem.*

Natalie's short hair and the chestnut colour make her look so different she thinks it'll be hard for anyone to recognise her now. And her appearance is a lot more child-friendly, she thinks. More fun. She quickly smooths on a bit of make-up to give her face a better colour and hide the dark rings under her eyes. All she needs now is a change of outfit, then she's ready to roll.

Quick, quick, she tells herself, moving as if she's on fast forward, stomach fluttering as she pulls a short denim skirt over leggings, then a faded black T-shirt, with a skull on the front and 'You Only Live Once' scrawled on the back. *Not bad,* she decides when she catches her reflection. Better than she'd hoped. And she's got Converse shoes, a baseball hat and over-sized sunglasses to finish it off. Now she's a skater girl and her slight frame makes her look younger than her years.

She's stuffing her belongings into her holdall when her phone rings. *Yes! That'll be Sasha.* Her heart lifts, confident of success if there's two of them.

'Hi!' she says, cheery and expectant. There's silence on the other end and she wonders for a moment if she's lost reception. But no, the little sign shows four bars. She listens again and hears a muffled cough. 'Hello,' she says. 'Hello. Who's this?'

'Natalie.' Her name stretches out into a long, whispered sigh. 'I thought so.'

She gasps, as if she's been hit, her body tingling with a sudden slap of rage. There's no mistaking that voice.

It's Tom.

CHAPTER THIRTY-SEVEN

Then

In prison, Natalie crossed off the date on the calendar that was stuck to the wall next to her bed. It was a present from Linda, who'd been released, and showed cheeky pictures of naked rugby players. It usually made her smile, but today was different. Today she didn't even see the images.

She was like a hive of bees coming to life in the spring, everything about her buzzing. Her pulse was a bit faster, her muscles a bit tighter, her stomach not sure if it wanted to hold on to breakfast or not. But it wasn't surprising, because her efforts today would determine her future. She got her writing pad out from her cabinet.

Little Munchkin,

It's an important day today because if Mummy passes this exam she can be a Personal Trainer. Won't that be great? It means I can earn money and buy you lovely clothes and toys and take you on holidays to fun places and get us somewhere nice to live. It's the start of our future, Harry, a future that is only eleven weeks away now. Oh my goodness, how slow the time is going, but the thought of us being together has driven me on, even on those dark days when every movement was like wading through treacle, my mind overflowing with everything that could go wrong. Days when even breathing seemed too much effort. The thought of you stopped me from giving up, Harry. You are my world, my life, my everything.

Wish me luck, little munchkin.

'Are you ready?' Mali poked her head round the door, her face looking drawn, shadows under her eyes, like she hadn't slept too well.

'Just finishing this off, won't be a sec.' She signed the letter 'Mummy' and added hugs and kisses along the bottom of the page.

'We can't be late or they won't let us do the exam and then it'll all be for nothing.'

'Don't be daft, they can't start without us. There's only you and me doing it. It's not like GCSEs, you know.' Natalie checked her watch. 'Anyway, there's plenty of time. It doesn't take half an hour to get to the gym, does it?'

She tucked her writing pad in her locker and flipped her thoughts to the exam, her mind crammed to overflowing with acronyms and medical conditions, Latin names for muscles and bones. *Please let me have done enough.* Her lips moved in a silent prayer, asking for help to remember as she slipped her feet into her trainers, hands shaking so much she could hardly tie the laces.

'Okay,' she stood up and stretched to ease out her back muscles, 'let's go then.'

The names of body parts streamed through her head as she followed Mali down the hall and she'd managed to work her way up from the feet to the lower back when she felt a tap on her shoulder. She tensed and spun round. A knot tightened at the back of her neck when she saw that it was Beryl, the prison officer.

Beryl never had good news. She was doing a stint on the Wing now and if she turned up, it was always with a warning. Something to do with Katya. Or Mags. The leaders of two warring factions within the prison, who both thought Natalie had access to over a million pounds and wanted a slice. But since Mags had been stuck on the Wing and Katya was still in the Unit, they often sent little messages via other women. Reminders. And Beryl would warn Natalie when someone difficult might be heading her way.

The idea of danger was a constant companion, sitting alert at the back of her mind. She watched and avoided, never allowed herself to be on her own with anyone, and attended the twice-weekly self-defence classes like a true disciple. Mali's crew had become her crew and they kept each other safe. So, on the whole, apart from a couple of skirmishes, life had been manageable.

Thankfully, Katya had remained in solitary confinement, regular reviews deeming her too unstable to mingle with other prisoners and Mags had been released two months ago. Since then, the choppy seas of prison life had taken on a new calm and Beryl hadn't pulled Natalie aside for several weeks.

'Just wanted to give you a heads up,' Beryl said, quietly.

'I've got an exam.' Natalie's mouth twitched as she watched Mali disappear down the stairs. 'I'll catch you up,' she called and turned back to Beryl, frowning.

Unusually, Beryl had a broad grin on her face. 'Good news for you, love. Katya's being transferred to Rampton.'

'Rampton?'

'Secure psychiatric hospital.' Beryl laughed. 'She got her lawyer to make a fuss about being in solitary for so long. Said it was against her human rights. So the Governor pulled a blinder and got her admitted to Rampton. She's off today sometime.'

Natalie's eyes widened. 'What? Really?'

Beryl grinned. 'Good news, eh?'

Natalie leant against the wall, her legs suddenly weak. 'Wow, that's just... it's...' She started to giggle.

'I know,' Beryl said. 'Exactly how we all feel about it. Anyway, don't want to keep you. Thought you'd want to know.'

Footsteps thundered up the stairs and Mali emerged, glowering. 'Natalie, what the fuck! We're going to be late.' She stopped and stared, eyes sliding from Beryl to Natalie and back again.

'Thanks,' Natalie said, her throat clogged with delight. 'You've made my day.'

'Made mine too.' Beryl laughed and made a shooing motion with her arms. 'Go on then, off you go.'

Natalie raised her eyebrows at Mali and hurried her down the stairs.

'So, what the fuck was that about?' Mali murmured.

'Good news. Tell you later,' Natalie said as they were met by another prison officer in the hall, ready to escort them to the gym.

The gym was housed in a Victorian red-brick structure with concrete columns holding up an entrance portico. An inscription, '*Ludis Pro Omes*', roughly translated as 'Sport for All' was carved in the stonework. Imposing double doors led into a square entrance hall and three doors led off this into the changing rooms, an office and the gym itself. The gym reminded Natalie of the assembly hall at her old school and was one large room, with a wooden floor marked out for different sports, and a raised stage at one end, which was sectioned off for gym equipment such as treadmills and loose weights.

'Okay, here we are then,' the prison officer said as she unlocked the door. She looked at them both and laughed. 'Don't look so worried, girls, I'm sure you'll be fine. The less you worry, the more you'll remember. That's what I've always found. And anyway, if you cock it up, it's not the end of the world, is it? You can always have another go.'

'We're going to do this, aren't we?' Mali said, voice wavering.

'Hell, yeah.' Natalie pushed Mali into the hallway, the door locking behind them. 'No stopping us now.'

But there was something stopping them.

A figure blocked their way, a sly smile on her face.

Natalie stared and wondered if she was seeing things. Mali grabbed Natalie's hand, tremors transmitting themselves from Mali's body all the way up Natalie's arm. She swallowed and remembered all the stories she'd heard over the last year. A level of brutality that she hadn't wanted to believe, but had been forced to accept was true.

It had been a long time since she'd seen her, and she looked thinner round the face, but she'd never forget those eyes. Such a dark brown they were almost black, and they were looking at Mali now, like a hawk latched on to its prey.

'Hello, girls,' Katya drawled. 'I've been waiting for you.'

CHAPTER THIRTY-EIGHT

Now

The sound of Tom's voice, familiar and unexpected, vibrates through Natalie's mind, setting off an avalanche of emotions. Her scalp feels tight, as though her skin has shrunk. Her teeth grind together.

'How did you get my number?' Her voice is low, accusing.

'My secretary gave it to me, said you'd rung a couple of times. Told her that it was a personal matter.' He gives a mirthless laugh. 'Then somebody said they thought they'd seen you on the island. I put two and two together, worked out it was you.'

I've been seen?

Her mind searches through the possibilities and she realises that it could be any number of people. People she's met on previous visits, people who work in Douglas. Or was Tom at the gig and she hadn't seen him? A weight settles in her stomach. Maybe she hasn't been as covert as she'd thought.

She can hear the quickness of his breath in her ear. *Is he nervous? Worried, maybe?* Seagulls screech in the background. *He's outside?* She looks out of the bedroom window, scans the promenade but can't see him or the silver estate.

'So… um, how can I help you?' She tries to make her voice sound curious, light, as if her trip to the island is of no consequence to him. She cringes. Even to her ears it sounds ridiculous.

'Oh, Natalie.' His voice is soft, wheedling its way into her mind, triggering memories of love and gentleness. *It's not real,* she tells herself, a sour taste in her mouth. *Don't let him fool you. It was never real.* He sighs. 'Let's not play games, Natalie. I know why you're here. Doesn't take a genius to work it out.' He sounds tired and she wonders if this could be an opportunity rather than a disaster.

'Are you okay, Tom? You sound a little… stressed.'

'Ha!' He starts to cough and it's a moment before he comes back on the line. 'Look, Natalie. I'll be straight with you. I can't cope with any more complications.' His voice cracks. 'Not at the moment.'

He sounds weaker than she'd imagined and she remembers what Jack had said about his marriage breakdown. Her hand tightens round the phone. She takes a breath and extracts the fury from her voice. 'I just want to see Harry. Please, Tom. I don't want any trouble. I just want to see him.' She sounds pathetic and feeble, no threat to anyone. But it goes against every grain of her being to have to beg to see her own son, the child she grew inside her, gave birth to and nurtured until he was stolen. Her body shakes with the effort of pretence.

'Natalie, look, I just want to say…' He gives another sigh. 'I'm sorry about… you know… about everything.'

She sucks in air.

Did he just apologise?

For a moment, she's floating, like a balloon that's been left to drift into the sky. *Sorry? Like I've lost a fiver on a bet?* She closes her eyes and puts a hand to her throat, strangling the urge to let three years' worth of anguish blast across the airwaves. He has no idea, not an inkling of the pain he's put her through. And now he thinks saying sorry will mend the cracks in her heart, fill the holes in her memory, where her son's childhood should be? She smacks the wall behind her with her fist.

'It wasn't… I didn't think…' Sadness drips from his voice and she can almost see his eyes, moist with tears. She hears him clear his throat before he comes back on the line. 'Natalie, please believe me when I say I never imagined things would play out the way they did. Honestly, I didn't. And if I could have my life again, I'd do things differently.'

The sincerity in his voice is a surprise and her mind picks at the possibilities. *Can I talk him into a meeting? Choose a place where I have a chance to get away without anyone seeing. Worth a try,* she decides. Her pulse quickens.

'Let me see Harry, then.' Her voice quivers. 'Please, Tom, let me see him.'

'No. I'm afraid that won't be possible.' He's regained his composure now, his voice clipped and resolute. 'Look, you need to leave the island, Natalie. My solicitor told me that the conditions of your parole mean you shouldn't be here. My next call is to the police, then you'll be back in prison. Is that what you want?'

Her body tenses from head to toe. *I knew it! I knew that's what he'd do.*

'And anyway, you're too late.'

'Too late? What do you mean?'

'We'll be gone tomorrow, so there's no point you being here.'

'Gone?' Her voice rises to a squeak. 'Gone where?'

'Somewhere you can't reach us.'

'I'll always reach you.' The threat is clear and she knows it to be true, knows she'll go anywhere, do anything to get her son back in her life.

'Not on Dad's estate, you won't.'

Which estate? she wonders, knowing that there are at least three.

'Dad's ready for retirement and I'm taking over the running of his business. I wasn't going to leave quite this soon, but…' He sighs. 'Life takes turns you don't anticipate.'

Kuwait. They're going to Kuwait. That's where his father's business has its headquarters and she thinks of the tight security around his father's compound, in a land that ensures women abide by a different set of rules. She sinks onto the bed, rocking backwards and forwards, arms hugging her body. *If I don't get Harry today, I may never see him again.* Her head seems to swell with the thought, as if it might explode.

'No! Tom, you can't!'

'I don't think you can stop me, Natalie.'

A sob fills her throat so she struggles to speak. 'Haven't you put me through enough already?'

The silence is long enough for her to rock her emotions into submission and she starts to wonder if he's still there. She grits her teeth. *He hasn't left the island yet,* she reminds herself, *there's still time.*

When Tom speaks again, his voice is more gentle, weary. 'I know it's been tough for you, Natalie. But you've got to understand that Harry's… well, he's not your son anymore. That's the reality. He doesn't know who you are. Doesn't even know you exist.' His words pierce her heart, draining the blood from her face. 'You don't need to worry about him, though. He's happy. A real daddy's boy, as it turns out. It's probably…' He lets out a long breath. 'Look, it's probably best if you just forget about him. Make a new start. You're still young enough, aren't you? Just forget and move on.'

Forget? Natalie's head rattles with rage. *How are you supposed to forget that you have a son, for Christ's sake?*

'I'm sorry, Natalie. Believe me. I am.'

'But you didn't even want him!'

'Things change. You of all people must know that. We spend a lot of time together, me and Harry. I love him more than life, Natalie.' He sounds like his teeth are clenched together. 'More than bloody life. And his happiness is why I'm leaving. It's all about him. Everything.'

Natalie lets out a silent scream. Tom has just articulated her own feelings in relation to Harry and in doing that, he's taken something from her, stolen an element of her confidence that what she's doing is right. If Tom's going tomorrow, then maybe Harry will be safe with him. *Maybe it's the best thing. Lech won't be able to get him in Kuwait.* In a couple of years she'll be completely free to go where she wants. She can visit.

But I'll be even more of a stranger.

It's not something she can contemplate. And anyway, how can Tom keep him safe when he won't acknowledge the threat from Lech?

Maybe he'll listen now. But she knows in her heart that he won't. When Tom's made his mind up about something there's no persuading him. And it's a long time between now and tomorrow, time enough for Lech to grab Harry. *He'll be safer with me,* she decides.

Her fist goes to her temples as she tries to compose herself for one last effort at persuasion. 'Just let me see him, Tom. Just see him, nothing else. I just… I want to know what he looks like. Don't you think I deserve to know that? What my own son looks like?'

Tom's breath crackles down the phone. Natalie waits, eyes squeezed shut, willing him to agree.

'I'm in the skatepark.'

Her heart skitters. 'Skatepark? Which skatepark? Where?'

'Peel. End of the promenade. If you can be here in fifteen minutes, you can see him. From a distance. Try to get close and we're out of there, you understand?'

CHAPTER THIRTY-NINE

Now

All Natalie can hear is silence. Tom has gone.

She can't begin to think this through, the urge to see Harry stronger than the need to breathe. Tom doesn't usually get upset, and he's as fragile and vulnerable as he's ever going to be. *So maybe I can persuade him to give me and Harry a bit of time together?*

She dashes downstairs, out of the front door, and turns right along the promenade towards a small headland, knowing this must be the right direction because she went the other way this morning and definitely didn't pass a skatepark. A few minutes later, she reaches a substantial Victorian terrace of red sandstone properties. Where these end, there's a sandstone wall, hiding a bowling green that can be glimpsed through a round opening, like the doorway to a hobbit home. At the end of the wall, three feet above the pavement, there's a mesh fence, enclosing a couple of tennis courts and then, metal railings surround the skatepark.

Natalie holds her breath as she slows and creeps along the pavement, like a wildlife enthusiast sneaking up on a rare animal. She crouches down and peeps through the railings, can see a half-pipe and a couple of curved ramps, then a smaller ramp, with flat, gentle slopes and on the other side of that is a large area of tarmac, the remnants of a basketball pitch, a couple of rusted hoops still in place.

A small boy, looking unsteady on a shiny Spiderman scooter is riding around, nobody else in sight. And there's Tom, sitting on a set of steps that run up to a path on a higher level, which leads to the top of the headland. The boy has to be Harry. Her heart clenches and releases as if it has forgotten how to pump blood round her body. She tries to breathe, but no air goes into her lungs. *Harry.* The moment she has longed for is here and now it doesn't seem real, feels like she's watching a movie, distanced from the action by a screen of disbelief.

'Watch me, Daddy!' Harry's voice is shrill with excitement, as he perches on top of the lowest ramp, waiting for Tom to turn and look. 'Watch me!' But Tom is on the phone, staring towards the horizon, having a heated conversation and Harry can't wait.

Natalie ducks down, so Tom can't see her, but she can see her son. Tears sting her eyes and she blinks to clear her blurry vision as Harry zooms down the ramp and hurtles towards her, making motorbike noises. Her heart lurches as she drinks in every feature of his face. A face that looks nothing like her composite picture, the one she has adjusted like a fine oil painting over the last three years.

There's no mistaking that he's her son, though. Her breath falters as he comes closer. At first glance, he appeared to be a mini Tom, his face a genetic copy of his father's, his hair short and blond, slightly wavy on the top where it has been left a bit longer, but as he gets closer, she can see that his mouth is more generous, like hers, his eyes a little further apart. And the closer he comes, the more she can see herself in him, in his expressions.

He's perfect. My little boy.

She stands up, like a jack-in-the-box and he stop a few yards away, staring with big round eyes. For a moment, she has no idea what to say, has no clue how to speak to a child who has just turned four, having little experience to draw on. Then she remembers all the children's programmes she's watched in prison, can hear the presenters talking, all over-jolly, smiley and wide-eyed and she copies them, focusing on the only thing that she knows for sure about this little boy.

'Hello, Harry!' She gives him her broadest smile and looks into familiar hazel eyes. Her eyes. She has to take a moment to compose herself before she can speak again, emotion filling her throat. 'Is that a new scooter? Did you get if for your birthday?'

Harry carries on staring, but now there's a frown on his tanned face, his mouth pressed into a thin line. She studies him, heart hammering in her chest, waiting for that moment, the one she has fantasised about, when he realises who she is and his face breaks into an ecstatic grin and he runs to her, desperate to be in her arms. But there's not a hint of recognition, not even a flicker. She feels weak, dizzy, her dreams of their reunion shrivelling inside her until they are nothing but dust. For a moment, she can't think, can't move, unable to believe that he doesn't know who she is. *He's too far away,* she tells herself, separated as they are by the railings.

Inside him there'll be a knowledge of me, she reassures herself, some primitive recognition of familiar pheromones, the sound of her voice, the feel of her hand, the smell of her. *If I can just pull him closer, get him into conversation, maybe get to touch him, hug him, then he'll start to remember.* Her throat is tight, her breathing shallow and she can feel her chin wobbling. *No, no, no,* she reprimands herself. *No crying. Keep it cool.*

She broadens her smile but Harry is losing interest in her and starts to shuffle his scooter round, ready to head off.

'That was so clever, Harry. Can you do any other tricks?'

He looks back at her and nods.

'Do you want to show me?'

He does another circuit, heading towards her and skidding to a halt just before he hits the railings, his face a picture of concentration that makes her heart feel it might burst.

She laughs and Harry gives her a little smile. *That's for me*, she thinks, *that smile is just for me*, and it's the best, most precious gift she has ever been given.

'High five,' she says, holding her hand up between the railings. He is just feet away from her now. But it's still too far.

Harry looks at her for a moment, then leans forwards and his little hand glances against hers, just for a second. She wants to hold it, feel the softness of his skin, the smallness of his fingers, the warmth of his flesh. This child's body, made from her own. She stares into his eyes, sure that now they have touched he will know who she is, but there is nothing and her heart is crushed.

'I'm Natalie,' she says, with a grin that could easily turn into a sob. It feels horrible, not being able to tell him she's his mummy, but she can't risk confusion and doesn't want to frighten him away. *Later, I can tell him,* she thinks, but what she needs to do now is get him to think of her as a friend.

She glances over at Tom, startled to find he is standing now and staring at her. Their eyes meet, her heart beats faster.

'Harry! Harry! Come back here.' Tom's voice is stern. 'What did I tell you about talking to strangers?'

Natalie's hopes tumble inside her, crashing to the ground as Harry runs to his father, who picks him up.

Harry looks over his shoulder at her, bottom lip poking out as if he's about to cry.

'But you weren't watching,' he says, in the pouty little voice that children use when they believe life is being unfair to them. 'And I did a really good trick, and the lady said it was so good. And asked me to do another one.'

Tom glares at her. She can't move. He storms over to the fence, puts Harry down and points to the scooter. 'Pick that up,' he says to Harry, who obeys. Tom leans down and gives his son a quick hug and a kiss on the top of his head, his voice gentle now. 'You go and play over there—' he points to the tarmac area '—while I have a chat with the lady.' He says 'lady' with a thick coating of distaste. Harry does as he's told, and pushes himself along, motorbike sounds revving again, the whole incident forgotten, along with Natalie.

She closes her eyes, battling to keep her composure and when she blinks them open, Tom's crouching down, clutching the railings, his face level with hers.

'Nice try, Natalie. Well, you've got what you wanted. You've seen him.' He gets his phone out of his pocket. 'Now leave before I call the police.'

She doesn't move, staring at Harry, telling him in her mind how much she loves him, her heart shredded by his indifference. Tom starts to dial. Natalie jolts to attention. Panic scatters her thoughts. She turns and runs.

CHAPTER FORTY

Then

The hallway of the prison gym felt suddenly cold. 'Katya,' Natalie said, trying to keep her voice steady. 'What are you doing here?' *Didn't Beryl say she was being transferred to Rampton today?*

She looked over Katya's shoulder, eyes searching for Fran, the woman who'd been teaching them, but the gym doors were open and the room was empty. That was odd. She should have been here by now, was always here before them. And where was Kirsty, the prison officer who managed the gym? *This feels all wrong*, Natalie thought. Hairs prickled on the back of her neck.

The three of them stood in silence, like mime artists in a tableau. Natalie waited for Katya to answer her question, senses alert, listening for sounds that would tell her that everything was normal. But all she could hear were her own shallow breaths. She noticed that Katya's gaze was focused on Mali, whose face had gone pale, a sheen of sweat visible on her forehead. She grabbed Natalie's hand, like a child reaching for its mother.

'Come on, ladies, let's have a little chat in here, shall we?' Katya said as she pushed open the changing-room doors. A false smile spread across her face, like an advert for toothpaste. Natalie could feel Mali's hand slipping from her own. She clasped it harder.

Mali moved backwards a step, then another, pulling Natalie with her. *Can we call the prison officer?* Natalie wondered. She'd only just gone and couldn't be far away. Then Mali bumped into the door and Natalie heard the lock rattle in its housing, a solid, final sort of a sound. A quick glance over her shoulder reminded her how thick and heavy the doors were. She swallowed. Nobody was going to hear them through those.

Mali whimpered. Katya had an amused gleam in her eyes, like a cat playing with its prey. *We're trapped,* thought Natalie, her heartbeat slow and heavy like the drumbeat that signals doom in a horror film.

'Jackie!' Katya called. 'Come out here, there's a good girl.' She sounded like she was calling a dog and they turned to see a woman standing in the doorway to the office. Big and square, she almost filled the opening. Her head was shaved, tattoos covering most of her scalp and down her neck. Her arms were as thick as Natalie's thighs, ending in meaty hands. She looked more like a man than a woman, her features prominent and heavy. Jackie smiled at them, an empty grin, her eyes just slits in the fat of her face. There was something about her expression that didn't look quite right, but there was no doubting her role in this scenario: she was Katya's enforcer.

Mali kicked the door, a donkey kick, as hard as she could, and started yelling for help, her fear transmitting itself to Natalie with every shake of her body. Katya laughed and Jackie joined in, the sound of her laugh high-pitched and ridiculous, like a hyena. Natalie felt sick. There was nowhere to hide, nowhere to run, nobody to help. They were on their own and Mali had turned from leader of the gang into a gibbering wreck.

It's up to me. Natalie's heart clenched. *I'm going to have to get us out of this.*

She thought back to her schooldays, before she'd met Sasha, when she'd won as many fights as she'd lost and had learned to look after herself out of necessity. Hanging out with Sasha had stopped the bullying and somewhere along the line, she'd forgotten how to be herself. She had allowed herself to live in the shadow of others, relying on them for her safety.

Until now.

Now there was nobody to hide behind.

Do not let fear dull your reactions. Isn't that what their self-defence instructor had taught them in their very first lesson? *Be the master not the victim.*

Natalie squared her shoulders and took a couple of calming breaths.

'What the hell's going on?' she said, keeping her voice light, thinking there might be a chance to talk their way out of trouble. 'We've got an exam in ten minutes. Can this wait till we've finished?'

'Just chill, Nat, you're safe,' Katya said. 'It's Mali here that I need to have a chat with. But you can come too if that'll make her feel better.' She stared at Mali, hate in her eyes.

Natalie frowned. *Did she mean it? Am I really safe?* A voice in her head told her she wasn't, Beryl's warning running on a loop in her mind. *These people are not your friends.*

'I've not done nothin',' Mali said and wedged her body behind Natalie's, using her as a shield. Her hands pressed against Natalie's back, her breath hot against her neck.

Natalie scanned the hallway, remembering the CCTV camera. Surely someone would be watching and would see what was happening. She looked up at the ceiling, her throat tightening when she saw that the camera lens had been broken. But there had to be a prison officer somewhere in the building. Maybe she'd popped to the loo or something, would be back any minute. So, if they just waited…

The silence ticked on for a few long moments until Jackie moved out of the shadows of the doorway and crunched her knuckles, like they do in films when they're getting ready for a fight. That was when Natalie saw the smudge on the front of Jackie's white T-shirt. A blood-red smudge. Her chest tightened as the last vestiges of hope were wiped from her mind, allowing her to see their situation with startling clarity. She had to assume the guard was out of action. Their exam was supposed to be an hour long, so the prison officer wouldn't be back for them before then. So, at least an hour until somebody turned up.

A lot can happen in an hour.

A chill crept through her like an invasive species, colonising her mind with premonitions of disaster. She took a deeper breath, and another. *There's no way I'm getting hurt*, she thought, pushing her panic down deep inside. *I've got to get through this for Harry. Play along*, she told herself. *It might be a storm in a teacup. Might be nothing.*

'Okay, so here's what we're going to do,' Katya said, as if she was talking to a couple of five year olds, her voice full of forced merriment. 'We're all going into the changing rooms.' Her eyes narrowed. 'Any problems, then Jackie will sort them out. Okay, ladies?' She clapped her hands together. 'Come on! We haven't got all day.'

CHAPTER FORTY-ONE

Now

Natalie runs back to Mary's house and dashes up to her bedroom, every nerve in her body on fire with the need to do something. *Tom's ringing the police.* How long until they arrive? Her hands grab at hair that is no longer there, tugging at the roots. *What to do? What to do?* The main thing, she decides, is not to panic. She takes a big breath, lets it out slowly and picks up her phone. One last try at contacting Sasha, then she has to go. She listens to it ringing, not expecting a response, waiting to leave a message.

'Nat? That you?'

She jolts upright. 'Sasha! At last.' Natalie paces the floor. She can hear talking in the background, music of some kind and wonders if Sasha's on set. Then she hears a door close and the music disappears.

'Christ, Nat, what's the matter?'

'I've just spoken to Tom.' Natalie hears a sharp intake of breath.

'Oh well that's great you've made contact. How did—'

'He rang me. Doesn't matter. But Sash, the thing is…' She has to stop and steady herself. 'The thing is, he's taking Harry away.'

'No, he isn't.' Sasha sounds dismissive and Natalie wonders if she's doing her usual multi-tasking and not actually listening.

'Yes, yes he is. Tomorrow. I've got to get Harry today, Sash, or it's all over.' Natalie's voice gallops along at an ever-higher pitch. 'I'll never get him back. And then, Mary—'

'Calm down, will you?' Sasha interrupts, all stern. 'Just calm down. You're not making sense. Where's he going to be heading off to when his business is here? He's probably lying. Have you thought of that? To get you off his back?'

'For Christ's sake, Sasha! Can't you just listen? He's going to Kuwait, to take over his dad's business. And he's taking Harry with him.'

'Kuwait?'

'That's what he said. And you know what his dad's estate is like. I told you, didn't I? It's like Fort Knox, with electric fences and security guards, CCTV cameras all over the place.'

'That's what he told you? He's taking Harry to Kuwait?'

'Yes. Yes. Tomorrow. And he's going to call the police, get them to arrest me. And they're already looking for me. I've only got until—'

'Okay, okay,' Sasha says, a heavy sigh in her voice. 'Look, let's not panic. Let's just… think about this for a minute. Tomorrow, you said? So, there's still plenty of time for us to get Harry today, isn't there?' Another sigh crackles down the phone. 'Just give me a sec…'

Natalie paces and waits, her eyes focused on the view out of the window. The tide is in and a gentle wave breaks in a lazy arc on the thin line of sand. A few people are strolling on the prom. Cars trundle to and fro beneath her window. It all seems ridiculously normal, another world, while Natalie's life spirals out of control. She clutches the phone tighter.

'Sash, you still there?'

'Yep. Still here. Just thinking. Right, so I'm going to have to work out how to reschedule this evening. That's the first thing. But don't you worry about that.' She huffs down the phone. 'Honestly, I really don't care about this bloody job anymore. Getting Harry back is much more important. And after what Tom's done to you, there's no way we're going to let that bastard run off to Kuwait, is there?'

Natalie stops pacing and leans against the wall. She can feel that Sasha is committed to the challenge now, can hear the determination in her voice. And once Sasha puts her mind to something, she's a force to be reckoned with. Natalie closes her eyes and takes a deep breath. *Thank God.* Her mind stops scuttling in circles, as she focuses on Sasha's voice.

'Look, as soon as I've sorted things at this end, I'll come and get you, okay? Nobody's looking for me, so that's going to be the safest thing. And we'll go and get Harry together. Tom's no match for the two of us, is he? The thing is not to panic. I'm sure the police are busy with real criminals. They're not going to be interested in chasing you, are they? It's not like you're a bloody murderer on the loose. They'll just contact your probation officer, hand it over to them to sort out.'

She sounds so sure of herself that Natalie doesn't contradict her. Doesn't try and tell her about the incident with the buggy, or the fact that the police seem to think she's a shoplifter, or that she has until eight o'clock tonight. Her breath steadies. *Together we'll think of something.* In the past, whatever scrape she and Sasha were in, they'd always got out of it, hadn't they? She hears the bang of a door down the phone, muffled voices in the background.

'Look, I've gotta go,' Sasha says, talking so quickly Natalie struggles to work out what she's saying. 'I'll call you later, a couple of hours max. Probably sooner. Give me time to finish up here, sort things my end, then I'll be with you. I promise. Just stay put and don't… don't do anything stupid.'

Natalie smacks her forehead with the heel of her hand as Sasha disappears again. *I can't wait a couple of hours, can I?* Natalie springs up off the bed.

'I'm off now, lovey,' Mary calls up the stairs. 'Good luck. And you take care, now.'

The front door clicks shut and Natalie watches Mary cross the road and walk along the prom. Past a silver car. Her eyes widen and she takes a closer look.

Isn't that the car that was following me? Her heart jumps. Her mind tells her to run. *It's got to be Lech, hasn't it? Or is it Tom? Did he follow me back here and now he's waiting to show the police where I am?* Either way, she can't stay here.

The back door's going to be her best escape route, through the alley and up the road to the car park. Adrenaline spikes in her bloodstream as she throws the rest of her stuff into her holdall, eyes glancing round the room to check that she's got everything.

She zips up her bag and runs along the hallway and down the stairs. But she forgets that the carpet is loose on the fourth step and her foot shoots out from under her. Suddenly, she's falling through the air, arms flailing as she tries to grasp hold of the banister but she misses and her arm goes through the railings. Her shoulder is trapped as her body continues its downwards momentum.

Muscles rip, ligaments snap, tendons twist and wrench from their moorings with a searing pain that burns through her body. She screams as she tumbles and bumps her way to the bottom of the stairs, landing upside down, her body crumpled on top of her right arm. Her head spins, black dots fill her vision and for a moment, she is no longer there, no longer anywhere.

A loud knock on the front door makes her eyes ping open and she remembers. *The silver car. Outside. Police on their way.*

The handle turns and the front door rattles as someone tries to get in.

Get up! Get up! she shouts in her head, but when she tries to move, pain scorches through her, blasting its way through damaged nerve endings. She retches onto the carpet, vomit trickling down her cheek and into her ear, burning the back of her throat.

The door handle stops moving.

She can scarcely breathe. *Did he hear me?*

There's still time to escape if she can only get herself off the floor. She tries to move again, slower this time, but her body has stiffened, mutated like molten lava when it reaches the sea, and she knows it's not going to happen.

Sweat breaks out on her forehead.

The letter box clatters open and a pair of eyes peer through.

Brown eyes.

It can't be Tom. Lech's found me.

CHAPTER FORTY-TWO

Then

Natalie tugged at Mali's hand and pulled her, like a reluctant donkey, towards the changing rooms where Katya stood with a plastic smile on her face.

'Come on, Mali, it'll be fine,' Natalie said, trying to communicate with her eyes that she wanted her to play along. That they'd think of something. What else could they do? Mali dug in her heels for a moment, then relented. She frowned at Natalie, her mouth clamped shut as she traipsed behind her.

'Good girl,' Katya said. She was using her body to prop open the changing-room door and as they walked past her, the smile twisted into a triumphant sneer. She snatched Mali's hand out of Natalie's grasp and grabbed hold of Natalie's wrist, pushing Mali forwards with a swift kick to the base of her spine.

Natalie winced as Katya's grip tightened, fingernails digging into her skin. She watched, helpless as Mali staggered into the room and out of her reach. Mali turned, her eyes big and round, her face pale. She looked tiny, frightened, like a little bird cornered by a cat. Natalie chewed on her lip as her heart thumped faster. *This is bad. Really bad.* Adrenaline coursed round her body, muscles ready to spring into action, but Katya seemed to sense it and tightened her grip further. Natalie gasped. *Wait for the right moment,* she told herself because two against one were not good odds. Not when one of them was built like a bulldozer.

Katya nodded at Mali. 'You go and sit over there, on that bench.' She pointed to a long wooden seat pushed up against the wall and watched as Mali obeyed, scrunching herself up, feet on the bench, knees to her chest, head tucked down, like an armadillo rolled into a ball.

'Jackie!' Katya called and the mountainous woman pushed past them. She stood in front of Mali, shifting from foot to foot, her fists flexing by her sides.

Natalie's heartbeat accelerated. It was all happening too quickly. *Think! Think!*

But there was no time.

Before she could do anything, Katya pulled Natalie outside the changing room, waiting for the door to close before letting her go. Natalie's hand tingled and she rubbed at her wrist, flexing her fingers to get the circulation going again. She looked up to see Katya staring at her. Her muscles tightened, ready to run.

Katya's hand reached out and grabbed her shoulder, pulling Natalie into a sudden hug. She froze, her body rigid for a moment before she decided that the best thing would be to hug Katya back.

'Natalie, it's been so long.' Katya pulled away from her, hands still holding her shoulders as she stared into Natalie's eyes. She was a different woman now, the one Natalie had thought of as a friend, her voice soft and warm.

'I didn't know you were still here,' Natalie said, forcing herself to keep eye contact, making her mouth smile. 'Nobody said. I thought you were long gone. Away. Free.'

'What, get out and not tell you?' Katya sounded surprised. 'No, I've got fucking ages yet. But the good news is that I don't have to stay in this shithole any longer. I'm off to Rampton today.' She gave a harsh bark of a laugh. 'Should be a blast.' She shook her head, slowly. 'Anyway, they left me with no choice; it was today or never and I couldn't leave without saying my goodbyes to Mali.'

A crafty grin lit up her face. 'But seeing you is a bit of a bonus. 'Cos I get to remind you.'

Natalie frowned. 'Remind me about what?'

Katya punched Natalie's shoulder and laughed as if she'd told a joke. 'About our money, of course.' Her eyes narrowed and she spoke slowly, deliberately. 'When you get out, my brother Lech will find you and help you get the money back.'

There was no mistaking the meaning behind her words. Natalie swallowed. 'Right. Yes. The money.'

Katya clasped Natalie's arms, gripping a pressure point near her biceps. 'I promised you I'd help you to get your money back, didn't I?'

Natalie winced, a sharp pain darting up towards her neck, her voice rising as Katya increased the pressure. 'Yes, yes, that's right. You did.'

'I never break my promises.' Katya's fingers dug deeper.

Natalie sucked in a breath. 'No,' she said. 'Thank you.'

Katya let go and patted her on the arm. 'Good girl. I knew I could rely on you.'

They stood staring at each other for a moment.

'So, what's happening?' Natalie looked over Katya's shoulder at the closed door, trying to keep her voice even. 'Like I said, we're supposed to be having an exam in ten minutes.'

'Not going to happen.' Katya folded her arms across her chest, blocking Natalie's path into the changing rooms. 'What's happening is that I got lucky today. Finally.' Katya smiled. 'Anyway, none of this needs to concern you. Why don't you run along and wait in the gym?' She gave Natalie a push, sending her towards the open door. 'There's a good girl. Just wait until we've finished, then you can go.'

Natalie looked into the gym. She studied the familiar equipment, the mats on the floor, loose weights set out ready and felt the pull of it. *It's not my problem, is it? I've got to think about what's best for Harry, not Mali.* Her conscience stamped on the thought, disgusted with herself for even entertaining the idea of leaving Mali to her fate. She couldn't let events unfold, could she? Mali was her friend. A proper friend, and she loved her like a little sister. *I've got to try. Maybe I can talk Katya round?* Talking wasn't going to put her in danger, was it?

'But... what about Mali?' Natalie said, turning to face Katya again.

Katya's face screwed into a mask of hatred. 'That fucking little shit is going to get what she deserves.'

Natalie fidgeted with her hands. She could see by Katya's face that she was taking a risk, but she couldn't stop herself. 'She's just a kid, Katya. You've got to make allowances, whatever she's done.'

'Oh yeah. A kid who'll snitch. A kid who'll get you banged up in solitary for a fucking year and your parole revoked.' Katya's hands were on her hips, face going red, her voice getting louder and louder. 'A kid whose evidence will get another few years slapped on to your sentence.' She sneered, eyes flashing. 'Nice sort of a kid, eh?'

Natalie chewed at her lip, suddenly understanding what was going on. It was Mali who'd seen Katya attack the girl, seen her stab her in the eye with a fork. It had happened when Katya had been out with the decorating team, when she was supposed to be supervised. Nobody else had admitted to seeing anything, and Mali must have given evidence secretly, to avoid repercussions while she was still in prison. Now she understood Mali's wariness, the desire to keep a small group around her. *Bodyguards.* And Natalie had been one of them. She wondered how that placed her in Katya's eyes. Wondered what would happen if she went into the gym, on her own. *Will Jackie come for me, ready to teach me a lesson too?* Her stomach clenched.

Maybe she could stall for time and a guard would turn up. Maybe. It was her best hope.

'You must have done things you regretted when you were Mali's age, didn't you?'

'Regret?' Katya sounded incredulous. 'Oh no.' She wagged her finger from side to side, like a metronome. 'No, no, no. I wasn't allowed to regret. What I had to do was learn never to do certain things again. Mali's a kid who needs teaching a lesson.' Her finger stabbed the air. 'That's what happened to me and it's what's going to happen to her.' Katya flicked her hand in the direction of the gym. 'Now you run along. I haven't got time for this.'

Natalie locked eyes with Katya for a moment and knew there was nothing more she could say, nothing that would change Katya's mind. She turned and walked into the gym.

What choice have I got?

She heard the changing-room door close and paced the floor, hands tugging at her hair as she tried to work out what to do. Raised voices made her stand still. A scream jangled her nerves. Then another. *Christ! That's Mali. I can't leave her, I can't.* Whatever the consequences, she had to try and stop whatever was going on in there. *Can I bribe Katya with the promise of more money?* Money that didn't exist, but she wasn't to know that.

Natalie ran into the changing room, hands flying to her mouth when she saw Mali lying on the floor, her face covered in blood. Jackie aimed another kick at Mali's head, her booted foot finding its target with a sickening thud. Mali groaned. Natalie gasped and pressed her back against the wall.

'I thought I told you to stay in the gym,' Katya said, slow and menacing as she walked over to where Natalie was standing. 'But I guess you want to watch.' Jackie aimed another kick. Mali grunted when it connected with her skull. She looked in a bad way, blood pooling under her head from a wound Natalie couldn't see, her face puffy and red, one eye almost shut.

'Stop it!' Natalie shouted, trembling from head to toe.

Instinct took over. She was sensitive to every movement, every sound and the world was stuck in slow motion. She saw Katya's expression change, saw the punch coming towards her face and was quick to block it with her forearm. At the same time, Natalie aimed her own quick punch at Katya's throat.

Katya let out a gurgled cry and staggered backwards. Natalie pounced. Her knee jerked hard into Katya's stomach and she crumpled, sucking in air. Natalie sidestepped her, dashed forwards and launched a sweeping kick that caught Jackie behind the knees, felling her like a tree. She crashed to the floor, her head hitting the edge of the bench as she dropped. She rolled from side to side, letting out staccato moans, like a chainsaw that wouldn't start, her hands holding her head, eyes squeezed shut.

Both of them down.

Natalie couldn't believe her luck. Breathing hard, she hunched over Mali, stroking her hair away from her face. Mali's mouth moved but she was unable to speak.

'Ssh, ssh,' Natalie said. 'It's okay. I'm here now. I'm going to get help.'

Mali's hand clasped Natalie's. Her open eye swivelled from side to side, and at the same moment that Natalie realised it was a message, a warning, a kick landed on the back of her head. Lights exploded in front of her eyes, and she sprawled forwards, her body slamming into the wall with a force that shuddered through every part of her.

It took a few seconds for her to gather herself.

A few seconds too long.

Katya jumped on her back, and pulled Natalie's hair with both hands, forcing her head backwards. A searing pain tore at Natalie's scalp, a ferocious scream ripped up her throat. *I won't let her win,* she told herself as she tensed against the pain. *Think about Harry. Win for him.*

'You stupid bitch!' Katya snarled. 'Why couldn't you just do what you were told, eh? Let us get on with the job and get out of here.' She banged Natalie's head against the floor in time with each word. 'Stupid. Stupid. Bitch.' Pain speared through Natalie's face and blood gushed into her mouth, clogging her throat. She coughed and spluttered, spitting blood so she could breathe, sure that her nose must be broken.

Katya tightened her grip on Natalie's hair.

'No, Katya. Please, no,' she begged, afraid there was more punishment to come. She glanced across at Mali, whose eyes were now closed, her breathing shallow and ragged. The pool of blood formed a red halo around her head and was growing bigger by the second.

'Please what?' Katya said, her words laced with a rage that Natalie couldn't begin to comprehend.

In that moment, Natalie understood. *There is no logic. No reasoning with her.* She wasn't going to stop. There was nobody coming to help. This was a fight to the end; it was her or Katya. One of them was going to die.

Harry.

The thought of him cleared her mind and she knew what she had to do. As soon as Katya tried to bang her head down on the floor again, she pushed herself backwards with all her strength, screaming through the pain as a clump of hair ripped from her scalp. Katya tipped forwards and her face smacked onto the floor, her body immobile for a moment. The only moment Natalie was going to get.

She rolled over and scrambled onto Katya's back, lying on top of her, holding her down with her body weight, pushing Katya's head against the floor with all her strength. But Katya was bigger, more solid than Natalie and she writhed and squirmed, trying to shake her off. A feral scream bubbled in Natalie's throat as she hung on, but it was like wrestling with a crocodile and it was only a matter of time, seconds, before Katya would break free.

Natalie's eyes raked the room for a weapon, something, anything, but the place was empty, everything bolted to the floor. The only loose object was Jackie's fleece, lying on the bench, and that wasn't going to hurt anyone.

Katya bucked, a powerful, sudden movement, the unexpected force sending Natalie falling sideward onto the floor. But as she fell, and Katya tried to push herself up onto her knees, she managed to wrap her legs round Katya's body, trapping her arms by her sides. She squeezed with all her might, grunting with the effort, her body slick with sweat. Katya clawed at her legs, her ankles, long fingernails gouging her skin. Natalie clenched her teeth, and focused her energy into her legs, squeezing and squeezing as hard as she could. But she knew she couldn't hold on for long, and with every second, her strength was fading.

Katya twisted and squirmed, biting any piece of flesh she could reach. Natalie tried to squeeze harder, but it was no good, Katya's arm was nearly free. *Do something! Do something!* Natalie snatched at the fleece, and flicked it over Katya's head. She twisted the arms of the jumper round each hand and pulled, while Katya writhed and spluttered as the cloth tightened around her neck.

CHAPTER FORTY-THREE

Now

'Natalie! Bloody hell… don't move. I'm coming around the back.'

It takes a moment for Natalie to realise that she knows the voice. And it's not Lech. It's Jack.

Am I safe? The back door opens and closes. *Or are we both in danger?*

Footsteps tap on the kitchen lino and the tiles of the hall. Then Jack is there, squatting by her head, stroking her hair and making shushing noises. She realises that she's whimpering and tries to stop, but the pain is insistent, relentless, and she can't.

'Hey, hey, it's okay,' he says. 'Good job my shifts got changed. You could have been stuck here for hours. Anyway, I've called an ambulance. Should be here soon.'

An ambulance.

So, what does that mean? Her thoughts tangle together like clothes in a washing machine. *Is it all over?*

The throbbing in her shoulder thumps along at a steady rhythm. Her eyes close and she breathes through her mouth, just as she was taught when she was giving birth. It helped then and it helps now, focusing her thoughts on nothing but her breath. She is aware of a damp cloth gently wiping her face, a hand stroking her hair, murmured words that she can't quite decipher. And all the time she waits for a bang or a crash, something to tell her that Lech has arrived. Because that's surely what's going to happen. *Any minute now.*

'Okay, love, can you hear me?' A new voice in her ear, loud and bossy. It startles Natalie out of her nether world and she opens her eyes to see a young female paramedic looking down at her, brown hair tied back in a short ponytail. Earnest grey eyes study Natalie's face.

'Just got to check you out,' she says.

Natalie hears Velcro tearing apart, something bump on the floor. Then another face looms over her, a middle-aged man with a shaven head, grey stubble on his jaw.

'Can you tell us what happened?' he says, all matter of fact. A light shines in her eyes.

'I…' Natalie's voice is a croak. She swallows and gives it another go. 'Shoulder,' she says, squinting into the light. 'Left shoulder. Caught in the railings. Fell down stairs.'

'Okay, love, now this may be uncomfortable,' the woman says, 'but I need to check you over before we can get you moved. Just be a couple of ticks.' She gently probes Natalie's body, from the head downwards and when she gets to her shoulder, Natalie slips into blackness.

She is vaguely away of being moved, rolling along on a stretcher, being loaded into the ambulance, people talking, injections. Drifting in and out of consciousness.

Nothing.

Then something.

The world is too bright, everything a blur, her eyelids so heavy they keep dragging themselves closed again.

'Hey, sleepyhead.' A man's voice, but Natalie can't reply. She appears to be in a different timescale, a step behind reality, aware of her surroundings but not in them. Her head is full of cotton wool, muffling the sound of her thoughts.

'Natalie, can you hear me?' A different voice, a woman. 'You're in Noble's Hospital.'

Natalie starts to remember what happened and her pulse quickens. She wonders if Tom went through with his threat. Do the police know she's here and it's just a matter of time until she's arrested? She forces her eyes to open, tongue licking dry lips as she tries to focus on her surroundings.

'Let's get you sitting up,' the nurse says as she adjusts the bed, fussing about with pillows. She hands Natalie a plastic cup of water and watches, hands on hips, while she takes a sip. Then another. She fights to get herself back to the present, her mind wandering around like a lost child, but once she's drunk all the water and has filled her lungs with a few deep breaths, she begins to feel more awake. Her thoughts get themselves organised, speed up. *I'm still free. And I can call Sasha to help me get Harry. I just have to get out of here first.*

'So,' the nurse says, 'you've dislocated your left shoulder, got a nasty bump on the back of your head, cracked a bone in your left hand and you're going to be pretty sore for a few days.'

Natalie looks down and sees her arm is in a sling, her left hand strapped up tight, touching her right collarbone.

'You've been given morphine for the pain and you were sedated while they popped your shoulder back in.' Natalie frowns, wondering how they did that without her really noticing. 'You'll have to wear the sling for three weeks and then you'll need physio to strengthen the muscles round the joint, just to make sure it doesn't pop out again.'

No, no, no! She shivers with a sudden chill.

'It's not so bad,' the nurse says, reading her expression. 'You'll soon get back to normal. But you need to rest for a few days. Let everything settle down.' She looks at Jack and smiles. 'I'm sure this lovely man of yours will look after you.'

That's when Natalie notices Jack, sitting in the chair next to the bed. He grins at her.

''Course I will,' he says. 'When can I take her home?'

Natalie's breath catches in her throat. *Home?* She doesn't have a home. *Does he mean Mary's?* She swallows. *Lech might still be there. Waiting. Or the police.* That's the last place she can go.

The nurse looks at her watch. 'I'll just check with the doctor. Back in a tick.'

Jack takes hold of Natalie's hand and squeezes. She squeezes back, without thinking, trying to work out what needs to happen next. She has until eight o'clock, then Mary will call the police. Which Tom might have done already. And Lech is out there somewhere, hunting her down. *He might be waiting outside the hospital. Or inside.* She shivers again and scans the room.

She has to get Harry today. But how is that going to happen when she's trussed up like a chicken? Even with Sasha's help, it's going to be nigh on impossible. She slumps into her pillows as the question rushes round her mind, looking for an answer that isn't there.

Half an hour later, when Jack wheels her out of the hospital to a waiting taxi, she still hasn't worked out a plan. The painkillers have made her woozy, her thinking disjointed. A knot tightens in her stomach.

'Where to?' the driver says as Jack gets in beside her. He starts to give Mary's address.

'No!' she shouts, surprising everyone, including herself. She can hear herself hyperventilating.

Jack gives her a sideways glance. 'Just a mo,' he says to the driver, who sighs and taps his fingers on the steering wheel. Jack turns to look at her, eyebrows raised.

'I can't…' Natalie says.

'You can't what?' Jack's voice is gentle, full of concern.

She stares at him for a moment, eyes wide. 'Stairs. I don't want to go up or down those stairs.'

'Oh, right.' His hand rasps over the stubble on his chin. 'Fair enough. Hmm.' They sit in silence for a moment while he thinks. 'Now I don't want you getting the wrong idea,' he says, shifting in his seat so he can look at her properly. 'But you can come and stay with me if you want.' He wags a finger at her. 'As long as you promise, no funny business.'

There's laughter in his eyes and her body sags with relief. She didn't see that one coming but it's not a bad idea. In fact, it's a great idea. *Who would think of looking for a fugitive in a prison officer's house?* She feels safe with this man and her heart gives a little flutter at the thought of spending some time with him. Although it won't be for long. Just until she can get Sasha to come and collect her.

'You can stay a few days, if you want. Till you feel better.' He looks hopeful. 'I've got plenty of space. Nice spare room.'

'Are you sure?' she says. 'I don't want to be a nuisance.'

'To be honest, it'll be nice to have some company.'

She gives a tentative smile. 'Okay then.' She allows herself to sink back into her seat, feeling the warmth of his body next to hers, so comforting, then her eyes are closing, lids so heavy.

After what seems like seconds Jack pats her on the knee. 'Here we are Natalie. Home sweet home.'

CHAPTER FORTY-FOUR

Now

So, where the hell is she?

Last thing I see is someone being loaded into an ambulance. I tried calling A & E but they have nobody of her name on their records. So, I'm thinking, what the hell? She must be using a false name, which could be anything. Can't even begin to guess.

Then I have to go and sort out some other bloody stupid problem, which takes hours and means a complete change of plans. Everything brought forward.

I don't know if she's still at the hospital.

I don't think she's dead. I'd feel it if she was. And if she's not dead, she's not very well, is she? Hospitals kick people out so fast these days. If she's not dying she'll be back at that guest house. Her stuff must still be there.

Yes.

I'll just have to be patient.

CHAPTER FORTY-FIVE

Now

It turns out Jack lives in a bungalow, on what looks like a housing development for the elderly. His place is tucked in a corner at the end of a cul-de-sac. Semi-detached with a neat lawn and flower beds at the front, a drive and garage to the left-hand side with a tall wooden gate leading into the back garden.

Jack helps Natalie inside, holding her good elbow like she's a geriatric. He leads her into a living room, which looks like it was last decorated in the seventies. A brown patterned carpet covers the floor, matched with green floral wallpaper and a faded pink sofa, two armchairs to match. An electric log-effect fire sits in a pretend-stone fireplace. Horse brasses hang in neat lines on either side of the fake chimney breast. The musky smell of incense hangs in the air. She sniffs. *Patchouli?* Three guitars are propped in a corner by the window. Pages of sheet music are scattered on the floor. A coffee table is littered with crisp packets, a pizza box and a collection of empty beer bottles.

No girlfriend then, she thinks as she glances round the room again, unable to reconcile the house with the man.

'Let's get you settled on the sofa,' Jack says, propping her in a corner with a variety of cushions, before draping a tartan blanket over her legs. He beams down at her. 'There you go, snug as a bug in a rug. I'll just er… tidy these up.' He gathers an armful of bottles and she sees a blush creeping up his neck. 'And… um. I'll get us a drink, shall I?'

He hurries out of the room before she can ask him about her phone. Because that's what she needs; more than anything else, she needs to phone Sasha, fill her in on what's happened and get her to come and pick her up.

She throws the blanket off her legs, and struggles to an upright position, no intention of relaxing because there's no time for luxuries like that. She has to find her bag. Her head swirls and she thinks she might be sick, or faint. Maybe both. She leans forwards, willing her brain to sort itself out. *It's the medication, of course it is.* But how long will that take to go out of her system? She's so far from fighting fit that any chance of getting Harry seems laughable. Except it's not funny. Not when his life is in danger. It's a disaster.

Stop it! she scolds herself. *Just get a grip. Where there's a will there's a way.* And Sasha's in perfect working order, so there's still a chance. She sits up, slowly, the dizziness gone for now. *One step at a time. Find the phone.*

Jack returns with mugs of hot chocolate, rather than the tea she was expecting, and sits in the armchair next to her.

'Thought you might need a chocolate fix after all that,' he says as he hands her a large mug, his eyes meeting hers for a second before flicking away. 'Got to apologise for the state of the place.' He looks around the room and pulls a face. 'Don't really see the mess until I have visitors. And I know it's a bit dated but… well, it was my grandad's house. Left it to me when he died.' He sighs. 'It's been a couple of years, now, but, I'm not ready to let him go just yet.' Jack blows on his drink and takes a sip. 'I miss him.'

Natalie can't look at him because she knows what it's like to miss someone you love and she doesn't want to cry. She needs to keep herself alert, not wrapped up in self-pity; an indulgence that can suck hours out of your life, days even. Time is marching on and she's got things to do. She thinks again about ringing Sasha. Then realises where her phone is.

'Jack?' She smiles at him. 'I don't suppose you know where my bag is, do you? Is it still at Mary's? It's just, I've got to ring my friend, you know the one I'm supposed to be meeting up with tonight. Let her know what's happened.' She takes a gulp of her drink in the hope that the sugar will start to counteract the drugs.

He frowns. 'Oh God, yeah, still at Mary's, I'm afraid. But don't worry, I'll nip down and get it for you when I've finished this, if you like?'

'Oh, would you?' Her smile broadens. 'Oh, I'd be so grateful. She's such a worrier and she'll be beside herself if I don't turn up and she can't get hold of me.'

'No problem,' he says. 'Only take ten minutes there and back. Not far at all.'

They sit in silence for a few minutes, until she asks about his grandad and he tells her about his family, losing his dad when he was young. His mum, a nurse, worked shifts and he spent a lot of time with his grandparents as well as with Mary, his friend's nan, who picked them up from school every day. He moved in with his grandad a few years ago, when he'd started with Alzheimer's, and had cared for him until his death.

His voice is melodic, soporific and she loses track of the conversation, silences opening up when she should be saying something. She struggles to keep her eyes open. Her thoughts weave in and out, blurring round the edges and seconds later, she's asleep.

Natalie wakes, hot and sweaty, immediately aware that something is not right. *What am I doing lying down?* She throws off the blanket and scans the room, eyes searching for a clock, heart jumping in her chest. *Harry. I've got to get Harry.* She has no idea what time it is, but guesses she must have been asleep for a little while. The smell of food fills the air, tomato and garlic and cheese. She hears singing, a guitar playing and decides Jack must be in the kitchen.

Has he been to get my bag? Surely he will have done by now?

There's a fierce, burning ache in her shoulder and her hand, a throbbing at the back of her head and she needs a minute to psych herself up before she can even consider standing. Then she's on her feet, swaying towards the door.

The floorboards creak as she pads down the hall, using the wall for support. When she enters the kitchen, Jack looks up from where he is sitting at the table. But something has changed. There's a hardness in his eyes that wasn't there before and Natalie stops, backs away, aware that she knows very little about this man and he is, after all, a prison officer.

'Ah, Natalie.' He puts the guitar down, gets up and walks towards her.

'Oh, I was just wondering…' Her back is against the wall now, Jack towering in front of her. He's quiet for a moment, anger smouldering in his eyes. Over his shoulder, she notices a clock on the wall. *Seven o'clock. What? Oh no.* Her T-shirt sticks to her back, sweat breaking out on her forehead. An hour until Mary tells the police. *I'll never make it.*

'Okay. I think it's time you told me what's really going on.' His voice is firm, jaw set as he leans against the doorway, blocking her exit from the kitchen. His expression holds a challenge and tells her that he knows something. *Of course he does. He's been trained to know when people are lying.* Her eyes fidget as she tries to work out what to say, settling back on Jack when he speaks.

'I rang Mary to tell her you're here, and to say I was going to pick up your bag. And she told me a very interesting story.'

'Story?' Her heart starts to gallop.

'Yes. Apparently, the police are looking for you. For a number of reasons.'

Christ! Her mouth forms words that fade away before they can be spoken. She tries to come up with a reasonable excuse, but the painkillers have dulled her mind and her imagination is fast asleep.

I'm trapped. That's it. Harry's gone. Forever.

She hangs her head, her legs lose their strength and her body slides down the wall until she's sitting on the floor, convulsed by great heaving sobs.

'Hey, hey, it can't be that bad.' Jack softens and crouches beside her, a comforting hand on her back, rubbing in small circles. 'Come on, let's have something to eat. You'll feel better for some food. Then you can tell me what's going on.'

But she doesn't move, the weight of her despair pressing down on her.

Jack sits beside her, takes her hand and holds it between both of his, such a comforting gesture that she has to swallow back a fresh swell of sadness.

'I'm not going to judge you, Natalie,' he says, softly. 'I just want to know what's going on. Be straight with me, so I know how to help you.' His hand squeezes hers and she wants to tell him, feels the words forming on her tongue.

'I don't know where to start,' she whispers.

'How about you tell me why the police are looking for you?'

'But Mary's already told you.'

'Yes, I know, but I want your version. In your words.'

'I… er… I…' The words slip back down her throat. *He'll hate me when he knows.* And somehow, that matters.

'Look, Natalie, I'm a prison officer and I don't think I'm going to be shocked by anything you have to say. Honestly, you'll have to trust me on this one.'

She looks into his eyes, and realises that she has no choice. If she's to have any chance of getting Harry, she has to hope that he'll believe her and be on her side. Then he might persuade Mary not to call the police. He also has her phone and without that, she has no access to Sasha, no hope of her plans coming to fruition.

So, she tells him the tale of her sad little life, the whole story, not the abridged version she'd told Mary, words tumbling out, as she rids herself of the secrets that have been eating her alive.

'And then…' she says, as she nears the end of her story, but it's as though she has come to the edge of a cliff and can't move any further forwards. She turns her head away. Images flash in front of her eyes, and it's still too shocking, too terrible to describe. Her breathing speeds up, fear squeezing her head, tighter and tighter as she relives the most terrible day of her life.

'Hey, it's okay,' Jack says, shifting closer. He pulls her to him and she lets her head rest on his shoulder, feels the warmth of his arms encircling her body. 'It's okay,' he murmurs into her hair, his cheek resting on the top of her head. 'I don't need all the details. I get it. You've skipped parole because you want to get your son back. You've been cheated and lied to in the worst of ways. If I was in your shoes, I think I'd be doing the same thing. That's not to say I think it's the right way to do things, but, you know… I understand.'

'No. No, you don't,' she says. 'That's the problem. You're nowhere near understanding. I've only told you half the story, the easy part. You need to know about… what happened in prison. I need to tell you about Katya.'

He pulls her closer. 'Okay, well, take your time. You just tell me when you're ready.'

She takes a deep breath and starts to speak.

CHAPTER FORTY-SIX

Now

When Natalie's almost at the end of her story, she stutters to a halt, reluctant to face the final chapter. Her mental scars have been slow to heal and now that she's scratched the surface, everything she would like to forget seeps into her thoughts, filling her mind with nightmare images that she can't bear to have in her head.

She hunches over, forehead resting on her knees, eyes squeezed shut, as if that might make everything go away. But it doesn't. Silence fills the kitchen, punctuated by the sound of her shallow breaths and the ticking of the clock.

'So…' he says, gently, 'was she… did you kill her?'

Natalie presses her lips together and thinks that might have been an easier outcome to accept.

'No,' she sighs. 'No, I didn't kill her.' She talks to her knees, unable to look Jack in the eye. 'I remember being pulled off her. Prison officers everywhere. Apparently, the officer at the gym had been knocked out and tied up. When she came round, she managed to raise the alarm.'

Natalie turns her head to glance at Jack, his expression stony. *He's judging me,* she thinks. *He's going to hand me in.*

Her chest reverberates with each thump of her heart as her future, and Harry's safety, teeter on the edge of a precipice. *I've got to convince him. Got to.* She grits her teeth and presses on, knowing that her life depends on it.

'They took Katya to hospital, did everything they could, but she'd suffered brain damage. She's in a wheelchair now. Can't talk. Doesn't know where she is, or what's going on. That's what I heard anyway.' Natalie sniffs. 'And Mali, well…' She closes her eyes and she's back there, in the changing rooms, watching an officer check for a pulse. Natalie's throat tightens and she can hardly speak. 'She died. Fractured skull.'

It takes a moment for Natalie to gather herself.

'There was no CCTV footage and the only witness was Jackie, who had a learning disability. She made up a story about me starting it, attacking them all. Improbable when you see the size of the woman.' Natalie wipes her eyes with her hand. 'But, you know, it was my word against hers, and at the end of the day, I was the only one standing when the officers came in. The prison officer who'd been knocked out couldn't remember anything and with no witnesses to what happened in the changing room, it was difficult.'

Jack is concentrating so hard on her face it feels like he's pulling the thoughts out of her head, testing each sentence to see if it's the truth. She looks away and winces as she scrapes the bump on the back of her head against the wall. She stumbles on, determined to convince him that the danger is real. That things need to happen right now.

'Nobody at the prison wanted to prosecute me. But Katya's brother insisted on charges being brought. Anyway, in the end, I was charged with GBH. Excessive force used in self-defence, they said, and I had to do an extra eighteen months.'

She adjusts her position, trying to ease the throbbing in her shoulder, the soreness in her limbs.

'Apparently, Lech was furious, thought it was too lenient. Then a few months before I was due to be released, I started getting threatening letters, saying he was going to torture me and hunt down and kill Harry.

'There was a scheme to reduce prison numbers and the authorities decided to let me out a couple of months before my official date. No fuss. Tucked me away in North Wales where they thought I'd be safe. But I knew he'd find me.' She looks at Jack. 'You know what goes on. Paying off prison officers or other inmates for information.'

'Yeah.' He nods. 'Unfortunately, I do.'

'So, I had to get Harry as quickly as I could, before Lech worked out where I was. And I knew I only had a matter of days. I had tried to contact Tom, my ex, through his old lawyer. But they wouldn't listen, said I was making it all up so I could have access or something. I knew I had to skip parole if I was going have a chance of getting to him, and keeping him safe.'

'Wow.' Jack whistles between his teeth. 'That's a hell of a tale. So now you're stuck between a rock and a hard place.'

She lets out the longest breath, overwhelmed for a moment by the sympathy in his voice. *Maybe,* she thinks, grasping at the thinnest slither of hope, *maybe he'll let me go. Give me my phone. That's all I need.*

'Yeah, that's about it. And the worst thing is, Lech's been following me.'

Jack's eyes widen. 'You sure about that?'

Natalie nods. 'Well, someone followed me from Douglas to Peel, even though I changed the number plates on the car. I don't know how, but whoever it is seems to know where I am. And then, I saw the same car parked outside Mary's. It's got to be him.' Having laid it all out for Jack, Natalie's even more sure of the danger she's in and her body gives an involuntary shiver as she thinks about her narrow escape. 'I'm pretty sure he was coming to get me when I fell downstairs.'

'Christ!' Jack stares at her, frowning. 'You think so?'

'I need to get Harry safe, Jack.' She reaches out and squeezes his hand to emphasise her point, to make him feel her fear. 'That's all I care about.'

Jack stares across the room, obviously deep in thought.

'Well, I think the first thing we've got to do is tip off the police about Lech. Get him out of the picture.' He looks at Natalie. 'I can do that anonymously, if you like, through Crimestoppers.'

Natalie nods. She hadn't thought about that, and it makes sense. But getting the police involved in any way is bound to spell trouble for her at some point and she's not ready to let that happen. Not when there's still time for her to get away on the fishing boat.

'Does Tom know Lech's been following you? Surely he must accept now that Harry's in danger?'

Natalie shakes her head, grimaces. 'He won't listen to me. He'll just think I'm pulling some sort of stunt. He might listen to my friend, though. But her number's on my phone and my phone's…'

Jack looks sheepish, finishes her sentence. 'Still at Mary's, I'm afraid. I got sidetracked by food. Honestly I was so hungry I could have eaten half a cow.'

Natalie feels helpless, because without her phone, she's completely dependent on Jack as to what happens next. And all this talking isn't getting them anywhere. Who knows how long the police will take to react to a tip-off. It could be days rather than the instant response she needs. She chews at her lip, tension pulling at her injured shoulder, sending spikes of pain up and down her neck.

'There's no time, Jack. Mary's going to—'

Jack speaks before she can finish her sentence. 'Mary said she wouldn't call the police, now she knows you're with me. So, there's no deadline tonight. And Tom's not heading off until tomorrow.' Jack stands and holds out a hand to help her up. 'You should have something to eat, keep your strength up. And while you're doing that, I've got an idea I want to check out. Something I heard that may or may not be right. But it might change things regarding Tom.'

'I just need my phone, Jack.' She pleads with her eyes. 'Let me ring Sasha. You don't have to be involved in any of this, she'll come and get me. Then I'll be out of your hair and none of this will be your problem.'

He squeezes her hand. 'Look, don't worry. I want to help, okay? I'll go and get your stuff when I've made the calls.' She looks at him, trying to assess his motivation. *Is he on my side, or is he my jailor?* 'I'll only be ten minutes or so. Then we'll sort out priorities. Together. I'm not going to do anything without telling you, okay?'

His eyes shift to the side as he's speaking, just a flick away but enough to make her wonder, *Can I trust this man?*

CHAPTER FORTY-SEVEN

Now

You think everything's sorted and then wham, literally, as it turns out, you have a different mess on your hands.

But it's definitely sorted now. And Harry's tucked away, ready, so I don't have to worry about that. Just her to think about.

Oh-oh, wait a minute.

Might have been a bit ahead of myself there. I do believe I heard something.

Yep, still gurgling.

Ha ha! Die a slow and horrible death, you pathetic bastard. Thought you were so big, didn't you? Someone to be frightened of. Oh, how the mighty are fallen.

CHAPTER FORTY-EIGHT

Now

Jack sits at the kitchen table with a notepad and pen, trying to sort through the muddle of information that Natalie has just dumped in his brain. It was quite a tale, that's for sure, and he wants to pick out the key points, so he can decide what to do for the best.

He's brewed himself a mug of coffee in the hope that a double shot of caffeine will get his mind focused and he sips it now, as he doodles on a blank sheet of paper, waiting for it to work. It's a bit late for coffee, but he has an inkling that he's going to need all his wits about him for quite a few hours yet because, at some point, in one way or another, shit will definitely hit the fan.

He's finally persuaded Natalie to go and rest in the lounge, and she's had a painkiller, which he hopes will make her drowsy and give him a bit of space to think. He can't make the phone calls with her listening. Wouldn't want her to think that he doesn't believe her story. Because he does, doesn't he? He thinks about the pain in her voice, that look in her eyes and knows that, to Natalie, her story is real. He runs a hand through his hair. *That's not the same as it being the truth, though, is it?* People start believing all sorts of things because they can't face reality. He's seen it at work. Many, many times.

But...

He taps his pen on the table while he thinks. And he comes back to the same conclusion. She's convinced him, right enough, but he'd be an idiot not to check it out before he calls in the troops.

With half his schoolmates employed in one line of public service or another, he doesn't want to be the butt of their jokes.

He imagines the smirk on Dan Corlett's face, standing in the pub telling anyone who'll listen what a jerk Jack is. How he let another woman make a fool out of him. Honestly, he quite liked the guy at one time, but since he's been promoted to sergeant, he's become a proper pain in the arse. Good at his job, all right, but that doesn't mean he isn't a tosser.

Jack finishes his coffee and starts to write, mapping out the main elements of Natalie's story, the chain of events. Then he makes a list of the things he needs to check out. Things that will make the police want to listen.

His sister, Fliss, works at the Treasury, in the tax department. And he's sure she mentioned an investigation into dodgy accounting practices with one of the wealth management companies. It's the biggest case she's dealt with and she was excited about some new piece of information that had made her case watertight. They were planning to make an arrest within days. Obviously, she couldn't say who they were after, but he has an inkling that it might be Tom. Just something she said that's made a connection in his mind. And it would explain Tom's rapid exit to Kuwait. A country which has no extradition treaty with the UK or the Isle of Man, where it would be easy to hide under his father's protection. So, if it is Tom they're after, he needs to tip off the police so they'll pick him up tonight.

The Katya and Lech side of things can be checked out by Ben, Jack's workmate. He's a sound guy, a proper friend, who won't ask too many questions and anyway, he owes Jack a favour or two. Jack knows that he's on security tonight, and it goes quiet after lock-up, so he'll have a bit of time to do the research. Shouldn't take long. And a bit more background on this Lech character will make it easier for Jack to get the police to take seriously the threat to Natalie's life, and that of her son.

Oh, and he needs to tell Mary not to go home just yet. Just in case. Lech might still be staking out Mary's house and it would be terrible if she got mixed up in this somehow. He'll do that first.

The other thing to check out is the car number plate. Natalie managed to remember it. It's Manx, so it shouldn't be too hard to trace. Probably a rental, but he's learned from experience not to make assumptions. Obviously, it would be an easy thing for the police to check, but he's not going to make that call to Sergeant Tosser until he's got all his ducks lined up in a nice neat row. His mate, Toby the Geek, should be able to get the info for him, no problem. He likes a bit of a challenge.

Jack looks at his list and puts down his pen. That should do it.

He goes to check on Natalie before he starts making his calls and smiles to himself when he finds she's already asleep. Her face, when relaxed, with all the worry smoothed out, is so striking, with those high cheekbones and her generous lips. So lovely, he wants to reach out and stroke her cheek, brush away her pain. He tucks his hands in his pockets and watches for a moment, heart swelling with a new determination to sort out this mess and help her in any way that he can.

He's not sure why he's such a sucker for a damsel in distress, but it's always been that way with him. A soft touch, his sister says. He reminds himself that things have never ended well, but bats the thought away. *The past is no predictor of the future.* That's what he tells his youngsters in prison. It's what his mum has always told him. And that's what he's going to believe.

He creeps out of the room, and closes the door behind him. Then sits himself down at the kitchen table and picks up his phone. It takes almost half an hour before he ends the last conversation and his mind purrs along like a well-tuned motorbike, now that caffeine and adrenaline have combined into a super-fuel for his brain.

It's a shame he couldn't get hold of Fliss, but he knows she'll ring back as soon as she can. His mates think he's gone a bit mad, given the story that he's just told them. Only part of the story, mind. Nobody knows the whole thing. It's not his story to tell, is it? He's just given enough to get the help he needs. Snippets, like parts of a crossword puzzle.

So…

He flicks the point of the pen in and out, in and out. There's nothing more he can do. His worker bees have their tasks and he just has to wait.

But he can't.

Retelling the story has increased the sense of danger that sits on his shoulders, urging him to do something.

He decides to go and get Natalie's stuff from Mary's, because they need her phone. He checks that she's still asleep. *She won't even know I've gone.* But he writes a note and puts it on the kitchen table under her packet of painkillers. Just in case. Then he puts on his leather jacket, grabs his helmet and sets off, closing the back door as quietly as he can behind him.

Five minutes later, he parks his bike in the alley behind Mary's house, finds the spare key under a flowerpot, where it's always been hidden, and lets himself in while his thoughts speed round his mind like bikes on the TT course. Questions and answers. Questions and answers.

It gives him heart that Mary believes Natalie's story and has agreed to stay with her daughter for the night. He might have joked that she was daft, but really he knows Mary's a shrewd lady and he'd trust her judgement over his any day of the week. His mates took a bit more convincing, though, and he supposes it does sound a bit melodramatic. But then, they haven't met Natalie, can't see how much she hurts inside or feel the fear that radiates from her. You can't fake that.

She lied to me. He presses his lips together and forces himself to address the challenge. *Not about things that matter,* he decides and carries on with his task.

He finds Natalie's bag, tumbled to a halt at the bottom of the stairs and checks her bedroom to make sure she hasn't left anything.

He can't resist a peep out of the window, looking up and down the prom but he can't see a silver estate of any make.

So if Lech isn't here, where the hell is he?

The question repeats itself, making him take notice. Natalie said Lech seemed to know where she was all the time. *A bug of some sort?* But Jack knows nothing about these things. *Maybe he knows where Natalie is now.* Jack stops, eyes wide, then hurries down the stairs. *Nah, no way can anyone know where she is.* Unless... He sucks in a breath. Unless Lech was waiting outside the hospital and followed them back to Jack's. It's not impossible. Jack wasn't watching, wasn't checking behind them, unaware that it might even be a possibility at that point.

He locks the back door, stashes the key and jogs back to his bike, Natalie's holdall slung on his back, like a rucksack. His pulse races. He scans the alley. Nobody there.

His phone tweets and buzzes and he looks at the screen before answering.

'Yeah, Ben. Got to be quick, mate.'

'Right. Okay. So, Lech Wozniaki is in HMP Manchester. Serving life for attempted murder. He was sent down a couple of weeks ago and won't be out for at least twelve years.'

'What?'

'Yeah. Definitely the same guy. Sister Katya is in a home in South Manchester.'

'You're sure about that? He's definitely in prison?'

'Yep. One hundred per cent. Nasty bastard. Tried to kill one of his prostitutes. And because he's a repeat offender, he's not likely to get out on licence.'

Jack whistles through his teeth. 'Okay, well, thanks for that, mate. I owe you one.'

They say their goodbyes and Jack sits on his bike. He rubs his chin, fingers pulling at his stubble. *So, if Lech isn't the one following Natalie, who is?*

CHAPTER FORTY-NINE

Now

Natalie wakes with a start, so stiff she can barely move. She feels woozy, like she's been drinking and it takes a moment to remember.

I'm at Jack's house. Safe.

She leans back against the sofa. A heavy ache makes her left shoulder feel twice its usual size. Her broken hand throbs and a pain spears the back of her head.

The house is silent. Too silent and she senses that she's alone.

She frowns while she listens for a moment.

Nothing.

She creaks across the hall and into the kitchen, little half steps because her hips don't want to move. The effort of walking pulls at nerve endings and she whimpers, like a hinge that needs oiling. *Don't be pathetic*, she tells herself, but it makes no difference.

Her packet of painkillers is propped in the middle of the table, next to a glass of water and she lurches towards them like a traveller in the desert who stumbles across an oasis. She fumbles the packet open, presses a couple of pills into her hand and swallows them down. It's probably too soon to be having more, but the last one has worn off already and if she's going to achieve anything at all, she needs the pain to go away.

She leans on the table, wondering how long they'll take to work. That's when she sees the note, written in a scrawl that any doctor would have been proud of.

Gone to get your stuff from Mary's. Be about 15 mins.

He's even put a time on it. She looks at the clock. He left ten minutes ago. She does a double-take when the time registers in her brain. Eight-forty. *Already?* The day is about to disappear and she's achieved nothing. *But Jack might have done,* she reminds herself and wonders what calls he's made, what he's found out. Thinks that it's kind of him to want to take an active part in a melodrama that's none of his business.

It's a bit odd, isn't it? Her hand pulls at her hair as a thought hisses through her. *Oh no! He's going to hand me in.*

She stands up, fully alert now and convinced that she's right. Why wouldn't he? It's the sensible thing to do. *I can't let that happen. Can't give up. Not without a fight.* She has to at least try things her way, doesn't she? Even with her injuries, she hasn't given up the hope that she can find a way to get Harry and take him to safety.

Sasha will help me. Her eyes widen and she feels in her back pocket for her phone. But it's not there. Just the piece of paper with Tom's address on it. She slaps her forehead with the palm of her hand. *Dammit! Phone's still at Mary's.* Yet again, Sasha's help is out of reach. In fact, all help is out of reach without her list of contacts and a means to get hold of them.

He'll be back anytime now.

I've got to go.

She looks at the address again. *I can walk there, can't I?* Thank goodness she didn't tell Jack she knows where Tom lives. It'll take him a while to work out where she's gone and by then, God willing, she'll be off the island. Exactly how that will happen, she has no idea. But she has to believe in herself. In her ability to think her way out of trouble.

And if it all goes wrong, the outcome can't be any worse than Jack's plan, can it?

She looks at the clock. Fourteen minutes since he left. Her heart picks up a pace. She takes a couple more painkillers and hobbles to the back door.

The back garden is unremarkable, a square of lawn bordered with overgrown flower beds, edged by a high fence. A gate leads to the front of the house and she's about to open it when she stops and recoils as if the latch has burnt her. *Lech might be there!* She'd almost forgotten about him in her haste to get away and she peeks through the slats of the gate. A few silent moments slide by before she allows herself to go through.

The evening is grey, the air full of drizzle, a sea mist that tickles her face and muffles sound. She flattens herself against the side of the house, her senses fizzing as she sneaks forwards until she has a view of the cul-de-sac. There's nobody about, all cars parked in their respective driveways. Nothing suspicious.

She's aware of the sound of her breath, heavy and laboured. All going to plan, she reassures herself.

Tom's address is short and easy to remember, the route there fairly simple from the centre of Peel. But she doesn't know where she is, doesn't know which direction she needs to go in. She dithers, sweating now. She's got to move, get away before Jack gets back. *Turn right.*

Every step makes her wince, but as her muscles warm up and the painkillers kick in, her aches dull to a manageable level. Her pace quickens as she turns corners, hoping to find a main road and somebody to ask for directions. A car door slams, a shout, the murmur of voices coming towards her. She crosses the road. A motorbike growls out of the gloom, swooshes past and disappears into the mist that envelops everything. *Was that Jack?* She hurries on.

A few minutes later, she finds herself at a roundabout, next to a pub and a row of shops. There's a convenience store that's open, bright lights drawing her towards it like a moth to a flame.

It's a small, narrow shop, crammed full of everyday necessities. There's a chiller by the door with sandwiches and drinks. And at the till, a young girl chats about the weather as she deals with an elderly lady. Natalie waits.

'I'm over on holiday for a few days,' Natalie says. 'And I want to look up my friend. I've got her address, and she explained where it is, but… well, I've got myself a bit lost and, to be honest with you, I haven't a clue where I am!' Natalie pulls a face, like she's stupid and the girl laughs. 'Do you think you could you give me directions?'

'No problem,' the girl says. 'We deliver papers all round here. So, what's the address?'

'Ballamona Cottage?' Natalie scrunches her face. 'I'm sorry, that's all I've got.'

'Peel?'

Natalie nods. 'Yes, that's right.'

The girl shakes her head, slowly. 'Sorry. Doesn't sound familiar, I'm afraid.'

'I checked on the map and it's off Poortown Road. But I don't know where that is.'

The girl's face brightens and she laughs. 'This main road out here is Poortown Road. Peel to the right. I know there's a few cottages dotted about, all the way along. Probably one of those.'

Natalie can picture the map in her head and she smiles. Down the main road for a mile or so and then turn right. Simple.

'Brilliant. Thank you, so much.' She leaves the shop, wanting to run, but unable to manage more than a brisk walk. *Not far, not far.* She urges herself on. *Fifteen minutes, tops.*

There's nothing to hear but the sound of her footsteps. Nothing to see but the mist. A few cars travel past and she flattens herself against a hedge every time she hears an engine, turning her back to the road. Just in case.

Soon, her hair is plastered to her head, her clothes damp and she's glad when she reaches the lane that leads to Tom's house.

There's renewed purpose in her stride and a few minutes later, she comes to a wonky wrought-iron gate, hung with a wooden sign that tells her she's found the right place. A curved drive leads to a shabby two-storey cottage that used to be white but is now flecked with green algae, paint peeling off the window frames. It's set in a scrubby lawn, edged by a tall, unkempt privet hedge. Large trees tower over the entrance, like sentries, the thick foliage creating an oppressive gloom. Water drips off the leaves, punctuating the silence.

Natalie shivers, her wet feet starting to go numb. She'd expected some sort of mansion, instead of this grotty little house and she wonders, for a moment, why he's living here. The curtains are closed, but lights glow from the windows. Her heart stutters. *This is it. He's home.*

Her eyes scan the house and garden, looking to see if there's another entrance, checking out places to hide. She sees something that draws her eye, making her take a second look. The back of a car. A silver estate. Parked in front of a garage.

Natalie sucks in a breath. *It's the same one.* Which can mean one of two things. Either Lech has beaten her to it. Or it's Tom who's been following her.

She moves behind the hedge, where she can't be seen, shuffling from foot to foot to keep warm as she tries to work out what to do. If it's Lech, she needs to go back and get Jack. Get the police involved, no question. Harry's safety has to come first. But if it's Tom's then that's a different matter.

Her thoughts are disturbed by a rustle behind her. Then another. *Footsteps?* The hairs stand up on the back of her neck. Adrenaline surges through her body.

She readies herself and turns.

CHAPTER FIFTY

Now

When he's almost home, Jack's phone buzzes against his chest. He waits until he gets to his driveway, and finds that he's missed a call from his sister.

'Hey, Fliss,' he says, when she answers. 'Got news?'

'There you are! I'm dashing out, so this has got to be quick.' She sounds out of breath, her words rushing over each other, as though she's keen to find out what her little brother needs from her so she can get on with her evening.

'So, it's about your big case – the fraud one you've been working on. I... well, I need to ask... Is it someone called Tom Wilson that you're investigating?'

'He's a person of interest.' She goes all proper, official. 'As is his wife. And that's all I can say.'

'Oh, come on, Fliss. Give me a little more than that.' Jack's voice is pleading. 'Don't play the big sis thing. I understand confidentiality just as well as you do, you know. And I can tell you that there's a child's life at stake here.'

'Okay, okay, keep your hair on.' She takes a deep breath. 'So. We think they're involved in skimming off clients' money. We're talking millions here. And filing false tax returns. She's a company director, even though she's not involved in the day-to-day running of things. More of a schmoozer, recruiting new clients, that sort of thing. There's some dodgy history over in England to do with him too, but we haven't got to the bottom of that yet.' Fliss is silent for a moment. 'Don't you dare repeat that. None of it. Not to anyone, okay. I'll be in so much trouble if—'

'Oh, Fliss,' Jack says gently. 'You know you can trust me. Anyway, who would I tell?'

Fliss sighs. 'That woman you've got staying with you, for one. You can't tell her you got any info from me, okay?'

'Yeah, yeah. Cross my heart and hope to die.'

Fliss tuts and he can imagine the pursed lips, a frown that makes a deep groove between her eyebrows. *What does she expect if she treats me like I'm a five-year old*, Jack thinks.

'So, what now?' he says.

'Well, I had to report the information about Tom Wilson threatening to leave the island to my boss. And things have gone into overdrive. He's asked me to go back into the office this evening. So, I'm thinking that things are going to happen pretty quickly.'

Jack thinks for a moment. 'But what if he was lying to Natalie? What if he's already off the island? He could be hundreds of miles away by now.'

'Oh, he's not gone anywhere. His passport and his wife's have both been flagged at the airport for a couple of weeks now and security at the ferry has been on alert as well, just in case. As I understand it, the police are organising a warrant for their arrests. That's why I've got to go in, you know, to make sure all the evidence is in order.'

'So, when do you think they'll go and get them?'

'Tonight, that's for sure. The authorities can move pretty fast when they need to. Maybe in the next hour, or so. That's what my boss reckoned, but he's a bit over-excited at the moment, so…'

'Wow, as soon as that?' Jack is eager to get off the phone now. 'Fliss, you're a star. Thanks.'

He disconnects before she has a chance to say goodbye, his thoughts scrambled.

Is it better for Natalie to have a conversation with Tom before or after he's arrested? And if his wife is going to be arrested too, does that give Natalie custody of Harry? Maybe there isn't a rush at all, now he knows that Lech isn't even on the island. He sighs. What a mess! Best thing is to talk it through with Natalie, see what she wants to do. But they'll need to make a decision fast.

CHAPTER FIFTY-ONE

Now

Natalie spins on her heel, thinking about the best means of attack, given her limitations. Her heart leaps like a trampolinist who's lost their rhythm, but when she sees who's behind her, she straightens up, hand to her chest and heaves a big sigh of relief.

'Christ, you frightened me.' She takes a few ragged breaths and leans back against the hedge, legs shaking. 'Phew.'

Sasha stands in front of her, dressed in a black tracksuit and trainers, hair tied up in a messy bun, no make-up on and she looks as jaded as Natalie feels.

But at least she's dressed for action, ready to help.

'Thank God you're here.' Natalie says. 'I was panicking a bit, wondering how I was going to get Harry on my own. I mean, look at the state of me.'

Sasha's eyes travel up and down Natalie's body and her hand goes to her mouth, eyes wide. 'Bloody hell, Nat, what the hell happened?'

Natalie takes a big breath. 'It's a bit of a long story. But there's no time to go through it all now. Someone's been following me and… I think it might have been Tom.'

Sasha frowns. 'Tom? Why would he be following you?'

Natalie puts a hand to her forehead, trying to think against the thudding pain. 'There's no time to explain, you'll just have to take my word for it. But the thing is, I think Harry's in danger. We've got to be quick.'

Sasha's frown deepens. 'I'm sorry, sweetie. But you're not making any sense. Someone following you? Don't you think that's a little, well… melodramatic?' Her face is full of concern. 'I really don't know what's going on here, Natalie, and I'm not exactly sure what you're planning, but you don't look as though you're fit for anything.' She gives a reassuring smile. 'And anyway, Harry's fine. I've been watching the house for a while now and I saw him.'

Natalie absorbs Sasha's words. *Harry's fine.* So the silver car must be Tom's. And Lech is nowhere in sight. Maybe she is being melodramatic. Maybe Lech doesn't know she's here after all. She lets out a long breath, her muscles sagging with relief.

She gives Sasha a feeble smile. 'Sorry, you're right. Just a bit worked up. It's been a hell of a day. But boy am I glad to see you.'

'Yeah, well, the producer's PA came up trumps for once and found the address. And when I couldn't get hold of you on the phone, I thought I'd come here. Suss out the lay of the land for you.' She steps forwards, and folds Natalie into a hug. 'The main thing is you're here now and so am I. So… we can get this whole thing sorted, can't we?' She squeezes Natalie, sending shards of ice-cold pain shooting down her arm.

Natalie groans, gasping as she tries to breathe through the pain and Sasha lets go, steps back, a horrified look in her eyes.

'I am *so, so* sorry, Nat. I thought it was your hand that was injured. I didn't realise you'd knackered your shoulder as well.' She shakes her head and grimaces. 'You poor thing. Christ you're a right old mess, aren't you? Lucky I'm here to help.'

She catches hold of Natalie's good hand. 'Anyway, the thing is, I've spoken to Tom.' Natalie's breath catches in her throat. Sasha nods. Her eyes gleam, a satisfied smile lighting up her face. 'I hope you don't mind, but I thought I could be like an intermediary, you know? Anyway, the upshot is, Tom wants a word with you.' She starts walking towards the driveway, beckons with her hand. 'Come on, let's go and talk this through.'

Natalie doesn't move. Her eyes narrow. 'It's not a trick, is it? He's not playing games? Got the police on standby or something? It's just… he wasn't too accommodating when I saw him earlier.'

Sasha closes her eyes for a moment then turns and walks back to Natalie, her voice soft when she speaks. 'Look, sweetie, it's probably not my place to say this, but somebody has to. I'm really not sure you've been thinking straight. Surely talking things through has got to be the best way forward, rather than trying to kidnap your son?' She gives a slow shake of the head. 'It's only going to lead to more trouble, isn't it? And think about Harry, he'd be so scared.'

Natalie's eyes flick to the ground, as her earlier doubts about her plans resurface, and Sasha carries on speaking.

'Maybe he's been gambling again or something? Got himself into financial trouble, like last time?'

Natalie looks at the house and suddenly, it all makes sense. *That's why his wife is leaving him. That's why he lives in a shithole.*

'But he's going to Kuwait,' Natalie says. 'To work for his dad. Any trouble here can't reach him there.'

'Look, maybe I shouldn't have, but I confronted him about it, said Harry would be better living with you than a gambler.' Natalie's eyes widen. 'And he admitted that he needs to escape, quickly, before the authorities catch up with him.' Sasha squeezes Natalie's hand. 'I honestly think this is the best way forward, sweetie. He seems open to negotiation and when I suggested letting the lawyers talk about access, you know, sorting it all out properly, well, he agreed.'

Sasha looks pleased with herself now, and Natalie can't quite believe what she's managed to achieve. If she's being honest with herself, her idea to take Harry and escape is a non-starter now, given the extent of her injuries, so maybe Sasha is right. Maybe talking is the best way forward.

Harry is safe. That's the important thing.

Sasha seems so sure, she's got to believe it's the truth. So now she just has to worry about herself, because safe is the last thing she feels. *Tom's in there. He wants to see me.* The thought of another face-to-face conversation with him makes her stomach quiver and she starts to work out what she wants to say.

There's a chance this might just work out okay, isn't there? A small glimmer of hope burns in her heart.

'Come on,' Sasha says, taking her hand. 'I'll be there as well, so you don't need to worry. It's two against one.'

Natalie stops. 'But what about his wife? Isn't she here?'

Sasha shakes her head. 'Oh no. Apparently she left a couple of weeks ago. There's only Tom to worry about.' She squeezes Natalie's hand. 'Don't you worry sweetie, we've got this. And if you feel uncomfortable at any time, then we'll revert to plan A, okay?'

Natalie nods and follows Sasha down the drive, past the garage and round to the back of the house where a kitchen extension runs across the width of the building. A patio door stands open, and Natalie follows Sasha inside, into a long, dingy room that smells musty and damp. Natalie scrunches her nose. There's another smell as well, pungent, like a bin that needs to be emptied.

Old units line the walls, the veneer chipped and peeling in places. The worktop is faded and worn. A square wooden table is pushed against the far wall, a washing basket on top of it, piled high with crumpled laundry. In the corner stands a huge, American-style fridge freezer, its doors covered with a child's pictures, secured with colourful magnets.

Harry's pictures.

Natalie is so focused on the pictures that she doesn't look where she's going and stumbles over something on the floor. She staggers a few steps, slams into the table and cries out, shaken by the jolt, shocked by the pain that whips through her.

'Ooh, careful,' Sasha says, making a grab for something on the worktop.

Natalie looks to see what she tripped over and struggles to breathe.

Tom lies on the floor, on his side. His outstretched hand is only a couple of feet away. That's what she stumbled over. His eyes are wide and staring, glazed over now and devoid of life. Blood is pooled under his head, still wet around his nose and mouth.

She understands what the smell is now. He's soiled himself. Her stomach heaves and she vomits on the floor, waves of nausea emptying her stomach until there's nothing left but bile.

She looks up to see Sasha holding a carving knife, pointed in Natalie's direction.

CHAPTER FIFTY-TWO

Now

'Wakey, wakey,' Jack calls as he pushes open the lounge door. He's halfway into the room when he realises that she's not there, the blanket crumpled on the floor. He spins round. 'Natalie!' he calls, thinking she must be in the bathroom. He listens. No reply. *Oh God, I hope she hasn't collapsed or anything.* He walks down the hall, calling her name, but the house is quiet and when he finds the bathroom empty he realises that she's gone.

He runs a hand through his hair.

How can she have gone when she can hardly walk?

A thought shimmers in front of his eyes, like a movie, playing out the worst-case scenario. *Maybe she's been taken?* Whoever was following her in the car. *That makes the most sense, doesn't it?* He scratches the back of his head. *Or does it sound like a load of made-up nonsense?* Not something he can go to Sergeant Tosser with, that's for sure. He looks at his watch and sees that he's only been out for twenty minutes so she can't be far away.

He pulls his phone out of his pocket and dials, cursing when he hears his call go to voicemail. 'Fliss, call me back. Please. I'm looking for the address of Tom Wilson, Excalibur Wealth Management. The guy you're investigating. It's really urgent so if you could ring me back, soon as poss. Cheers.'

He's certain it's the only place she can be.

Before he can move, his phone buzzes and when he sees who's calling, he accepts the call, knowing that it'll be quick. 'Tobes, mate. What you got?'

'God, that was too easy, you know, man. Make it harder next time, will ya?'

Jack laughs. 'Alright, clever clogs. So, who owns the car?'

'The car is registered to one Blue Cougar. Our very own celebrity.'

Jack frowns. 'Who? That doesn't even sound like a real name.'

Toby laughs. 'You must have heard of her, man. She's an actress. Adult films, I think they call them these days. They did an article about her in the papers when she was on that reality TV show a couple of weeks back. Don't tell me you didn't see it. Dude, she is hot! And that picture, well, it's on my wall here.'

Jack did see the picture. He remembers it well.

And his brain makes a connection that jolts through him like an electric shock.

He can't wait for Fliss to call him back.

'New mission, mate,' he says to Toby.

CHAPTER FIFTY-THREE

Now

A look of disgust twists Sasha's mouth into an ugly gash as she stares at the splatter of sick on the floor.

'Seriously? Did you really have to do that?' There's a meanness in Sasha's eyes that Natalie has never seen before, a look that suggests a dozen things she might like to do with a carving knife.

Natalie feels a shiver in the pit of her stomach. She flashes a glance at the open patio door, just for a second, but Sasha catches her eye, steps over Tom's body and closes the door, making sure it's locked before tucking the key into her pocket. Then she pulls out a chair, away from the puddle of sick, and steps towards Natalie, placing the point of the knife under her chin.

'Have a seat,' she says, walking Natalie backwards until her legs hit the chair and she has no option but to sit.

Keep calm. Keep calm, Natalie tells herself, aware that she's not going to get many opportunities to escape, and there's a limit as to what she can do with her injuries. She has to be ready for the merest hint of a chance and can't let her resolve be fractured by panic. But her body isn't listening, is nothing close to calm, and her heart hammers in her chest.

She keeps Sasha's gaze, wary of what she's going to do next, watching her jaw work from side to side.

'So, what exactly happened to your arm?' Sasha says, head cocked to one side. She runs the point of the knife down Natalie's throat until it rests in the hollow at its base. The blade drags through her skin, the point digging in when she swallows. Natalie winces. She feels blood trickle from the cut, inching its way between her breasts. The sound of her pulse fills her ears.

Without warning, Sasha punches Natalie's bad shoulder with the force of a boxer going for a knockout blow. The chair rocks back, almost tipping over before righting itself. Natalie howls, her eyes stinging but she's determined not to cry. Because crying means she's given up. And giving up is not something she's going to be doing. Not until she and Harry are safe.

Oh God, that hurts. That really bloody hurts. Her good hand clutches her shoulder and she groans inside. *It feels weird.* Knobbly in the wrong places. *Has the joint popped out again?* Whatever has happened, she knows her shoulder is now useless, that the sling has to stay in place and she only has one useful arm to fight with. Do anything with.

Sasha cackles, like she's watching a comedy act.

'Ooh, sorry, did that hurt?' She gazes at Natalie. 'Let me see… is it dislocated?'

Natalie blinks and chews her lip.

Sasha scrunches her nose. 'Now that's a bit of a disappointment, you see. Sort of slims down the options.'

Options? Options for what? A bead of sweat works its way down Natalie's spine.

'Ho hum. Never freakin' simple, is it?' Sasha shakes her head, and puts the knife back at Natalie's throat. 'I'll just have to improvise, I suppose.'

She stretches a hand to open a drawer behind her and rummages around, eyes on Natalie all the time. 'One move and this is going right through your throat, okay?'

Natalie blinks.

Sasha takes out a roll of masking tape, looks at it and scowls. 'That's no bloody good, is it?' She rummages again, pulls out a hammer and studies it for a moment. 'Hmm, this might work. I just need you immobilised, you see, while I set everything up.'

You can do a lot of damage with a hammer, Natalie thinks, wondering how she can defend herself against a tool like that. A fresh burst of adrenaline floods into her bloodstream and, after a moment, her thoughts settle, like mud in a lake, allowing her to view the situation with a new clarity.

I've got to talk to her. Because if Sasha has a weakness, it's that she always has to have the last word. And if she's talking, not paying attention, then an opportunity will surely come along.

'What have you done with Harry?' Natalie says the words without moving her lips, like a ventriloquist, no movement in her throat. 'Where's my son?'

Sasha's eyes narrow. 'Your son?' Her voice is low, menacing. The knife waves in front of Natalie's face. 'You really don't understand, do you?' There's fire in Sasha's eyes and she leans forwards until her face is inches from Natalie's. 'He's not been your son for years, you stupid bitch. Harry is my son. Mine. I'm the one he calls Mummy. I'm the one who saw his first steps, who heard his first words. I'm the one who nursed him through chicken pox and scarlet fever and all those colds. It's me he comes to for a cuddle when he's tired and upset. Me who reads to him at bedtime. You don't even know him.' Her chin quivers as she wrestles with her emotions. 'He's my little man, the child I thought I'd never have. I'm the one he loves, not you.' She hawks up phlegm and spits in Natalie's face. 'You're nothing to him, d'ya hear me? Nothing.'

Natalie recoils as the gob of spit slides down her cheek and drips off her chin. Her eyes slide towards Tom, then back to Sasha and things click into place.

Sasha married Tom?

Natalie can hardly bear to have the thought in her head, the taste of betrayal coating her tongue like poison. She clenches her arms against her chest, hands gripping each other as if she will fall out of the world if she dares to let go. Her best friend married her lying, scheming ex-husband? *Then pretended we were still friends. All those letters slagging him off. And none of it was real?*

She can feel the rage building inside her, heat in her throat, fiery words ready to blast out of her mouth. *No, no, no!* she screams at herself. *You'll make it worse. Give her an audience, that's what she likes. Use distraction as a weapon.*

She brings her focus back to Sasha, who is still speaking.

'Let's face it, you couldn't look after Harry properly. I had to come and help you, didn't I?'

Fury fizzes on Natalie's lips but she swallows it down. *Play along. Be the person you used to be around her.* After all, Sasha has no idea who Natalie is now. No idea what she's capable of. And there are no limits as to what she'll do to get Harry back.

'Only while I was poorly,' Natalie says, in a pitiful voice.

Sasha slams the hammer down on the table, leaving an indentation in the surface.

'A month! I was there for a month. Plenty of time to see what was really going on in your perfect little life. In your big, posh freakin' house with your high-flyer of a fucking gorgeous husband.'

Sasha waves the knife around as she talks, her voice getting louder. Natalie takes a deep breath. *Pick a moment,* she tells herself, keeping her eyes locked on Sasha's. *You've got one arm and you can still use your legs, can't you?*

But the knife is over her heart now. Piercing her clothes, pressing into her skin. She hardly dares to breathe and speaks in little gasps, so her chest doesn't move.

'I was exhausted, you know that. You've no idea what hard work it was when Harry was poorly.'

Sasha sneers, the knife flashing in the air again, to emphasis her point. 'Tom said you couldn't cope with motherhood. He didn't know what to do with you.'

Natalie gasps. 'What? That's not true! Tom was never there, so he doesn't… didn't know what I had to cope with. We were in separate rooms, so he could get a proper night's sleep. He didn't—'

'Oh, spare me the sob story,' Sasha snaps. 'You had your chance and you blew it.'

She delves in the drawer and her hand comes out clutching several nails. She looks at them, a slow smile creeping onto her lips. She lowers the knife. 'Yeah, I think these will do nicely.'

Images flick through Natalie's head. Terrible things you could do with a hammer and nails. She needs to act quickly. *Now!* But before she can move, Sasha drops the knife on the table, grabs a sheet out of the washing basket and flicks it round Natalie's body, strapping Natalie's arms to her chest, her body to the chair. Sasha wraps it round again and pulls it even tighter. Natalie tries to wriggle free, but can hardly move.

She's trapped.

Panic rears its head, threatening to overwhelm her in one swift gulp. She closes her eyes for a moment and sees Harry's face. *How can I let this monster have him?* She can't, not while she's still got breath in her body. When she blinks her eyes open, she feels sharper, bolder, more alive. *I won't let her win. For Harry's sake.*

Sasha picks up the hammer and starts nailing the sheet to the back of the wooden chair. Tap, tap. Bang. Bang. Bang. She whacks at the nails and each blow judders into Natalie's back, the vibrations finding their way into her shredded nerves like the worst kind of toothache. She groans and tries to lean forwards, but Sasha has pinned her tight.

'Aw, is that hurting?' Sasha's voice drips with mock sympathy. 'Nearly finished.' She gives the fifth nail one last whack and stands back to survey her handiwork. 'This is just temporary, you know. While I get the noose set up on the stairs.'

Noose? Natalie's eyes widen.

Sasha leans forwards, hands on her knees, her face level with Natalie's. 'I think it's possible that you could manage to hang yourself, don't you? Even with your injuries. It was going to be drugs, alcohol and slit wrists in the bath, but I'm not sure you could do that with a dislocated shoulder and a knackered hand.'

She's going to kill me!

Bile rushes up Natalie's throat, the chance of escape more remote than ever. It all seems surreal. *Or is she just trying to frighten me?* Her eyes slide to Tom's lifeless body and fear wraps itself round her chest. There's no doubt that he's dead. And no doubt, either that Sasha had something to do with it. And if you've killed one person, then why not two?

'Yes, I think hanging is probably better,' Sasha says. 'We'll write out a nice note. Couldn't cope with life without Harry. Couldn't face going back to prison. And that will be that.' She slaps her hands together and smiles. 'All over.'

She stands up and pouts. 'You do understand, don't you? I can't live like this, waiting to see if you'll turn up. Always thinking you'll try and take Harry away. Having you chase after us wherever I take him. Honestly, my nerves are shot to pieces.' She shakes her head. 'I have to say, I underestimated you. I thought prison would break you. I thought you'd give up, would abide by the law and leave us alone.' She gazes at Natalie. 'There is no other way, sweetie. And I think, in all honesty, death will be a blessing for you.'

CHAPTER FIFTY-FOUR

Now

Jack checks his watch again. Ten minutes since he called Toby. He paces another lap round the kitchen then rings him back.

'Got anything?'

'Nah, mate.' Toby sighs. 'Bit tricky, this one. Nothing under the wife's maiden name, before she changed her name by Deed Poll, or her married name, Sasha Wilson.'

'What?' Jack's eyes widen as he recognises the name. 'Did you say Sasha?'

'Yeah, that's right.'

Jack whistles between his teeth. *Isn't Sasha the name of Natalie's friend? Can't be a coincidence, can it?* 'Oh God, that's not good.'

'No?'

'Anything for Tom Wilson?'

'Nah, mate. Nothing under his name, rented or owned.'

'But they've got to be living somewhere?'

'Probably a private rental. That's the most likely thing. Or staying with a friend? But I wouldn't know where to start with that. All I know is that everything I would normally use has just come up with their old address, you know, his parents' house.'

Jack thanks Toby for trying and asks him to keep looking.

Is it time to ring the police? He cringes as he runs through the story he would have to tell them. And he doesn't know for certain that she's in danger, does he? But he feels it, wrapping its icy fingers round his heart. He shivers and tries to call Fliss again.

CHAPTER FIFTY-FIVE

Now

Sasha grabs hold of the chair that Natalie's sitting on and tips it backwards, so it's resting on the two back legs and starts to drag it across the floor, heaving it first this way, then that, the legs screeching and scraping on the quarry tiles. Sasha grunts with the effort and Natalie tries to make herself heavy by relaxing her muscles, but it's not working because her body has already been primed to fight.

She's going to kill me!

The words are on a loop going around and round in Natalie's head, getting louder and louder until they are shrieking at her, and she can hardly stand it. Her stomach roils and gripes and she thinks she might be sick again.

Get a grip, will you? She takes a deep breath. Then another. *Engage the enemy, isn't that what they say?*

'Sasha, stop this!' Natalie shouts. 'It's madness. Come on. It's all got out of hand, let's talk this through. Work out a solution.'

Sasha keeps on tugging, snarling like a wild animal.

Natalie grits her teeth. 'You're right,' she says. 'Harry isn't my son anymore. I can see that now.' Her voice quivers. 'I promise you, I'll just go away, leave you alone.'

Sasha stops, and the chair bangs down onto four legs sending fresh splinters of agony through Natalie's body. Sasha leans over to catch her breath, hands on her knees. Natalie closes her eyes, lets out a long, slow breath to settle her thoughts. *There's got to be a way out of this.*

Sasha straightens up, goes to the sink and runs a glass of water. She gulps it down, then pulls out a chair and sits in front of Natalie, wiping her brow with the back of her hand.

'You know, they say you should be careful what you wish for?' Sasha looks over at Tom. 'He wanted me so badly, you've no idea. He needed support and you couldn't give it, you were so wrapped up in yourself. Honestly, it was pathetic. He came to me, desperate for a shoulder to cry on, knowing that he was making a mess of everything and you weren't there to help him. And I—' her voice wavers and she stops, her mouth a thin line, eyes glistening '—I so desperately wanted a child. But… as you know, I couldn't have one. I was thinking about adoption, but who would choose me as an adoptive mother? And I just looked at you with your wonderful husband, who you didn't love and your beautiful child who enjoyed being with me more than he wanted to be with you…'

She shakes her head, lips drawn back as she sneers at Natalie.

'You always had everything I ever wanted. There I was slogging away, trying to make it in the movies and ending up doing crappy porn and you just landed on your feet. Married into a shedload of money, given a fabulous job by your husband. Wonderful house. Yet there you were, wallowing around like a freakin' beached whale, all moany and miserable, not looking after your husband or your baby. You were making both of them unhappy and I knew… I knew that they needed me.' She jabs a finger at Natalie. 'I *had* to make your life into my life. Because you didn't deserve it. And they deserved better.'

Natalie is quiet, patient as a cat, sensing that an opportunity is about to unfold.

This is it. She's going off on one, playing to the crowd.

'It was so easy to take what I wanted.' She flings her arms wide. 'So easy that I just knew it was meant to be. The cosmos was with me. Call it Karma.' Sasha shrugs and holds up her hands. 'I don't know. But Tom didn't need much persuasion, that's for sure.' Her eyes shine. 'He was so grateful I was there. So happy that I worked out how to get him out of the mess he was in.'

'Mess?' *Keep it going, keep it going.* 'What mess?'

Sasha snorts and looks at the ceiling. 'There you go, just shows how little you knew about your husband. How unaware of his needs.' While Sasha isn't looking, Natalie pushes against her bindings with as much force as she can muster.

She hears a slight tearing sound.

Did Sasha hear it too?

Natalie doesn't think so because she's still talking to the ceiling.

'I could see that as soon as I came to stay. Two days it took, for him to come to my bed.' She looks at Natalie again, a triumphant gleam in her eyes.

'No!' Natalie's jaw clenches. *They were having an affair while I was in the house.* 'I don't believe you.'

'Well, obviously there's nobody to corroborate my story now that Tom's dead.' Sasha looks at him as if to check, then sniggers and sings, 'Dead. Dead. Dead as a dodo.' She closes her eyes, wrapped in a fit of giggles. Natalie pushes against the sheet again and hears another tear.

Sasha's eyes flick open.

Natalie's heart skips a beat and she stares at Sasha, keeps her body completely still.

'You'll just have to take my word for it. Your husband had massive gambling debts. He had no idea what to do. Panicking he was, really panicking. Felt he was a failure, let his family down and all that shit.' She flaps a dismissive hand. 'Anyway, once the drugs had started working, you were even more hopeless, then you started spending money on frivolous things, and… well, he lost his patience. It took a while, of course. Rome wasn't built in a day, was it? But finally he saw that my plan was the only way out for him. And a couple of years in prison wasn't too bad for you, a palatable trade-off.' She smiles. 'Stealing money off a client and setting you up was the only way he was going to get himself out of trouble. He couldn't go crawling to his father for money, now could he? It would have killed Tom for his dad to know about his gambling. So, you see, he needed me.'

She leans back in her chair. 'I posed as you to make it look like you'd been in the office and transferred the money. Did loads of stuff to make you think you were going mad.' She laughs, a harsh, mirthless sound. 'Now I have to admit that was a lot of fun. The oxy in the tonic was a brainwave, even if I do say so myself.' She laughs again. 'I set it all up. All of it. And you thought it was Tom! I'll have to admit I had a good giggle when I read your letters.'

She gives a satisfied smile, but it falls from her lips and she frowns. 'But then I could see you were so determined to get Harry back that I started to get worried. You weren't broken at all, even after serving the extra time. I thought that was going to be the final nail in the coffin as far as your ambitions to be Harry's mother were concerned, I really did, but it seemed to make you even more determined.' Her expression turns to puzzlement. 'How could you not realise he wouldn't know you? Wouldn't want anything to do with you? Anyway, you kept telling me you'd come for him, so I had to keep in touch to know what you were planning. Very handy that was. But then they let you out early and all my plans were shot to pieces.' She throws her hands up, exasperated. 'I should have been gone before you were released, moved away where you couldn't find me. I had it all sorted. Not that Tom had a clue.'

Sasha sits back and looks down at her hands, twiddles a ring round her finger, lost in her thoughts for a moment. Natalie pushes against her bindings again and hears a ping as a nail hits the floor.

Sasha looks up.

Natalie looks down and shuffles her feet. *Did she hear?*

But Sasha's gaze shifts back to Tom. Natalie breathes again.

'Anyway. It's all history now.' She looks at Natalie, gives a dismissive flap of her hand and stands up. 'The past is the past.

And Harry's future is nothing to do with you. He's safe and sound. We've got a lovely new life waiting for us. You honestly don't need to worry.'

Sasha says it as if she's taken Natalie's favourite lipstick, rather than her son.

Words jam in Natalie's throat. She glares at Sasha, wishing she would shrivel up and die, right there, in front of her eyes. But the only person who's likely to be dying is Natalie.

Sasha paces up and down, in her element now, as the last act plays out to a captive audience.

'It's your fault he's dead, you know.' She nods towards Tom.

Natalie frowns.

'Nobody was supposed to die. Not even you.' She jabs a finger at Natalie. 'This is all your fault. You told me he was taking Harry to Kuwait.' She looks at Natalie with wild eyes. 'I didn't even know he was leaving me. Can you believe it? The sneaky bastard was just going to go. Text me when he got there or something. He knew that I had to go away to work for a few days and wouldn't notice until it was too late.'

She stops, eyes staring at the cooker, where an omelette pan sits on the hob. 'I hit him with that pan. Cast iron. Smashed his head in.' She makes it sound of no consequence, like she chipped a plate taking it out of the dishwasher.

Sasha turns, her hands balled into fists. 'But he deserved to die, you know. Making me live in a rented shithole like this because he gambled away all our money. Then—' her voice hitches '—then he thinks he can take my son away from me. The most precious thing I have in the world.'

She flicks a glance across the room.

'I put the steps up over there. Tried to make it look like he fell off changing a lightbulb.' She scrunches up her face. 'But I'm not sure it looks too convincing.'

She frowns, then smiles. 'Ooh, I've just had a better idea. Duh!' She slaps her forehead with the heel of her hand. 'Bit slow on the uptake with this one.' She walks over to the cooker and picks up the pan.

'Let's make it look like you killed him. Then it'll be all tidy.'

Sasha goes to the sink to wash her fingerprints off the pan handle and while her back is turned, Natalie pushes against the sheet with all her strength. It tears, quite a lot this time and another nail pings to the floor, the noise drowned out by the sound of the tap. Natalie lets out a slow breath, the sheet so slack around her body now, she has to hold it in place.

Wait, till you can grab her, she tells herself, knowing that she needs an element of surprise.

Music suddenly fills the room, and Sasha looks up. She reaches over and takes her phone out of her handbag, which sits on the worktop next to the cooker.

'Yep,' she says, then listens, her eyes on Natalie all the time. 'Well, just give him a snack if he's hungry… I don't mind, whatever you've got.' She nods, lips pursed. 'Well, if it's got to be Candy Crush, let him play on my iPad.' She sighs and puts a hand to her forehead. 'What? No… no, I don't know when I'll be finished. Not too long.' She looks at her watch. 'You're kidding me! I can't… right, right. Yes, I know. Yep. Okay.' Her voice rises. 'Twenty minutes? Are you serious?' She nods, teeth gnawing at her bottom lip. Her stare hardens. 'Yes, okay. Don't worry. I'll be there.'

Sasha walks over to where she dropped the knife and picks it up. 'Change of plan,' she says, walking towards Natalie, an expression of grim determination on her face. 'Turns out I haven't got time for plan A. So, we'll have to go with plan B. You and Tom had a domestic and fatally wounded each other.' Her lips are stretched into a tight line. 'So much easier, I don't know why I didn't think of it before.'

CHAPTER FIFTY-SIX

Now

Natalie yanks at the sheet with all the power she can muster. It falls to her waist, but a couple of nails hold it to the chair.

Still trapped!

Her heart flips, but her mind is focused. Because what she does next will determine if she lives or dies.

Sasha lunges towards her with the knife. Natalie throws her weight sideways.

Just in time.

Sasha misses, losing her balance when the knife doesn't hit its expected target and she stumbles, catching hold of the worktop to stop herself from falling.

Natalie curls her body as the chair crashes to the floor. She manages to keep her head from smacking against the tiles, thankful that she's falling onto her undamaged shoulder. The wood splinters and the back of the chair breaks away from the seat. *Oh, thank God!* Natalie is free and she rolls, using the momentum of the fall to get herself back up on to her knees. Just like they practised in self-defence classes.

Quick as a flash, she swivels round and kicks the chair seat towards Sasha. The wood skitters across the tiles and smacks into Sasha's shins, making her howl. It halts her for a second, enough time for Natalie to scramble to her feet, stumbling backwards as Sasha advances, lips curled in a snarl, the knife raised above her head like a Samurai sword.

'Sasha, stop it!' Natalie shouts, retreating until she is blocked by a door that must lead into the hallway. Her best means of escape.

But Sasha has no intention of stopping.

She takes a wild slash at Natalie's neck.

Aware of every twitch of Sasha's body, Natalie ducks down low, out of the way. The knife hits the door and spins out of Sasha's hand. It clatters to the floor and skids under the cooker. And while Sasha watches it fall, Natalie dives forwards, headbutting Sasha in the stomach, using all the power in her legs to push Sasha backwards, slamming the edge of the worktop into her kidneys. Sasha grunts, groans, shocked into stillness and Natalie takes her chance and dashes through the door into a narrow hallway.

She slams the kitchen door behind her and glances around, puffing and panting, her body fizzing with adrenaline. Stairs run up the right-hand side of the entrance hall, the front door is ahead of her.

She lunges towards the door, grabs the knob on the Yale lock and turns, but no matter how hard she pulls, it won't open. She grunts, frowns and pulls harder, eyes flicking around to work out what she might be doing wrong. That's when she notices the bolts, one at the top and one at the bottom.

Footsteps slap on the floor behind her.

No time, no time, she tells herself, spinning round to face Sasha, her back against the door.

'There's no way out, you stupid bitch.' Sasha prowls towards Natalie, teeth bared, panting hard, the knife in her hand. 'This is going to end right now.'

Natalie's heart stutters, like an engine that's run out of fuel. Her chest heaves. She can't keep this up, knows that at some point soon, the pain will win.

She dodges towards the stairs, but Sasha is quick, and before she knows what's happening, Natalie's legs are taken from under her by a swift kick and she smacks to the ground. The confined space makes for an awkward landing, and she ends up on her back, like a beetle, unable to right herself.

'Ha ha! Look at you, grovelling on the floor.' Sasha walks towards her, a predator closing in on its prey. 'You're pathetic.'

'Sasha, don't do this.' Natalie's voice wavers.

Legs. Use your legs. Just wait till she's close enough.

'Please. Let's work it out.' Natalie uses her words as bait to reel Sasha in.

Sasha halts, a step away, a triumphant look on her face. She cocks her head. 'Aw, now. Don't go all whiny on me.'

Come on, just a little closer.

Natalie whimpers.

Sasha takes another step.

Natalie's foot smashes into Sasha's kneecap and she crumples to the floor, landing hard on her hip with a whoomph as the air is forced out of her.

Get up, get up!

Natalie urges her body to move and she pushes herself with her feet, sliding along the lino on her back until she can use the stairs to haul herself upright.

She stumbles up the steps, not daring to look behind.

A hand grabs her ankle, yanking her backwards.

She grabs the banister, holding on with all her strength, but she only has one useful arm and her hand is sweaty, her grasp insecure. Her hand slides downwards. Her body starts to go with it as Sasha's fingernails dig into her skin, clawing and tugging.

A sudden, burning pain erupts in her thigh, searing down her leg. Natalie screams and looks down to see blood seeping through her clothes. Her stomach heaves. Her hand slides further. Sasha raises the knife, ready for another strike.

No, no, no.

With the last of her strength, Natalie lashes out with her foot, a powerful kick that connects with something hard. *Sasha's head?*

She hears a grunt and does it again. Something crunches. The hand on her ankle lets go and Natalie hurtles up the remaining stairs as though she's been fired from a catapult.

Her breath pumps in and out so fast she feels lightheaded, pain stabs at her thigh, blood trickles down her leg and into her shoe.

At the top of the stairs, she ricochets off the walls, down a short hall and into a bathroom at the end. She slams the door shut and turns the key in the lock. *Thank God,* she thinks, as she leans on the door, looking at the hefty, old-fashioned ironmongery.

Seconds later, Sasha slams against the door and rattles the handle. But Natalie knows she is safe for now and she perches on the edge of the bath, her vision fizzing with little black dots, her body hot and sticky, as she gulps in big mouthfuls of air.

'Fucking, fucking, fucking bitch!' Sasha screams.

She starts kicking the door. It's an old-fashioned one, with two frosted glass panels at the top and two wooden panels beneath. Natalie watches it shake, but all the fixings seem secure, despite the onslaught. She starts to tremble, her body weary beyond exhaustion, hurting beyond the boundaries of any pain she's experienced before. But her mind is sharp. Life or death; when there's only those two options it tends to clear your thoughts.

I've got to keep going. Get Harry safe.

Her eyes scan the room. There's a white bath with a shower over it, toilet, sink, and a built-in airing cupboard by the door. A mirrored cabinet is fixed above the sink and on the far wall, between the toilet and the bath, there's a window.

The onslaught of rattling and banging stops.

Natalie listens and hears footsteps. Not running, but steady. Thump, thump, thump, as they go down the stairs, echoing the beat of Natalie's heart.

Has she given up?

Wishful thinking, Natalie cautions herself. *You can't relax.* Not when Sasha knows she has her cornered.

Natalie presses a hand to her forehead and looks around for something she can use as a weapon. Plastic toys hang in a basket on the tiled wall behind the bath. A bathmat shaped like a whale. Towels on a rail by the door. The windowsill is cluttered with toiletries. She opens the cabinet over the sink and rifles through the contents, but all she can find is a small pair of nail scissors. Not much use, but they go in her back pocket anyway.

The window is the only way out.

She sweeps the jars and bottles off the windowsill, sending them clattering to the floor, opens the window and peers out. Below her is the flat roof of the kitchen extension. At least a four-foot drop.

Can I get out of there? Feet first and hope for the best?

It's a possibility.

With one arm?

But there isn't an alternative.

Don't think, just do it, she tells herself. She tries to step on to the edge of the bath, her leg sticky with blood, but the muscles refuse to work properly, shaking uncontrollably when she tries to step up. She grabs on to the windowsill to stop herself falling, collects herself for a moment and tries with the other leg, but with her arm in a sling, her balance is all off kilter.

This is impossible.

Her heart races faster.

She grits her teeth and by using her knees, she manages to heave herself to standing with the aid of the shower curtain. In her mind, the manoeuvre to get herself out of the window had seemed so straightforward, but now, as she edges herself on to the windowsill she's beginning to wonder. Sweat beads on her forehead. She tries to twist her body round, legs scrunched up to her chest but the windowsill is too narrow.

Tears of frustration sting her eyes. *It's not going to work.*

She hears footsteps running up the stairs and tries again.

Crash!

The air fills with the tinkle of broken glass.

Natalie's head spins towards the door, mouth open in horror as Sasha glowers at her through the broken panel. There's murder in her eyes, blood trickling from her nose and into her mouth.

Wedged in the window, Natalie watches Sasha's arm reach through the broken panel, feeling for the lock. Jagged shards of glass make the job too treacherous and after a moment, she retrieves her arm, lifts the hammer and starts to clear a bigger hole.

Natalie slithers off the windowsill and lurches towards the door. Sasha's hand snakes through the panel, reaching for the key.

Kick her hand, quick. But Natalie's leg won't move properly and she stumbles, bouncing off the sink, then the bath, like she's in a pinball machine, her forward momentum throwing her against the door.

The key rattles in the lock.

Natalie grabs at Sasha's hand and finds the pressure point at the base of her thumb. She squeezes with all her strength and Sasha squeals. Her fingers straighten for a second, enough time for Natalie to yank the key out of the lock and throw it across the floor.

Waves of pain flow through her, the floor undulating beneath her feet, like the surface of the sea. Overwhelmed by nausea, she clings to the door handle, unable to move while the world shifts around her.

A hand slams across Natalie's neck, pinning her against the door, fingers gripping her windpipe tighter and tighter. Sasha has stuffed her arm through the open panel, right up to her shoulder, her face pressed against the other side of door and although Natalie writhes and struggles, her strength is waning fast and Sasha's grasp is too tight. In vain, she gasps for breath, dredging her lungs for air.

Natalie starts to see black dots crowding her vison, darkness invading her head. She struggles harder, her hand slapping at Sasha's fingers, scratching and clawing at her skin.

She thinks about Harry, living with this witch, her wickedness infecting his life. Never knowing his real mother and the love she can bring to his world.

It can't happen. It can't.

With her last mouthful of air, the words of her self-defence instructor march into her mind. *Use your head, not your strength.*

And suddenly, she knows what to do.

Against all her instincts, she makes her body go limp, her dead-weight dragging at Sasha's outstretched arm. Sasha grunts with the effort of holding on and the pressure on Natalie's windpipe eases slightly, allowing her to draw in air. Minute breaths, so shallow her chest hardly moves, but it's enough.

Enough for her to remember.

The scissors.

In her back pocket.

She pulls them out, fingers shaking. Her last hope. With the handles of the scissors clenched in her fist, she jerks her arm towards the hole in the door, smacking the points into Sasha's flesh with all her might. She can't see what she's doing. Can't see where she's made her strike. But she feels the slap of Sasha's skin against her own.

A spine-chilling scream confirms that she's hit her mark and Sasha's hand slackens. Natalie stabs again. And again, knowing that Sasha is unable to defend herself while her shoulder is wedged through the door panel.

Finally, Sasha lets go and Natalie slides to the floor, rolls out of Sasha's reach, great gulps of air rushing in and out of her lungs.

Blood, warm and wet, dribbles down her leg, and her foot squelches in her shoe. But there's no time to think about it. This is only a temporary respite. The only chance of escape she's going to get. She crawls across the floor towards the window and drags herself up to standing, body shaking.

She pulls in a few good breaths and tries to clamber on to the edge of the bath again, biting her lip to make herself concentrate. The sound of her pulse whooshes in her ears and she moves at a snail-like speed as the life drains out of her.

It takes a few attempts, but eventually, she manages to stand on the edge of the bath and lean out through the open window. She studies the drop to the roof below and her stomach clenches. It looks so much further than it did before and everything is spinning around, like she's on a fairground ride. Bile rises up her throat and her stomach heaves. She steadies herself, closes her eyes and pictures what she has to do.

Head first? Is it even possible?

Feet run down the stairs.

Natalie's eyes flick open.

Christ, what's she going to do now? There's a whole garage full of tools down there.

Natalie grits her teeth and heaves herself through the opening, but her sling gets caught on the window catch and with all her body weight lying on top of it, she can't work it free.

No, no, no.

Her heart pounds so hard its beating rises up her throat. Seconds turn into minutes as she tugs and twists, trying to free herself. She tries to go backwards, but that doesn't work and her body is fast running out of energy. She rests for a little while before trying to go forwards again. It's her only chance and she grits her teeth and increases her efforts.

Exhaustion slows her struggles and she has to stop again. A car engine starts up, the sound thrumming through the mist before it disappears into the distance.

Has she gone?

She listens, her head spinning, heart pounding, and for a few minutes, she thinks she might be safe. Thinks it might be over. Her body starts to relax, her eyes close and her pulse slows.

Until… there's the sound of the engine again. A door slams.

Christ, it's not over! She's come back.

She starts to struggle again, trying to free herself.

The sound of footsteps thumping up the stairs makes her efforts more frantic.

The lock rattles. There's a heavy thump, then a bang as the door bursts opens, the handle bouncing off the airing cupboard.

She whimpers, every nerve in her body alive to the fact that she's going to die if she doesn't move. And finally, with a fresh bout of wriggling and squirming, the sling rips free. With all her remaining strength, she pushes against the windowsill, oblivious to the pain as she fights to get away.

Her weight starts to pull her downwards.

She feels her legs sliding over the windowsill and she tucks her head down, getting ready to push herself off the wall as she falls, and roll when she lands.

But a hand grabs her skirt.

Another grabs her belt and pulls her backwards.

CHAPTER FIFTY-SEVEN

Now

Jack tugs at his hair, his sense of foreboding growing by the minute. Fliss still isn't answering and Toby has drawn a blank.

Where the hell is she?

He decides he has only one option left and cringes at the thought. But it's got to be done. He dials Sergeant Tosser's mobile.

'Yeah, bro, can't really speak now. Up to my neck in something with the Treasury.' *Bro? Since when did they call each other bro?* The guy was developing affectations like an outbreak of acne. 'Call you later. Gotta go.'

'No wait, Dan! Wait. This is urgent.'

'What, in like urgent police stuff, or urgent, gotta get some lads together for a night out?'

'Trust me, Dan. It's in connection with the Treasury case you've got going. Fliss is involved, right?'

There's a moment's silence and Jack wonders if Dan has disconnected. Then he hears muffled voices, and realises Dan's hand is over the receiver. *He's talking to someone*. Jack clenches his fists as he paces up and down and is wondering whether to hang up when Dan comes back on the line.

'Sorry about that. So, the answer to your question is yes. But Fliss shouldn't be talking to you about it. It's highly confidential. It could damage the case.' He sounds superior now, bossy, and Jack wonders if it was a mistake to call. *Should have gone for nine-nine-nine.* But he's talking to a policeman, so he decides to plough on.

'Shut up and listen, will you! I think someone's been kidnapped. You were looking for her earlier. In connection with an incident in town. Anyway, I need some help.'

'What? Sorry? I didn't quite catch that. There's a lot going on here.'

Jack shakes his head, jaw clenched. He takes a deep breath.

'Tom Wilson and his wife. Or just his wife. One of them. Or maybe both of them, I don't know.' Jack wonders how to shrink the story into a couple of sentences that will make Dan take notice. 'Anyway, they've been following my friend around. And now she's disappeared.' Jack can hear raised voices in the background.

Is he even listening or am I just talking to myself here?

Dan is issuing instructions and Jack rubs the back of his neck as he waits.

Two minutes, he thinks. *Then I'm gone.*

'Sorry, can you run that by me again?' Dan says, when he comes back on the line.

Jack takes a deep breath to calm himself down before he speaks. 'She's disappeared and I think they've taken her. I haven't got time to give you all the details now, I just need some help because I can't find out where Tom Wilson lives and I thought you'd have his address. That's all I need. Tom Wilson's address.'

Dan gives a staccato laugh. 'Yeah, bro. We'd like to know that as well. Seems they've moved out of the address the Treasury have got. We've just been to their old place, looking for them. Right palaver going on.'

The receiver is filled with the chatter of conversation.

Jack rings off. *Probably better to go through official channels,* he decides. *Then they can't ignore me.* He's about to dial the emergency services when his phone rings.

'Fliss, thank God! There's something—'

'No, no, it's not Fliss, it's Mary.' Jack grimaces. 'I wanted to make sure it's alright for me to go home now. It's just that I'm going to miss my bus if I don't set off soon.'

Jack sighs. 'Yes, sorry, Mary. I should have rung earlier. It's just… I, um…'

'Something the matter, lovey? You sound all of a dither.'

'Oh, Mary.' Jack sits down at the kitchen table, his knee jiggling up and down. 'Natalie's disappeared. I think her ex might have taken her, but I can't find out where he lives and—'

'Taken? What do you mean, taken?'

'There's something weird going on. Someone's been following her and…' *I haven't got time for this.* 'Thing is I need to ring emergency services. Get the police looking for her. So… look, I don't mean to be rude but I've got to go.'

'Oi, just a minute,' Mary says, in a tone that Jack recognises from his youth. 'I know where she'll be. Tom Wilson's house.'

Jack grinds his teeth. *Patience,* he tells himself. *She's an old lady.* 'I know that's where she probably is. But nobody seems to know where he lives at present. Not the Treasury. Or the police. And I've tried all the normal databases. But—'

'I know.'

'What?'

'I said, I know. Well, my friend Margaret is friends with Judy Kennish. She was nanny to Tom Wilson when he was a baby and she's been looking after Tom's little boy these past few years. Anyway, I remembered her saying something last month when we were—'

Jack raises his eyes to the ceiling. 'Mary, sorry to interrupt, but this is urgent. I just need the address.'

'Oh, right, yes. Ballamona Cottage, it is. You remember. Belongs to Maurice Fairburn, that grumpy old git of a farmer who tried to shoot—'

'No, I don't remember.' He snaps. 'Where is it?'

'Ooh, you're in a right tizz, aren't you? Well, it's on that little lane, just off Poortown Road. On the right. After the cattery, I think.'

'Mary, that's brilliant.' His heart races. He knows just where she means now. 'Gotta go.'

He rings nine-nine-nine, gives them Tom's address and tells them it's a suspected kidnapping and he thinks the woman involved is the person the police were looking for earlier in the day. Then he texts the address to Dan and Fliss. *Double whammy. That should get them going.* He shrugs on his jacket, grabs his helmet and runs out of the door.

The mist has thickened to a fog and he has to make himself drive slower than he'd like through the estate. Dusk has come early and the street lights glisten like golden globes in the gloom, the light sparkling on the droplets of water that fill the air. Thankfully, it doesn't take long before he's out into the countryside and he allows himself to accelerate.

It only takes a few minutes to get to Tom's house and he pulls up by the gate and turns off his engine. The house lights are on, dim squares of yellow in the greyness. He decides that he needs a stealthy approach, because he has no idea who's in there. Or what's happening.

He pushes his motorbike next to the hedge, out of sight and is just resting it on its stand when the roar of an engine makes him look up. *Is that the police?* He hopes so, but fog bounces sound around in a peculiar way and it's hard to tell which direction the sound is coming from. He takes off his helmet and realises that the noise is closer than he thought. In fact, it's coming from the other side of the hedge.

He peers round into the driveway just as a car speeds through the gates, making him jump back out of the way.

A silver estate car.

He stares after it. Checks the number plate.

That's the car that was following Natalie.

He looks at the house, then back down the lane, where he can see the red tail lights getting smaller. He has to make a decision. Fast. Check out the house or follow the car?

Maybe Natalie's in the car?

The thought gets him back on his motorbike and he speeds down the lane. The tail lights turn left, towards Peel and he holds back a little, his lights off, so he won't be seen. His mind races. *Was that the right decision? Should I have made sure Natalie wasn't in the house first?* But then he would have lost the car. And the police will be at the house soon. *Just focus on the car,* he tells himself. He's made his choice and his gut tells him it's the right one.

They twist down the streets until they reach the marina. The road is a dead end and there's no chance of losing them now. He parks up, deciding he can be stealthier on foot, and runs after the vehicle.

It turns into the car park by Fenella Beach and he presses himself against the sea wall, peering over the top. Someone gets out. Dressed in black. Long hair. It must be Sasha or Blue or whatever she calls herself. The car lights blink and he hears the locks engage.

Sasha hurries past his hiding place, back towards the marina and before he can make a conscious decision, he springs out, grabbing her arm.

She cries out, spins round and the hairs lift on the back of his neck when he sees her bloodied face. *How the hell did that happen?*

'What the fuck? Get off me!' She kicks at his legs, but he dodges out of the way and they stagger across the road grunting and grappling, like wrestlers. 'Marco! Marco!' she shouts. 'Help! I'm being attacked.'

Who's Marco? Jack wonders as he tries to grab her other arm, but she whips it out of his reach.

'Where's Natalie?' he demands. 'What have you done with her?'

'Marco!'

She writhes like a snake and it takes all of Jack's strength to hold on. But he does. Until a blow to his back sends him falling forwards. Sasha pulls her arm out of his grasp, and for a moment, he loses his balance. He teeters on the edge of the marina. The tide is in, and the footbridge has been swung back, to let boats in and out. He has just about regained his footing when a powerful push to the small of his back sends him sprawling forwards, into the dark, glassy water.

He tumbles head over heels, his heavy biker gear dragging him down. Water trickles down his neck, into his suit and his boots. It starts to fill his helmet. The weight of his clothes make it a struggle to lift his limbs out of the water. Swimming is not an option. He grasps for the surface, then sinks, down, down to the bottom.

CHAPTER FIFTY-EIGHT

Now

Natalie tries to kick out, but her legs are wedged against the body of the person holding her. *This is it,* she thinks, holding her breath, eyes closed tight, steeling herself for the final stab of the knife. The end of her life.

Thoughts of Harry flow into her mind, the child she has never been allowed to know and a sob fills her chest, her last memory of him being his indifference towards her. *Sasha did that*, she thinks, and now she will taint his pure little soul with her evil and greed. The pain in her heart is worse than any pain caused by her injuries. Tears roll down her cheeks and drip off her chin while she waits for Sasha's final blow. *I love you, Harry,* she thinks. *I'll always love you.*

'Oh, no you don't.'

Natalie's eyes flick open. It's a man's voice. One she doesn't recognise.

'Nige!' The man shouts. 'Need some help up here!' The man tightens his grip.

She hears footsteps running up the stairs. More hands grab her and heave her back through the window. The men set her on her feet and when she sees the black uniforms, she almost chokes on her breath, unable to decide whether to laugh or cry.

Police. It's over. I'm safe.

Her legs decide they can't cope with the confusion of emotions and she crumples to the floor. A policeman crouches next to her and she tries to focus on his face, but it keeps moving. She closes her eyes, nauseous and hot, shaking with relief.

'Okay, love, can you tell me your name?'

She tries to remember the name she used for her ferry tickets, but decides that things have got too far out of hand to bother with lies.

'Natalie.' She whispers. 'Natalie Wil… No, sorry, it's not that anymore. It's Natalie Patterson.'

Natalie's eyes stare at the sink in front of her. She feels like her batteries are running out, every movement such an effort, even thinking requires too much energy.

'Okay, Natalie. So, I'm Sergeant Corlett and this here is Constable Waters.'

Her head is too heavy for her neck and she leans it against the bath.

'Right, Natalie, there's a lot of blood here. I'm just going to put a dressing on your leg.' He nods to the other policeman, who keys his mike.

'We need an ambulance,' he says when it squawks into life. 'Urgent. Female patient, lost a lot of blood.'

Natalie is shaking so much she can hear her teeth chattering, her body banging against the bath panel. She clings on to herself, the sink swaying back and forth.

'I think you might be in shock,' she hears Sergeant Corlett say, as if he's half a mile away. 'Let's just get you lying on the floor. Feet up on the bath.'

Sergeant Corlett is gentle and she's grateful for the support of the floor as he manoeuvres her into position. Her heart bangs along to a crazy beat, fluttering and skipping before finding a rhythm and losing it again. Sergeant Corlett frowns and turns to his colleague. 'Nige, get a pillow and a blanket or something, will you? We need to keep her warm till the paramedics get here.'

He grabs a towel and wraps it round her leg. She winces as he pulls it tight. 'Sorry, Natalie. Just trying to stem the bleeding.

Ambulance won't be long.' He goes to join his colleague in the hallway, where the Constable murmurs an update.

'So, we've got a dead male in the kitchen. ID says he's Tom Wilson. Looks like there's been a fight. He's got a carving knife in his hand. Head's been bashed in with something. I've left it for SOCOs to do their bit.'

'Okay. Thanks, Nige.'

'Then there's blood stains on the stairs. And here outside the door.'

Natalie tries to concentrate on what they're saying, but her mind is caught up in an avalanche of thoughts, tumbling on top of each other. *Stay with it,* she urges herself, trying to catch the thing that's bothering her and dig it out of the confusion. *Harry. Get him safe.*

'Where's Sasha?' she says it with as much force as she can muster, but it sounds like a whimper, rather than words.

The policemen turn and look at her. The sergeant comes closer. 'Sorry, did you say something?'

She clears her throat. 'Sasha. Did you get her?

He frowns. 'Who's Sasha?'

'She was here. Tom's wife. She killed him. Then tried to kill me.'

Dan Corlett crouches next to her. 'Tom Wilson's wife, you say?'

She nods, panic thrashing in her head. 'You've got to find her. She's got my son.'

The policemen look at each other. One goes out into the hallway and she can hear him talking into his mike.

'Nige, have another look round,' Sergeant Corlett calls. 'Make sure she's not hiding anywhere. Check outside as well while you're at it.' He turns his attention back to Natalie and pulls a little black notebook from his top pocket. 'Right, then. Let's see if you can tell me what's been going on here?'

Her mind rewinds and replays everything that just happened. She begins to speak, the story flowing out in one long sentence before the last of her energy drains away, her voice so quiet, the policeman has to lean close to hear.

A little while later, the Constable comes back, grim-faced. 'Nobody else here. But it looks like someone might have escaped from the rear exit in the kitchen. There's a trail of bloodspots going out to the driveway.'

'Okay,' Sergeant Corlett swallows hard. 'Right, well, we've already got the exit routes covered. The ferry and the airport. She's not going to get away.'

Natalie's own plans to sneak Harry off the island drift into her mind. *Private boats.* Her eyes widen as she remembers.

She clutches at the policeman's arm. 'But what about the harbours? Are you watching them as well?'

Sergeant Corlett frowns.

'I saw her, you see. In Peel. She was with a bloke on this yacht. Maybe she's gone to him?' Her voice is fading, but she forces herself to go on. 'It was called *Smooth Talker.* Big motor yacht, moored right by the entrance to the marina.' Her breath hitches in her throat. *As if it was getting ready to leave.*

Sergeant Corlett gets to his feet and goes out into the hall. The chatter fades into the distance. Cold and clammy, Natalie shivers under the duvet that has been draped over her. She prays that they'll reach the yacht before it leaves. Prays that they'll find Harry for her. There's nothing more she can do. Darkness invades her vision and she slips into the blackness.

CHAPTER FIFTY-NINE

Now

Marco looks at the water, his mouth hanging open.

What just happened? Did she just push him in? Really?

He turns to Sasha, who is running towards his yacht, moored not more than twenty feet away. He can hear splashing and peers through the mist. He sees an arm, a hand grasping at the surface. Then it sinks beneath the water. And then he can see nothing. Not a splash, nor a ripple. Just the cloak of the mist as it twists and weaves through the air.

He stares, holding his breath, willing the man to pop up to the surface. He listens, but all he can hear is the muted sound of chatter coming from the pub on the other side of the marina. Yellow light seeps through the mist and it seems like another world, not real. Because reality says a man just fell in the water and he hasn't come back up again.

Marco's medical training kicks in. The compulsion to save lives. It doesn't matter that his work is now more cosmetic in its focus. What matters is why he became a doctor in the first place. He cannot and will not stand by and watch a man drown.

'Sasha, get the lifebelt!' He points to a post at the side of the road. 'Over there. Quick.'

But Sasha ignores him.

He looks at the water, then runs after Sasha, grabs her arm and spins her round.

'Seriously? We can't leave him in the water, for heaven's sake. Can't you see that he's drowning?'

Sasha snatches her arm away and glares at him.

This is their first row, their first ever disagreement of any kind. Marco doesn't do confrontation, has never been good at it and up to now he's made every effort to accommodate Sasha's whims. Ever since he met her in his consulting room, he's been addicted to her, obsessed with the idea that he can save her from the terrible life that her husband makes her live. She's such a sweet person, so loving and she deserves so much more than that loser can give her. Tom is just trouble and he's going to drag Sasha down with him. How can Marco let that happen? He can't, not when he has the means to give her a new life. That's what this is all about. Escaping the clutches of her awful husband and his criminal activities and getting her away somewhere safe.

Marco glares back as if the force of his stare will make her reconsider. In surgery, everyone does exactly what he says, without hesitation and this situation is completely alien to him.

In fact, Sasha's behaviour is pretty alien. His eyes narrow. And so is her face.

Now she's under the street light, he can see her properly. He takes in the shattered nose, the cut lip, and the swelling on her cheek, decorated by a large bruise. There's blood smeared all over her. She looks like a cage fighter.

He blinks and slaps the back of his neck, as if he's swatting the bad feeling that's settled there.

'My God, Sasha! What happened to you?' He runs an expert eye over the damage and swallows as plans for their new life sink into the harbour along with the stranger.

'He attacked me.' She points to her face, eyes fierce. 'This is what he did. And you want to save the fucker?'

He glances at the water, then back at Sasha. Time is running out for the guy. And Sasha needs medical attention. She needs those broken bones set. A couple of stitches in her lip and that wound in her neck looks nasty. He clamps his jaw shut. Tells himself to sort out his priorities. A man's life is in danger and that has to come before anything else.

A day won't make any difference, he tells himself as he runs past Sasha and wrenches the lifebelt from its post. He throws it into the water where the man went under and peers over the edge of the marina, hands clenching and unclenching as he watches for signs of life.

Must be five minutes since he went in. But he knows that, with the water being cold, there's still a slim chance that the man can be resuscitated.

'I can't see him. Sasha, call the Harbour Master.' He rips off his jacket. Pulls off his shoes. She hasn't moved. He glares at her. 'Now. Go on.'

'No. No, I won't.' She runs over to him and tugs at his sleeve, trying to get him to go with her. 'We can call once we're out at sea.' She sounds frantic. 'You said we've got to go. Now. Or we'll miss high tide. And then we'll be stuck here… Marco, please, please, let's go.' Her eyes flick to the yacht. 'We can't leave Harry on there on his own. He might… he might fall in or something. It's not safe. Please, let's just go.'

Marco stares at her. *What the hell is going on here?*

Her eyes plead with him. His eyes go back to the water. Still no sign of the man.

He pushes her away and starts to take off his trousers. 'I'll have to go in. It would kill me if I didn't try and save him.' He looks at Sasha. 'Ring the Harbour Master. Then call for an ambulance. We'll go tomorrow. No big deal, is it?'

'Please, darling. Let's just go. While we've still got time.' Her hands are clasped together, like she's praying. 'Five minutes. Then we'll ring.' She starts sobbing, a revolting mixture of snot, blood and tears streaming down her face. 'Please. I'll do anything. But please, please, let's just go.'

In an instant, her whole demeanour has changed, from being a cold-hearted bitch to a woman who needs looking after. Just like that. And he realises what a fool he's been. How easily she's played him.

Sasha glares at him as he tosses his trousers on the floor. There's a meanness in her eyes that makes him shudder. *It wasn't an accident.* He saw her do it. She pushed him in.

The day has gone to hell. In fact, his life, as he'd planned it, has gone to hell too, but he puts those thoughts aside. *I've got to save that guy.*

He dives underwater, into the murky blackness, feeling the soft silt of the bottom of the marina with his hands. He circles round for as long as he can hold his breath, then comes up for air. He dives under again. His methodical brain makes him work in a grid pattern, up to the marina entrance. After four attempts, his legs are going numb with the cold, his fingers too, but he's not going to give up. Not until he's got that man to safety. His teeth chatter and he looks to see if there's any sign of someone coming to help.

No. Nobody. She hasn't called for help, has she? Because they'd be here by now.

'Help!' he calls, thinking that the people outside the pub will hear. He listens, but all he can hear is the gentle slap of water against the boats. *Crap,* he thinks. *Smokers. They've gone back inside.*

He knows that time is of the essence with a drowning. And there's still a hope for the guy if he can just find him. 'Help!' he calls again, because there must be other people about. People on other boats. Walking dogs. But he's so cold he can hardly keep himself afloat and his mouth fills with water. He coughs and splutters and decides he's wasting time.

I'll run to the Harbour Master, he decides. *It's not far.*

He tries to grab the edge of the marina, but the cold has zapped his strength. His hands won't hold on, his arm muscles won't pull and after a few attempts, he realises it's not going to happen.

He looks around, studying the concrete walls. *There must be something I can use to climb up.* Out of the mist, something floats towards him. He squints then breathes a sigh of relief. *The lifebelt.* He grabs hold of it, ducks underwater and puts his arms through, letting it take the weight of his body. He tries to organise his thoughts. *Mind over matter*, he tells himself. But his body shakes from head to toe and for a moment, being cold to the bone is all he can think about.

He feels safe in the lifebelt and as his muscles relax a bit, he has an idea. He's next to his yacht. All he has to do is paddle round the back and then he can get up the steps. *Twenty feet. That's all.* He turns and gets his arms working in some sort of a rhythm and with limbs like rubber, he inches forwards.

He thinks about Sasha's behaviour. And her lies. *Why would someone attack her, for God's sake? And that blood on her face wasn't fresh. Nor was the bruise. And what the hell has she been up to for the last four hours?*

He's nearly at the back of the boat now and grits his teeth while he makes one last effort. A familiar noise makes his eyes widen, and he sees the water start to churn. His stomach clenches. *She's turned the engines on.* He looks up and sees her in the wheelhouse. The yacht starts to move past him towards the marina entrance. The propellers create a current in the water, which sucks at his legs, pulling him towards them.

He kicks as hard as he can and strikes out with his arms, but it's no use, he's going backwards instead of forwards.

'Help!' he shrieks, so loud it scrapes the back of his throat. 'Sasha, turn the engine off. Sasha!'

She turns and he thinks she must have heard him, seen the danger he's in. But she looks away and the engines thrum louder, the propellers pulling him closer and closer.

CHAPTER SIXTY

Now

Jack hopes that his drowning man act was believable enough. He's been in and out of this marina on fishing trips since he was a young lad and knows it well. It's not wide. Maybe forty feet and he's always been a strong swimmer.

He pulls himself along the bottom, across the width of the marina towards the steps, which he knows are on the other side. He has to be slick as a seal when he comes out, careful not to make too much noise. He creeps up the steps, which are hidden behind the wheelhouse of a large fishing boat, and listens. He can hear the man shouting at Sasha, telling her to get a lifebelt.

He pulls off his helmet and cringes when water splashes to the floor. But Sasha's yelling now, so he doesn't think they heard him. He runs towards the Harbour Master's office and bursts through the door.

'Mike! You need to close the gates. Get the bridge back across. Shut the marina off. Right now.'

He drips on the floor. Mike stares at him, his hand dipped into a bag of crisps.

'Bloody hell, Jack, look at the mess you're making. What the hell's going on?'

'People wanted by the police are trying to get out of the harbour.' Jack points behind him. 'On that motor yacht, just by the entrance.'

Mike chews and swallows.

Jack's voice gets louder, more urgent. 'Please, Mike. I'm helping the police. Just do it, will you?'

Mike purses his lips and frowns. 'This isn't some practical joke again, is it?'

'Oh, for God's sake!' Jack shouts. 'I'm not twelve anymore, am I? Do I look like I'm playing a joke?'

He lurches for the controls but Mike smacks him away. 'Oi, you're not allowed. Only I'm allowed.' He turns his back and Jack hears the deep groan of the mechanism as it comes to life.

He dashes outside and peers through the mist. The yacht is moving. It's at the entrance. He chews a nail as he watches, heart racing. *Did I get here in time?*

Mike comes out and stands next to him. There's a scratching, scraping sound as the gate rises up from the bottom of the marina and catches the hull of the yacht. It seesaws for a moment, engines revving.

Jack grips Mike's arm. *Can it get over?* It looks like it might.

Then the propellers catch on something and shudder to a halt. The yacht hovers for a moment, looks like it will fall forwards and escape. Until the footbridge swings into place and smacks through the wheelhouse, shattering the glass, splintering the fibreglass and pushing the yacht backwards into the marina.

'Oh my God,' Mike says, scratching his head, his face quite pale. 'I am in such big trouble. Such big, big trouble.'

'Call the police,' Jack shouts over his shoulder as he hurtles across the footbridge. The yacht bobs up and down, and sways from side to side as if it's in a washing machine. He can see Sasha, slumped over the wheel and he slows down. She doesn't appear to be moving and is covered in debris. As he jogs alongside the yacht, a small face, with big scared eyes peers out from a porthole. *Harry?*

'It's okay,' Jack shouts to the boy. 'I'll soon have you off there. Just hang on.'

Jack jumps into the water and grabs the yacht's mooring rope, which has fallen over the side. He throws a loop over a mooring post, heaves himself on to dry land and pulls the yacht next to the marina wall. He fixes the rope tight and leans over, panting with the effort.

He hears the tap of little feet coming up wooden steps and the boy emerges from the cabin. Tears stain his pale cheeks. He's clutching a toy rabbit to his chest, one of its ears in his mouth.

'Harry, isn't it?' Jack says, holding out his hand. He beckons to the boy. 'Come on, let's get you on dry land, shall we? There's been a bit of an accident.'

'Who are you?' Harry says, not moving.

'A friend of your mum's.'

Harry looks up at the wheelhouse and Sasha's immobile body. He starts to cry.

'Hey, it's going to be okay. Nothing for you to worry about. The ambulance will be here soon.' Jack steps on to the yacht. 'Everything's going to be fine.'

In the distance, he can hear sirens and he waits, watching as the blue flashing lights come over the bridge and head towards him. The boy's hand curls into his and he gives it a squeeze.

CHAPTER SIXTY-ONE

Now

Natalie's eyes blink open and the first thing she sees is Jack, wrapped in a silver blanket, sitting next to her bed. The second is the drip attached to her hand. She tries to move her head, so she can see him better but her body feels like it has been set in concrete.

It takes her a moment to remember why she might be here. Again. Or maybe she didn't leave? But then the events of the evening come rushing back in a terrifying blur, images flashing into her mind, melding into each other so she isn't sure if they're real or some half-remembered nightmare.

'Hey,' Jack says.

She smiles and tries to make her eyes stay open.

Sasha escaped with Harry.

The smile shrivels on her lips as the memory hovers at the front of her mind. She frowns and tries to sit up, sees that she's in a room, not a ward and the other bed is empty. Jack stands to help her, raising the end of the bed, propping a pillow behind her. But she has no intention of staying in bed. She tries to throw off the cover but even that small action is too much and her head spins.

'Oh, no you don't,' he says, gently pushing her back against the pillow. 'You're not going anywhere. You lost three pints of blood. They put fifteen stitches in your leg and they had to put your shoulder back in again. And the doctor said—'

'But Harry... I need to find him.' Her pulse quickens, and her head throbs. She puts a hand to her forehead, squinting in the bright lights.

'I know, I know,' he says. His sits on the bed, his voice soothing. 'It's okay.' He grins. 'We've got him.'

Her eyes widen. She claws at the cannula. 'I want to see him. Now, I've got to—'

'No!' The force of his voice stops her hand in mid-air. She stares at him, shocked. He's a bit of a Viking when he's cross.

'Look,' he says, more gently. 'You're suffering from shock. You need to rest.' His voice falls to a whisper, his mouth close to her ear. 'You've got to stay here. Police guard outside.'

Her eyes widen.

He sighs. 'I'm afraid you're under arrest. And until they can sort out exactly what happened to Tom, you're technically a suspect.'

She leans back against the pillow, not caring that she's under investigation. She has more important things to think about. 'Where is he?'

'Oh, the Family Liaison Officer is entertaining him for the moment, just until they sort out a foster placement.'

'Foster placement?' She closes her eyes, dismayed by the idea and he seems as far away as ever.

Natalie blinks as an unwelcome thought pushes into her mind.

'What about Sasha? Did they get her?'

Jack nods. 'Oh yes. In fact, she's in A & E right now. A few stitches and broken bones to patch up. Then she'll be straight to prison on remand.'

They sit in silence for a moment and Natalie allows herself to imagine that Harry will be hers again. Once all the formalities are sorted out. Surely, now that the truth is about to come out, she'll be allowed to be his mother. The thought swells in her heart, filling her chest.

'There's a way to go yet, you know that, don't you?' Jack says.

She glances at him and looks away, picking at the blanket that covers the bed. 'Yes, yes. I know. So, what's going to happen to me? Do you know?'

Jack sighs. 'Bad news, I'm afraid.'

Natalie swallows. *Back to that stinking rotten prison.* A weight settles in her stomach.

'You're going to be in hospital for a few days. But I've got a lawyer for you and we're seeing if you can come and stay with me, while the police complete their investigations. If you want to, that is.'

He gazes at her with an expression that makes her heart monitor beep a little faster. The colour rises in her cheeks and she covers her confusion with a shaky laugh. 'What? For real?'

He nods, his thumb stroking the back of her hand. 'Between you and me, they know that Sasha killed Tom. The sergeant, Dan Corlett, told me that the pathologist has given them an estimated time of death for Tom, which makes it impossible for you to have killed him. Because you were here. They're waiting for the autopsy report, so it's all official. And they need your statement. Then they can dot all the "i"s and cross all the "t"s.'

Natalie gasps. 'I just can't… I didn't think… But what about skipping parole?'

'Oh, I've got the lawyer on to that as well. Extenuating circumstances.' Jack waves her concerns away. 'I wouldn't worry about it. Honestly. He's amazing, this guy. You'll like him.' Natalie nods, sure that she will. 'Old school mate.' Jack laughs. 'He was the clever one.'

Silence settles around them again, while Natalie takes it all in, but there's only one question in her mind.

'When can I see Harry? Please, Jack, I've got to see him.'

'Oh well, there's a lot of legal stuff to sort through, but the liaison officer thinks you'll be able to see him in a few days. When you're out of hospital. Start to get to know each other. You're his next of kin, after all, now that Tom is dead.'

He gets his phone out of his pocket, taps and swipes, then turns it to show her. 'I thought you might like to see this.'

Her hand goes to her mouth as she watches the video of a little boy, sitting on the floor, playing with a train set, clearly engrossed in what he's doing. She recognises that expression on his face, remembers it from when he was a baby. And lying next to him is Mr Bunny, the first toy she ever bought for him, a little bit of her love that he has carried with him for all those years that she has been away.

A tear trickles down her cheek. But she's laughing, unable to stop now that she's started. She reaches her arm up to Jack and he hesitates, then leans forward and she hugs him tight.

'Thank you,' she whispers, not wanting to let go.

He hugs her back, pulling her close as she laughs and cries, unable to believe that it's all over and she has a new beginning to look forward to. A new beginning with her son.

Jack sits on the bed, his arm round her shoulders as they watch the video again and again. He kisses her hair and she tilts her head until she's looking into his eyes. He hesitates for a moment, then his lips are on hers and she knows, with that first, lingering kiss, that Jack is going to be part of her new beginning too.

CHAPTER SIXTY-TWO

Two Years Later

Natalie hangs out the washing, in the enclosed garden at the back of Mary's house, enjoying the order of things; Jack's work clothes at the far end, then her jeans and T-shirts, Harry's school uniform and last, but definitely not least, Rosie's little baby clothes. Her family, right there, hanging on the line. Her family. Her house, now that Mary has done a swap with Jack, finding the bungalow much easier to manage. Her wedding present to them, Mary said.

After all that she's been through, Natalie still finds it hard to believe. In the space of two years, she has a husband, a baby girl and Harry back living with her again.

'Are you there, lovey?'

Mary pokes her head out of the kitchen door, ignores Natalie and goes straight to the pushchair, gazing down at Rosie, her crinkled hand reaching out, stroking the cheek of the sleeping child.

'You're early,' Natalie says, hanging the last of the clothes on the line.

'Couldn't wait to see this little mite,' Mary says. 'And I've brought chocolate brownies for Harry. They're on the table. And my John says he's got a BMX bike off a friend that he can mend. So that'll do grand for Harry's birthday. And I've knitted a couple of cardies for this little one. Lemon and white this time. You can have too much pink, can't you?'

Natalie laughs. 'Mary, you're terrible. These kids are so spoilt!'

Mary beams and Natalie gives her a hug, enjoying the soft, cuddliness of this old lady who's come to be such an important part of her life.

'Okay, so milk's on the side, just needs warming up when she's ready,' Natalie says, picking up the washing basket and taking it inside, Mary at her heels. 'And she's got some pureed veg there too. She's not that keen, but give it a go and I'll be back in a couple of hours.'

'Righto.' Mary puts the kettle on and gets her 'World's Greatest Nana' mug down from the shelf, a present from Harry the previous Christmas. 'You have a good class.' She smiles. 'No need to hurry back.'

Natalie picks up her bag and sets off up the hill to the residential home where she's doing armchair aerobics with the residents.

'Morning, Norma,' she calls to the receptionist as she walks towards the day room.

'Oh, Natalie, just a minute,' Norma says, bustling out of her office. 'We were wondering… I mean, just say no if it's not going to work. But we wondered if you could do another couple of sessions a week for us? Everyone so looks forward to you coming, it really brightens their day, you know. So…' She looks hopeful. 'We were hoping you might be able to do alternate days for us.'

Natalie smiles, a rush of happiness warming her heart. 'Well, thank you, Norma. I'll have to check with Mary, see if she minds doing another couple of days. But…' She laughs, picturing Mary's delight at being able to spend more time with the children. 'I don't think there'll be a problem.'

'So, can we sort out a contract then?'

'A contract?' *Yes! Finally, a steady source of income.* The classes she does for pregnant ladies on Thursday mornings and postnatal classes in the afternoons are on a pay-as-you-go basis and are just taking off. But, a contract. How genuinely marvellous! Yes, her business is developing very nicely and it all fits perfectly round the children, with Mary as a willing babysitter.

She thinks about Harry, how he loves school with a passion she can't even begin to comprehend, replays the conversations they have about anything and everything in her mind. She pictures him wrestling with Jack, snuggling up between them on the sofa, trying to feed his sister, flying kites on the beach, searching rock pools for crabs, and she wraps herself in the joy that he's brought into her life. She wonders if she'd feel like this if she'd never lost him. Would she experience everything about him in luminous, brilliant Technicolor like this? Or would she have taken him for granted? She'll never know. But what she does know is that every day she's grateful to have this little person in her life, along with the rest of her new family.

It never ceases to amaze her how quickly children adapt. It only took a few months for Harry to accept her version of reality; that Sasha was just looking after him while Natalie had been away. She showed him in the mirror, how he and Natalie had the same eyes, the same shaped eyebrows, the same mouth. Showed him pictures of them together when he was a baby. It took a little longer for the legal machinations to grind their way through all the necessary processes and allow him to come and live with her. But he settled in quickly and fell in love with Jack as soon as he heard him sing. And now the past feels like a terrible nightmare that never really happened.

Harry used to talk about Sasha. She came to be known as Auntie Sasha. Now he hardly mentions her at all. But he does miss his father and it's clear that he had a strong bond with Tom, which is a surprise to Natalie, because he struggled to know what to do with Harry when he was a baby. But then some men, she knows, can't cope well with the baby stage of a child's life, finding they get closer to them when they can communicate. It must have been like that with Tom and Harry. They talk about Tom when Harry wants to and Natalie tells her son what he needs to know, lets him remember his father with love. Because he must have done a lot of things right for Harry to be such a loving and well-balanced child.

Tom's parents are still in touch and Natalie has met up with them a few times when they have visited the island; meetings that have been stilted and awkward from Natalie's point of view, but Harry seems genuinely fond of them, having shared their lives for several years. Now that Tom is dead, he will one day be heir to his grandparents' fortune, so at least she knows his future is secure.

Sasha has been charged with Tom's murder. And Marco's manslaughter. Plus the attempted murder of Natalie. All adding up to a life sentence. Sasha is also facing charges for fraud and embezzlement, the authorities having taken a while to untangle Tom's affairs and realise that Sasha had a part to play in the disappearance of clients' funds.

The sentences for the crimes against Marco and Natalie were given to run concurrently, because life is life, isn't it? Or it should be. Tom's parents, along with Marco's family are appealing to ensure that the full sentence is served, and no parole given, but the process is slow.

Natalie satisfies herself with the knowledge that Harry will be an adult by the time Sasha gets out of prison. Hopefully, she'll have to serve the full thirty years, but whenever she's released, she'll just be a shadowy figure from his past. Nobody important. Nobody he loved.

In time, when Harry is old enough, he'll know the full story and then he can keep himself safe if she ever tries to contact him.

Jack persuaded her to sue for wrongful arrest and, although at first resistant, she accepts now that it had been the right thing to do. The compensation has given them a very useful nest egg. She'd thought they'd buy a new house, somewhere bigger, with a proper garden, but she can't bring herself to move from Mary's and it's big enough for now, handy for the beach, which Harry loves. And it was a gift from Mary, so it's special.

She thinks they'll stay because she has another idea for some of the money. Jack doesn't know it yet, but she's found a little building that would make a perfect recording studio. She's just waiting for some quotes to come back for equipment, get it put together as a complete package and then that will be his first anniversary present. No less than he deserves because he's saved her life in so many ways.

Natalie finishes her class a little late, because the ladies do love to chat and she doesn't like to hurry them. She checks her watch and half runs, half walks to the school, children already streaming out of the door as she draws close.

'Mummy! Mummy!'

She turns and there's Harry, running towards her, a picture flapping in his hand. His hair is tousled, shoes are on the wrong feet, and his PE bag bounces on his shoulder.

'Hey, little munchkin,' she says, laughing as he jumps up and down on the spot. She crouches and his little arms clasp around her neck. He plants a wet kiss on her cheek.

'Love you, Mummy,' he says. 'Look, I drew a dinosaur eating SpongeBob.'

She pulls him to her, his words never losing their magic, their ability to make her heart swell until her chest is fit to burst. 'Love you too, little munchkin,' she says, kissing him back, holding him tight.

EPILOGUE

Thirteen years, two months and fifteen days to go.

I'm being good. Ever so freakin' good. But any actress will tell you that life is simpler when you've got a role to play.

Thank God for the Internet, that's all I can say. And friends who know how to hack into Facebook accounts. And have illegal phones, SIM cards, Wi-Fi passwords.

I can look at him, my boy. Watch him grow up. At least I have that. And when he's older, and has his own account, I'll be able to talk to him. Not as myself, of course. But I can be a cyber pal. The best pal he'll ever have.

He'll always be my son.

Of course he will. He's mine.

Mine, mine, mine.

It's me he loves. Me. Not her. That drippy waste of space. Look at the goofy grin on her stupid face. And she's holding him all wrong. He doesn't like being held like that. And that's not a proper smile on his face. That's a smile for the camera. I can tell.

Poor boy. I cry for him sometimes, when I imagine how much he must be missing me.

But we'll get through it. I know we will.

The good news is that I know where he is.

And, when the time is right, I'll make him mine again.

She'll pay for what she's done to me. Oh yes, she'll pay, alright.

A LETTER FROM RONA

I want to say a huge thank you for choosing to read *Keep You Safe*. If you did enjoy it, and want to keep up-to-date with all my latest releases, just sign up at the following link. Your email address will never be shared and you can unsubscribe at any time

www.bookouture.com/rona-halsall

The inspiration for this story came from my own experiences of being temporarily separated from my children during my divorce and, although I can reassure you that my story was nowhere near as extreme as Natalie's (I promise I didn't go to prison!), it still came as a tremendous shock and has made me value every moment with them ever since.

In writing this novel I wanted to explore how shocking it might be to have a child taken away and really think about how far we would go to protect them, even if it meant putting ourselves in danger.

I hope you loved *Keep You Safe* and if you did I would be very grateful if you could write a review. I'd love to hear what you think, and it makes such a difference helping new readers to discover one of my books for the first time.

I love hearing from my readers – you can get in touch on my Facebook page, through Twitter, Goodreads or my website.

Thanks,
Rona Halsall

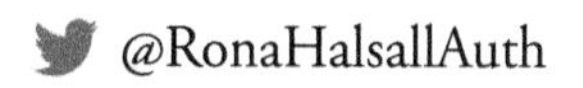

ACKNOWLEDGEMENTS

This book has been through several incarnations and there are many people to thank for different stages in its evolution.

First and foremost I have to thank my husband, David, for being my first reader and telling me it was great, when I knew it wasn't. His unfailing support has been a tremendous boost at every wobble. Thanks must also go to my daughter, Amy, along with her university housemates, who took the time to read and make suggestions for improvement. Thank you, girls, for your awesomeness! And while we're talking reading buddies, I have to thank Kerry-Ann Mitchell for providing invaluable nudges as to where the clues were too obvious and for helping me find a better way.

At a professional level, Manx Litfest put on a fabulous event every year, which spurred me on and provided the chance to pitch to agent Joanna Swainson, who gave me invaluable editorial support right at the beginning as well as giving me the confidence to believe that I could actually write a psychological thriller.

Huge thanks have to go to everyone at my fabulous agents, Madeleine Milburn Literary, Film and TV Agency, especially Hayley Steed, who has been so enthusiastic and supportive from the start, Anna Hogarty for her excellent editorial work and Alice Sutherland-Hawes for selling overseas rights.

Last but definitely not least, I have to thank everyone at Bookouture who has been instrumental in welcoming me to the family with such enthusiasm. What a lovely bunch of people you are. I feel so blessed to be with such a friendly and forward-thinking publisher and to have Isobel Akenhead as my editor, whose laser-minded attention to detail is nothing short of remarkable. You are a joy to work with, all of you!

CPSIA information can be obtained
at www.ICGtesting.com
Printed in the USA
LVHW080858280920
667211LV00021BA/3209